MIDNIGHT'S
SUN

MIDNIGHT'S SUN

A Story of Wolves

Garry Kilworth

UNWIN

HYMAN

LONDON   SYDNEY   WELLINGTON

First published in Great Britain by the Trade Division of Unwin
Hyman Limited, 1990

UNWIN HYMAN LIMITED
15–17 Broadwick Street
London W1V 1FP

Allen & Unwin Australia Pty Ltd
8 Napier Street, North Sydney, NSW 2060, Australia

Allen & Unwin New Zealand Pty Ltd with the Port Nicholson
Press, Compusales Building, 75 Ghuznee Street, Wellington, New
Zealand.

British Library Cataloguing in Publication Data
Kilworth, Garry, *1941–*
  Midnight's sun.
  I. Title
  823'.914 [F]
  ISBN 0–04–440683–5

Typeset in 11 on 13 point Palatino
Printed in Great Britain at the
University Press, Cambridge

To Pete and Peggy

Once upon a time
there was a lonely wolf
lonelier than angels.

Fable by Janos Pilinszky
(Trans. from the Hungarian
by Ted Hughes)

Contents

Author's Note

This is a work of fiction, a story, a folk tale. It has to be, for no one knows the mind-set of a wolf, nor how it views its world. Were the story about primitive men however, I would have to say the same, for who can tell how such creatures thought and reasoned? Perhaps the earliest of them were wolves in all but features. We know as little about much of the human race as we know about wolves. The history of the wolf, persecuted for seasons out of time, might well be the history of primitive peoples.

Where possible I have tried to ensure that the physical behaviour of the animal characters in this story does not deviate from that of the wild creatures in the real world. For this information I have to thank Barry Holstun Lopez's book *Of Wolves and Men* (Dent), *The Arctic Wolf* by L. David Mech (Airlife), Peggy Wayburn's *Adventuring in Alaska* (Sierra Club Books) and *The Wolves of Mount McKinley* by Adolph Murie (University of Washington Press). These authors are naturalists, possibly purists. They have spent many years studying creatures I have chosen to use simply in order to write about fortitude, endurance, comradeship and other abstracts that interest creative writers. I wanted to write about wolves because their way of life intrigues me and because I believe the wolf, through folklore and fairy tales, has had a bad press which it does not necessarily deserve. It is time for a tale in which the wolf is the good guy.

Finally, thanks to Anita and David Bray, Hong Kong friends and neighbours, whose natural enthusiasm for the place and subject refired my own, week by week, at a time when the unwritten majority of the book stretched ahead, seemingly into infinity.

Garry Kilworth, 1989

PART ONE

The Day of the Wolf

Chapter One

The wolf Meshiska gave birth to five pups on the night before the full moon. Outside the den a storm was lashing the spruce trees. The sky and the land had become part of each other: a scatter-wind night swirling with fragments of white and black. There were walls of snow piled against rock-faces and deep pits where seconds before there had been flat land. Snow became darkness and the darkness snow, and any creature lost between the two found a rock or tree and lay down beside it to wait until the world had formed again.

Inside the den the pups whimpered and nuzzled close to their warm mother, blindly seeking milk. They could not hear the storm, but they could sense it, beyond the dog-leg tunnel that led to their hollow. Curled in the safe world of fur they either slept or fed according to their needs and dispositions: no feelings of fear stirred in their breasts. The world outside might rage and tear itself apart but mother was there to keep them from harm.

Meshiska was also warm with maternal feelings. She licked the pups continually as they rolled and slithered over each other in a tangled heap in her belly fur. They were hers. Hers! She would kill in defence of them, die in defence of them. No mother ever had such beautiful mewling puppies as she had at that moment. Each one of them was as precious to her as her own life. She was even glad that Aksishem was out hunting for food so she did not have to share this moment, even with her he-wolf. She lay with her muzzle on the ground and smelled the earth of her ancestors.

There were three female pups and two male.

Meshiska was a *headwolf*, as was her mate. Together they led the pack in most enterprises. They were mainly headwolves for hunting and choosing the place for the den. Since she was the dominant partner of the two it could be said that she led the pack, but not in *all* things. The pack's pecking order was not rigid; it changed to suit circumstances and situations, and Meshiska was its leader only by the agreement of the others. At certain times, skills others than those she possessed might be needed and she would defer to one of the shoulderwolves in the pack. Leadership was also subject to alternation in the seasons. What was necessary in the pack was that they worked as a team. The pack that was not fluid, with members that fought amongst themselves over such petty issues as who was going to make the decision to stand or run, was a pack that did not survive.

In Meshiska's pack there were those whose senses were primed for the scent of man, there were those whose knowledge of water-holes surpassed her own, there were those who knew the weather and its ways, who saw the coming of the storm, who sensed a long drought in the air. To these she and Aksishem deferred when necessary.

Each pack had a hierarchy of females and a separate hierarchy of males. Each hierarchy had its own head and these two heads became the breeding pair. One of the two, either male or female, would be the dominant headwolf. There was also an interwoven tribal structure to the pack, consisting of pups, *undermegas* (yearlings to three year olds) and *megas*, who were wolves that had undergone an initiation at the age of three years.

There were packs that were skewed in some way, either in part or completely. Meshiska had come across those that were wild and undisciplined, recognising in them a sense of doom. She had heard of packs that had spawned megalomaniacs: tyrants who were strong enough to brook any opposition and did so out of pure pride. Such packs had been wiped out in a single day. Packs, like wolves, were subject to personalities. To survive, a pack had to subject itself to controlled change. She was the dominant headwolf of such a pack.

One of the small privileges of such a position was that she could name her own pups.

Meshiska called the females Tesha, Kinska and Koska.

She named the two males Athaba and Okrino.

The first two weeks were tumbledown time when the pups crawled all over each other and Meshiska, and rolled, and flopped, and gradually grew in strength. They developed hearing and sight, though neither sense was of much interest to them in the darkness and peace of the den. Grey shapes moved around them, silver-hazy and indistinct, and the murmurings of their father, or the occasional protests from their mother when her teats became too sore, these were the sights and sounds from their closed world. Koska was the strongest of the five and consequently grew even stronger since she was first at the teat, shouldering her weaker siblings aside. There was no brotherly or sisterly love when it came to food: survival took precedence over all emotions.

Okrino was the clown of the group, his floppings and sprawlings more pronounced than those of the rest of the litter. The markings on his face gave him a permanently earnest expression, as if he were either in a mood of constant concern for the welfare of the world or in an uncomfortable state of constipation. His parents thought him a strange little pup, though not unusual enough to cause them undue worry. Meshiska just hoped he would not grow into one of those wolves that irritate the rest of the pack by unwittingly acting the fool. Such wolves were dangerous, accident prone and apt to lose concentration at crucial times. To be a clever clown was something else entirely; that sort of wolf kept the pack amused during hard times. Even at this early age, though, Okrino appeared to enjoy being the centre of attention, and sometimes repeated a roll or flip which had brought forth a wry comment from his father. No doubt he would be a clever clown.

Kinska was the smallest of the pups, the runt, and though there were only four siblings to contend with she had to battle hard to get her share of the milk. During the first few days of life she hardly put on any weight at all.

Tesha was the next smallest, but this cub had a determination which Kinska seemed to lack. You could see by her expression that she was ready to take on a bear if she had to in order to get her milk. There was a haughty little tilt to her jaw and a gritty look in her eyes. When Koska shouldered her out of the way sometimes, Tesha would throw herself right back at the bigger cub time and time again in an attempt to remove her big sister from the teat. Koska often looked very puzzled by this behaviour. She knew she was the strongest and couldn't understand why Tesha took no notice of that fact. Sometimes, after Tesha had come back at her for about the fifth time, Koska would look up at one of her parents with an exasperated expression, as if to say, 'What is it with this half-pint? Why isn't she afraid of me? What do I have to do to teach Tesha her place?' But Tesha didn't recognise

5

places. She only knew she became furious when thwarted at the teat and size didn't mean a diddle in the den when she had her hackles up.

Finally, there was Athaba, who though he put on weight tended to be much more wiry than the other four. Quiet and thoughtful looking, he had a far deeper curiosity than his siblings. The dog-leg tunnel interested him, especially when he got to the curve and could see the silver-grey light at the end, before his mother jerked him back again. He sensed there was a much larger world beyond that hole, a place full of happenings. Out there were monsters and fiends, but great wonders also. He wanted to be the first to investigate this mystery before his brothers and sisters. Unlike them he could not believe this was all there was to life: milk and sleep and an occasional tumble. The world could not just consist of a hollow of earth and two giant slaves that catered for your every need. There had to be more beyond that hazy bright stuff than a few smells where one of his brothers or sisters had urinated. After all, his father and mother occasionally went along that tunnel and disappeared for long periods of time – so long sometimes the youngsters thought them dead. Often Athaba would take himself off into a remote corner of the den to consider these happenings. The others, especially Koska, did not like this behaviour. There was something not quite right about one of them thinking he was better than the rest of his family. She would waddle over to him sometimes and grip him by the jaw to pull him back into the group. Athaba only half resisted this because, though he preferred to be alone, he also liked to please. He was not a pup to court rejection.

Two weeks after the birth Kinska died from hypothermia, despite the efforts of Meshiska and Aksishem to keep her alive.

At four weeks the pups' ears became erect, standing up from their heads like arrowheads. It was at this time that Okrino let out his first howl. He not only startled his brother and sisters, he also made himself jump. The little pup looked around him nervously, then glared, as if it were one of the others that had made the sound and he was not too happy about it.

'Did you see that?' said Aksishem to his mate. 'Okrino was the first. He almost hit the ceiling.'

Meshiska replied, 'I saw. Wonder which one will be next . . .'

It was Tesha. She let out a long thin note which had Athaba cowering in the corner of the den. Then the he-pup tried himself, and found his own voice. Finally, Koska joined them.

Aksishem buried his head between his front paws.

'There'll be no peace in the den *tonight*,' he grumbled. 'I only hope they get tired quickly, so we can get some rest. Listen to it!'

By seven weeks they had been weaned and were mauling each other in the entrance to the den. They were now seriously into mock combat which sometimes left one of them with wounds. There was no organisation to their fights at that point, they just threw themselves at each other and tried to gnaw a leg or a tail, or they would battle jaw to jaw, trying to grip their opponent and force him or her to the ground. Naturally, Koska won most of the fights she had with her brothers and sister.

They were in the middle of such play one day when something happened which would haunt Athaba's dreams for many nights and days to come. Their mother was down in the den, their father out on a hunt. As they fought each other, they gradually worked themselves some distance from the opening to the den. In a short while Meshiska would be out to herd them back inside again, but on this particular day she was unwell and her reactions somewhat slower than normal. Suddenly, a creature with a flat face and terrible narrow eyes dropped from a nearby fir tree and ran across to the pups. Its legs were stumpy and its body thick and round, but its movements were fast, agile. Athaba saw some vicious claws spring magically from previously innocent-looking soft paws. They were quite unlike his own scratchers, being long, curved and extremely sharp, resembling large thorns. The marauder's flat face opened to reveal many pointed teeth and the jaws snatched a pup. The beast ran off, leaving the other pups startled for a moment. Then they set up a wailing which brought their mother out immediately. A swift assessment told her that Tesha was missing. She then called for assistance from the pack. A team of four set out in pursuit of the predator, but returned a day later without having caught it. Tesha was gone forever.

Meshiska's pups were down to three.

The incident disturbed Athaba more than the other pups. Koska and Okrino soon forgot about their sister and the monster that

7

snatched her away to oblivion. Athaba, however, missed Tesha quite a lot. He was closer to her than the other two and had been very fond of the stubborn, determined pup who refused to acknowledge the fact that she was smaller than her siblings. There was something to admire in such feisty behaviour, though Koska had continually tried to put her sister down. Athaba, in his way, had recognised that physical prowess, strength alone, was not the end of all achievements. Spirit, too, was important. In fact he had seen in Tesha that no matter what the state of the body, the spirit could enable one to triumph. He himself had mock-battled for hours with Tesha, finally becoming disheartened because his sister just *would not* give in. Wherever she was, he thought, she was giving somebody a puzzling time with her pugnacious will.

The beast that had stolen his sister was also much in his thoughts, both sleeping and waking. He had guessed there were monstrous creatures in the world, but never did his imagination produce a furry fiend such as this robber of siblings. It had come out of nowhere fast, and went back there even quicker. It was all yellow eyes, teeth, claws and wild fur. Even its ears had wispy hair going up into little curled points. Such a demon had been spewed by the dark rocks and swallowed again by the trees. It surely had not come from the wholesome world of wolves? Not from the forests or the tundra? Not from the mountains? The boggy muskegs with their gaseous smells must have spawned such a devil.

It was a long time before he thought to ask the creature's name and learned that it was called a lynx.

Koska, Okrino and Athaba grew strong and healthy until the summer season was upon them. The still mock-fought each other and their parents, improving their skills by the day. Koska was the natural leader and something of a bully. Once she wounded Athaba quite badly and the he-pup had to lie up for a few days until the gash in his rump healed.

Aksishem would arrive home after a hunt with a slab of meat and eat it in front of the pups. Then all of them would begin a strange writhing dance, their supple bodies twisting. The pups would squeak and jab at Aksishem's muzzle in impatience, trying to get him to regurgitate the food so that they could eat sooner rather than later. Occasionally, Okrino would go for the meat before one of his parents had devoured it, only to be knocked firmly away. Koska was even bolder and would try to growl the adult away from the raw food like a fully initiated *mega*, which amused both Meshiska and Aksishem.

'You'll be a great hunter, one day,' said Meshiska to her daughter. 'That growl's coming on nicely. I shouldn't be surprised if your teeth are growing too.'

One time Meshiska went off hunting, as usual, leaving the pups in the entrance to the den. Koska said to the other two, 'I'm going to follow her. See where she goes. Anyone coming?'

The other two shook their heads. They had been told to stay in the den. Their mother's anger was not a thing they witnessed very often, but when it came it was decidedly unpleasant.

'Cowards,' said the she-pup. 'I'm going anyway.'

She went trotting down the trail after her parent.

As she rounded a rock, she came slap up against a large ochre-coloured lump of fur. Koska was slightly annoyed for a moment, wondering who or what was blocking the trail when it should be an open road, for the use of all. Then she looked up.

It was her mother.

Meshiska was sitting in the middle of the track, obviously waiting for her.

'Yes?' said her mother. 'Did you want something?'

Koska nosed around the pine needles, as if looking for something, then gradually made her way back to the den. Mother followed behind and gave her rump a sharp nip just before they got back to where the other pups were waiting.

Then without another word, the adult went off down the trail again.

'I bet she's not there a second time,' said Koska, after licking the sore patch on her bottom.

'You want to test it?' asked Okrino.

'Not today,' replied his sister. 'But I bet she's not, all the same . . .'

The incident was never forgotten, by any of the three pups. Despite Koska's bravado, she never tried the same trick again.

That was not to say they respected the grown wolves so much that they were afraid of them. They loved to sneak up on one of the adult wolves and grip it by the ruff, hanging on while the adult shook them around trying to loosen their hold. Their father was a particular favourite, he would allow himself to be gripped by three pups simultaneously and would rise with them dangling from his fur like cones from a pine. Once or twice they chose the wrong adult, of course, and were firmly held by the muzzle and pinned to the ground for a moment or two to teach them a lesson. They learned which of the pack were to be avoided.

Athaba was feeling frisky one morning and was, as usual, engaging in mock-combat with his siblings. They were belly crawling through the grasses, stalking each other and pouncing when they came within range. Though some of the adult wolves were busy at small tasks, most of them were sprawled around the entrance to the den, watching the pups indulgently. It was a fine day, full of butterflies and birds, which often distracted the fickle pups.

Athaba was by this time a slate-blue coloured wolf with blond and grey hairs flecking his pelt. His eyes were bright, searching, though the inherent curiosity in them was not too obvious now. He had learned to hide what others might think to be a flaw in his character. His jaw was strong and firm and his brow deep. A handsome wolf, some said. He had a pleasant disposition and was not too cocky, and was therefore well liked by most other members of the pack.

At one point in the game, Koska was stalking Athaba, and the he-pup was waiting for her, hidden by the tall wispy foliage. He was watching, as he had been taught, for movement amongst the grasses. Then he saw it, a twitching of some stems, and when he thought the time was right, he leapt.

Even before he hit the wolf he knew it was not Koska, but an *undermega* whom the youngsters never played with simply because he always looked so serious. Athaba, now in mid-leap, went in anyway, full of bravado.

The wolf he had unfortunatley jumped at was a yearling called Skassi, a very ambitious young male who seemed eternally pre-occupied with something very important. Athaba gripped this *undermega* by the ruff and attempted to pull him to the ground. Ordinarily such play was encouraged by adults, but this occasion was not one of them. Skassi rolled and flipped, sending Athaba flying through the air. The pup landed heavily and had the wind knocked out of him. Before Athaba could get to his feet, Skassi was standing over him, and the yearling's eyes were hot with anger. He administered a savage bite to Athaba's rump.

10

The pup squealed and took up the submissive position as his only line of defence. He raised one paw, curled his tail under, lowered his body and flattened his ears. As Skassi stood over him, he flashed the whites of his eyes and produced his most submissive 'grin'.

The yearling's ears were forward, his tail erect and his hackles raised. His lips were retracted, up and down, so that his front teeth were revealed. He looked what he was, a ferocious killer who could tear the throat from the he-pup in an instant.

Meshiska came running and confronted the *undermega*.

'That was unnecessary,' she snapped. 'Get away from my pup. He's not old enough to understand yet.'

For a moment the three wolves formed a tableau as they stood there in the soft light of the forest, each caught in a dramatic pose. Everything was still.

The first movement came from Skassi. Athaba saw a gradual change come over the male yearling. In seconds, he went from a dominant posture to a submissive one.

Skassi went forward on his belly and licked Meshiska's muzzle, nipping it lightly. Then he tried to slink away, but as he moved off Meshiska stepped forward and body-slammed the young male, knocking him over.

Skassi recovered his feet and said, 'I wasn't ready for him. I just reacted.' He then slunk away, but not without a malevolent glance at Athaba, who knew he had somehow made an enemy. It was an incident that was going to have a strong effect on the rest of the pup's life. He scratched his fleas out of nervousness. An *undermega* was not a very important member of the pack, especially a yearling, but to a pup such a wolf was more dangerous than an adult. Yearlings had everything to prove, especially to their peers.

Later Meshiska spoke to Athaba.

'I was nearby this time, but there will come a time when you'll need to fight wolves like Skassi. I can't be a mother to you forever. You're very young yet and I will protect you throughout the summer, but eat well and grow strong. The yearling may not let it rest at this. One day it might be between you and him and I might not be around to intervene. Even if I were, the pack might not let me. You're my pup and I don't want to see you hurt. Attend to me and your father and we'll teach you all we know – after that, you'll have to find

11

your own place in the hierarchy of the pack. Do you understand?'

Her words were firm but her eyes were soft. There was a torment in her breast which a young pup could not hope to understand. It was a mother's knowledge that however hard she tried she could not keep the world from her young ones and eventually they would have to be able to fend for themselves. All she could hope to do was prepare them to withstand the onslaught. There would be harsh conditions, starvation, storms and enemies to contend with and a mother could not hope to live forever, nor could she expect to ignore the laws of the pack. When her pup was a year old he would be outside the protection of his parents. That did not mean Meshiska would *not* go to his defence, but she would risk a great deal by doing so. Many a headwolf has become a tailwolf overnight. The tailwolf is the lowest member of a pack, despised by all, chased and bitten, tormented and left only the barest scraps of meat. Only the *utlahs*, those that have been banished from the pack forever, are lower than the tailwolves. The *utlah*, or outsider, is not even considered to be a wolf any more, but becomes a raven. The outsider eats with the parasites, the black scavengers that follow the pack, contending with these crazy birds for carrion.

'One day,' said Athaba, stoutly, 'I shall become a *mega* like you and Aksishem – once I reach three years and go through initiation. Then I'll be able to fight Skassi and . . .'

'And Skassi will be a *mega* too, long before you are. Don't dream too much of revenge, little one. Try to think about getting around Skassi, getting him to accept you. It'll be a long time before you're strong enough to tackle him in the way that you're talking about.'

'But you said I had to learn to fight!'

'So you must, but you must also learn to *wait*. If you start nurturing thoughts of revenge now, you'll become too impatient and he'll be the one to choose the time. The wolf who chooses the time and place is most often the victor. You must be submissive until you are strong and ready, and thhe time is right. It may be that you will make friends anddd therefore such a fight will not be necessary. It happens, more often than not. Skassi's a young wolf, wanting to make his mark early and like many ambitious *undermega* he's becoming frustrated with having to wait two more years for his *mega*. By the time he gets it, his personality will have matured and I doubt he will be concerned with you any longer.

'For the moment, he's chosen you as a target, which is foolish of him. You're not even an *undermega* yet, and no credit would come of him harming you. We'll see. Just don't show any hate too early, my son. It may yet all melt away like the winter snows.'

For his part, Athaba hoped it would.

Fortunately for Athaba, as they moved into summer the pack became looser and covered a wider area. The pups hardly saw their father and mother together, let alone other members of the pack. Each wolf, or sometimes pair, went off in search of the plentiful game. There was less need for group concentration during the summer and privacy could be had. Athaba was safe until the autumn, when the pack began to pull together again into the tight knot that would take it through winter.

The summer was a good one. Voles and lemmings were plentiful and the pups developed, learned their hunting skills, and stayed away from other predators like the lynx and the bear. They found birds' eggs and feasted until they were fat, then lay around for days until the feeling of fullness wore off and they needed food again. They played in the sedge and amongst the stunted larch, spruce and alder. There were hot springs to watch bubble and hiss. The light was strong, glancing off shallow pools and scattering itself amongst the rocks. Sometimes it was a blinding gold that hurt the eyes and the pups had to turn their heads. Out on the tundra, where the permafrost still lay beneath layers of ground water and mosses, herbs gave the air a rich fragrance – saxifrages, bluebells, campions, shinleaf and poppies. There were dwarf willows out there, and flowering shrubs, but every step was a disgusting squelch and the wolves soon went back to the high country where it was dry.

Athaba saw the mighty moose and the formidable caribou, and wondered how a wolf could ever bring one these creatures down. He chased hares, and lost the race. He crept up on lakes of geese and jumped them, just to see them rise in the air like a single cloud of feathers, making a noise to wake his ancestors from their long sleep. He fed on the brilliant coloured bearberries which grew on the moorlands.

One day Aksishem found Athaba alone and told him a riddle which he said must remain a secret between the two of them. It went like this:

I am –

the stone that floats,
the wood that sinks,
the rock that runs,
the air that stinks.

What am I?

No matter how Athaba pleaded, his father would not tell him the answer.

'One day you'll work it out for yourself,' he said. 'It's more satisfying that way. If I tell you, you'll just say, "Oh no, I would have guessed that, if you gave me more time" and you'll get nothing satisfying out of it at all. You wait and see. I know I'm right.'

Even though his father had said it was a secret, Athaba mentioned it to his mother. The she-wolf looked shocked and told Athaba not to repeat the riddle to *anyone*, to forget about it altogether. Later Athaba heard her remonstrating with his father, though he could not understand what anyone had done wrong.

When they were a few months old, the pups underwent a rigorous programme of indoctrination. Play time was over. The serious stuff of life began.

'Repeat after me,' said their father. '*Every action, every thought, every word, must be for the good of the pack.*'

'. . . *for the good of the pack,*' they chorused.

And this was to be their watchword until they died. For the individual was unimportant, except as a member of the whole. Only by ensuring the safety of the pack could the individual hope to survive. Teamwork. Cohesiveness. The pack worked together, ate together, slept together. They did not watch over each *other*, each watched over the *pack*. No wolf was expected to lay down his life for his brother or sister, but he was *bound*, if required, to give up his life for the pack. Their songs were of comradeship but not of individual friendships. Unity. The good of the pack.

14

When he was four months old Okrino had an epileptic fit. Two months later he had a second fit. Such an affliction made a wolf a liability to the pack.

The other *megas* heard about these fits. A midsummer meeting took place by Waterfall Rock. Were he a fully grown wolf, Okrino might have been banished, but as a pup and not yet an *undermega* a more definite and immediate fate was in store for him. Two days later two large shoulderwolves came to collect Okrino. He was taken away into the darkness of the trees and Athaba never saw his brother again. When he asked his parents what had happened to him, they told him Okrino had gone to the Far Forests.

Why? he asked.

For the good of the pack, they replied.

Chapter Two

During the summer human hunters pushed the loosely formed pack northeastwards. Under the guidance of the two headwolves, their efforts to stay out of range of those that hunted on foot were successful. Shoulderwolves and flankwolves led the pack over rugged ground to make it difficult for pursuers. Tailwolves laid false trails with their droppings, trying to confuse the men and send them in the wrong direction. The narrow-eyed native hunters, usually on foot, were good at tracking and excellent marksmen, but their weapons were not as powerful as the wide-eyed southern hunters. Those that travelled the land in noisy machines were an unavoidable phenomenon. This second group, however, were not such good shots, and you could smell them from the far side of a mountain.

On the other hand, avoiding the native trackers was a matter of technique, learned from centuries of such lessons in survival. As soon as one trick had been used a couple of times it had to be discarded because the native men soon devised counter-moves, no matter how ingenious it seemed at first.

That season only one wolf was killed by the guns, an elderly male called Rikkva.

The pack at this time numbered about sixteen, not counting the pups. They studiously avoided areas marked by other packs in their search for new territory. Man is enough of an enemy for a wolf without antagonising his own kind.

The time of the light was drawing in, and darkness drawing out, especially since they had moved farther north than they had been before. Summers are swiftly over in the land of midnight suns. Autumn brought cutting winds and coats thickened in preparation for the coming of the deep cold. The landscape took on a russet hue in forest and on tundra. Skies and surface waters were inseparable in their weak colours. Once more the pack became a tight-knit group, moving and working as one.

During the autumnal time there was a trial of a wolf accused of mysticism and magic. Athaba witnessed this event which took place on a rocky outcrop under the light of a pale moon. The atmosphere as the wolves gathered and took their places, the important *megas* on the most prominent rock, was deadly serious. The jaundiced light which seemed to trickle through the spruce created a frightening scene to the young pup. The only comforting aspect was the scent of the forest floor on which Athaba and Koska lay, which smelled of ordinary crisp leaves and pine needles.

The wolf who was on trial, an *undermega* flankwolf by the name of Judra, was escorted from the den and brought to face her inquisitors. The precise nature of her crime was that she had been caught telling stories of an improper nature to Koska, who was too young to understand the seriousness of this transgression.

Meshiska, as headwolf, opened the trial.

'A charge has been brought here of a particularly offensive nature. One of instilling the young with mysticism and magic, which we are all aware are corrupting influences on a pack. Let us be quite sure what we are talking about here. We are not speaking of religion, which is an established fact. The Far Forests, that land of tranquillity to which we go after death, is held firmly in place by reason not magic. It is entirely reasonable that we go to another land after we leave this one.

'We are not speaking, either, of the Old Ways, when wolves roamed the earth in great numbers. The stories of our ancestors are historical in nature, not mystical. Whether such things as evil spirits may have inhabited the landscape in those times is not our concern, but the business of our heroic forebears. That such things are part of some traditional stories does not make them acceptable to the enlightened wolves of today.

'No, what we are talking about here is the *invention* of new tales containing unacceptable elements. Judra was overheard telling one of our impressionable young that there were such creatures as tree spirits, which came out in half-light and swallowed shadows for food . . .'

There was a gasp from the onlookers and Koska shifted her weight so that her side was touching Athaba's. She was shivering.

'. . . it must be obvious to all intelligent wolves,' continued Meshiska, 'that such things just cannot be. We cannot afford to have to look over our shoulders for things that are not there, when we have to concentrate on the danger that *is* there. If our attention is taken up with so-called 'tree spirits' it will not be on the scent or sound of men, the *real* danger in our lives.

'So, we have Judra before us and must decide on her fate.'

Judra was then allowed to plead her case but it was a pathetic defence: simply a stream of chatter about how the twilight played tricks with her eyes and that she was sorry she had caused such distress, and she certainly hadn't intended to *corrupt* the pup. Koska was simply the first wolf she had met after her 'experience' in the dawn light. She just had to tell someone. It would not happen again. Judra announced that she realised now how wrong she had been in even *thinking* she saw what she had said she had seen. In her heart she knew that there were no such things as spirits of the forest and had been on double-sentry that night, was tired and dispirited by the time the dawn arrived, and her mind was not itself . . .'

Her speech went on in like vein until it trickled to a stop. The *megas* put their heads together and an air of gravity pervaded the whole scene. Athaba's heart was pounding in his chest as he imagined himself in the same position as Judra. The whole experience was very frightening for a young pup. He could feel Koska still trembling beside him, knowing she had had a narrow escape. Had his sister been a yearling, she would probably have been castigated alongside Judra for being the recipient of such tales.

The *megas* came up with the verdict: guilty but with mitigating circumstances. Judra had remained to perform a second duty as sentry that night because her relief had been ill. She had not vacated her post and had consequently entered a period of mental exhaustion. This state of mind had brought on 'visions' which she should have ignored as unbelievable and ridiculous. Her crime was that she allowed herself to be seduced by the daydreams created by a strange light.

She was sentenced to be reduced from flankwolf to tailwolf and informed that she was fortunate to have escaped banishment.

Athaba was still shaking when he went to his bed.

Now that the pack was together and tight again, Athaba felt he needed to be wary of Skassi once more. The cinnamon-coated *undermega* showed little interest in him, however, and Athaba began to think that his mother's words had been right: perhaps

Skassi had matured over the summer and no longer needed to prove himself? Also, although Skassi ignored Athaba, the yearling seemed to find great sport in the company of Koska. Since it was not mating time, it was nothing to do with pairing. It seemed they liked each other and were often seen together. Athaba found it strange that Skassi should treat one pup with contempt, yet find another acceptable company. He had previously believed that the *undermega* despised *all* wolves younger than himself, but it seemed it was a personality problem, just between the two of them. When Athaba mentioned Skassi to his sister one time, asking her why it was that Skassi did not like him, she told him he was imagining things, that Skassi was a popular wolf and well liked, and consequently had no need to make enemies.

'But he was going to kill me once,' said Athaba.

Koska snorted. 'Don't be silly. He was probably playing with you. We were very young then, don't forget.'

His sister would not accept that the yearling had any animosity towards members of his own pack. This left Athaba in some doubt himself, and since Skassi had not even thrown him a single hostile glance now they were in each other's company again, he felt perhaps the others were right.

After an evening of story-telling, when Aksishem had related some of the history and mythology of the Old Ways, Athaba mentioned Skassi's enmity to his father. The older wolf just shook his head.

'I can't fight your battles for you and I can't get inside Skassi's head to find out why he dislikes you so much. You'll just have to weather it yourself. The only way I can help you, Athaba, is to teach you how to defend and attack . . .' and they proceeded to have the rough and tumble that was normal between a parent and his pup but which did little to help solve Athaba's problems.

The next day three wolves went out hunting after a caribou. They tracked it across open country, keeping pace with the beast until they felt it was time to attack. The first wolf to go in was Athaba's father. The story of the outcome was told by another member of the hunting party as the pack was gathered in a depression, out of the wind, later in the day.

'It was this way,' said the she-wolf, Urkati. 'Since Meshiska was not with us, Aksishem naturally assumed the lead and gave instructions. He suggested we should follow the caribou, down to the tree line if necessary, but to wait until it was exhausted before we attacked.

'This seemed sensible to us all and we deerwalked behind the prey, stopping when it stopped, and generally keeping pace with it, though not closing the gap. Occasionally, it turned its head to bellow something at us, but you know what caribou insults sound like – hollow and empty – anyway, we didn't heed it, thinking it was just trying to distract us.

'So, we went across marsh and over rise, just tagging along behind, occasionally stepping into a loping run when the caribou attempted to break from us. It kept shaking its head and stamping and we guessed something was bothering it – warble flies, we think.

'Eventually, the caribou stopped by some water and hung its head, scraping the ground with one hoof. That's when Aksishem cried, 'NOW!' and ran forward to head the attack. I was right behind at first, but a hare leapt up in front of me and stole my mind . . .'

There were murmurs of understanding from the rest of the pack. This was an unfortunate occurrence, but they did not question Urkati's phrase since it was not rare for a hunter to be surprised by another creature, a bird whirring up from behind a tuft, or a hare starting. When such a thing happened, of course the creature took the hunter's attention with it – *stole* his or her mind – and it was always a few moments, usually precious, irrecoverable moments, before the wolf could get it back again.

'Consequently,' continued the shoulderwolf, 'I lost ground. Kossiti was behind me and being distracted I got in his path too.

'The result of all this was that Aksishem reached the caribou seconds before we did and leaped for its throat. The prey turned at the last minute, almost by accident I think, and Aksishem drove himself straight on to the beast's antlers. He didn't stand a chance. I won't go into a gory account of his wounds, except to say that after the caribou had shaken him off he only managed to drag himself three body lengths before collapsing and dying.'

Urkati turned towards where Meshiska sat.

'I'm sorry Meshiska. We could do nothing. Killed in the course of the hunt. It could happen to any wolf and certainly Aksishem did not discredit himself. There was no stupidity involved and the plan was a good one. It was unfortunate, that's all.'

'And the caribou?' asked Meshiska, softly.

The other hunter, the flankwolf Kossiti, answered for both of them.

'A caribou that has killed is not going to be taken easily. This one was almost crazy with warble flies. When it ran, we did not follow. To abandon it was for the good of the pack.'

This, too, was good judgement. A mad beast is not an easy prey and had they known how badly affected the caribou really was, they might never have followed it across country in the first place.

Throughout the meeting, consisting of a loose circle of *megas*, with *undermegas* further back and behind, Athaba and his sister were huddled together under a small rock overhang. They heard the words but did not look at each other. Koska pretended she was watching the Howling Sentry, posted up on the rise to keep watch. They could see the wolf's silhouette against the light night sky.

At first, Athaba was stunned, and could not believe what he was hearing. His father – the one who used to let him roll all over him, grabbing his ruff, chewing his ear, biting his tail – could not be dead. It wasn't possible. This morning Aksishem had played with a fir cone, showing Athaba how to growl it into submission, then, with a savage shaking of the head, toss it high in the air. The night before, Aksishem had told him and his sister historical stories about the beginning of the time of wolves and *Firstdark*, when dogs, foxes and wolves were closer than cousins. He had told them of the hybrid swarms, to the south, where wolves mated with feral dogs to produce a creature that was something in between the two. How these hybrid swarms ranged over the lower lands stealing and killing and generally giving both the feral dogs and wolves a bad name. How they were considered to be the outlaws of the canid family.

His father had told them this just a short time ago. How could that same father be cold and stiff, his soul gone to the Far Forests where their ancestors roamed in packs of great number? No, it wasn't possible. Aksishem would come back, stroll into the camp, his tongue lolling out and that funny look on his face which said, 'Tricked you, young 'uns. Thought I was *dead*? What, your old wolfer, dead? Just shows, you'll believe anything at your age.'

But he did not stroll into camp, nor did he slip back in, or come bounding in. He was somewhere out in the night, his

21

heart turned to ice and his fur stiff and brittle. His eyes had glazed and whitened and his great chest was now like a frozen lump of wood. If you body-slammed him now, he would roll over with a sound like a hollow log. He was gone to a place Athaba could not follow, where the fir trees were taller and thicker and the sun shone all the time. Athaba's body began to ache for the return of his father.

He wanted to do something – he did not know what – but there seemed nothing he could do that was acceptable. He could have run, yelling and shouting his grief, out into the night, but he knew this would have shocked and astonished the *megas* with its inappropriateness. Punishment would have followed swiftly. His mother might have understood, but she would hardly tolerate ill-advised behaviour which might be regarded as disrespectful towards Aksishem. There were dirges to help the bereaved, solemn laments to show that they mourned the passing of his father.

These did not seem enough, and besides, in this pack even the *undermegas* were not permitted to join the Howling Circle. Athaba was not allowed to do anything but sit and watch. He did so with a heavy and resentful heart. He wanted to show *his* grief. It was his father, after all, and he knew he was going to miss him a great deal.

The pack *megas* gathered together and began the funeral songs, mourning the parting of the hunter. There was no formal body position for such a ceremony: wolves could lie, sit or stand, as they wished. There were, however, set repertoires depending on the status of the deceased and the general regard for that wolf. Aksishem was considered a good-great hunter-warrior, which was one down from the pinnacle of achievement, a great-great hunter-warrior, and of course better than a good-good hunter warrior. Then there was his prowess as a breeding wolf, a secret held by Meshiska who had (naturally) passed it on to each and every wolf in the pack, so that all knew it but none spoke openly of it. Finally, there was his disposition and general sociability to take into account: by no means unimportant in a group of creatures which depend on cooperation for survival. There were other smaller aspects: his ability as a Howling Sentry, his efforts at group teaching, his mock ferocity in establishing his position as a headwolf. There was the strength of his jaws, the breadth of his shoulders, the length of his stride. To this was added the power of his nose, which even amongst wolves was enviably strong. It was said that Aksishem could smell a deer-mouse at a distance of three days.

All these points were considered, discussed and generally appraised, before a repertoire of appropriate funeral songs was chosen.

The singing went on throughout the night.

In the dark-light hours, Athaba retraced the steps of the hunt across country. It was a dangerous thing to do for a pup. If he were to be attacked by a hostile animal, he would not stand a chance. But he was determined to settle something in his mind and the thought of being chased by some stronger beast was pushed to the back of his thoughts. He crossed freezing streams and still patches of icy water. He travelled across the eerily lit tundra, feeling the soft mosses between his pads and the permafrost. He skipped over lichen-covered rocks. The skies swirled in a turmoil of wispy clouds above him.

Once, a great bird circled around him, descending in slow revolutions, until it was directly above him. He did not heed it, except for a quick turn of the head, a glance. Then he continued his journey through the willow scrub. A few months previously he might have had cause to worry, but Athaba did not think the eagle would swoop on him now. He had grown considerably. A second later the flier obviously came to the same conclusion and wheeled away to the south, where it had been heading in the first place. The creature was apparently not in its normal territory and birds, too, feel insecure out of their usual habitat.

Athaba travelled through a thousand odours but always keeping the scent of his father in his nostrils.

Finally, he came upon the carcass and knelt down beside it. The poor body was broken and the pelt torn and punctured. Aksishem's head lay to one side and Athaba could see the eye sockets were empty. He guessed the ravens had been there, cleaning up after the pack. Athaba felt an unreasonable anger towards the ravens who normally ate any carrion left by the pack. Ravens had a special relationship with the wolves and it seemed quite wrong that they should mutilate Aksishem's remains. However, Athaba knew that the pack *megas* would not agree with him. Once the wolf's spirit had departed from him, the skin and bone left behind was nothing more or less than the dead bark on a rotten log, or withered grass, or a pine cone floating on a river. It was one of those things that was once something else, something with a *use*, and now it had been shuffled off and was no longer that thing.

Athaba gripped his father's body by the hind leg and dragged it towards a bog. He wanted his father's corpse out of the way of scavengers. He was *doing something* at last and the pain of his grief became bearable.

In the distant south was a pinnacle which commanded a view of the whole territory. In all their history only one wolf had stood on the top of the tall rock tower. Wolf legend had it that when *Groff* led the armies of men out of the sea-of-chaos and began the slaughter of the wolves, an *undermega* called Lograna made a mighty leap from the ground and caught a cloud by its tail. The cloud rose into the air with the *undermega* still clinging on by its determined teeth. As the cloud was floating over the tor now known as Howler's Rock, the wolf let go her hold and dropped on to the high peak. From this magnificent vantage point Lograna was able to act as the Howling Sentry for the whole wolf population of her part of the world, warning all the packs in the forests, mountains and flatlands of the north-west, while in other areas, especially beyond the seas, wolves were being slaughtered to the last pup.

Every victory of this kind has some cost, however, and the tragedy of Lograna was her own self-sacrifice. Although she had managed to attain the place where only eagles had dared, she was unable to descend. Once the danger was past, the young she-wolf died of hunger and thirst upon the rock. Her bones were still up there. They howled with triumph every time the wind blew.

Athaba turned his father's body to face the direction of Howler's Rock and then, as the carcass sank in the dark bog, crooned to the guardian of that holy place to watch over the soul of Aksishem and see that it reached the Far Forest.

When he finally gave up the howling, Athaba turned from the muskeg swamp to find that two pack members, sent out after the pup by Meshiska when he was found to be missing, had witnessed this strange rite. They took Athaba back with them and reported to the rest of the *megas*. They spoke contemptuously of gnatwinged magic and goatsucker mysticism.

Meshiska was ordered to absent herself from the trial. Athaba was taken before the *megas* and given a thorough 'staring-out' by

24

each of the adults in turn. Unlike Koska's involvement with the deviant Judra, Athaba was being accused of directly initiating a mystical rite, something far more serious than Judra's crime of 'story-telling'. The pup was in fact on trial for his life. They told him they could look into his heart and see if there were any weaknesses there, which might be harmful to the pack in the future.

Inside, faced by those terrible accusative eyes, Athaba quaked in fear. Now he regretted his actions but it was far too late for that: now that those grey eyes looked right down into his spirit, searching for corrosion of the soul. Terrified as he was he had the sense to know that he had to stare back, unblinking, and think thoughts of purity. He had to fill his own eyes with such innocence that his accusers would be impressed by his confidence in himself. His thoughts went out to the tundra, the flatlands where the wildfowl filled the air and lakes, and the stunted alder grew. He thought of the white and yellow flowers that populated the air with their seeds, and the star mosses, the grasses and the braided streams. His head was empty of everything except beautiful scenery. Not once did he blink or look down, or make any movement that might be construed as a sign of a guilty conscience.

Finally, the staring-out was over and the questioning began.

'We have to consider the good of the pack, of which your mother is the present headwolf,' stated Urkati. 'We have no wish to intimidate you, pup, but there may come a time when others are relying on you. If you are given to daydreaming or any of that mystical stuff, you may be inattentive at a crucial time and cost us lives. Now, why did you return to your father's corpse?'

Athaba was terrified and now thoroughly regretted his attempt at thwarting his grief. He lied.

'I didn't believe my father was dead. I wanted to be sure.'

Since Urkati was the one who reported the accident she looked a little shocked and offended.

'Are you trying to say that you didn't believe me? When I gave my report before the *whole* pack? Are you telling me,' her voice rose in anger, 'that you, a *pup*, considered I might be a liar!'

'No, not that. I thought – I was *hoping* that you might have been mistaken, that perhaps he was not quite dead . . .'

Now Ragisthor, the wolf with a twist of humour, gave voice. He was lying with his paws crossed, towards the back of the group and he tilted his head as he spoke.

'I don't think you quite understand the nature of death, my little sapling. To be *dead* means to be lifeless. There is a distinct lack of movement discernible in the creature that once bounded through the forests and across the tundra. This absence of any motion, activity, excitement, agitation or progress of any sort, extends right through the breast to the very heart itself. Nothing beats, palpitates or pulses. In short, one cannot be "not quite dead" – one is either dead, or not dead. Understand me, little shrub?'

Athaba, young as he was, seethed, while at the same time tried not to show it.

'What I meant was, I couldn't really *see* my father as dead, until I was able to feel the coldness and stiffness of his body. I was a bit dazed. I'm over it now though . . .'

Urkati said, 'You were seen *crooning* over your father . . . wolves heard you calling.'

'For help,' said Athaba, quickly. 'I was lost. I needed someone to point the way home. I was confused.'

'So confused,' said Itakru, another *mega*, 'that you dragged Aksishem to the bog and there let him sink. Can you explain these actions?'

'I thought I could smell man in the vicinity. I've been told that the barking ones need strong confirmation of the presence of wolves and I thought if hunters found Aksishem's body they would know they were on the right track and persist until they caught up with us. Did I do wrong?'

They let him live. He owed his life to the words that came to him from some region of his mind that was only accessible while the adrenalin flowed. He hardly knew what he was saying, yet the words were right. (Later in his life, he thought that perhaps his father had been speaking through him, so deep were his heresies by that time.)

He owed his life, also, to his own strength of spirit. If he had once looked away, or worse still *down*, during the 'staring out' they would have fallen on him and torn him to pieces.

Finally, he owed his life to the wolf Ragisthor who argued on his behalf when the time came to debate his fate. Ragisthor was known to dislike pups intensely, so even though his standing in

26

the pack was only at balance – he was considered neither a great wolf nor an inadequate one – his words were taken seriously.

'Of course, it is possible that there may be something wrong with the pup,' he said to the *megas*, 'but if he were lacking in some way, or eccentric, his tongue and his eyes would have made us sure of that fact. *I'm* certainly not that sure. Are any of you?'

It seemed they were not.

When the ordeal was over, Athaba staggered away to recover his composure. He went in amongst some rocks, out of range of his mother's enquiring eyes.

She knew he was not in the perfect mould of the hunter-warrior. Yes, he would have laid down his life in defence of the pack, for the pack, with the pack, but *inside* there was a stain on his spirit. He had not the purity of a clean practical hunter-warrior. The wind to him was more than a bearer of scent and sound, it was the breath of the earth. Rivers, streams, lakes and ponds were more than water sources where a wolf might drink; they were places where magic light dwelt. The forests were not just places to hide; they were the haunts of ancient darknesses. *She* knew that her pup was blemished in some way. What she didn't know, and what he did not wish her to guess, was the depth of that flaw. Meshiska would not like to cause the death of her offspring, but the season of maternal feelings was almost over and her position as headwolf was swiftly regaining its former importance to her. She was the 'mother' of the whole pack – they were all her charges – and she might easily sacrifice a pup for the good of the whole.

While Athaba lay behind the rock, realising how stupid he had been, Skassi found him out. The *undermega* began by body-slamming the pup against the rock, several times, while saying, 'Your mother won't help you now. I've been biding my time, waiting for you to fall. I knew it would happen in the end. You're in disgrace. I could *kill* you now and get away with it. I'm glad Aksishem is dead. Any wolf that produces a creature like you deserves to be dead. I can't think why the *megas* didn't destroy you. You stink of *unwolfiness*. We need no shamans or priests.'

Skassi savaged Athaba on the flank and left him to lick his wounds. When he had gone, Athaba stared in the direction of Agus Rock.

In wolf mythology, there is a time coming when all accounts will be settled. This time is known as the *Lastlight* when the world will afterwards revert to that initial darkness enjoyed by wolves and foxes before the giant *Groff* had made the light of day. In the *Lastlight* men will finally turn all their force against men, and wipe the earth clean of human presence. The canids – the wolves, coyotes, foxes, dogs, dingoes, jackals – will rise from their graves and settle old scores with each other. They will come from the Far Forests, from the Perfect Here, from the Unplace, those lands, beyond death, to do battle with their erstwhile enemies. The formerly weak will triumph over the formerly strong. There will be a reckoning, a balancing of rights and wrongs. And after the *Lastlight* there shall be no more bitterness, no more hatred, only satisfaction. Enemy will lie with enemy, licking each other's wounds. All strife will be ended, the mighty shall have fallen, the meek raised up, and they shall meet in the new life after the end of life.

For wolves like Athaba, who had strong undefeatable enemies such as Skassi, the *Lastlight* was something to look forward to, to nurture in the place of bitterness and hatred. The *Lastlight* was a saving grace that kept wolves like Athaba from the self-destructive pit of enmity.

It was unfortunate for Athaba that he had crossed with the one wolf in the pack who was having problems of his own that day in his early puppyhood. At the time, and for a long while afterwards, Skassi had been having troublesome dreams which bothered him when he was awake, and he had been lost in thought. Then, suddenly, this *creature* on the track, right in front of his nose, had leapt at him, clung to his ruff! Of course, Skassi had been startled: anyone would be.

And where had the young idiot come from, unless, of course, he did have the ability to change shape and form? Was it possible they had a mystic amongst them? Skassi had thereafter decided to keep an eye on Athaba. If there *was* something strange about him, Skassi intended to be the first to know, and to denounce the creature. After all, what stronger evidence did one need than the fact that a wolf pup could manifest itself out of thin air? Now this thing with Athaba's father had confirmed Skassi's suspicions. He was determined to cause Athaba's downfall, one way or another, and had decided that patience would deliver the pup into his jaws.

Skassi had made it one of his tasks in life to protect the pack from the occult or indeed any kind of sorcery. No one had asked him to do this, but he found duties where others avoided them. He intended to be headwolf one day, and those destined for such high places needed to seek out opportunities to invest effort into the pack, for the good of the pack. His work in warding off evil *thinkers* (just as bad as those who *practised* evil) was only a small part of what he saw as his complete duty, but it was still an important part for all that. Once he became headwolf he intended to initiate a purge, to divest the pack of all those even tainted with mysticism. If they refused to purify themselves, then they would have to pay the consequences.

There were days when Skassi found himself out alone amongst the black spruce and he could feel the spirit of the forest moving against him, trying to get him to renounce his duty as a hunter of bad souls. Shadows linked themselves against him, and there were cold draughts of air in places where he knew the forces of devilry were gathering. Sometimes he felt as though he would be overcome by their sheer power of presence, and once or twice went into a swoon as his mind whirled with repetitive thoughts. At such times he did not dare go back to the pack, for fear that other wolves might see his fear and know it to be a spiritual thing. He knew the forces of evil were trying to discredit him and drive him away from his purpose of purging the pack, for how can you be the scourge of those possessed by demons, if the demons have taken your own soul?

'They try to trap me,' he said to himself, as the branches locked overhead, and the wind screamed through the crazed patterns of their shadows. 'But I will drive them out, drive them from within me and my kind.'

At night he would often wake from a dream, suddenly, and know that the forces of the forest had been trying to wreak their ugly vengeance on him while he slept. He woke, trembling and covered in sweat, sure in the knowledge that they had come and worked their foul magic on him. He would have to sneak off, as if for a drink, to wash himself, purify himself, in the nearest clear water. It had to be running stream water, down from the mountains. Rainwater or muddy river water was useless for cleansing his soul, he knew, though *how* he knew was another matter. He felt he had been born with this kind of knowledge: he had been chosen in the womb for these tasks.

So, Skassi watched the young Athaba, closely. He found he could not make up his mind about the creature. One moment Athaba seemed like a wolf corrupted by mystical foxes, the next a pure wolf, an asset to the pack. It was really very frustrating and there were times when Skassi wondered whether the 'good' side of Athaba was merely there to throw his elders off the track.

Once, just after becoming an *undermega*, Skassi had doubts about himself. Perhaps, he thought, as he woke violently from a deep sleep, I am wrong about myself? Maybe I am not one of those chosen to keep the pack unstained by cabbalism? This worried him a great deal and he went to a grove of dwarf alder to consider the matter. While lying amongst the stunted trees, he suddenly became aware that he was in a holy place. The light angled through the weak branches of the alders and patterned the ground with strange wavering symbols. He thought he could hear a voice, coming from within the grove, and it whispered to him that he was the chosen one who would one day lead a pack quite unlike any that had gone before. He did not see this experience as a mystical thing but as a practical fight against the forces of destruction. All that had happened to him was very *real*, nothing imagined. If he compared himself with the chastised Judra, for instance, he knew their two experiences to be quite different. Judra had *thought* she saw spirits amongst the forest, had been alarmed by them and had been in danger of forsaking her duty because of them. He, on the other side, had been confronted by actual demons, had stood steadfastly against them, and had triumphed over them. There were wolves who *deliberately* courted mysticism, were seduced by it, indulged in it. This was where the terrible dangers lay. He had not set out with the intention of seeking the demons, they had come to find him. They had gathered together in their squadrons and attacked *him*. His was a very different case from a wolf who allowed the spirits to possess her, such as Judra, or the wolf who practised mystical rites because he had been corrupted by the desire for power through evil.

Skassi was now certain that he was a very special wolf and basked in his own purity and strength of spirit. The demons had gone from him.

Thus he continued his secret crusade, not just against Athaba, but against *all* evil.

Chapter Three

Winter came screaming through the darkness.

Now the night was endless. The human hunters had gone back to their dens, to rub their paws and to bark into their fires. The wolves continued to forage and hunt, envying the bear, asleep in his warm den. It was a time when perspectives sharpened and objectives were clarified. The world was a heavier place. Its creatures slowed, sometimes to a standstill, to freeze in their tracks. Ice clogged the paws and clung to shank hair. Snow softened any sounds.

After the 'mystical' incident Athaba was determined to become a model wolf. He set about making relationships with his brother and sister wolves, proclaiming good comradeship to be the highest of aspirations and renouncing the poetry which stained his soul. He was attentive to the teachings of the *megas*. How to hunt and fight, as an individual and as part of a team. How to walk flank, rear and forward, in order to warn the pack of any danger. How to sing the stirring songs whose words reaffirmed the unity of the pack. How to show respect for *megas* and *undermegas*. How it was possible both to intuit and anticipate a role within the pack during a joint operation, yet still show individual initiative.

At a slight risk of being considered 'different' he formed a group of pups and *undermegas* which be named *The Good Companions*. He explained its purpose to be a special guard or set of runners for use of the headwolves in emergencies. He himself did not lead this group – that was unthinkable for a pup – the top position was given to an *undermega*, but credit went to him for the original idea. Only two *undermegas* declined to join *The Good Companions*, and one of these was Skassi. Skassi explained to the *megas* that he was grooming himself to become headwolf one day and therefore had to concentrate as much on individual skills as team work. This was perfectly acceptable and not regarded as presumptuous. Grooming yourself did not mean you expected to become headwolf, only that you were preparing yourself for the event *should* it come to pass.

Even before he was a yearling Athaba was chosen once or twice for the duties of a flankwolf, at times when the pack was stretched. Athaba discharged his duty without a murmur or any show of fear, even though as a flankwolf it meant he was often quite far away from the core of the pack, and vulnerable. Some of the *megas* were beginning to comment, first on his willingness, then on his stability, and finally on his considerable *ability*.

He became a yearling and an *undermega*.

Becoming an *undermega* was by no means automatic. Most wolves did, but then most wolves had to live through their first year without being killed by the weather, a ritual execution by the pack, or by enemies of the pack. Sixty per cent of all pups did not make it through that first year. Having made it, there were circumstances whereby the *megas* might not grant the promotion. It was not unknown for a wolf, devoid of all privileges, to be addressed as 'pup' until it proved its competence in at least *one* of the tasks set for it.

Aksishem had told his pups (as a warning?) that he had known a toothless old wolf called Bidaka, who was a pup from his birth to his death. Such a wolf had to be healthy and willing, for the good of the pack of course, and be forever on the verge of showing promise. Otherwise it was reduced to the dreaded position of tailwolf. Young pups and first-year *undermegas* would tease a tailwolf unmercifully. They would walk around it, shouting abuse.

'Look at the ragged tailender. Want some rotten bits of skin? Here, have a dry old bone. Who's afraid of *this* old wolf? Hop, hop, hop amongst the stools . . .'

Pups would bite the legs of the tailwolf and pull all the hair out of its flanks.

Such a wolf might not last long in the pack but would end its days as a raven-wolf, an outcast. The treatment of a tailwolf and a wolf that had been banished was quite different. No one ever went close to or spoke with an *utlah*. Such a creature was outside the pale and completely ignored, provided it did not try to re-enter the pack. If it approached the pack, it was fallen on and torn to pieces. A raven-wolf was reduced to a pathetic creature, driven mad by torment and hunger, which would indeed wonder whether it was animal or bird. It had to fight with other scavengers, not just the real ravens, for the tiniest morsel. Outcasts did not have long lives, unless they kept their hearts burning with hate.

At the end of a hard winter, during which he had acquitted himself very favourably, Athaba's mother told him she was proud of him. Koska, envious at first, followed her mother's example. Skassi remained aloof but at a distance. There seemed to be a mutual understanding between them. That unvoiced understanding was, *don't get in my way and we have no need to fight*. There was not a great deal of difference in their bodyweights now. Skassi was a little taller and broader, but not remarkably so.

Meshiska was no longer headwolf as often as she had been in the past. The pack was tending to favour Urkati and her mate Itakru. There was no loss of face in this development. Meshiska had been headwolf for many years and was happy to relinquish her responsibilities. She drifted away from her high position with grace and dignity. Urkati was pregnant and her status always increased throughout the months of darkness, since she was a good night hunter.

One day in spring, when the smells of the awakening moss and lichen were filling pockets in the air, Athaba was out hunting with Ragisthor. He liked being with the older wolf, whose nonchalance and bonhomie, his dry wit and graceful manner, made him an unusual wolf companion. Ragisthor told Athaba he had invented 'taste' which was nothing to do with food.

'Mention good taste to most wolves,' he remarked, as they deer-trotted along, 'and they will look at you with wide eyes and hurry away to some blistering chore they say needs tending. Somehow I feel you will understand, young sapling, when I say that an elk is a much more elegant prey than a moose or musk ox; that a wolverine looks more refined than a coyote; that ravens are distasteful birds; and that bringing down a caribou in full flight, with one leap, is more stylish than gutting a wild sheep after several tries . . .'

Somehow Ragisthor had got away with being 'different' all his life. Athaba was beginning to understand that personality and punishment, not to say justice, were closely linked. If you appeared mysterious and quiet, the slightest infringement of the pack's vague rules brought you before the *megas*. If you were cocky but engaging, you could get away with a great deal more. A wolf with a sullen appearance had to discharge its duties with perfection. A wolf cub that cheeked its elders but was full of zest or, like Ragisthor, had a quick clever mind, was likely to have its faults overlooked.

Athaba did not fully understand, but he liked to please and made an affirmative sound. They were near the sea and his attention was taken up by great skuas, the predators and pirates of the air, who at this time of year were even fierce towards each other. Once the breeding season was past, they tolerated skua company but still practised thuggery and banditry on other birds. Athaba was thinking how different it would be if he were a gull or a skua. They had no use for teamwork. Survival depended upon how well you could beat up your neighbour, preferably when his back was turned and he was least expecting a visit.

'I wonder what it's like to be a bird,' he said in an unguarded moment, and too late he realised his tone had been wistful. Ragisthor, however, seemed disturbed for both of them. The older wolf looked around, carefully inspecting a patch of stunted willows to the south.

'Careful, my little shrub,' said Ragisthor, 'the rocks tell tales.'

He glanced behind him, then continued, 'I should think it would be a very *graceful* existence, if you were a hawk or falcon, but a pretty grubby one if a sparrow. More specifically, it might be a *change*, though,' he glanced around him again, 'an *inferior* one of course, if one were to sprout swan-like wings and be able to view the world from above.'

'Why not gulls' wings? They can glide and cut.'

Ragisthor gave a slight shudder.

'Gulls, my curled fern, are ghastly creatures that will eat dead herrings. Have you ever smelled a dead herring? I thought not. It is an experience to be missed, I can assure you. The world would not be a poorer place without dead herrings. Swans, on the other hand, are graceful creatures . . .'

'They dip their beaks in *mud*,' protested Athaba.

'Out of sight, young sapling, out of sight. They do it under the water where, I am reliably informed, there are no odours and few witnesses. It is like picking the dirt out of one's pads. One waits for darkness before carrying out these necessary but offensive tasks.'

'You do, but the rest don't.'

'Quite. Which is why I have taste and they do not.'

Athaba said, 'Ragisthor, have you ever taken a mate?'

34

'Certainly not. Too much responsibility. And if one takes a mate one is expected to propagate. *Ugh!* All that to-ing and fro-ing, fetching and carrying, after the pups are born.' He gave a little shudder. 'Nasty little creatures, pups. Puking and mewling half the time. You have to eat their food first and then bring it up for them. Disgusting business. I'm glad I was never one myself. Eating regurgitated food – '

'But, Ragisthor. You must have been a pup, once upon a time?'

'No, never. I utterly refute it. I was born a yearling. I could never have been one of those blind deaf blobs with the appearance of pink rats. Never. I reject the notion completely. The statement is made. Let it stand. Desist. I cannot abide little *pups.'*

'But I've seen you playing with Urkati's new little ones. You enjoy yourself. And you used to tumble with me, when I was a pup.'

'Only for the good of the pack. Without my tuition you young-sters would never survive. The other wolves are all right, in their way, but they haven't my intelligence, poor fools.'

'Have you ever been headwolf?'

Ragisthor stopped and stared into Athaba's eyes.

'Are you quite mad, sapling? If I were ever made headwolf, perish the thought, I would throw myself over the nearest cliff. For the good of the pack, don't ever say that again.'

For the good of the pack. How often Athaba heard that phrase. Everything had to be *for the good of the pack.*

Suddenly, Athaba started. There was a scent on the wind. Man. The distinct odour of man. It was one of those from the south, smelling like sickly flowers. A hunter on foot, thankfully.

His legs 'went spider' and his underhairs touched the ground. Ragisthor still stood, but his nose was up and his head tilted to one side.

'To the north-west,' said the *mega*. 'I hear him now. He's very close. He must have started downwind, but the direction's changed and caught him out. Knows we've got his scent. Prob-ably aiming right now, to get one of us before we run . . .' there was a zithering sound in the grasses, followed a moment later by the distant noise of an explosion.

'Run!' said Ragisthor. 'Warn the pack.'

'What about you?'

'I'll distract him.'

Something skimmed Athaba's flank and left a thin line of searing pain behind. He nipped at the surface wound, a brown mark along his pelt. He had almost been shot! This was enough to set the yearling's legs working. He ran straight across the tundra with Ragisthor yelling after him, 'Zig-zag, like a hare, you gannet's brain! This is no time for style.'

He did as he was told, glancing back only once, to see Ragisthor creeping furtively around a rise. Incredibly, he seemed to be stalking the human. Athaba's skull buzzed as if it had a mosquito trapped inside. *Was he going to attack the hunter*? Athaba had heard of such a thing, a wolf attacking a man, but usually it was a last ditch attempt at self-defence, or the wolf was driven by hunger.

Athaba wondered if the hunter had a machine with him. Wolves knew from experience that there were two distinctly different things that moved on the landscape: a living thing, like a wolf or caribou or man; or the things that some men brought with them, which the wolves had single word for, though they qualified it: the *flying machine* and the *ground machine*. The machines were easily identified by their smell and noise. Both would carry men.

If the hunter had a ground machine with him, Ragisthor would have to be very, very quick.

When Athaba reached camp he found the *megas* in conference with six or seven strangers. They had been making overtures for days, wanting to join Athaba's pack, their own having been depleted in numbers. It was possible, of course, to have a pack consisting of only two members, but there were definite advantages to having packs around twenty strong. The addition of these strangers would put Athaba's pack at twenty-three.

Athaba ran immediately to his mother.

'Meshiska,' he cried, 'there are hunters behind me. Ragisthor's trying to draw them off.'

'How many?'

'I only smelled one, but you've often said only the tundra dwellers hunt alone. Outsiders usually come in two, three or more.'

'It was an outsider?'

'A poor marksman. He missed twice.'

She nodded.

'Sounds like an outsider. We must move.'

She turned to the group of *megas*.

'You heard that. We must make a decision fast and be on our way. I say we absorb the newcomers. Urkati? Itakru? Seven is not too many. We don't need them, but they need us.'

There was general agreement that the new wolves should join the pack. Once said, it was done. The whole pack including the new members then began to move westwards, towards a distant tree line. Pelts ranging from slate blue to white, through chocolate and brown, ochre, cinnamon and grey and blond, moved quietly but swiftly over the landscape.

Meshiska was not headwolf that day. Itakru was the wolf directing the retreat. He carried out his duties efficiently, making sure that the new pups born to Urkati were carried, and that the elderly were herded in the middle of the pack.

Athaba was posted as the south rear flankwolf. It was a dangerous position, way out on the periphery of the pack. If the hunters blundered across country, as they very well might being outsiders, and they happened by accident to be on the correct lateral course, the first wolf they would meet would be the south rear flankwolf.

However, Athaba accepted the post without a murmur. Not that it would have gained him any credit to have argued. For the good of the pack Ragisthor was down there amongst the hunters, doing what he could to pull them away from the area. How could Athaba quarrel over a position *within* the pack? All he hoped was that Ragisthor would outsmart the hunters. They were outsiders. Ragisthor had always held human outsiders in contempt. He scorned them, he said. The local hunters were considered extremely dangerous and not to be taken lightly. But outsiders? Their weapons were powerful and accurate, but their eyes were close and their vision poor. Sometimes they came on foot with a local tracker, but mostly they used vehicles which could be smelled miles away. They often smelled themselves, of fermented berries. They stank of firesmoke, made loud noises, clinked things, tripped over stones and turfs. They snatched shots at targets too distant for their guns.

Occasionally, one would come who was indistinguishable from the tundra-dwelling humans in his ability to hunt. But that was very rare. Athaba hoped these were contemptibles, for Ragisthor's sake.

The pack travelled twenty miles with unbroken stride, into high timber country. Once amongst the trees they found a place to rest.

The two rear flankwolves were sent back, along the trail to scout for signs of Ragisthor and to keep a nose to the wind for the smell of the men.

When night came there was still no sign of Ragisthor. Athaba and the other flankwolf returned to the pack. Now that the immediate danger was behind them, Athaba was given a hero's welcome for his part in running the guns to bring word to the pack. Itakru came forward and gave him a 'comrade's body-slam', to show how pleased he was with him. Urkati gripped his muzzle between her great jaws and then released him. His mother stood by, the pride evident in her eyes, then came forward to lick his brown wound. Skassi was nowhere to be seen: he was on Howling Sentry.

They made a great fuss of him, because he had done right, done well for the good of the pack. Itakru whispered a promised position of shoulderwolf 'just occasionally' which was almost unheard of for a junior *undermega*.

No one spoke of Ragisthor.

All night and for two days afterwards, Athaba watched for the coming of the *mega* he now regarded as a close friend. The trees held their shadows close to them and the skies were mottled, swirling like ice formed in a sea of slow currents. Dragonflies whispered messages to each other, their voices too small for a wolf to hear. Ground squirrels watched from distant rises. Islands in the tarns of the wetlands, peppered with snow-coloured balls of seed, held thousands of geese all shouting to each other about the danger of foxes. Terns dive-bombed the seals along the coast. Frogs, at their northern limit, propagated.

In short, the world went on, even though the best friend of a young wolf was lost in the wilderness.

On the third night of Ragisthor's absence, the Howling Sentry woke the whole pack with an alarm. Instantly, every wolf was on its feet, ready for flight. Then the alarm tone changed suddenly, to one of welcome to a lost comrade. Finally, through the trees came a weary-looking but unmarked wolf.

Ragisthor.

He entered the camp in triumph, his poise and manner that of a conquering hero. Ragisthor was a large wolf and his presence could never be ignored. He stood in a shaft of moonlight and looked about him quizzically for a moment, before seemingly noticing Urkati and Itakru. He continued towards these two.

There was just a slight roll to his shoulders. Not a *swagger* – Ragisthor would never stoop to such artificial postures – more an easing of the muscles as he walked. He was haughty, of course, as he nodded greetings to each of the *megas*. Occasionally, he tilted his head at a pup, to show that even great wolves acknowledge the new generation. His large dark-ringed eyes took in Athaba as he passed him. The *undermega* thought he noticed an expression of faint amusement in them but was willing to grant that he might be mistaken.

'Sapling?' Ragisthor murmured.

When he reached the two headwolves, he stopped.

'You will gather from my presence here that the hunters failed in their efforts to kill even one of our pack. They were in fact quite happy with the caribou I led them to, further south. The sort of hunters that will shoot at anything that moves, though whether they ever hit their target is another matter. I fancy that little harm will come to caribou, despite their bulk. To these hunters, *nothing* is an easy target. Now, if you will excuse me, I shall get some rest.'

Urkati nodded.

'Ragisthor, the pack is grateful.'

'I thank the pack for its gratitude, but I was merely doing my duty. The youngster – his name escapes me for the moment – ?'

'You mean Athaba?'

'Exactly. Gratitude should be hurled in his direction, if it is to be sent anywhere. He kept his head under fire, sustained a slight wound I understand, and managed to break through to give the warning.' He turned his head, to nod at Athaba. 'Well done, *undermega*.'

With that, Ragisthor curled up in a warm hollow between two roots at the base of a tree and closed his eyes.

Athaba knew that the *mega* hadn't forgotten his name, but it was just like Ragisthor to play to the pack. He went across to the wolf in question and lay down beside him. Eventually the whole camp turned in and the Howling Watch was changed. Later, when no one was paying attention, Athaba whispered, 'You didn't forget my name. Was it so you couldn't be accused of partisanship?'

Ragisthor opened one eye.

'Partly that, my little shrub, and partly the fact that if you get someone else to say the name, they are more likely to remember

39

it in the future. Had it slipped glibly off my own tongue, it might have failed to stick sufficiently strongly.'

'*You* deserve the credit. You're the one that drew the hunters off. Why do you want me to get the biggest share of the glory?'

Ragisthor sighed.

'I have no use for *glory*. I'm seven years of age. But you, you're young and ambitious. This will look well on your record of achievements. You want to be headwolf one day, don't you?'

Athaba tried to sound surprised.

'Headwolf,' he said. 'I hadn't thought about it. I'm far too young to consider such things yet . . .'

'Liar,' murmured Ragisthor, his eyes closed again. 'I was never a pup but I know your dreams. Every night you have visions of yourself leading the pack.'

True. It was true. Ragisthor was one of the wisest wolves Athaba had ever known, except perhaps for his father.

Athaba whispered his father's riddle into Ragisthor's twitching ear.

'What does it mean?' he asked.

Ragisthor sighed. 'I have no idea. Floating stone? Sinking wood? Let me sleep, please. I've had a hard three days.'

'Oh, yes,' said Athaba, 'drawing those hunters southward. I can imagine what a terrifying ordeal that was – or perhaps you were too exhausted, to concerned with the task, to be frightened?'

Ragisthor, was half asleep.

'What?' he muttered. 'Oh! Oh, yes. Ran rings round those hunters in half a day.'

Athaba thought about this, then said.

'Two or three days, surely?'

'No,' murmured the voice. 'Only half a day. It was the she-wolf that wore me out . . . insistent . . .'

'Ragisthor?' said Athaba, firmly.

The older wolf's eyes opened. There was a shine to them that Athaba had not noticed before. He slid a little closer to the *undermega*.

'You may have thought me invulnerable, little sapling, to all things under the sun. True, I may be immortal so far as the hunter's gun is concerned, but alas, I am not impervious to the attractions of a she-wolf in spring. I have to tell *someone* –

experiences of this kind are like that – and you're the only wolf I can trust to keep it to himself.'

Ragisthor's jaws were close Athaba's ear now. He could feel the hot excited breath on his face. He could smell the herbs caught in Ragisthor's coat. There was a crushed beetle trapped by its legs in Ragisthor's cuff. Clearly, he had been rolling on some soft bank somewhere, collecting seeds in his pelt.

'Listen, sapling. It only took me half a day to get rid of those fools with the guns. Then I went across country and sneaked into forbidden territories until I found myself a willing female. It is *spring* after all. Do I not have desires, like any headwolf? Do I not feel the turf stirring beneath my paws? Quivering? Do I not . . .'

'But you said propagating was obnoxious to you?'

'Only if one has to look after the pups,' murmured Ragisthor.

'Some other wolf will have that pleasure. In any case, there are no available females in our own pack. They are all spoken for and I have no wish to demean myself by fighting some half-witted block-shouldered oaf for the pleasure. No, no, this was the only way.'

Athaba was not sure he approved.

'But everybody thinks you behaved like a *hero!*'

Ragisthor looked a little hurt.

'Oh, but I did. You should have seen me, sapling. I was truly heroic. You would have been proud of me. I spoke with the tongues of kittiwakes. I was as gentle as a roundworm. I was as passionate as a lynx. I was – *magnificent*. A hero indeed.'

'It isn't even the mating season!' Athaba retorted.

'You sound indignant about it. There *are* those who will mate out of season. I am one. I found another. Now go to sleep. You're boring me, sapling.'

And with that, Ragisthor fell asleep himself. He was obviously exhausted. Athaba stared at the great grey animal lying on its side, its ribcage rising and falling slowly, with each breath, and wondered how on earth he had survived all these years.

Chapter Four

Wolves tell a tale of one of their kind who found a flock of geese lying dead, scattered amongst the grasses of a hillside. Thinking himself fortunate the wolf took each goose and cached it somewhere: one he put in a hollow log, another he buried just beneath the turf in some soft soil where it would be easy to retrieve, a third was placed in the space beneath two rocks that touched brows. And so on, until at least twelve hiding places held a future meal. The wolf then went back and reported to the pack.

When he returned later that day with some extra jaws to help carry some of the cached geese, he found the hollow log empty, the turf disturbed with nothing beneath it, and between the two rocks was just air. And so on, until every hiding place was checked and not a goose was to be found. The wolf was very angry with himself because as he discovered empty cache, he *gradually* realised what had happened.

There are some things that wolves as a group never learn. One of the reasons for this – perhaps the main reason – is that individuals amongst them *hate* admitting to a mistake. They would rather keep absolutely quiet about an error than pass on valuable information at the risk of losing face. Therefore, they have these stories which they pass on to their young in which something happened to another wolf (not to *them*) which the young ones should be wary of. Young wolves, being what they are, take everything literally, and as far as they are concerned, geese are geese and ducks are ducks.

Athaba was out hunting on his own one day when he spied a lone duck. Although a supreme harrier with a zig-zag that many wolves envied, he was not normally good at catching birds. With birds a lot of patience was required. You have to come at them from down wind, of course, but in little spurts, sticking close to the ground. Every move was done with a hunched-down crouch, except when you were lying flat in the grass. *Up* dink-

dink-dink-dink-dink-dink *down*. Stay-absolutely-rock-stone-still-until-you-are-sure-you-haven't-been-seen. Then – *up* dink-dink-dink-dink-dink-dink-dink *down*. And so on, for perhaps half a dozen times, then just as you get near enough to taste fowl, more often than not the duck takes to the air. You make a last desperate leap, which does not come easy after being crouchy and dinking along on tiptoe, hoping to get a mouthful of plump bird. It was all a bit too slow and careful (not to say uncertain) for a wolf like Athaba who liked zipping over the scrub with the adrenalin racing through his body and his nerves tingling with electricity.

So on first seeing the duck, he was not all that enthusiastic about attempting the catch. At first, he just strolled in the general direction of the bird which was prodding about in some weed at the edge of a shallow stretch of water. However, as Athaba got closer, he realised that the duck was so intent on feeding itself it had not noticed him at all. He crouched, he dinked, crouched-and-dinked, crouched-and-dinked, l-e-a-p-t – and the bird was in his mouth. He was about to close his jaws on it, when it suddenly went all limp and floppy. It had died, like so many small creatures, of a heart attack. Voles did it all the time.

So, with the feast undamaged, Athaba trotted back to where the pack were gathering for the evening. He was very pleased with himself. The first person he wanted to show the bird to was Ragisthor, who was always telling Athaba he was the worst bird hunter in wolf history.

When Athaba had said, 'I'm not interested in hunting birds,' Ragisthor had replied, 'Little green shoot, you should be. You should be interested in hunting anything and everything that a wolf hunts, or one day you'll find yourself in no-hare country with no voles or deer-mice in sight. A place where the moose and caribou never venture. In this strange land there will only be one thing to eat, unless you count snow amongst your favourite foods. That something will be *birds*. In that land, precious fern, you will starve to death, because you cannot catch birds. For shame. For shame that a wolf should die because he likes to do only those things he is good at and scorns those things which he has to practise, over and over, merely to be adequate. Sometimes adequate is enough to prevent you from that ignominious death of which I speak. You can't chase hares which do not exist, no matter how skilled a harrier you might be.'

43

Athaba saw Ragisthor standing on the edge of a group. He dropped the duck to call to his friend, filling his chest for a loud victory howl. As he threw his head back, the note just about to be loosed from his throat, something took to the air in front of his eyes. It was the duck, that had been doing something ducks – and geese – were famous for. Feigning death. When a waterfowl has nothing else to lose, when the jaws are closing on it and there is no hope, why *not* pretend dead? Athaba had heard the story about the flock of geese who had seen a wolf coming, knew that hunters were over the brow of the hill so could not take flight, and had feigned death. Athaba had heard about the chagrin of the wolf, who when finding all his caches empty, had realised what had happened. Had then guessed that the geese had fooled him, had got up and shook the soil and twigs from their feathers, had a good snigger and waddled away to some hiding place. Athaba had heard that story all right. Had tucked it away somewhere in is mind, thinking, 'Mustn't forget. Geese feign death sometimes, when you sneak upon them.' No one had said anything about ducks, or any other birds or animals for that matter.

Ragisthor came strolling over to him, a puzzled expression around his jaws and in the position of his tail.

'What was that?' he asked.

'What?' replied, Athaba innocently.

'I saw a bird fly up from under your very nose. A duck, it seemed. Was I wrong? Perhaps I've been looking into too many sunsets?'

'Yes.'

'Yes what? Bird, or one sunset too many?'

Athaba cringed inside.

'Well, actually, yes there was a bird, and it was a duck.'

Ragisthor looked closely at his protégé.

'Ah, I see. Sneaking up on the pack, was it? Ready to peck the lot of us to death in one fowl stoop? Got it, little blade. Got it. And *you* the courageous hero managed to thwart this dastardly creature. Caught its measure on the wind, sallied forth and went for it despite the terrible danger. I see it barely escaped with its life . . .'

'What do you mean?' said Athaba, his heart sinking at every word Ragisthor uttered. He was envisaging later revelations to the pack and his standing amongst them deteriorating beyond recovery.

Ragisthor replied, 'You have a feather on your jaw.'

Athaba brushed rapidly at his jaws with his right paw and a small downy feather floated to the ground. He stared at it in dismay, knowing that Ragisthor must have guessed what had happened. The older wolf cocked his head on one side.

'I think this brave act of yours should be kept to ourselves, young sapling. We don't want Skassi to get too envious of your exploits, do we? Saving a wolf or two here and there is all very well for your image, but glory due for saving the whole pack is a bit hard for any rival to swallow. Yes?'

'Yes,' he replied in a very small voice.

Ragisthor turned to leave, then said over his shoulder.

'Don't be too despondent, my little fern. At least you're catching them now.'

Once Ragisthor had settled himself, Athaba joined the pack. Several seasons had gone by since his father had been killed by the caribou and his subsequent foolishness was now forgotten by most. Possibly Skassi still remembered but it was doubtful if any other wolf had bothered to retain the memory. Athaba's standing in the pack was very high. Amongst the senior *undermegas* his ranking was equalled only by that of a she-wolf whose pack had joined Athaba's. Skassi himself was now a *mega*, a good shoulderwolf and in strong contention for the position of hunter-warrior headwolf. He had brought down a caribou in full flight, had beaten another *mega* in a battle for a contested place in the inner circle next to Urkati and Itakru, and his howling skills, the range and quality of his tones, were enviable. Thankfully, Skassi had no time for quarrels that would not advance him further in the hierarchy of the pack.

Athaba was also frequently chosen as a shoulderwolf, though this was not unusual for an *undermega* shortly to become a *mega*. He was almost three years of age now: twelve seasons. Despite the appalling duck incident, he rarely made major errors out in the field. He knew his territory well, from the tundra flatlands to the subalpine fir-covered mountains. He knew its shades of light, its warm pockets during the cold winters, the likely position of quarry given the time of year and type of weather. He was sensitive to subtle changes in temperature, to odours beyond number, to the changing landscape. One of the things that Ragisthor had taught him (among many) was to maintain a flexible mentality.

'A closed mind, sapling, is a dead one. We are by nature rigid beasts. The structure of our society may seem flexible on the surface – headwolves that move aside for others in changing circumstances – but we shatter on impact with the unusual. We are disciplined and regimented from birth: necessary for pack survival but often destructive with regards to the individual. One day you may need to survive as Athaba, not as a member of a pack, and then you will need individuality . . .'

For the good of the pack, Athaba carried out his duties in the field and around camp assiduously. For the good of himself, he sometimes lay watching the landscape from a high vantage point. He observed differing patterns of light that fell on various parts of the tundra. Most wolves would have settled for the fact that there was light, or half-light, or dark. Athaba was poetically in love with light, hazy or clear, soft or hard. The shadows had a shallowness or depth to them which intrigued him. In the forests, shafts of hard light dazzled him, glades of soft light seduced him. Out on the tundra the slanted light had an ethereal quality with a power to influence travellers. Owl-light, gloaming magic, twilighted wetlands.

To most wolves, certainly to his own pack, a study of rock formations was more important than the nature of light. Each scar, crag, stack, tor, sill and overhang had its personal name. Every rock and stone was once a wolf heroine or hero, an ancestor from the *Firstdark*, caught in a dramatic death pose. These were the wolves that died in the initial great battles with the new creatures, the *men* that the giant *Groff* and his dogs helped out of the sea-of-chaos. In those days, the first men did not have guns but were bigger, stronger creatures who fought with sticks and stones. In their battles with these muscled, grisly people, the wolves were seized and their forelegs wrenched apart so that their hearts were split in two. The shock of such a sudden end transformed the heroes and heroines to stone. The bodies were flung far and wide across the landscape, the agony of their death-throes evident in the angled features of each petrified corpse. Such were these wolves from the *Firstdark* that even in death they were of use, forming landmarks to navigate by and pinnacles to use as watchtowers. They had such names as *Ooolhralahan, Aarwanlillaa, Uuraqahiiri*. All four-syllabled names which gave themselves to a distinctive howl. The sound of their titles crooned out of the throat smoothly and hung over the

46

moonlit landscape for many moments after the call. They were names to drift as droplets of moisture over the treetops, and fall like delicate rain upon the ears of waiting wolves many miles away.

These battles were not fought *during* the *Firstdark* but immediately after, since on leaving the sea-of-chaos men had ensured they would have light to hunt by. *Groff*, their provider, had given them a sun and moon at one throw. However, when the great open battles had been fought and lost on the plains, the wolves took to the high cold country where there was more cover. They were hunted down by the more ferocious of the men with dogs for trackers and scouts. By now men had discovered metal and killed with spears, arrows, axes and swords. True to their devious nature men devised tricks to entice wolves from hiding and to draw them into traps. They sent their young females out, dressed in hooded riding cloaks, to draw curious lone wolves to a place where men with axes were waiting to cut them to pieces. They placed domestic pigs as lures in stockades, which became increasingly more difficult to enter and leave: the first stockade was made of straw, which was easy to breach; the second made of sticks, which took more effort; but the third was made of stones and held a dozen men, ready with fire and sword. Once inside the stone stockade, the wolf could not escape and was at the mercy of his captors.

Wolves, unused to chicanery of any kind, tried to fight back in like manner. They sent in some of their number, smaller wolves posing as alsatians, to stalk the alleys and streets. The light of day was too revealing, and on the darkest of nights men carried lanterns which threw out powerful beams, so wolves waited for the moon. Then they sent these agents amongst the men, to discover their ways and report on any future plans to destroy the wolf population. However, wolves are wolves and find deceit very difficult. The time of the full moon is when wolves generally celebrate with each other in their comradeship, and they would forget where they were and lick a domestic dog's jaws in greeting, or nip his shoulder as a sign of friendship. Dogs rarely exchange such gestures, especially not at the time of the full moon, which is a wolf time. The dogs would raise a hue and cry which would spread to the men and human barking could be heard throughout the world. In the beginning the wolves often escaped. Men rely on vision and were not used to hunting in half-light. Thus they fumbled with their dull metal bullets, dropping them on the ground and mishandling them. Such things do not deter the most devious creatures on this earth for long. Soon men began to make bullets of silver, even though this metal is precious to them, because it shines under the moonlight and is more easily seen at such an hour. So wolves gave up their practice of spying and retired to even colder climes, in the far north, where men were loath to follow. There were still some who would chase them, even through blizzards and over difficult terrain, but their numbers were few.

Canids are very proud of their history: wolves arrogantly so. It is a past full of suffering and valour with almost all the credit going to the canids. Even dogs, though traitorous to their own kind, are faithful to death once new loyalties have been established. It has caused others to speculate on whether the dingoes, jackals, dogs, foxes and wolves once got together and made it all up. Such speculations have given rise to many alternatives, one of which states that wolves and their cousins were originally long-legged otters that lived in trees, who only came down once the dust had settled under men's feet. But that story was probably spread around by a cynical lemming.

In years when vegetation on the tundra is abundant, the ground seethes with rapidly breeding voles and lemmings. There are several species of both which burrow through snow in the winter or scramble over the moss in the summer. In such years there might be fifty lemmings where two seasons before stood a single pair. Their breeding overtakes the food supply, and multitudes of vole and lemming refugees can be witnessed crossing sea ice, tundra and mountain ranges, going no one knows where. In such years, the canid predators, the coyotes, foxes and wolves, eat well.

Unlike the savage shrew families, who are entirely carnivorous and crunch away happily on beetles and bugs, the lemmings and voles depend on good quality vegetation. If this is not there, the numbers shrink. In such years, the wolves seriously have to consider each hunt and cannot rely on small rodents to fill their larder.

Itakru gathered together four wolves for an attack on some musk oxen to the south. One of the shoulderwolves was Skassi, the other Athaba. There was a junior *undermega* on one flank and the *mega* Rennedati, whose hunting skills were on the wane, on the left. The rest of the pack were assigned tasks by Urkati, from hunting smaller ground prey, to pathfinding for the next camp.

'We're off after a musk ox,' Athaba told Ragisthor, not without a trace of excitement in his voice. His hunting blood was up and that peculiar heady feeling which overtakes wolves when their adrenalin is racing was already beginning to have an affect on him. It was as if he were in someone else's body: he experienced a feeling of detachment from himself. It was almost as if he were ill. Yet his senses remained keen. In fact this feeling seemed to sharpen his senses and hone the edge of his brain. There was the dangerous thought that he could do anything, was invincible.

Ragisthor said, 'You be careful. Those muskies are not as docile as they seem, young fern. Their horns are sharp. I know. I've had a punctured shank and two cracked ribs from those beasts. They want to live too, you know.'

'Right. I'll remember,' cried Athaba, eager to be on his way. How could he ignore this flame in his breast? Ragisthor was getting old and cautious, naturally, in his middle age. But such sentiments did not do for a young wolf about to become a *mega* in just over a season. He left Ragisthor, standing elegantly on a horizontal slab of stone, looking as if he had been carved by artistic hands.

The five wolves set off, deerwalking across the rough rocky ground. With the wind in his nostrils and riffling his shank hair, Athaba felt good. The light was sharp and bright, the air clear. Only one or two clouds like fine underhair floated across the sky. It was a curiously flimsy day with airborne seeds drifting by. There was a silence balanced delicately on the ridge which threatened to slip away at any moment.

Athaba remembered he had not taken leave of his mother, Meshiska, but then realised she would understand. He glanced across at Skassi, stiff-legged and high-headed. There was no doubt about it, the bully of his earlier seasons was a handsome-looking wolf. He had strength, and intelligence too. But what was it that Ragisthor had said about him? *He lacks imagination. Never underestimate the potential of good creative thinking, young shrub. You have it. Nurture it.* Athaba was not quite sure how to 'nurture it' but it pleased him that he had something Skassi had not, whatever it was. Still, Athaba was anxious to remain on the right side of the cinnamon-coated Skassi, which seemed easy to do so long as one showed deference. When Skassi and he came too close together and Skassi produced dominant gestures, then Athaba would follow with submissive ones: the raised paw, the curled under tail, grin, lowered body, eye-whites and flattened ears. The lot. This was not cowardice or even servility, it was protocol. He still suffered the occasional body-slam, or bite, from a senior wolf, though Skassi had not gone this far for a long time.

They came across an old kill from two days previously. The ravens were still working at the dried streaks of meat on bones which had once been a wild sheep.

'Ghood ghunting,' cried the beaked ones, stamping over the carcass and flapping their black shiny wings. 'Crussh 'em, keell 'em, make 'em dedid!' They shouted. 'Ghood wolkfers. Ghood wolfers. Niyse sharp teethings. Haaaaaaak!'

The wolves, as they always did, ignored the scavengers that followed their pack. The ravens considered themselves part of the family, but the wolves pretended there were no such creatures on earth as the revolting little parasites that tagged along behind the pack.

'Ghed 'em throtes!' screamed a raven, as a parting call. 'Ghed 'em throte and rippit 'em opens! Haaaak! Haaaak! Haaaaaaaaak!'

After half a day's travel they came across the musk oxen, who had unfortunately caught the wolves' scent when the wind veered sharply without warning. The great beasts, looking like a cross between a yak and a bison, immediately formed a tight defensive ring with the young animals in the centre, and their horns outward. They stood on the plain, their fear evident, and long shaggy guard hairs brushed the ground as they swayed from side to side. The smell of their matted underfelt wafted up the ridge to the wolves, who knew that the wind had again changed but that the quarry was now warned and on edge.

The wolves showed themselves, and began to circle the prey. Athaba, the *gentle* Athaba, was somewhere else now. Inside his skin was the *hunting* Athaba who had scented the kill. His brain was bone-white light, with blood red. The air came out of his nostrils in short tight breaths. His body was primed, every neuron charged. Scent, sound, sight, touch, all alert to a fine hair's end, finely quivering. Every subtle change was noted instantly, judged, muscle adjustments made to shadow-thin precision. Ice-keen, thorn sharp. Athaba the hunter-killer.

Even as he began circumnavigating the quarry, Athaba sensed their restlessness was due to more than the presence of the wolves. Of course, predators like himself disturbed them and put them on the defensive, but they had been alert and edgy when the hunting party arrived. There was something else bothering them, some other animal in the vicinity which had the musk oxen nervously stamping at the ground. Athaba lifted his nose and tried for a scent.

As he was doing so, the herd suddenly broke and the animals began to stampede across the plain. Athaba, in the act of cutting off any retreat, had not quite closed the surrounding circle. He jumped desperately for a passing bull, struck the creature's shoulder, failed to get a grip and somersaulted over the top to land on his feet again. Itakru and Skassi had singled out a another single quarry and were harassing it, but failed to bring it down.

'Follow close!' cried Itakru, and set off in pursuit, though he was not running flat out by any means. The wolves were faster than the musk oxen but needed to conserve strength for the kill.

The muskies disappeared over the gentle ridge and the wolves followed after, only to discover another creature on the far side, a fisher that had just landed a catch from the plain's river. It was a brown bear, the largest of all bears, and it had already been disturbed by the musk oxen. It stood on its hindlegs and faced the oncoming wolves.

Athaba had seen brown bears from a distance, but at such close quarters this giant beast looked as formidable and impassable as a high rock face with claws and teeth. When it reared and stood tall, it seemed to block out the whole sky. Its shadow covered the land. It spread its great arms as if to enfold the whole hunting party and crush them into a single ball of pulp. Its long claws slashed at the air. Its eyes reflected its fury. Athaba was too stunned by the sheer size of the bear to be afraid.

Athaba knew that ferocious as brown bears could be, they were normally mild mannered and easy to avoid. This one, however, was in Skassi's path, who in his zeal seemed incapable of stopping or finding a way around the beast. He charged ahead, regardless of the danger. When the bear made a move across, Skassi leapt like a salmon, up and sideways, his athletic muscled body twisting to reach the bear's throat.

51

The bear was of course incensed at this unjustified attack. She had been quietly gathering together a fish and vegetable meal when surprised first by a thundering group of dense-skulled muskies, followed by several uncivil snarling wolves. She felt she was entitled to be up on her hind legs in protest, defending her catch. Then to be attacked! Not good. Not good at all.

She let out a roar of rage in her own language, as Skassi's teeth skimmed her throat fur, and with surprising speed and agility for her bulk gripped the wolf around the chest with her great arms. Holding him captive with one arm, she raked Skassi down his flank with her right claws as he tried to bite her face. He screamed and struggled, now realising how great was his danger. Athaba guessed that until then Skassi had been working on instinct, attacking blindly the thing that was between him and his quarry and not thinking about the consequences. His eyes had been 'full of blood' as they say. Now he knew he was in terrible straits and wanted to be out of them quickly.

Athaba, Itakru and the terrified youngest wolf ran in to harry her legs, snarling and snapping, while the experienced Rennedati ran behind to divert her. They played head-dart tactics, trying to make her let go of their pack-member. She refused. Now that her blood was up, she was going to see gore. She began to crush the wolf in her arms. Her jaw twisted sideways with the effort. Athaba heard one of Skassi's ribs go, as loud as the cracking of pack ice, and the bear's victim howled pitifully.

Itakru jumped for her right shoulder, but she managed to ward him off with a sweep of her great paw while still keeping a grip on Skassi. The shoulderwolf had however wriggled down a little. Athaba tried for a leg bite and was marginally successful. Then he was kicked backwards, head over heels, on to the soft moss. He was on his feet instantly but somewhat shaken. The power behind that limb had been tremendous and it had been nothing more than a flick which had sent him flying. Surely Skassi was lost? How could creatures like themselves deal with such strength?

Another rib cracked, louder than before.

Skassi had gone limp now, his eyes rolling into white. Athaba could see the pain in his expression. Although Skassi had bullied him in the past, he felt nothing but compassion for his rival. He could feel Skassi's agony just by looking at him. If they did not get him away from the bear soon, Skassi would suffer serious internal damage and there would be no saving him.

The fifth wolf, Rennedati, was now behind the bear and she leapt to grip its ear for a second. The brown creature let out another great roar, this time of pain, and swung sideways, sending Rennedati flying through the air. She landed on her rump, but was immediately on her feet. Athaba guessed what was going through her mind. *Got to keep out of the way of those arms!* The bear, having dropped Skassi at last, was soon after her, running on all fours. Rennedati was away like a cat, her hindlegs reaching so far between her forelegs she was knocking herself under her chin with her shins. Athaba could see by her skidding over-reactions that Rennedati was desperate to keep clear of the claws. She darted, she twisted, she leapt and turned. She made more telemarks on that tundra than a hare with a fox on its tail. Twice the great claws lashed out, and twice they skimmed Rennedati's hind quarters by a fraction. She was the oldest wolf among the hunting party, but at that moment an *undermega* would have had difficulty in matching her acrobatics.

The youngest wolf was watching his superior with wide frightened eyes and Athaba could hear the yearling whispering under his breath, but whether it was encouragement to Rennedati or a prayer to some ancestor to intervene and save them all from destruction was not clear.

Athaba joined Itakru in trying to divert the attention of the she-bear from Rennedati. They raced around the beast, snapping and snarling at it, yet trying to remain out of range of its claws. Athaba went in too close, racing across between the bear and the retreating Rennedati. Even as he was carrying out the action he knew he had misjudged it. A huge paw swung out and lifted him off his feet.

He never felt the rock that his head struck. He simply gave himself up to blackness.

Chapter Five

When Athaba opened his eyes, the land was covered in a light fall of snow. He tried to lift his head but at first the pain was so sharp he felt it was wiser to remain still, lying flat on his side. It began to get dark around him and the whiteness less hurtful on his eyes. From his right ear, down the side of his eye, and on to his jaws, was a matted stiffness of hair. He knew this to be dried blood and extended his tongue carefully to lick away at the clotted material. He did not want to return to camp with an exposed wound which would concern the other wolves of the pack.

As the time passed his body began to chill and he knew he would have to move if he was to survive. He climbed unsteadily to his feet and tottered to a stream, a thin sliver of water, not far away. There he dipped his head in the freezing beck. He lapped some of the water, filling his empty belly with cold liquid. Finding a space between two rocks, he settled down to rest again. Dizziness overcame him and he slipped away for a while into the twilight world he had previously inhabited.

The daylight hours were short. One night stretched into another. He found the strength to hunt small creatures on the wide tundra: lemmings that had begun to burrow beneath the snow. Frequently, he had to lie on his side as a feeling of giddy sickness overtook him which did not suit his normal eating habits, that of feast or famine. It was not Athaba's nature to have a bit here and a bit there, with pieces of grass or herbs from under the snow in between. Yet, that was the way in which he was having to conduct his meals. It brought home to him how sick he was.

On the next day he began to recover properly. The wound on his head had stopped seeping every time he moved and he managed to mouth-spear some grayling from the stream. Once he had eaten the fish he surveyed the landscape, intending to set out in search of the pack.

It was a murky day, with poor light, and the darkness touched upon both sides of noon. Athaba went forth, retracing his movements of a few days previously. When he reached the place where the dens were supposed to be, he found them empty, however. There was a strong smell of humans around and he guessed the pack had moved because of the presence of man. He attempted to follow the trail which had almost gone cold. Once again he collapsed but came to as the light was fading. He felt strange, a little dreamy and not fully himself, but still he decided he was strong enough, physically, to continue.

On the way he came across some blood on the snow which might have belonged to a wolf. He also found a kill which had been abandoned. There was very little meat on it. Another wolf had been there. He saw some hairs on the snow which might have come from his own coat, had he not been sure that it was his first time in the area. He broke some old bones which the ravens had not yet found and sucked the marrow from their hollows.

Towards morning he had one of his dizzy spells and flopped at the base of a pine to rest. Then he smelled the smoke from the nearby fire, which normally he would have scented earlier had he not been ill, and crawled closer to see that there were humans, three of them. They were huddled around a small smouldering pile of logs, breathing heavily inside their coverings. Athaba realised they were all asleep. There was also a small lean-to, under which was a fourth prone body. The pelts that they slept in smelled of grease and fat. Athaba could not see guns but knew they would be around somewhere, probably inside the sleeping furs being kept warm and ready to shoot. Athaba was happy that he could smell no huskies, nor could he see a sled of any sort. Obviously the men had set out before the snow started. They appeared to be on foot, but it was known to wolves that hunters were often dropped and picked up by machines. Some of these machines came from the air, some across country leaving twin tracks in the snow.

Athaba sniffed, looked around, and spied some burned meat at the edge of the fire ashes. He began to salivate. The odour of the meat made his stomach churn. Climbing to his feet he stepped out and entered the men's camp. He padded softly between the sleepers, knowing he could be away in an instant. Just as he was lowering his head to snatch up the meat, he heard a small movement from the lean-to. Looking across, a pair of grey eyes met his. For a moment the two creatures, wolf and man, were locked and lost in one another.

Then Athaba grabbed the hunk of meat and darted out of the camp while the human was struggling inside his sleeping furs. Athaba guessed that the hunter was trying to get at his gun, but when he looked back the man had a small black box in his hands and was aiming this at the young wolf instead.

What? A new weapon? Athaba did not intend waiting around to find out. He sought a place amongst some trees where the wind was broken and diverted. There he tore at the meat, filling his belly. It tasted strange but good. He wished there were more of it.

Within a short time he was back on the trail of his pack. At first the air was smoky with windblown snow that swirled up into the murky skies, but by noon it had cleared a little. The pack was heading north again, into the oncoming winter. He followed.

At one point a gyr falcon came dropping out of the heavens and snatched a rock ptarmigan from the ground not far in front of the wolf. Athaba watched the bird climb with its prey in its talons, then it turned, no doubt heading for a high place. He lost it quickly, amongst the greyness above.

It seemed to grow colder by the minute. The long hours of summer had gone, the whistling swans had flown south again leaving the greenish waters of the tundra lakes to freeze over. Snowy owls had ceased to gather and now hunted singly, patrolling the silent skies, on the watch for small birds. Athaba could also smell lynx on the wind and kept his nose keen for stronger scents of creatures with black tufted ears and side-whiskers. These narrow-eyed cats would not attack a fully grown wolf but could be formidable if surprised.

Athaba came to a shallow valley and there below him was a wolf pup playing with a piece of stiff hide. It was taking the frozen patch of leather and skimming it across some thin ice, watching it spin as it slid along. Then the youngster would race after it, catch it in its jaws, and repeat the exercise.

Athaba called.

'Navista!'

The pup looked up, seemed startled, then ran away. Athaba followed it, into another narrow valley. There he could see the pack gathered. Navista had run into camp ahead of him, shouting that he had seen an ancestor come back from the dead. There were one or two alarmed looks and some of the youngsters were up on their paws ready for flight, but Ragisthor called for calm.

He came out to meet Athaba.

'Well, well, sapling. We thought you dead.'

'No, I survived. I was unconscious for a while.'

The older wolf appeared a little perturbed.

'So it seems. Yet, you were definitely reported as dead. The bear chased away the rest of the hunter-warriors, leaving you and Skassi behind. Apparently, Skassi's ribs were hurting too much for him to be able to take flight instantly. When he had recovered enough to make good his escape, he found you lying – dead – not far away.'

Athaba nodded.

'Not dead, Ragisthor, as you can see.'

Now the warmth returned to Ragisthor's eyes.

'Skassi will be disappointed,' he murmured. 'Welcome home, little shrub. It's good to see you. I grieved, I mourned, and here you are, standing as strong as a willow wand in the spring. What are you trying to do? Thaw an ice-hard heart? One can't afford these feelings of affection. They lead to one's downfall, eventually.'

Athaba gave him a gentle shoulder-slam.

'You didn't grieve for me?'

'I swear. I was in a state of grey collapse. The light had gone out of the sky and a cold wind had entered my world.'

Athaba said, 'That was just the winter coming on.'

Ragisthor looked around him.

'Really? I hadn't noticed. I thought it was the absence of my friend that had robbed the world of light and warmth. It just goes to show one can't trust one's emotions. The winter? Well, well.'

'You're an old fake, Ragisthor. Still, I missed you.'

This time Ragisthor was serious.

'I missed you too. It would not have done to show it, of course. I have my reputation to consider. The hardened cynic.' His expression became lighter. 'Now, step alongside me, and we'll walk into camp together. They're a little worried by you, of course, coming back from the dead. But we'll show them there's nothing to fear from our old *undermega* Athaba. There's not much news to tell. We moved, of course, as you found out. Skassi has been impossible, utterly impossible, since he attacked the bear.

57

It's my guess that Itakru wasn't sure whether to report it as a foolish, not to say, stupid confrontation, or as an act of courage and audacity. He chose the latter because it enhanced his own subsequent actions. To lead an unnecessary attack on a bear does not do much for one's reputation, even given that one is making the best of a bad situation. So Skassi come out a hero.

'You'll have to lick goodbye to your thoughts of becoming hunter-warrior headwolf one day, unless of course something happens to Skassi. I think he's got it nearly cornered. You, my little friend, have got a little climb ahead of you, to get back your status. It is all very heroic to be wounded and manage to crawl back to the pack on the day, but you have been gone some time. You have gathered some *foreignness* about you, which will need to be seen as nothing more than the residue of your convalescence.'

'What do you mean?' asked Athaba, as they neared the others. He could see the wolves of his own pack, eyeing him warily, as if he were a stranger trying to intrude, or was bringing bad odours from the outside world back into the camp.

Ragisthor turned to glance at him.

'There's something different about you, sapling. It might be that you have grown in spirit, but you have something about you which was not there before. You would do well to hide it.' His voice grew louder. 'Look at this. Our Athaba, come home to us. It seems it takes more than a bear to kill one of us, eh? Here he is, fit and well, after his long convalescence out on the tundra.'

Urkati came forward, sniffing the air.

'You have the smell of man about you,' she said.

Athaba shook his head.

'Not man, his meat. I stole some from his campfire. I was weak and hungry and it was a last resort.'

'I see. And you're fit now? You were reported dead.'

Athaba looked across to where Skassi was standing.

'An understandable error,' he said, 'the report was almost true. Somehow I managed to retain my strength.'

There was still a hardness in Urkati's eyes.

'But you have been gone some twenty-three days . . .'

Inside, Athaba felt the alarm go through his torso and limbs, though he tried to keep it from his face. Twenty-three days! He had thought he had been away for four, or five days at the most. Twenty-three days! Something was wrong inside his

58

head. Either his giddy spells stretched over days, instead of a single day, or he was losing days in his memory. Whichever it was, he needed to keep such a thing secret. The pack did not like wolves with strange heads. His brother had been killed because of such strangeness.

'Well,' said Urkati, after a staring-out during which Athaba's mind screamed to be released, 'we'll see. You say you've spent all that time recovering?'

'Yes. Catching marmots and voles, eating grass. I'm quite well now.'

This was reluctantly accepted by Urkati and Athaba was allowed take his place within the pack again. However, his standing amongst the wolves was never the same again. No matter what he did, how well he performed his duties, he was always regarded with a certain suspicion, sometimes faint, sometimes strong. If he was spoken of behind his back for any reason, there would be a wrinkling of the nose, as if a slightly unpleasant smell were in the air.

From that time on it was noticed he took himself off occasionally, to be on his own. This he did when he felt one of his dizzy spells coming on. Though he learned to control these bouts to a certain degree, and the periods between them became longer, they never completely went away. He knew it was essential to keep his problem from public knowledge and did not even trust Ragisthor with the secret. His mother – well, his mother had raised him, but she had raised other pups too. He was not *that* special to her. In short, he did not trust his mother either.

Skassi had recently been called a great-great hunter-warrior and was too full of himself at that time to bother with Athaba, though when the subject of Athaba's initiation ceremony into the circle of *megas* came up, Skassi was adamant.

'The wolf, I seem to remember, has been under scrutiny not once, but *twice* since his birth. You will recall the time he went off and carried out strange rituals, the meanings of which are known only to him, at the time of the hunter-warrior Aksishem's death? Then there was his more recent behaviour. I am reluctant to brand any wolf a *mystic* without irrefutable evidence, but I am equally reluctant to allow a wolf with such a damning history into the circle of *megas* . . .'

For once, Ragisthor did not defend him. The older wolf was beginning to grow tired – the exhaustion of age – and no doubt he felt Athaba's position was indefensible. He made no explanations to Athaba, and Athaba asked for none.

So, Athaba's initiation day came and went without reference to him becoming a *mega*. He awoke in the morning (at this time unaware that the decision had been taken to exclude him) full of hope and promise. Once the status of *mega* had been attained, he felt he could begin to work his way back to his former position once again. There would be a renewed respect for him, so he thought, when he joined the inner circle.

Gradually, he realised he was being shunned out of embarrassment, even by those who normally would have passed a few words with him. He went to his mother.

'Meshiska,' he said, 'is there to be no ceremony?'

At first his mother would not even look at him.

'Go away,' she said at last, her eyes full of weary anger. 'You've shamed your father's memory with your strange antics. I disown you.'

'I have shamed no one,' said Athaba. 'I have lived, hunted and fought as well as any wolf – better than most – and have always had the good of the pack at heart. It's you who should be ashamed, that you turn from your son when he needs support, because there is a wolf with power who is my enemy.'

Meshiska turned on him fiercely.

'Don't – speak – to – me – that – way! I can still take you to task and I will, make no mistake!'

'I doubt it mother. I have grown stronger since I have had to rely on myself and not on the pack.'

He flexed his broad shoulders, which were indeed hard and muscled. Athaba knew he was a match for any wolf in the pack, even Skassi, if it came to one to one combat. He had spent a winter hunting by himself, having to go out alone into the teeth of blizzards, while others were resting, knowing he had to prove himself worthy. It had all been futile. No matter what kills he brought back, they were taken from him grudgingly and distributed without a word of praise to him. And, of course, the scrag ends of the carcasses always ended in his belly.

'However,' he continued, 'I would no more harm you than I would bite off my own paw.'

He turned and left her then, knowing that without a ceremony, with its howls and songs, without his vigil on the rock, without the *acceptance* of the rest of the pack, he could not be called a

60

mega. Equally, since he was now over three years of age, he was no longer an *undermega*. He was nothing, nothing at all. Soon the youngsters would begin to jibe. Soon the kills he brought in would be spurned, no matter how hungry the pack was.

He would have been better off dead.

He carried out the vigil on his own that night, travelling overland to a high-tower rock, and there meditating on his life. He thought about what he had done and what he would do. He considered his faults and made promises to himself to overcome them. When he descended in the morning, he felt spiritually cleansed and ready to withstand the contempt and ridicule of the pack. Life was quite different now, from what it had been just a few months previously, but he knew he had to stop himself from growing bitter. Such feelings eat away at the spirit until there is nothing left inside either.

He returned to the pack and no one commented on his absence. His mother, when she acknowledged his existence at all, looked at him with accusing eyes. It was as if he, Athaba, had done something terrible to the pack. His unjust punishment became more bearable when Meshiska died a natural death in the middle of the summer. It was at the time of the loose pack, when only the two of them were in the vicinity. She contracted dysentery, became dehydrated, and dried into a husk from which the breath eventually ceased to whisper. At the height of the illness, Athaba tried bringing her mouthfuls of water, but she rejected any help from him. Her eyes had yellowed and had lost their moisture, but they still held her disdain for him. He found her one morning, stiff, her hair coarse and lifeless. Her neck was extended and her mouth partially open, as if reaching for a drink.

When the pack came together in the autumn, Athaba found that the summer had not been kind to Ragisthor either. The wolf looked old and worn, his eyes pouched and his jaw grizzled. He snapped at others when addressed and no longer seemed inclined to seek Athaba's company. Athaba sought him out one morning, when the dew was like spittle upon the plants.

Athaba said, 'You have rejected me, along with all the others. I thought I could trust you to remain my friend.'

Ragisthor shook his head.

'These are selfish thoughts, sapling. You judge things always with regard to yourself. It's not you I've drawn away from, but life. I'm in pain. There's a burning inside me which won't go away.'

Immediately, Athaba apologised to the older wolf.

'I'm sorry. You're right, I was just thinking of myself. I'm alone so much now that I've come to believe the only one in the world with troubles is me. Can I help?'

'No one can help. If it goes on, I shall not see the end of the summer.' He turned his soulful eyes on Athaba. 'But don't feel sorry for me, sapling. I've had a good life – you too. None of us is guaranteed happiness from the moment we are born. You could have been your brother, killed not long after leaving the womb. Would that have been better?'

'It might have been.'

'No, no. We had some fine times together, little shrub, would you have them be nothing? Just one of these days is surely worth many of these? Yes, these are bad days for you, but who knows, they may change again tomorrow. And you have had the good ones. Skassi can't take those away from you. You may not believe this but Skassi has *always* been unhappy, and he always will be. You are much more fortunate than he. You have known many days of joy. He has known few, if any at all. His ambition has burned his spirit to nothing. You must not envy Skassi, rather he should envy you.

'And look at these new experiences you are going through. They are turning you into the strongest wolf I've ever seen. Strong in body and limb, strong in spirit. Why, you don't even need *me* any longer. Once upon a time you relied on me so much I was afraid to die. Now I'm not.'

Athaba was alarmed by the tone of Ragisthor's words.

'You're not going to die?' he said. 'Not so soon after my mother?'

The evening began to melt into darkness. Shadows chased each other across the land, amongst the grasses. The clouds turned on one another.

'You're being selfish again,' murmured Ragisthor. 'If I want to die, then surely it's up to me. I think I shall go tonight.'

But he did not die that night. The winter was almost through before he finally sighed his last. In the end, he was whispering blasphemies about the red people that had once covered the land and how they would return and bring the old ways with them. Ragisthor had never known those times, though they were part of wolf history, before the new white hunters, but he spoke as if he had lived then. His eyes burned hotter than fires the night he died and he unnerved the whole pack by going down to a stream and rolling in the ochre clay, so that he looked like something not-wolf. The pack shunned him, when he walked into camp, his coat stiff with shiny river clay and those two eyes burning deep in their sockets. He was like something cast from the earth.

When Athaba asked him why he had done it, he rambled about always having done the expected, so why not when going out to where no one could touch him, why not do the unexpected?

'You're a master at that, Athaba. Eccentric wolfery. I always admired that in you. Brave sapling. I can only find the courage in death. Look at them!' he nodded contemptuously to where the others were cowering, each of them hoping one would come forward and denounce this strange behaviour. 'Creatures of correctness. How I despise them. Don't judge all packs by this one, sapling. There are those more enlightened. GRHAAAAAA!' he yelled, at the eyes in front of him. The he sighed and rolled over.

Athaba howled over his body the whole night. In the morning Skassi came and told him to leave the corpse alone. It was a mistake on the part of the new headwolf. The pressure in Athaba's chest had reached the point of explosion. Athaba was just looking for someone on whom to vent all that tightly contained emotion. Skassi was the perfect target.

'Make me!' he said.

Skassi had left himself no choice. He attacked, probably thinking that Athaba would humble himself, as he had always done in the past. Athaba did no such thing. He met the attack with such ferocity that the fear immediately sprang to Skassi's features. In the first hit their leaping bodies struck each other in mid air and they cracked skulls. Both wolves fell to the ground dazed.

Skassi was first on his feet, a trickle of blood finding a pathway down his brow and across his eye. He blinked away the blood and then made a rush for Athaba who was now struggling to his feet. A powerful body-slam sent Athaba spinning into a tree, which knocked the wind out of his lungs. He knew he was in trouble and somehow had to give himself a few seconds respite. He rolled down a slope and lay still at the bottom, his lungs heaving.

Skassi started down the incline, obviously still a little dizzy from the clash of heads himself. Once, he tripped and staggered, but quickly found his feet again.

By the time he reached the bottom of the slope, Athaba was a little recovered and got up to face his opponent.

'You piece of meat,' snarled Skassi, 'you've gone too far this time. I'm going to tear your hide open.'

Some of the rest of the pack had been alerted to the fight and were standing, watching, from the top of the incline. Athaba could sense their hostility towards him. To them he was a wolf who did strange things, who had fits and was not to be trusted in times of emergency. Skassi, on the other hand, was headwolf of the moment. There was little doubt that the majority of the pack were rooting for Skassi, whatever they thought of him personally.

'Not this time,' replied Athaba with the same determination his dead sister Tesha might have shown in the circumstances, 'not in front of those miserable wretches up there. This is *my* time.'

And with that he flung himself at Skassi, gripping the headwolf by the ruff and spinning him round. He let go and watched as Skassi lost his footing and struck a half-buried rock. Skassi was on his feet again in an instant and the pair of them began circling one another, looking for an opening. Twice Skassi leapt forwards, only to find his jaws clashing on air. Once Athaba went for the flank but came away with only fur in his mouth.

Finally, they both went in together again, but this time two pairs of scissor jaws locked on each other, like forked sticks rammed together. Both wolves had a grip of the soft sides of his opponent's mouth. Athaba felt intense pain flooding from his face: he knew if he relaxed his grip Skassi would crack the joints of his jaws and cripple him. Instead, he attempted to force his adversary down to his knees and hopefully on to his back.

Skassi seemed equally determined that he should not be the one to go down. They were like a couple of wild bulls, locked together, of equal strength. They pushed against one another, their teeth deep into flesh, and swayed back and forth.

Then suddenly, Skassi's legs went from under him. He went sliding backwards over the forest floor, his legs skittering, trying to get a grip on the loose pine needles. Athaba then transferred his grip to the other wolf's throat and Skassi's eyes opened wide, knowing that he was a moment away from death.

At that point a *mega* broke from the group of spectators and shoulder-slammed Athaba away from his kill. Exhausted, Athaba rolled away. Other *megas* came for him, driving him away from their headwolf. They called Athaba mad. They said he was rabid, out of his mind, not fit to live with other wolves.

Skassi, limping and dropping blood onto the snow, called:

'You are *utlah*! Outcast. Outlaw.'

Athaba knew then that he could never go back to the pack. He was banished, without friends or family, and could be torn to pieces by his former kin if he even tried. A horror settled on his heart. This was worse than death, to be cast out. From this point on he would have to walk alone.

He raved at his persecutors, running at them, attempting to breach their lines. They stood fast against him, their eyes hard, and a panic took hold of Athaba. He ran off, into the forest, and kept going until his legs gave out and he fell exhausted to the ground. He felt wretched and spiritually disabled. A great misery was in him and he was hollow. When he had regained his breath he just lay there and howled and howled until his throat was sore and his voice was hoarse. None of this did him any good at all. It did not heal his spirit, nor did it mend his hurt. He remained an empty thing, a walking pelt, a bitter soulless being.

From that time on Athaba followed behind the pack with the ravens. He ate carrion with the black birds and the coyotes. He was truly alone in the world, having no pack. The young wolves taunted him from the safety of the ridges, as if he were an old ragged musk ox, silly in his brain. They called him weakling and coward. He could have broken their puppy necks with one snap of his jaws, but he took their jeers, knowing that the young will always find a scapegoat for their own fears. If it had not been him, it would have been one of themselves, and he did not care any longer.

The ravens and coyotes treated him warily, with a kind of respect. They could see he was no broken-down reprobate or a wolf whose brain had addled. They were aware of his strength.

'*Utlah*,' the ravens said, 'whaat you do? Why you by *utlah*? You keel him someone? Eh?'

He was a king amongst the scavengers, a chief among bone-pickers, and he was answerable only to himself. He had the satisfaction of knowing that with his expulsion from the pack had come the downfall of Skassi. Athaba had lost his place with the pack, but Skassi had lost his status.

Skassi's wounds, first by the bear and then by Athaba, had reduced his skills as a hunter. His reactions were far from sharp and there was sometimes a momentary delay when going in for the kill. The bear and Athaba had created a psychological problem for Skassi which muted his zeal. He no longer threw himself vigorously into a situation. He paused, just a moment, assessing things first. That moment was enough to take away his edge over other ambitious wolves.

And of course, he had lost in single combat. No wolf's reputation remains undamaged after being beaten by another wolf in a one-to-one fight. He had lost the respect he needed to remain as headwolf hunter-warrior. He retained, above all, a cold hatred towards the wolf that had brought him down. The only thing that stopped him from going out and killing Athaba, as that outcast slept, was the fact that he knew banishment was a worse punishment than death.

Finding a new position in the pack was not as easy as Skassi thought it would be. There were only so many places, for so many wolves, and they all had their ambitions. It was not a case of naturally slotting into the position vacated by the new headwolf, because others had been waiting for that opening too, and the competition was fierce. There were other aspects, which contributed to his problems of finding a new position. When a headwolf lost his status, as dramatically as Skassi had done, he or she automatically lost a great deal of face. When a headwolf fell, enemies suddenly emerged from the shadows, and took their small vengeances. These were, of course, wolves who had at some time or another stepped out of line and had had to be reprimanded or punished by the headwolf Skassi. Some felt they had been victims of injustice. There were grudges to contend with, and petty jealousies that could now be voiced.

Thus, Skassi found himself with quite a battle on his hands, simply to keep from being pushed back as far as tailwolf. One night, as he was licking his paws and reflecting on his lot, he thought how Athaba would have gloried a little in the results of his single combat. Not only had he beaten Skassi in a one-to-one, but his victory had shattered Skassi's life.

Skassi, through straightforward determination, managed to hold on to the status of flankwolf. In time he hoped to work his way back to a shoulderwolf position (though not the top one, of course) and pursued these ends. He was diligent in his duties, though he had lost a lot of his former flair for insider politics, and fiercely pro-pack. When his turn came round to lead the Howling, he always chose the most traditional of songs and grew dangerously close to becoming maudlin. He was indeed once accused of mawkishness. He responded to the charge with such formal dignity that the council of *megas* who had called him to task almost ended up praising his patriotism.

It was at that interview that Skassi realised the value of chauvinism, in real terms, and he fell into the role of the aggressive patriot with such vigour, that by the time he made shoulderwolf again he believed in it himself. The pack was not only a good pack, it was the *best* pack that was or ever had been. Its only faults were the trivial flaws in a few of its members and these could bullied out of them, until it was perfect. He made this his sole object in life: to raise the pack to perfection. The individual members of the pack hated him for attempting to scourge them of their slight faults, though they were afraid to speak out because his patriotism was an almost impenetrable defence. An individual would expose himself to the body, and his enemies would take the opportunity to crush him, even though each one of them secretly agreed with his view.

So, Skassi was despised by all.

Yet, he loved *them*, and displayed this love so violently that he was safe from their hatred.

He was unerringly devoted to them and the removal of their sins, their small stains, their tiny blemishes, and had Athaba known what it was like in the pack, during the seasons that followed his banishment, he would have been glad to be the outcast he had become.

PART TWO

The Night of the Raven

Chapter Six

Ravens are large and formidable birds, almost twice the size of kestrels. Athaba was surprised by their intelligence, thinking that because they were scavengers they must be stupid, because creatures with any brain at all can hunt their own food. After he had been with them for a while, he began to revise his opinion. The ravens lived very well, without having to hunt. They knew how to get the very last piece of meat from carcass. He watched in amazement the first time he saw one using its intelligence to get at meat that would have been inaccessible to a wolf.

It was the carcass of an elk and when every scrap had been stripped from the bones, and Athaba had used his jaws to break open the last of the weaker bones to get at the marrow, he said to the ravens:

'It's finished.'

One of the black birds hopped forward.

'Nein, nein. No finish-shed. More meats.'

The raven picked up one of the thicker bones in its beak, carried it, staggering, to a high piece of ground with a sheer drop on to some rocks, and let the bone go. It fell, and bounced. Undeterred, the raven went through the same exercise again. This time the big bone cracked open on a rock, revealing the marrow. The ravens began to feed again.

Athaba was amazed.

'What did you do? I've never seen that before.'

'Ach, I bash this bones on rock. Raven do this all time. Come crrrrrackking opens. Gut, ja?'

'I've never seen that before,' repeated Athaba, still a little perplexed by the use of tools to get at previously inaccessible food.

When they came across a camping place where man had left some of his food containers, a raven kept picking one up with its beak, tossing it away from itself with a shake of the head, and pecking up the beans that fell out on to the snow. Again,

Athaba was very impressed. It made his brain spin when he tried thinking of such things. Of course, he would *play* with objects, and if something fell out by accident, all well and good. And he would stick his nose in a can (at the risk of getting it stuck!). But what the ravens were doing seemed to be a different thing altogether.

Life with the ravens was a dreary day to day existence, tracking his own pack through the snows, following spoor he once printed himself. He grew very lonely and depressed. Sometimes he would sit for hours just staring at the stark shape of a rock formation against the dark-light sky. He would lift his head and put his nose to the breeze, drawing on the scent of the pack, a few miles ahead. The ravens would watch him with their heads cocked, on such occasions, and nudge each other, saying 'Vot shames, vot shames,' and then spoil it by breaking out into a cackle of laughter.

They were irrepressible birds whose minds were not made for serious contemplation. Everything had a humorous side to it and they ensured that side was fully illuminated on all occasions.

Much as he needed their company, Athaba often felt the need to get away from them, to walk off on his own.

When the next summer came, and the midnight sun returned, the hunting was good. Athaba did not need to share with the ravens. He went out on his own and caught what he needed, allowing the black birds to feast later. The pack under its new leaders, whoever they were, had dispersed and was loosely roaming the countryside. Whenever one of them encountered Athaba, there would be an embarrassed turning away. They were not so brave on their own.

One day he surprised a *mega* in the forest. She came through the slanted shafts of light, tripping amongst the mosses and lichen, the sunbeams picking out the red hairs amongst the grey. Since he was resting amongst some ferns, downwind, she had not caught his scent.

He moved, giving away his position.

She came to a halt, startled, and her expression was one of surprise.

It was his sister, Koska, and she stepped back, with a cry of, 'Who's that?'

Athaba felt a wave of tenderness flow through his body. He had never been very fond of his sister, since she seemed always

72

to prefer the company of others to his own, even when he had been a successful wolf. Since leaving the pack, he had begun to think more about her though, and understood that she had needed to distance herself from him. He had never been, after all, the very model of a wolf. Even in his heyday, there had been the taint of mysticism about him, which he could hide from all those but his close friend Ragisthor and his mother and sister. Koska was, after all, his only surviving litter-sibling: they had shared the womb together.

He moved up, into the path of the wind, so she could catch his scent.

'There's no need to be afraid. It's only me, Athaba.'

She wrinkled her nose as if there were a disgusting smell in the glade. A shudder went through her frame. Clearly, her brother was not someone she had been looking forward to meeting again.

'There is no Athaba. You are the *utlah*.'

There was genuine hate in her grey eyes. It struck him then that she had suffered a little because of him. Other wolves, even other litters with the same mother and father, would regard her with distaste. She was as closely connected to a raven-wolf as one could get.

Her eyes burned into his.

'Yes, I am the outcast,' he said, 'and I have no name.'

He realised then that he had lost his status, not just as a wolf, but as a natural creature. The pack would have been told he was not the wolf that had been born Athaba, but some alien beast, which had possessed Athaba's body. Since wolves considered it impossible that one of their own kind would practise mysticism, then there must be some other creature inside the grey pelt. Koska would have been told that another animal (probably a fox, since the redcoats were often into devilish arts) had entered and was using the body which had once belonged to Athaba. With the brand of the *utlah*, or outlaw, on his hide he was nothing, nobody. From that moment on he began to call himself 'the Outcast'. The ravens had at first referred to him as 'the *utlah*' which was the archaic word. He himself preferred 'the Outcast' and encouraged all in the use of this term.

'Get away from here,' said Koska, in a choked voice. 'Go away, far away. You have made my life miserable.'

'If you had stood up for me, like a womb-sister should, I might never have been banished, and you would not need to say such things to me. You're a coward, Koska, and one of Skassi's instruments. He uses wolves like you to further his ambitions – or used to.'

'Why – couldn't – you be *normal*, like any other wolf?'

'Because I'm *not* normal. I was destined to be great, or nothing. At the moment, I'm nothing, but I shall leap back, and when I do you'll be proud to be of the same litter.'

He didn't believe it himself, but he needed to recover some of his lost pride. He was not going to hang his head before his sister and beg her forgiveness for being her brother.

'Never,' she spat. 'You will never come back!'

With that, she turned on her pads, and walked off into the waves of mosquitoes and gnats which moved ravenously through the forest looking for blood. The Outcast watched her go, fighting back a feeling of intense sadness. She had always been very proud, his sister, and a proud wolf hurts easily, is prey to a bitterness that is sharp and cold, and comes too early in life. A bitterness like an unseasonal autumn frost.

It was a mosquito summer that year. Most years the insects ruled the evenings, roaming like dustclouds in their millions. They were irritating thunderbugs which blackened the sky with their numbers. Birds feasted on them, but beasts were tormented by them. The only good thing about the mosquitoes was that the females liked sucking the blood of men more than any other creature and this kept the numbers of human hunters down for at least one month of the year. There were times out on the tundra, or in the forest, when you swallowed a hundred lives with each new breath.

Athaba lay and panted in the heat of summer sun, hating his coat even without its extra thickness, and thought that the mosquitoes had moved inside his brain. There was a buzzing there, which had nothing to do with the blackouts he sometimes suffered. His head felt as if it were floating over the streams and runnels with their fringes of sedge. Sometimes he wondered whether it might not be better to walk down into some valley where hunters were camped and offer himself to the guns. The Far Forests were surely not as lonely as a long hot summer full of dry insects and dust. But something stopped him. A feeling that there was a lord of the ladders, somewhere, who was

74

cutting a stone staircase in the wall of rock that surrounded him. This mystical god, who pushed wolves from high places, could also restore them to their pinnacles once again, so long as they were patient. So, he waited for the lord of the ladders to finish his work.

When a new autumn came, with its soul-stirring russets and whisperings of winter, the pack came together again. Bigger hunting parties would soon be needed, to find and bring down the larger quarry. The Outcast was surprised to find he could not tear himself away from his old pack. When he thought about striking out completely on his own, or trying to join another pack, his heart went cold on him. It was extremely unlikely that another pack would allow an outcast into its hierarchy and the thought of living completely cut off from all society filled him with despair. There seemed to be an invisible umbilical cord connecting him with his former relations, which was impossible to sever. He remained a raven-wolf, dragging along behind the pack, and suffering intense loneliness. If he got too close to the pack – close enough to catch whiffs of his puppyhood – they sent out a war party to chase him away again.

The Outcast came to learn that exile was sometimes more terrible than death. He began talking to himself and would wake from some dream to find he was ranting. Coyotes began to fear him for his savage appearance and wild eyes, and refused to pass the time in conversation, hurrying away to find some other carrion rather than share a carcass with *crazy-face*.

The ravens didn't care, of course. They were all half-mad themselves, and considered their new companion only mildly eccentric compared with some of their own kind. They thought he was hilarious when he pretended to be dead one day, so that some of his pack came to sniff him and he could hear them talking over him. They stood off from the wolves and chortled:

'Ja, ja. Is a dedder, this Outcastings. We eat him, ja?'

The wolves did not think much of the joke. When the Outcast leapt to his feet they attacked him, chasing him over a nearby hill on to a frozen lake, where they spent the next few moments in a weird skating dance, trying to catch him. The ravens enjoyed this scene immensely and asked the Outcast to do it again, the next day, and were not put out when he told them to fly into the nearest rock.

75

'Is good with wordings, this Outcast,' they yelled with ear-splitting volume to a neighbour only inches away, as they tore pieces from the hide of a caribou. 'Is good. Very funnys. Fly into stonings. Caaaaaaak! Caaaaaak!'

These were small events in a long period of solitary roamings for the Outcast. He moved through the night months with despair gnawing away inside him. The ravens were no real company: nor would any other creature but a wolf fill his inner emptiness. When the darkness was upon him, he cursed himself many times, for his pride. If he had only showed servility, acknowledged Skassi's place above his in the pack, he might have been with them now. At such times, had he seen Skassi on the horizon, he would have run to his erstwhile rival and begged to be allowed to pass a few words with him. No such opportunity presented itself. There was just the ice and darkness. The Outcast's heart began to harden to stone. He would rise after a rest and eat snow, if there was no unfrozen water available. Then he would put his nose to the wind and seek the scent of those he had known. The tracks would be found and he would follow behind, pausing only to eat, sometimes with the ravens. Once he found indentations in the snow where some huskies had been lying. There was no sign of men, so the Outcast decided the dogs had gone wild. Perhaps their owner had died, out in the wilderness? Anyway, he considered trying to find them, to see if he could join their numbers. They would need a good hunter, being domestic creatures, unused to feeding themselves.

When he caught up with them, he found them going south, returning to the place from whence they had come. They mistrusted him, chasing him away. When he called to them and said he wanted to join their group they told him to go and look for a hybrid swarm.

He considered doing this, but eventually decided against it. The hybrids were much further south and he was afraid of losing all contact with his pack.

The winter was cruel to him. It raked his belly inside with hunger pangs. It froze him, the ice clinging to his pelt, painfully sticking to pads, in between his claws. The shaggy musk oxen with their matted knotted strings of fur hanging from them, looking for all the world as if they were already dead and rotting, seemed to be becoming fewer. Certainly they were harder to find than they had ever been and there was no reason to suppose

76

they had become more intelligent or cunning. They were dull creatures who spoke in deep mournful voices about how good it would all be when *something happened*. None of them was sure what that something was, but it would improve life no end once it did come about. Musk oxen were always complaining, wishing for the past or the future, or simply sullen.

That winter the pack, which had been whittled down to about fourteen in number, moved further north than ever in order to avoid the hunting parties that were being dropped by air and used snow machines in order to chase the wolves. The Outcast followed his kind up into the frozen world where the plant eaters, the lemmings, hares, musk oxen and caribou had to keep on the move all the time in order to find food. They left their beloved trees far in the south. This was the place of the five-month night and five-month day with a month in between them when the change took place. This was the land of the northern wolf. There were few hunters here, though there was a human group of dwellings where men lived.

These harmless humans played with toys that spun in the wind, and sent inflated bladders up into the sky with metal objects dangling from them. (The Outcast found one of these coloured objects one day, lying on the snow, and he worried it for an hour trying to get some sense of what it was, but in the end he gave up and left it as one of those useless toys of which humans were so fond.) Occasionally, the pack would scavenge from the bins outside the group of huts, and when they were not there, the Outcast would go. Sometimes the food was frozen to a block of ice and he had to chew at the corners to break it down. Sometimes he would see one of the humans, covered from head to toe and wearing a mask, battle his way in an ungainly fashion from one hut to another, braving the wind.

Even in this desolate land, this wilderness of wildernesses, the pack would not allow the Outcast back into its protection. He lived out on the snow, digging himself hollows when the wind was strong and howled in his face. The wind in the north was a constant force, never completely dying out to that occasional and precious stillness he had once experienced in the timberlands. He missed the mornings when the light drifted down from the treetops like soft fine mist and the quiet was so profound it made you wonder whether the foxes were right, that there was something in their idea of a spirit of the landscape. On those still days the very earth and stones seemed possessed of soul.

Now he was in a place where the darkness moved and wailed, and the light, when it came, was jagged and sharp and angled off mountains and hills that had voices. He roamed the glaciers and icefields, and the hares stood on their hindlegs and saw him coming from a long way off. He crossed paths with foxes and ermines, his rivals for the running meat.

One ermine in particular, he came to know as well as any wolf might *know* another creature who is in competition with him.

They passed each other, a few times in the area of the human huts, wary at first. The ermine was more interested in smaller vermin that scavenged around the bins, but like the Outcast it did not disdain the discarded offal either. The Outcast, hungry for social contact, especially since the ravens were no longer with him, began attempting conversation with the ermine.

At first their exchanges amounted to grunts and nods and facial expressions, but gradually the Outcast began to learn words from the language of the wiry creature: *Mustelidae*. Since the language of the canids had evolved from *Mustelidae* it was not such a difficult task as the Outcast expected, even though the ermine showed no interest in learning any *Canidae*. After three months the Outcast was able to understand a great deal of what the savage little ermine had to say, and could speak a little himself.

'It's not the meat so much as the killing I enjoy,' said the ermine one day. 'You know the feeling – sinking one's teeth into soft flesh and feeling it squirm in one's mouth.'

'Can't say that I do,' said the Outcast, as usual revolted but fascinated in a horrified way by this bloodthirsty creature with its little beady eyes. 'I really only think of filling my stomach.'

The ermine shivered from the top of his head to the tip of his tail, the feeling rippling along his white body fur.

'Oh, yes, filling the stomach's important, friend' (he always called the Outcast 'friend', probably in order to remind the wolf that he was for talking to, not for eating), 'but you and I, we are of the *tooth and claw*. We are born to be killers, to stalk, to hunt, to suck the life from the throats of our prey. It stirs me to a feverpitch of excitement, the thought of the final pounce, the screaming of the dying . . .'

'Well, I think we are a little different in that respect.'

78

The ermine conceded the argument, seemingly eager (as always) to please.

'Of course, of course. You are the *great* wolf, the mighty hunter – not so mighty as the bear, of course, but fairly mighty just the same – you do not need to bother with the passion of killing, the colour of death. For you no prey is too large, or too fearsome. Take me, for instance. Can you imagine me trying to bring down a musk ox?'

The Outcast regarded the narrow fiend with its bright eyes like chips of ice.

'As a matter of fact, I can and I can't. I mean, you seem to have the spirit for the job, but you lack the stature, if you know what I mean.'

'The *spirit*? Ah, I've got that all right, friend. The spirit of the kill is in me. If sheer ferocity and tenaciousness were all that was required of a hunter, I would have left a trail of slaughtered musk oxen from here to the warm south. But alas,' he sighed, 'I shall never have the necessary bulk for the task. How I would love to tear the throat out of one of those giants. Imagine the amount of blood! I suppose you can stain whole glaciers with the blood of a musk ox, eh?'

'I've never really thought about it.'

'Oh, but you should. I would have measured each patch with my length, to see if I could better it the next time. I've dragged away their intestines from time to time, once the kill has been made, but I've never actually been there when the life is bubbling from a dying musk ox's mouth. I expect they scream for mercy, don't they? I like it when they plead for quarter. *You* know they're not going to get it – *they* know they're not going to get it – but they scream anyway. I suppose it's an automatic reaction, to yell like that?'

'I'm not sure . . . that is, I don't understand the language, and anyway, musk oxen are usually out of breath when they're brought down.'

'Hares scream,' said the ermine, confidentially.

'Do they?'

'Oh, yes, scream like billy-o. They act tough, hares do, until the old fangs pierce the jugular, *then* you want to hear them yell! I remember one you could hear for miles. Really highpitched. I tried killing the next one I caught the same way, but you know, I never ever did get another scream to match it. Funny really, you would have thought they were much of muchness, hares. They all look the same, don't they, with those ridiculous back legs, but in fact they're all different in a subtle way. I've made a particular study of the death rattle of hares and the scream varies both in pitch and tone quite dramatically, some of them almost low and hoarse. You wouldn't think it, would you?'

'Not all all,' said the Outcast, wondering what hellish creature had spawned this white devil with its tiny sharp teeth and unhealthy obsessions.

The ermine shook himself free of snow.

'Well,' he said, 'I really enjoy our little talks. I learn a lot from you, one way and another. You're the first wolf I've had the pleasure of conversing with and I must say I *really* admire the shape of your jawline – did I mention that before – so firm.' The ermine sighed. 'I could crunch a few heads with a jaw like that, to be sure.'

Then it rolled and lolloped away, over the snow, leaving the Outcast feeling that it was a good thing their sizes were not reversed or he would have been attacked and killed (though not necessarily eaten) long before now. The ermine called back through the darkness, 'One last question. In the scale, does a musk ox scream from top to bottom, or from bottom to top?'

The Outcast, who had not been devoid of a sense of humour in better times, replied, 'Depends, which way to rip open its throat, left to right, or right to left.'

'Oh. I'll have to think about that one.'

These interludes, diverting as they were, did not occur often in the Outcast's life in northern latitudes. Much of the time was spent in the hungry quest for food. There were few leavings from the pack in this land where game was so scarce. The Outcast grew thin, his fur hanging from him like the loose clothes of a human, and his cheeks grew sunken. His eyes seemed to shrink back into his skull and they burned there. Often his head ached or buzzed as if it were full of flies. Once or twice during that winter he had one of his fits and blacked out, to wake cold and stiff in the snows. He had the feeling at such times that there were eyes out there in the darkness, waiting for him to remain where he was, to expire.

From time to time, he caught a glimpse of northern wolves or saw their tracks in the snow. The packs were fewer up here in the north and their hunting circles that much larger. There was no doubt that the timber wolves' hunting area overlapped that of a neighbour and he had dreams of a clash between the two groups. In this dream Skassi would be fighting to the death with a matched male and his sister beset by two she-wolves, when the Outcast would arrive and tip the balance of victory. He would fall on the largest of the aggressors and save his own pack from annihilation. Their gratitude would leave them with guilty feelings as they turned him out into the dark winter once again (as they would) and their attitude towards him would soften. He would go away again, feeling noble and good, and the pack would gradually turn a blind eye to him as he approached the den (by accident, of course) on the odd occasion.

These were false dreams. These were the dreams of a wolf with a burning head.

Once, he told the ermine the rhyme his father had taught him, but the little creature scoffed at wood that sank and stones that floated.

'Sounds like a fox riddle,' he said. 'I don't have anything to do with foxes. They'll convert you, soon as look at you. Mysticism and magic – they've got it coming out of their ears. They use tricks like that to get you interested, then they start trying to get you to admit that yooouuu have doubts about death, whether it's the end or the beginning. I can't be having any patience with stuff like that. Death is death. The heart melts like snow in heat, the mind trickles away. Simple as that. No more wolf, no more ermine, no more fox if it comes to that. Just because they believe in that waffle, doesn't mean they're special. They're just cowardly fools, who're afraid of dying. I'm not scared of death. I spit in its eye.'

Ask a question, thought the Outcast, and you get a lecture in return.

Chapter Seven

Near the end of the winter, as the light was creeping back to purple the sky, the Outcast met Skassi on a whale-back ridge. It was an accidental meeting, since the wind was leaden that morning, refusing to carry scents very far and letting them drop to cold ground. It had snowed during the night and there was a light fluffy covering of shinbone depth, which softened the sound of any approach. Consequently, they were not aware of each other until they rounded a boulder, one from either side.

The two wolves both stiffened and then the Outcast instinctively went into the submissive role: head down, ears flat, back arched. Almost immediately he had adopted the pose, he straightened and pricked up his ears, angry with his body for betraying him. Since he was not a member of the pack, he had no need to placate this *mega* that had caused him so much grief. And he had beaten the other in a one-to-one: even more reason for not humbling himself.

They were both lean from the winter months under their thick coats.

Skassi was the first to speak. His voice had changed from the Outcast's memory of it. It sounded softer but firmer. There was more confidence in the tone, less aggressiveness.

'Is that the wolf Athaba?'

His name! How strange it sounded after all this time. Something fluttered inside him: a kind of hope. It was the use of his name that awakened this sensation, and not the thought that he might be readmitted to the pack. Such a thing was highly improbable, virtually impossible. He did not know whether he even wanted to go back to the pack now. He had been away too long, was used to being a loner, a 'raven', an *utlah*. His mind was set in a certain way now and he would find it difficult to live with other wolves. One became used to one's own company and doing things in a particular way. The pack would never approve of his lifestyle: he would have to fit in with the others, carry out certain duties, set an example to the young. All that kind of thing was behind him. Out on the white wastes he was his own master, to do with himself as he pleased, not answerable to anyone. Still, it would be good to be asked.

'I am the Outcast,' he said, surprised at his own calmness in the situation. 'Is that the wolf Skassi?'

Skassi came forward a few paces, his paws crunching now on the patch of brittle snow that always forms on the exposed saddle of a ridge. Then he stopped at a respectable distance, regarding the Outcast. The pack wolf had fared better than the Outcast. His eyes were clear and his coat was in better condition. The Outcast hoped he himself did not appear too thin and scraggy. He wanted Skassi to go away with the impression that he could take care of himself, and had no need of the pack.

'I would not have recognised your scent, or indeed your coat, except that it would be strange to find another lone timber wolf up here in the high country. You look lean and fit.'

Athaba could not detect any overt hostility in Skassi's tone, only a strong reserve: the sort of coldness one might use towards the member of a rival pack. Had his arch enemy mellowed a little since they last confronted one another? Perhaps Athaba had caught Skassi offguard, and the *mega* was having trouble adjusting to an unexpected situation? This was more likely than a reformed Skassi.

'We hear of you from time to time,' continued Skassi. 'The youngsters . . .'

'Treat my name with scorn no doubt!'

He had not meant to sound so bitter. A lack of control was starting to seep through. Some of the ancient feelings were beginning to rise up from the dregs now. He wanted to retain the clarity of his initial emotions, but the sludge was starting to bubble, deep down.

Skassi looked surprised. Then an expression crossed his face which made him appear more like the wolf Athaba remembered. When the *mega* spoke his voice had an undercurrent of contempt.

'Of course. What did you expect? We can't allow you to become a hero you know. They'll all want to go it alone. Nevertheless, you've become something of a, shall we say, *dark force*? Something of a legend in the pack. You roam the hills, solitary, haunting the landscapes as a lone silhouette. The youngsters see you and whisper to each other . . .'

The Outcast was suddenly amused.

'You mean the mothers use me to scare the pups? "If you don't go to sleep the raven-wolf will come and take you away to eat you." So they scream to each other, "Watch out, the *utlah* will get you!" and run from each other.'

'Perhaps – you know the games. You were a pup once. But you've gained a sort of "respectable notoriety" – you are quietly and subversively admired as a survivor. Not many wolves would have lasted as long as you, outside the protection of the pack. I discourage such thinking, of course, it's not in accordance with our ways. We must think of the good of the pack. However, we could have done with your skills this winter. We've had a hard time of it. Some have perished – young and old mostly. A very hard time. This land is cruel and we've had one or two brushes with a wolf pack that overlaps our own hunting territory.' His jaw twisted. 'You could say that life within the pack is not that much better than your own in these times.'

'You are headwolf again?'

'No, I've never got back to that exalted position. Not sure it's what I want these days and nights. Too much responsibility. I'm not the wolf that you knew – the wolf full of ambition. Those were the strong times.'

The Outcast let the wind riffle through his fur.

'It's a great pity we could not have had a conversation like this when we were rivals,' he said, letting another trace of bitterness escape. 'Perhaps we may have prevented many things from happening which injured us both.'

Skassi shook his head.

'Athaba, you could *not* have stayed in the pack, whether I was for or against you. My opinion of you, my fear of you – oh, yes I can admit that now – had nothing to do with you being ostracised. You were beginning to exhibit strange mannerisms. Do you still get fits?'

'Yes.'

'Well, there you are then. You're a deviant, Athaba, always have been. My animosity towards you is not without foundation: I don't waste my time bringing down innocents. I don't waste my efforts on destroying those who are worthy.' Skassi's tone began to enter lofty regions. 'I don't hate you now. What would be the point? You're nothing – an *utlah* – a ragged piece of skin and bone. The battle between *us* is over. You are where I always thought you should be: outside the pack. You are a decadent influence on the young. You would have eroded the moral fibre of the group in time, with your mystical air . . .'

'I'm not a mystic,' said the Outcast, his voice full of disgust.

'You say, but then you can't see yourself in the same light that I see you standing. You, with your airy-fairy ways, full of your own self-importance, full of secrets, whispering with wolves like Ragisthor, trying to undermine the structure of the pack, corrupting the young with your false stories. You're a destructive element, Athaba, I recognised that from the start. You hated me because I stood for the old values, for convention, something you saw fit to laugh at, to despise.'

'That just isn't true,' cried the Outcast. 'None of that is true.'

Skassi's voice fell to a condescending tone.

'Athaba, you were always destined to be a loner, to end up this way. Can't you see? You're too independent, always have been. You're not a pack animal. In other circumstances these might be admirable traits, but not in a wolf pack. Wolves have to look to the good of the pack. The fact that you have survived out here, for so long on your own, points to an aspect of your character which is out of place in a pack. Any decent wolf, with real pack feelings, would have died of loneliness by now. He would not have been able to help it. A proper wolf needs his pack around him. You're not normal, you're a loner. You should have been born a fox.'

'That's not true either,' said the Outcast. 'I am a sociable creature. It wasn't me that was wrong, it was the pack. It's too tight, too inflexible.'

The Outcast was aghast at the insults that were being heaped on his head – a *fox* – but the proper words to defend himself just wouldn't come. He had been too long outside the pack and his use of language had deserted him. He wished at that moment he was as eloquent as Ragisthor, so that he could put Skassi in his place with solid argument, indisputable logic. All he could do was deny the charges, which was a weak way to counter such accusations. The worst of it was that Skassi actually believed these things he was saying – the *mega* had convinced himself that the old Athaba had been a destroyer of moral values, without any respect for convention.

'I'm innocent . . .' he blustered, but Skassi came in again, ignoring his protest.

'You expect the pack to suit *you*, fit around you, rather than the other way?'

The Outcast hunched his shoulders.

'You see,' said Skassi, 'you *are* an individual. The world must bend to Athaba, not Athaba bend to the world. As I said, under certain conditions you might be an asset to a pack, but they would have to be very abnormal circumstances. A time of open warfare – something like that.'

The Outcast saw no way to counter Skassi.

'You'll never understand me,' he said, turning away, 'and I certainly don't understand *you*. What I mean is, there must be packs who would accept me for what I am, fits or not. There must be packs where the thinking is less narrow and any talent I have to offer – or any wolf has to offer – is recognised and used . . . yes, for the good of all. Your pack, well, in your pack wolves are pushed into responsibilities that are not suited to their personalities, their character, their natural skills. Instead of finding an opening which fits the wolf's form, you squeeze the wolf out of shape to push him into the wrong hole.'

He had said his piece at last.

He turned away and walked the length of the ridge, feeling Skassi's eyes still on him. Then he heard the other wolf call, 'Good hunting Athaba,' but he did not acknowledge the compliment. He did not want Skassi to know how strongly those words affected him and his voice would be sure to give him away.

They tore the heart out of him.

Not long after this encounter, the Outcast met another wolf, only this time the meeting was between two canids who did not know each other.

The Outcast was trotting over an icefield when the scent of wolf came to him faintly on the wind. He stopped and listened and could hear sounds of distress coming from the near distance. Since he was moving in that direction, he continued his journey, and eventually sighted a wolf lying on its side on the ice. By her scent, she was a female, and she appeared to be struggling with something.

Moving in warily, the Outcast called to her.

'Are you in trouble?'

Her head went back, and she whimpered.

He moved in closer, until he could see that her paws were entangled. He went close and smelled. It was an old fishing line. The Outcast had often witnessed humans using these lines, pulling fish through holes in the ice, and occasionally they left the tangled sections which had been cut away, lying around on the icefields. These were virtually invisible on the white surface and extremely dangerous to a running wolf; dangerous to any creature, especially birds. If you did get caught up in one of these nets of fine twine, they seemed to tighten with your struggles, rather than loosen. The cord cut into your legs until it disappeared beneath your fur and it was difficult to get your teeth to it.

The Outcast stood over the she-wolf. He guessed she was a *mega*, in about her third or fourth year. Her paws were bleeding where the line was cutting deeply into her flesh.

'Lie still,' he said, 'I'll do what I can.'

He crouched at her feet and began to nip and nibble at the line between your hindlegs. She watched him, silently. The cord was tough and impossible to gnaw through. He had to nip it sharply, between two teeth, which took time. In fact the whole morning passed by before she could eventually stand on her feet and the last pieces of line fell from her legs. She stared at him for a few moments while getting the feeling back in her limbs, then she turned to leave.

The Outcast was a little offended.

'Don't I get some sort of acknowledgement?'

She turned. Her eyes were wide and deep.

'I was trapped, you set me free. What else is there to say? I know you've helped me, and you know it too. I don't like to be in your debt, but I am.'

'Well, that's something, I suppose.'

'Did you want a reward? Perhaps you think I ought to give you something? My next kill, for instance?'

He felt uncomfortable. She was obviously genuinely distressed at not being able to return his kindness. He shook his head.

'No, I just wanted to hear you say *something*. I mean, you've been lying there looking into my face for I don't know how long, without a word. Which pack are you from?'

'The one that clashes occasionally with yours.'

He sat on the ice. It was cold on his haunches.

'I don't have a pack. I'm an outcast.'

'I know. I meant the pack to which you once belonged. I've seen your tracks, following behind the timber wolves. What are they doing so far north anyway? Don't they know this is our country?'

He was amused by her arrogance.

'*Your* country?'

'These are our traditional hunting grounds. They are not usually the haunt of timber wolves.'

'We were having hunter trouble in the south. For the last few years they've been pushing us further and further north. It was either move or die. I suppose the pack would rather face your hostility than come under the guns. As for myself, I don't care what happens to any of you.'

Now she sat down and faced him. This was encouraging.

'Yet you set me free. That valuable time could have been spent in hunting.'

'It was a diversion. I get bored easily.'

'Why were you banished from your pack?' she asked. 'Did you commit some terrible crime?'

He hesitated for a moment and then decided to tell her the truth.

'Yes, I get fits. I black out and have dreams. I'm told during these bouts I shake and convulse, and it's very frightening to watch me.'

'That doesn't seem so terrible.'

He was surprised by her answer.

'Would *your* pack permit a sick wolf to remain?'

'No, but that doesn't mean I agree with them. To my mind it depends on what kind of sickness. If it's something to harm the pups, then of course, the wolf has to go. What's your name?'

'The Outcast.'

'Your real name.'

'Athaba – it means "endurance".'

'My name is Ulaala. It's something to do with the wind, but I don't think it has a precise meaning.'

'If it did, it would be "the one with wind-coloured coat",' he said gallantly, and against all protocol he reached forward with his nose and nuzzled her gently.

She stood up quickly.

'Time for me to leave. The pack would not like me sitting here talking with one of our rivals.'

'I'm glad you didn't say "enemies". I feel we only have one real enemy – the man with the gun. Without him there would be room enough and prey enough for all. Will I see you again?'

She looked about to deliver a firm denial, but then she faltered.

'I don't know. Possibly we may run into each other on the trail.'

Then she turned and began trotting away. When she was a good distance from him, she turned and howled into the wind. He thought he caught the words, but he could not be sure. It sounded like 'the north ridge'. What did that mean?

He spent the rest of his waking hours hunting and managed to run down a caribou. Then he lay under the shelter of a rockhang, where the snow was not so deep, and began to think of the past. It was not something he (or any other wolf) normally indulged in, there being little enough time to think of the present and its needs. That evening the aurora lit the sky with its splendour, flickering and shimmering, hanging curtains of light in the heavens. Athaba viewed it disinterestedly. Lights in the sky were commonplace. He was much more concerned with subtle scents and the nuances of shadow and shade.

The Outcast could hear the Howling Chorus of one of the packs (his own, or hers?) and for the first time in a long while an acute feeling of loneliness came over him. He missed his old friend, Ragisthor, and his wry comments, his cynical remarks.

'I'm getting old,' he said to himself. 'My mind's beginning to walk backwards.'

He had witnessed, as an *undermega*, wolves of the pack deteriorating as old age overtook them. They became grey-muzzled, crusty and bad tempered, and were always muttering about the past. Was that happening to him? He ran his tongue around the edge of his mouth. Perhaps he was grizzled too? She (What was her name – Ulaala? – strange word – he could hardly get his tongue around it) must have thought him a grandfather.

His head jerked up. Suddenly, suddenly he realised he was not even a father. Not just that. He *wanted* to be a father. He wanted pups. He wanted a mate.

His head went back down on to his paws.

What chance was there of that? He was the Outcast, a ravenwolf. Where would he find another wolf, a she-wolf, like himself? They all belonged to packs. There must be female *utlahs* but the possibility of finding one out on the snowy wastes was, well, very remote to say the least. He knew which female he wanted. The light grey one, with the ears that were more rounded than his own, and a shorter muzzle, and shorter legs. But he would be killed by her pack if he ever tried coaxing her away. It was an impossiblee dream.

He was destined to live his life out, in the high country, where the massive snouts of glaciers pushed slowly across the land, gathering moraine as they went. The moving land, that was never still, creaking and groaning as if it were trapped and forever trying to escape. Here, in the ice kingdom with its blue light and sculptured snow, he would end his days alone.

That night the blizzard began which lasted two days. He stayed hunched under the rockhang, thankful that he had eatenn just before the storm broke and would not starve if it blew into several days. The wind had lost its reason and was screaming in every direction, blowing drifts against obstacles one minute and removing them the next. This was the ultimate loneliness of the high country of the north. Everything went crazy up here from time to time, and the wind was no exception. There was no malice in it. It had simply gone temporarily insane.

When the white air had cleared and a bluelit day came, he trotted out on to the unmarked surface of the snow, printing his spoor on the crisp upper layer. He could smell his old pack, not a great distance away, upwind. That umbilical cord tugged on him again, and he began to follow in their wake, eventually sighting them. There were small gusts of wind still, kicking up snow spume and spraying his coat where it remained for a time. One wolf turned to face him, probably by instinct. It stared at him for a moment, then recognising him as the Outcast, whirled and joined the other members of the pack. They were closely bunched, not strung out, as if they were expecting an attack or something. The Outcast wondered if a rival pack was in the area and there might be trouble. He himself sensed danger of some kind, but having sniffed the air several times, and cocked an ear in every direction, he could not locate the direction of the potential peril.

The pack continued up a gravel mound that rose sharply from the flat icefield, the gravel showing through the snow in one or two places like dark stretch marks. One of them, probably the headwolf, reached the highest point and turned its head south, testing for danger.

The Outcast waited at the foot the hill. The pack began to descend the steep slope, some of them sliding on their rumps. The Outcast moved back, to let them down, and waited some distance away. The youngsters were in the middle of the flankwolves: one of them took a tumble on the way and almost bowled over a shoulderwolf who snapped at its tail, playfully.

It was when they were halfway down that the unexpected occurred.

The Outcast heard the roaring, but could not understand where it was coming from. It seemed to be everywhere and nowhere. It was deafening, filling the heavens. Then a dark shadow passed over him. He looked up to see a black bulbous shape, like a giant swollen dragonfly, sweeping low across the landscape. The wind from its whirling wings raised snow flurries along its route. It grew in size until it filled the sky. The wind ripped and tore at his coat, driving against his eyeballs. He sucked air and tried to get his head out of the blast.

The dragonfly swooped upwards and did a half-circle above the pack, its tail swinging round, buzzing loudly. The Outcast half-crouched, fear almost making him defecate on the spot. He sensed that something terrible was about to happen. He wanted to run, hide, but there was nowhere to go. The landscape had no cover. There were no large rocks and no deep depressions.

The pack, too, was in a state of terror. They began to bunch, running into each other in their fright. One youngster was just sitting, bewildered, looking up at the monstrous shape now hovering above his head. An older female was trying to dig down, into the hard snow. The Outcast could see there was no escape for them. They were all exposed on the ridge, stark against the whiteness. He had difficulty in filling his lungs. He wanted to shout warnings, *scatter, scatter*! He wanted to help them, but he knew they were lost. There was nothing he could do.

A *mega* had broken from the knot of panicking wolves and was coming down the slope, his forelegs long, his hindlegs short. Once he rolled, and then was up again, quickly. The Outcast could see his eyes, wide and white. The Outcast willed him to move faster, outrun the wind from the whirling wings. There was a dak-dak-dak-dak-dak-dak-dak-dak-dak-dak sound below the roaring in the sky. Pockmarks followed the running wolf. An invisible bird chased him, caught him, ran along his spine. It left bloody footprints. The wounded creature twisted sideways, almost folding in the middle, and slid the rest of the way to the bottom of the slope. The broken body landed sprawling some distance away from where the Outcast was crouched.

The dragonfly, its eyes glinting, hurtled down towards the rest of the pack and began spitting viciously. Heavy rain began to flatten the snows in and around the pack. The Outcast watched as spattering in the middle of the pack, saw youngsters running, somersaulting, belly-flopping on the ground. Sometimes their momentum carried them on without legs. They slid gracefully across ice patches leaving red streaks on the white. The flankwolves moved in, as if they thought they could protect the yearlings, and they too were killed in the spray. One managed to break free of the group, ran, than sank to its knees slowly. Finally, it just keeled over and was still.

– dak - dak - dak - dak - dak - dak - dak - dak - dak - dak - dak - dak -
dak - dak - dak - dak - dak - dak - dak - dak - dak - dak - dak - dak - dak -
dak - dak - dak - dak - dak - dak - dak - dak - dak - dak - dak - dak - dak -
dak - dak - dak - dak - dak - dak - dak - dak - dak - dak - dak - dak - dak -
dak - dak - dak - dak - dak - dak - dak - dak - dak - dak - dak - dak - dak -
dak - dak - dak - dak - dak - dak - dak - dak - dak - dak - dak - dak - dak -
dak - dak - dak - dak - dak - dak - dak - dak - dak - dak - dak - dak - dak -
dak - dak - dak - dak - dak - dak - dak - dak - dak - dak - dak - dak - dak -
dak - dak - dak - dak - dak - dak - dak - dak - dak - dak - dak - dak - dak -
dak - dak - dak - dak - dak - dak - dak - dak - dak - dak - dak - dak - dak -
dak - dak - dak - dak - dak - dak - dak - dak - dak - dak - dak - dak - dak -
dak - dak - dak - dak - dak - dak - dak - dak - dak - dak - dak - dak - dak -
dak - dak - dak - dak - dak - dak - dak - dak - dak - dak - dak - dak - dak -
dak - dak - dak - dak - dak - dak - dak - dak - dak - dak - dak - dak - dak -
dak - dak - dak - dak - dak - dak - dak - dak - dak - dak - dak - dak - dak -
dak - dak - dak - dak - dak - dak - dak - dak - dak - dak - dak - dak - dak -
dak - dak - dak - dak - dak - dak - dak - dak - dak - dak - dak - dak - dak -
dak - dak - dak - dak - dak - dak - dak - dak - dak - dak - dak - dak - dak -
dak - dak - dak - dak - dak - dak - dak - dak - dak - dak - dak - dak - dak -
dak - dak - dak - dak - dak - dak - dak - dak - dak - dak - dak - dak - dak -
dak - dak - dak - dak - dak - dak - dak - dak - dak - dak - dak - dak - dak -
dak - dak - dak - dak - dak - dak - dak - dak - dak - dak - dak - dak - dak -
dak - dak - dak - dak - dak - dak - dak - dak - dak - dak - dak - dak - dak -
dak - dak - dak - dak - dak - dak - dak - dak - dak - dak - dak - dak - dak -
dak - dak - dak - dak - dak - dak - dak - dak - dak - dak - dak - dak - dak -
dak - dak - dak - dak - dak - dak - dak - dak - dak - dak - dak - dak - dak -
dak - dak - dak - dak - dak - dak - dak - dak - dak - dak - dak - dak - dak -

dak - dak - dak - dak - dak - dak - dak - dak - dak - dak - dak - dak - dak -
dak - dak - dak - dak - dak - dak - dak - dak - dak - dak - dak - dak - dak -
dak - dak - dak - dak - dak - dak - dak - dak - dak - dak - dak - dak - dak -
dak - dak - dak - dak - dak - dak - dak - dak - dak - dak - dak - dak - dak -
dak - dak - dak - dak - dak - dak - dak - dak - dak - dak - dak - dak - dak -
dak - dak - dak - dak - dak - dak - dak - dak - dak - dak - dak - dak - dak -
dak - dak - dak - dak - dak - dak - dak - dak - dak - dak - dak - dak - dak
– barely audible above the sound of the sky machine. This was
the storm that fell upon the pack, the metal raindrops showered
upon them.

The pack lay broken and bloody all over the slope. The air
machine had made only a single pass. Every wolf, struck down,
inside a minute. The blood of the first one to be hit had not had
time to stain the snow before the last one to be brought down
jerked and convulsed in the throes of death. Nothing moved
except for one youngster, crawling downhill using only his front
paws, dragging his mangled hindquarters through the snow. The
Outcast could smell the pain and fear on the yearling. He felt a
need to go and lick this youngster, offer a few words of comfort,
but still his legs would not move. The yearling gave a pathetic
whine. Its movements became slower and slower. Its head sank
to the snow. The cries coming from its throat ceased. Eventually
even this last drop of life amongst the pack had drained away.

The engine of the machine raised the snow in clouds as it went
in low over the corpses. The Outcast found himself shaking,
staring and shaking, and he knew if he did not move soon he
would have a fit.

The great bulbous shape turned in a wide circle. It was coming
back, its eyes shining with blankness, its needle mouth ready to
spit metal all over the snowscape once again. It was greedy for
more death. Its appetite was insatiable. Not one, not several, but
all. It wanted every wolf that ever cast a shadow. It lapped the
air with its whirling blades, drinking the slaughter. It tongued
the wind, savouring the massacre.

The black machine curved down towards him, not like a hawk
stoops in a straight dipping arc, but peeling away to one side. It
was dark, with a tiny elongated mouth, like the proboscis of a
mosquito. Its smooth shiny eyes rippled with lunatic light.

The Outcast's heart began to race. His legs moved at last and
he ran, sightless and witless, away from the carnage towards a
cliff edge. He heard some small sounds behind him, pucking the

snow and ice. He knew that an invisible bird was tripping after him, its tiny feet eager to dance daintily along his spine.

Then he was flying through the air. The ground had gone from beneath him. There was a white world of rushing ice, whirlwind snow, spinning about his head. He turned several times, then landed in a deep drift, was buried in it. The sounds of the world became muffled and there was a kind of comforting darkness around him, though mind-numbing panic still surged through his veins. His brain was blind in his skull with the terror that possessed him.

Chapter Eight

The Outcast lay for a long time, shivering in his pit of snow. His ears were so finely tuned to the sounds of the world that he could hear a nearby glacier calving its icebergs. He was not cold. His heart was numb with fear inside, but his flesh succumbed to fits of shaking. He could hear the wind above him, whispering over the hole he had made. At any moment he expected that monster to blacken the sky above the hole and start spitting at him.

It never returned.

When the Outcast finally summoned the courage to leave his hiding place, he found he had to dig a tunnel and crawl along it for quite a distance. As he emerged from the opening, he looked back to see the cliff, the edge of which he had leapt over in his panic. It was very high. The drop was frightening and he considered himself to be lucky to be alive. If the snow had not been so deep, or he had hit a rock projection, he would certainly have broken his back.

He circumnavigated the cliff, finding a path up one side, to reach the top again. It took a little courage to make his way towards the slope where he had left the bodies, but he wanted to be sure all were dead.

His own spoor had gone. A strong wind had rearranged the surface snow. He had been in his pit on the far side of the cliff for a long time and the wind had since scoured the surface.

The Outcast continued his journey to the slope.

When he reached the spot where most of the wolves had died, he found it empty. There was nothing there. It was as if he had dreamed the whole thing.

The hunters had taken the carcasses away with them. Sometimes they skinned their quarry on the spot, but presumably there were too many for that this time. They had taken the whole pack somewhere up in the sky. There were humans that lived in the clouds and humans that lived on the ground. There were hunters and non-hunters amongst both types. Those humans in the huts, who barked at the wolves and showed their teeth sometimes, were non-hunters. The ground hunters were sometimes men from the south with guns that could kill at a very long distance, but more often they were northern men who actually lived in or close to the snows. These two types smelled differently.

The northern men had the smell of the tundra or woods about them and they moved in on their quarry like wolves. They would shoot a wolf, but they tracked mostly caribou. They fished the lakes and sea and called to wolves in a language which sounded almost like real speech.

The men who came up from the south only barked. They wore a variety of false smells, most of them sweet and sickly, and you could scent them coming from a day away. The only way a southern hunter could kill a wolf was to come on it suddenly in a fast ground machine. It happened, but quite rarely.

The non-hunters who lived in the clouds were rarely seen. There was one that visited the group of huts from time to time, and when the Outcast had caught his odours as he was walking from his bird towards the huts, the human had smelled mostly of machine himself. The Outcast wondered if the men from the sky *were* machines of some kind. Certainly they walked stiffly when they emerged from their metal birds.

Finally, there were the cloud-dwelling hunters in their flying machines, who were death itself. They came down out of the sun and hovered over their prey, shooting them from the air. There was no way a wolf could escape, if it was in open country. The machine would follow, spitting all the time, until the wolf went down. Only trees or caves offered any kind of safety whatsoever.

The Outcast left the slope and wandered in a bemused way over the icefields, his brain buzzing. Long-tailed jaeger birds dive-bombed him, as they will do from time to time, and he had to duck continually to avoid them. They were getting their own back for the times when wolves raided their nests. They must have been puzzled by his lack of interest in their audacious attacks.

His head was still full of the *dak-dak-dak* sound, and wolves continually tumbled down the slope in front of his eyes, leaving bloody streaks on the snow. His pack was gone! His pack. What could he do now? Follow that invisible umbilical cord into the land of the dead? It had been so long since he had been one of their number, that he had forgotten what pack life was like. Yet he felt an enormous sense of loss, as though the whole world were a vacuum and he the only living thing on it. There was no sense to life without the pack. It was true that he would probably have gone on until death without ever getting back into its ranks, but it was always *there*, and there was ever that faint unquenchable flame of hope which burned in his breast, that one day, *one* day he might achieve some great status through an act, a deed so heroic that they would *have* to let him back in.

He walked, he did not know where, until the cold began to hammer his brain, and hunger forced him to stop, whereupon he blacked out.

'What's the matter?' asked a voice. 'Why were you shaking so violently?'

He opened his eyes, and *she* was there. Ulaala, of the wind-coloured coat. He sniffed her fur for a moment. Had she come to him by accident or design? He felt weak from his fit, as though a giant had picked him up by his forelegs and shaken him violently for a long time. There was an enormous hollow inside him, and he turned from her to lick the ice, to get some liquid into his empty stomach. Once his thirst had been satisfied, he felt a little better, but still craved food. However, he could not just get up and walk away. She had asked him a question. What was it? Something about the shakes.

'I probably had a fit,' he said. 'I told you, before, I have these things. A bear mauled me when I was younger and now I black out sometimes and my body shakes. It's what they banished me from the pack for . . .'

Then he remembered: the sound of thunder in the sky, the sudden swoop of the mechanical bird, *dak-dak-dak-dak-dak*, snow-spurts on the ridge, wolves dropping where they stood, the whole pack, dead.

The horror of those moments returned to him and he threw back his head. They filled his mind. He lifted his head and let out a high mournful howl, which rang out over the icefields.

She backed away from him, startled.

'That's the Death Howl,' she said. 'Are you dying? Here, I have a hare.' She indicated a stiff corpse some distance away from the pair of them. 'You may eat it. You seem to be starved.'

He had not had any food since before the storm and gratefully he took the carcass from her and began to feast. As he ate he told her about what had happened on the gravel mound, how the attack was so sudden it was over almost before it began, how he had managed to save himself only by falling a great distance into a snowdrift. She was guardedly sympathetic. He imagined this was because she had not known any of the victims.

'I can't imagine my whole pack being slaughtered,' she said. 'I've heard of these massacres of course, but it's never happened around here before.'

She then added in a more cautious tone.

'You must be feeling revenged. The wolves that banished you and caused you so much grief are now all dead.'

He had not even considered that way of looking at it.

'No,' he said truthfully. 'At one time, if you said such a thing might happen, I may have indulged in a little satisfaction – but when it actually *does* happen you just feel . . . empty. Well, they're in the Far Forests now, if you believe in that sort of thing, which I'm not sure I do. I'd like to think it was true, but when you think about it, it doesn't make sense . . .'

She interrupted him.

'That's the trouble, you shouldn't – not in that way. It's not a place to be *thought* of, to understand. It's a place to be *felt*, to be approached emotionally. Why should things make sense in a material way in the world of the spirit? *That* doesn't make sense. You won't *have* a brain to think with in the Far Forests.'

Well, he hadn't asked for a lecture, but he had got one anyway. He decided he would be more careful in choosing his subjects in future. She was obviously a wolf with strong opinions. He pitied her mate, whoever he was, because she did not seem a wolf fond of making compromises. A little too strong-headed.

'What are you going to do now?' she asked.

The wind was lifting the surface snow around the icefield and blowing it gently over the ground in the form of veils. The low sun burned with a dull polished sheen on the landscape and the light was the colour of dying leaves. Out there were a million possibilities, and none. What *was* he going to do? He was free. There was no cord tying him to a group now. He had to make his own judgements. There was no headwolf in front, making decisions on behalf of the pack – where to go, what to do – decisions that he could follow blindly, without responsibility.

'I don't know,' he said honestly.

'Why not,' she began, her voice seeming to drift away with the rising wind, 'why not start your own pack?'

At first the words did not register. After all, the idea was so ludicrous, so impossible, he hadn't considered it, not for a second. When he did understand what she was saying, he was puzzled. She was far from foolish, yet it sounded like a stupid solution to his problems.

'Start my own pack? What do I do, go out and gather recruits. Gather in all the outcasts and outlaws roaming around the countryside and weld them into an obedient group? Tell them that I'm the headwolf and they are obliged to do as I say?'

She raised her eyes into her skull.

'No, you idiot. I mean, start your own pack. There's nothing wrong with you is there? . . . I mean, you have fits, but that doesn't mean you can't have pups, does it?'

'What?'

'It's the breeding season,' she said bluntly. 'Do I have to say more? Are you really that dim?'

He still couldn't get it into his head. The idea had been thrown at him too suddenly. He needed time.

'You mean, you and I . . .'

'Yes, exactly.'

'Do you know what you'd be taking on?'

'I think so. A tired old outcast who's lost his pack and doesn't know which from what. On the other hand, I see great things in him. I see a spark of youth that hasn't quite gone out. I see strength – certainly strength – and fortitude. I see loyalty. You've never had much chance to be loyal, have you Athaba? I think you could be one of nature's constant wolves. A wolf who would die for his own. Furthermore . . .

'. . . I *want* you,' she said, simply.

Excitement stirred in his breast. He could see the rolling dunes of snow stretching out to the base of low hills. Somewhere out there the hares were dancing their mystical dances. Somewhere out there a bloodthirsty stoat had banished all thoughts of killing from his mind and was gorged with another kind of lust. Somewhere out there, further away still, weasels were standing on hindlegs and swaying rhythmically.

'What about your pack?' he said. 'Won't they object?'

'Ours is not a strict, regimented pack. The leadership is a little loose, has been for some time. There's no really strong member. It's kind of drifting at the moment. One day a wolf will emerge with leadership qualities. Perhaps more than one? That's the way it usually happens – you need a strong personality – you wait and wait – then three come along at once and there're battles fought over what could have been had for the taking a few months previously.

'Anyway, what I'm saying is, no one will miss me. We can leave right now.'

'Leave for where?'

'I suggest we go back south. This is a hard land to rear pups. Once we have our pack, we can move north again.'

'What about the hunters down there?'

'There're only two of us, not twenty-two. We should be able to keep low and hidden. If it's too bad, we can always come back.'

'True.'

'Well?'

He felt full.

'Of course, of course. But I still don't understand why you chose me. You could have had one of your own kind, one of the northern wolves.'

'Some of us like to be different. There's something about you – I can't put it into words. Something a little strange, but attractive.'

'And the fits? They don't worry you?'

'I would worry for our pups, but you told me the fits came because of an injury. You weren't born with them. In which case there's no reason why our pups shouldn't be healthy. As for the two of us, you have coped with your fits now for many seasons, and you've survived outside the protection of the pack. You'll do, Athaba. You'll do.'

He finished the hare and then stood up, his hunger appeased. He could see a flock of long-tailed jaegers getting ready to mob the two of them. This would normally have irritated him, but suddenly he saw an amusing side to their behaviour. He wondered what his new mate would think of him, once his coat had been soiled by those birds. (They were extremely accurate.) It took a while to get the mess out of his fur after they had dive-bombed him.

100

However, if the two of them hurried, they might get out of range.

'Let's go somewhere now,' he said, 'away from the birds.'

They found a place out of the wind where they could be together. In the hollow, they nuzzled one another, fur touching fur. It was the first time, for both of them, though both had approached, been approached before. The feelings were almost frightening in their intensity, especially for the Outcast, who always believed in being in control, in keeping his reserve.

They stayed in the hollow for over a day before he reluctantly went out to hunt. The hare had satisfied him only in part. He was now hungry enough for a feast: a feast which might last him several days. He felt light, buoyant, as though if he just flicked himself off the ground he might float. It was a tremendous feeling, of confidence and strength.

That day he caught three hares in quick succession. The hare population did not know what had hit them. One was for her. The other two he devoured himself.

Back in the hollow again, he settled beside her. He saw no reason why they could not stay as they were for ever. It was all so comfortable. But then, when he thought about it hard enough, he realised that, as Ulaala had said, it would be better if the pups were born further south, where the cold was less like a blow in the chest every time one left the den.

Lying beside her, he felt it was a time for cleansing his spirit. The pack, his pack, had gone now. There was no Skassi to despise, to help nourish a red burning in his breast during a long winter. He missed Skassi now. Missed having someone in the world to blame, when the scavenging and hunting was bad, and the ice was creeping into his veins. Enemies have their uses. They give us a reason for living, for battling through the hard times. No one wants their foe to hear that they have gone under, given up, so they pretend that all is well. There is the story of the wolf caught by its hindleg in a gin trap, who says to the birds, 'Tell my enemy, I am quite well'. And the birds say to him, 'But you're caught in a trap!' The wolf looks down casually and shrugs. 'Only a tiny section of my *leg*,' he says. 'The rest of me is in wonderful health.'

The state of one's mind is much more important than the state of one's body. The wolf who refuses to acknowledge that she is sick, that the cough is only a temporary lodger, which will eventually be evicted and sent back where it belongs, will often live many seasons longer than the wolf who sees his illness as part of *him*.

The Outcast had for many seasons now been ignoring the actual state of his physical health. He was run down. Since he was not looking his best, it was strange that Ulaala found him so attractive. Perhaps she saw the potential in him? And, of course, he was an *experienced* wolf in more ways than one. Still, he was sure she would prefer a less lean mate: one with a sleek coat. He now set about putting himself on the path to full health, by getting back on a good diet. Otherwise, he was likely to lose this female who was mad enough to take him on.

'You'll soon be completely fit again,' she said.

They spent a few more days preparing themselves for the long journey south.

Chapter Nine

In the beginning, just after the *Firstdark*, the wolves were being slaughtered by the hundreds. Man, with the help of his slaves the dogs, spent much of his time discovering the whereabouts of wolf packs. Once a pack had been found, men would mount those horses whose spirits had been broken, and run down the wolves, cutting them to pieces with spear and sword, with lance and arrow.

This state of affairs was, of course, extremely distressing to the wolves and they sought some way of living in peace. They sent emissaries to man's creation, the giant *Groff*, pleading with him to intercede for them. The giant said he was willing to help, but what he needed from the wolves was a promise of complete capitulation, a surrender without terms, a willingness to be subjugated. Naturally, the wolves could not agree to this, and went away again. None knew at the time whether *Groff*, having become very powerful since his success on behalf of the humans, was taking things on his own shoulders without first consulting his masters. It was possible that man *wanted* some kind of peace with the wolves. After all, the wolves made it difficult for lone men and their children to walk through the woodlands without being attacked. Since they stood no chance against the horsemen and their superior weapons, some wolves had taken to raiding the woodsmen who lived in the great forests that then covered the earth. Left to themselves the woodsmen would have quietly gone about their business of cutting down trees and making carts, furniture and ploughs, and may not have bothered the wolves. But an enemy driven to desperate measures will attack the opposition at its weakest point, and in this case it was the shacks and cabins of the men of the forest.

The woodsmen in their turn were incensed at these raids by the wolves and called on the horsemen and their weapons to annihilate *Canis lupus* from the face of the world. This served to initiate revenge attacks from the packs and the whole bloody cycle continued.

It was thus possible that man might listen to the wolf and offer some sort of compromise in order that their forests remain safe for travellers and woodsfolk. But first the wolves had to get past *Groff*, the intermediary who had grown too big for his boots and who was taking it on himself to presume the wishes of men.

One day, from the far north, there came a wolf by the name of Magitar, whose intention it was to seek out another path to the ears of men. He came down from a stronghold in the mountains, from the place of parched rocklands and rushing torrents, through the low foothills of rounded earth and stone, to the plains beneath where the rivers were wide and lazy and the reeds rustled in their beds. Down from the high citadel where the winds had teeth that tore through thick fur, to the quiet country of warm breezes that ruffled his tail. Down from the treeless walls and crags, to the land where the skies were vast stretches of blue.

The first creature that Magitar met was a dog, out on its own, and on its way between towns. It hesitated when it saw the wolf, but had nowhere to run. Magitar called out to the hound that it had nothing to fear, that he was on a peaceful mission and merely wanted to talk. The dog approached him warily.

'Might I ask who you are?' said the wolf, 'and what is your position in the world of men?'

'I used to be a sheep dog,' was the reply. 'My breed is Border Collie. I helped men round up their sheep from the hillsides and watched over them. I helped protect them from bears and wol . . .'

The dog stopped abruptly.

The wolf chose to ignore the slight.

'What I would like to ask you,' he said, 'is whether you see any way of wolves coming to terms with men, without losing their freedom? Tell me, what freedom do you and other animals who live with or closely to man enjoy?'

The dog sat on its haunches and scratched behind its ear with its hindleg, clearly nervous.

'Well, I wouldn't recommend the life of a dog,' he said, 'if it's freedom you want. We used to hunt for our own food before man came, but now it's given to us. Some of us have to work for it, like myself, driving sheep or cattle. We don't have to live in houses, but we are usually chained outside in a tiny wooden place we call a kennel. Then there are those who are forced to live in houses, who are retained to guard property. Then there are pretty-pretty dogs, who are overfed on cream chicken and who are kept simply for what they are. Some of these never see green fields or proper trees, but are carried or led on a leash through concrete towns. In all cases the freedom is very limited. I suppose hunting dogs, pointers and such, are the closest to what you want, but I wouldn't say that they had any more freedom than the rest of us, really. They are still kept in kennels or houses, and only let out when their masters are ready.'

'None of this sounds very appealing,' said Magitar, 'to say the least. Can you recommend I talk to some other creature?'

'Why not try a cat?' said the Border Collie, clearly relieved to be let off the hook.'The cats have more freedom than the dogs. It's no good speaking with horses or donkeys. They have a worse time than we do. Pigs are killed in their prime. Cows, goats and chickens buy their way into men's favour by giving them milk and eggs. I take it you would have trouble delivering milk in the right quantities and you would have even more difficulty in producing eggs?'

The wolf nodded, grimly. 'Eggs would be difficult.'

'In that case, your best bet is a cat.'

The wolf left the dog and went in search of a tabby. He found one on the edges of a town. The cat seemed less afraid of him than the dog had been, but stood a way off with its escape routes all open.

'Cat,' said Magitar, 'what kind of freedom do you have under men?'

'Complete,' said the cat. 'No other beast, man or otherwise, is my master. I come and go as I please, and I offer no man my absolute allegiance.'

'This sounds more like it,' said the wolf, 'but there must be more to it than that. Men do not feed other creatures for nothing. What do you give them in return for your right to wander at will, without being hunted and slaughtered?'

'Nothing,' bragged the cat. 'We are their equals.'

Still, the wolf was not convinced. He could not see how such a small creature could be regarded as an equal by man, despite it's renowned courage.

'I take it you are fed by man?'

'Correct,' said the tabby, licking her fur. 'I allow one to feed me.'

'And you live in this house?'

'That's right. I deign to honour him with my presence from time to time, but only when I feel in the mood. Most of the time I go there to sleep.'

'How did you first come to know this man?'

'He took me home as a kitten, to play with his young. I got pulled about a bit, of course, and had to undergo certain humiliations, but that's all part of the initiation ceremony.'

The wolf nodded.

'The initiation ceremony.'

'That's right.'

Magitar then asked, 'And later, when you matured and were no longer needed to play with the man's young, what did you do to keep yourself fit?'

'Well, I was expected to hunt mice and rats of course, in the coal cellar.'

'And if you refused, or were a poor hunter?'

'Probably been out on my ear,' she replied, then hastily added, 'but of course I wouldn't have minded that.'

'No?'

The tabby looked uncomfortable.

'Well, not much. The only thing is, it's a hard life being a feral cat.'

'What's one of those?'

'A domestic cat gone wild. You have to forage round waste bins and the food's disgusting. You have to fight other cats for scraps. I've seen ferals and most of them are thin – ribs coming through the fur – that sort of thing.'

'So,' said Magitar, 'you are in fact dependent on man?'

The tabby shook herself.

'Not *entirely* dependent. No, I wouldn't say that. I mean, I hunt my own birds. Oh yes, I hunt my own birds. Robins and sparrows and wrens. They don't like that, men. They don't like finding a dead robin on their kitchen floor.'

'Then you don't actually *eat* these birds you hunt?'

'No need. We get far more tasty food from our mas . . . from our equals. It's a partnership you see.'

Magitar nodded.

'I see.'

106

And he did see. He saw that cats were really in no better position than the dogs. The only difference was that dogs had accepted their inferior position and cats had fooled themselves into thinking they were independent. It seemed there was no creature amongst men which had an honourable status, which retained some link with the natural world and could boast a certain amount of freedom.

Magitar turned back towards the mountains, but on the way he passed a goshawk sitting on a post. The hawk had leather thongs hanging from its ankles: clearly the trappings of man.

'What are those strap things, on your legs?' asked Magitar.

'These?' said the hawk, looking down. 'They're called jesses. My man uses them to hold me when he doesn't want me to fly off.'

'Yet here you are, free,' said Magitar.

'Well, I'll go back when I'm ready to. I just needed a bit of space to sit and meditate for a while. Sometimes you've got to get away from them, if only for a couple of days.'

'But you're *free*. You need never go back.'

'Not if I don't want to, but when you've got the choice, well it doesn't matter, does it? I mean, if I did get desperate, I could fly off the next time he took me out, and never return.'

This sounded much more like it.

'What does he take you out for, in the first place?'

'To hunt for him, and for me. He likes to see me stoop on the prey. Gives him some sort of thrill, I don't know. Then he gives me some of the bird, and take the rest home to eat for himself. I suppose you could say I should get *all* the bird if I caught it for myself, but the fact is I can't eat it all in one sitting, and I get some choice meats from him when we get back. Sort of partnership, you might say. I give him something, he gives me something.'

'Is he kind to you? Does he beat you, like he does his dog sometimes. Or starve you like a cat?'

'If he did, I wouldn't stay around would I? No, he knows he's got to treat me with respect or I'd be off, quick as that.'

'Where do you live?'

'I've got a place outside in the grounds. Its called a mews. I have my own perch in there. It's where we first became friends. I was taken there as an eyass, straight out of the nest. We went through the manning – that's where the waking took place.'

'What's that?' asked Magitar.

'Well, the falconer keeps you awake for a long period of time, in order to get you to know him. He stays awake too, of course. He offers you food, but only when you go on to his wrist. That's just to get you used to the feel and smell of him. When it's all over, you're friends.'

'And you have to wear those "jesses"?'

The goshawk looked down.

'Oh yes, but they're not uncomfortable. Kind of badge of office really. I meet wild hawks who're quite jealous. Sometimes I wear bells too, and swivels, and a varvel – all sorts of things – none of them limit me in any way. I mean, it would be pointless to make me wear things that would hamper my flight, wouldn't it?'

'I suppose so. What else can you tell me?'

'What, about our relationship? Not much, really. Oh, yes, when I rake away – that means flying wide – of the falconer, he sometimes uses a lure to get me to come down. It's usually when we've had a disappointing hunt. I get a bit petulant and tend to blame it on him. The lure is a bit of meat, a titbit really, which he whirls around his head on a piece of string. Kind of compensation for not putting out any quarry.'

'What about when you're taken from the mews. Don't you feel like taking to the air straight away?'

'Sure, but he puts a hood on me until we're out in the country.'

Magitar nodded his head thoughtfully.

'Oh, a *hood*.'

'Yes, but you needn't think I don't like it. It's kind of comforting, that darkness. Sometimes we go through areas where there are a lot of other humans – not falconers – and then there are the horses stamping and snorting away. I'd rather not see these things. They're a bit distracting. We're nervous, highly strung creatures, us hawks. Sudden movements startle us. It's best for us both that I wear the hood. I've got leather hoods and velvet hoods, with little plumes. Quite dramatic in some ways.'

'Do they ever let you get fat, like they do the cats and dogs sometimes?'

'Never,' said the hawk emphatically. 'If we put on too much weight they put us through what we call enseame treatment, to make us lean again. A fat hawk is no good as a hunter.'

The hawk's brilliant orange eyes regarded the wolf for a long time as Magitar digested all this information. It certainly seemed as if the raptors had the answer to living with man. They were allowed to hunt in their old ways – indeed that was their job – so the skill never left them. They could leave at any time and never need go back, without causing a hue and cry. They retained their natural diet and were not fattened and made useless on cream chicken. They had a freedom occasionally, when things got on top of them and they wanted space to think.

They had to wear certain things at certain times, of course, but you had to bend a little if you were going to form this kind of relationship with men.

'It sounds,' said Magitar, 'as if hawks and falcons have the answer we wolves have been looking for. I shall go back to *Groff* and demand that he take the same terms to man on behalf of the wolves.'

'That's fine,' said the tercel on the post, 'but where are your sails?'

'My – sails?' asked Magitar.

'Yes,' replied the hawk, taking to the air, 'your *wings*! Where are your wings, to circle, to stoop with, to fall on the quarry? Where are your wings which enable us to do all those things in which man finds his excitement? How will you get up into the sky, where he can watch you check and drop and kill without his vision being hampered by trees or rocks? Your *sails*, you son of the trail, you earthbound fourlegged, wingless wolf. Your saaaiiiiiiilsss!'

And then the goshawk was gone, riding the thermals and climbing in spirals up to the sun.

Magitar sighed and turned his head towards the distant white peaks of his homeland.

He knew when he was beaten.

He settled his heart to looking forward, to the *Lastlight*, when the reckoning would come.

PART THREE

The Birth of New Songs

Chapter Ten

It was her time. He arose one night to find her scent in the air. They had been lying in close-together depressions in the snow and her patch was empty. She was standing not far away, on a slight rise, looking down to where he now stood. Trembling a little, he walked stiffly towards her trying to shake the cold out of his limbs as he did so.

Halfway there he stopped, for her stance seemed hostile. It seemed she had changed overnight into a wolf he did not know. Her physical appearance was the same but her whole demeanour, her bearing, her poise, seemed passionately intent. There was another she-wolf under that recognisable fur. It was as if she were bridling a savagery not previously shown him, holding in check a fierce side to her nature, one she had not previously revealed. It seemed not to come from within but from earth around her, beneath her. He did not know whether he would be torn to pieces or received by her. He was at that moment afraid of her, the way she stared at him. He could tell by those eyes that she was in control, while all knowledge had gone from him. His confidence ebbed and flowed by the moment. At the same time, he was sexually aroused almost to the point of desperation. He could not decide whether to advance or retreat.

While he stood there, undecided, she took a few paces upwind. Then she turned, and looked again.

She wanted him to follow her!

He moved forward now, surer of himself, his feelings becoming increasingly more fervid by the second. He inhaled. The smell of her earth was pungent, biting sharply into his sensitive nostrils. He followed that scent to a hollow in the rocks, out of the wind. A burning sensation travelled to every part of his body, along his limbs, even to the tip of his tail. He could taste its hotness in his mouth. A white-hot flame sprang from beneath his body.

The earth opened for him and his fire flared into her, touching the centre of her being. He knew he had scorched her, for she lifted her head and tried to swallow the moon. His tongue turned to flame, his eyes were scorched, his nostrils were seared, his mind raged out of control. The midnight sun locked with the earth. It engulfed the earth, and the earth too burned with the moment.

When they were able to look into each other's eyes, he knew they had no more natural secrets to hide, and he was happy.

Athaba, time-ravaged as an ancient rockface, did not fully understand why the she-wolf Ulaala had chosen him as a mate. He knew what he was: an outcast of a pack which no longer existed. Apart from his general appearance, there was also the question of his behaviour towards her.

She had been out on the icefields and had caught her prey, dragging it down to the foothill. He came across her as she was feeding. Going up to her, he shoulder-slammed her roughly out of the way and snatched a choice piece of meat, treating her like he would a coyote. She was bowled over, tumbling in the snow. There was no thought behind the action. It was done instinctively: a survival mechanism. Then, as he chewed, he realised what he had done.

'I didn't mean . . .' he began appalled with himself.

He had been out of company for so long he could not stop himself, in unguarded moments, from such actions. It was true there were only the two of them and they could dive in together, grabbing at the meat, without getting in one another's way and causing annoyance. It was not as if there was supposed to be any kind of feeding manners at a carcass: the idea was to fill your belly as quickly as possible. In a pack situation, there would be an order of priority, of course, with the seniors snatching their chunks of meat, before the juniors were allowed in. Sometimes there were arguments between those of near equal rank.

But Athaba's action had been deliberately provocative. He had gone in hard and aggressively, banged her aside in a manner which was designed to intimidate, to make her think twice the next time before she ate the best bits. She was supposed to be wary of him. A coyote must be taught its place at the feeding.

But she was not a coyote. She was Ulaala. He had no right to treat her that way, especially since it had been her kill.

He tried to explain to her.

114

'You see, when you're battling against other scavengers, you've got to get to the meat first, or it's all gone. I mean, normally there's just a few scraps left on the bone, and the ravens and coyotes were so quick . . . I'd have starved if I hadn't asserted myself, showed a bit of aggression. You see?'

'I think so,' she said, a little coldly.

'No, you don't really, and I can't blame you. A little pushing and shoving is all in the game, but I smashed you out of the way. I'll try not to let it happen again.'

Her voice became a bit warmer.

'If you do, you'll get some back.'

'That's the spirit,' he said, relieved.

He was afraid he was going to lose her, before they had even started their life together. Why was she doing this in the first place? She was such a handsome animal she could surely have any male in her pack? Instead, she had asked a scruffy outlaw to become her mate and undergo the hazardous business of starting a new pack. It did not make a lot of sense. There had to be something more, something he was missing.

To make up for his mistake at the carcass, he took her to the huts where the humans lived, to ensure they had a good feed before beginning the long trek south-east. At the bins she was understandably nervous, and when a man came out of a shack and saw them, she almost bolted. The human stood, stock still, and stared at them through the eye-covers they all wore up in the cold high country.

'Pretend you haven't seen him,' muttered Athaba, crunching away on something he had found in the bin. 'He's just as scared of us as we are of him.'

'I don't believe that,' said Ulaala.

'It's true. You walk straight towards him and he'll turn and run to the nearest hut. It's happened before. They're only dangerous when they're carrying weapons. Believe me.'

'If you say so.'

The man held his ground, watching them all the time they ate. It was as if he were fascinated by the sight: something Athaba had always wondered about. I mean, what was so interesting about an animal eating? Nothing, so far as he knew. These humans had worms in their brains. They were all mad.

There was a movement from behind a bin and a head appeared. It was the ermine. The snaky little creature emerged and flowed

115

over to them. Its bright little eyes were never still. Its nose twitched continually.

'Hello, brother,' said the ermine in its own language.

'I'm not your brother,' Athaba replied.

'Who's the local?' asked the ermine, ignoring the attempted put-down. 'You teamed up with another wolf? What's his name?'

'*Her* name. She's my new mate.' It was difficult to keep the pride out of his voice.

That much was lost on the ermine though.

'Oh? Her pack kick her out, did they?'

'Not so far as I know,' said Athaba stiffly, and then in *Canidae* to Ulaala. 'This is an ermine I befriended some time ago. It's a bloodthirsty little beast.'

Athaba then explained to the ermine he and Ulaala were heading for the south.

'Crunch a few eyeballs for me,' said the ermine, by way of a farewell, then he waddled over to the bins and began gnawing at some unrecognisable piece of frozen swill.

'What's the matter with *him*?' called the ermine, as Athaba and Ulaala were leaving. The wolf looked back and saw that he was indicating the human, still standing with a frozen stance some distance away. 'Got ice in his veins, has he?'

'You know what they're like,' replied Athaba.

He and Ulaala soon left the compound behind and were trotting over ridges and down gentle slopes, still snow-covered despite the season they had entered. Athaba felt toned. Inside, he was full of strength, full of vigour. His eyes scanned the landscape for possible dangers. His nose was alert for unusual odours. His ears keen. He loved to be travelling, feeling land move beneath his pads, his sinews stretching, his muscles rolling.

There was a fresh wind at their backs, travelling in the same direction. Perhaps it was because it was behind them that they failed to pick up the scent of the wolves in front.

When they came over a rise between two shoulders of rock, a pair of wolves were waiting for them. Lean-shouldered northern wolves. They blocked a pass through which Athaba and Ulaala had to go.

'Are they from your pack?' asked Athaba of Ulaala.

'I'm afraid so,' she said. 'They've been out hunting. They must have caught my scent and wondered why it was mingled with

116

yours. Look, their's a third – it's Uneega. They're definitely waiting for us.'

One of the three wolves in their path was a large male with a dark smudge over his left eye. A *mega* in his fifth year by the look of him. The other two looked like senior *undermegas*, and they flanked the big one. Athaba decided there was only one way to get through them, and that was to brazen it out. In his experience, most battles *between* wolves were won with the mind. If you had enough front, you could get away with anything. The problem was when your opponent called your bluff, or seemed even more formidable. Physical strength was important, but even if you were sure you were superior in this aspect, yet the wolf in front of you looked prepared to fight to the death, no holds barred, and appeared to have the courage of a thousand weasels, physical prowess lost its edge.

There was no way to circumnavigate and outrun this small group, and once you *began* running you *definitely* lost the advantage and had to keep going and win, or go down.

'Let's go through,' he said.

Ulaala stayed by his side as they descended.

'Are you scared?' she whispered.

'No,' he lied.'I'm not afraid.'

Out of the corner of his eye, he saw her lift her head at these words.

'Neither am I,' she replied.

When they were about ten body lengths from the waiting trio Athaba paused.

'Are you going to get out of the way,' he snarled, 'or do we have to come through you?'

One of the *undermegas* took a step back, but the big male did not even twitch. Instead, it spoke to Ulaala.

'Where are you going, *mega*? It's not your day for a hunt. You leave a lot to be desired in your choice of companions. That's the outcast from the grey ones . . .'

'I know who he is,' she interrupted sharply.

'Then you must have an explanation? This is strange behaviour. Not a good example for these *undermegas*.'

'The explanation is simple,' said Ulaala, and Athaba noticed the heat in her voice, 'I'm weary of your bullying, Agraaga. I'm leaving the pack. This . . . this wolf has lost his own pack to the hunters. We are going south, to begin again.'

117

This conversation had revealed some of the reasons behind Ulaala's decision to run away with Athaba and he felt that given any more space she was going to dig a pit for the both of them. If she antagonised the big male further, he might have no choice but to stop them, whether it meant losing his life or not.

'Enough talk,' interrupted Athaba. 'The fact is, Agraaga, we have decided to leave. We – *we* have decided. I am a free agent. My pack . . .'

'I've heard about your pack.'

'Then you know they have been wiped out. I have nothing to lose. I wasn't banished because I couldn't fight. Don't make that mistake. They turned me out because they thought I was crazy. Maybe I am. I repeat, I have nothing to lose. I'm coming through. If you try to stop me, I'll tear some throats. What does it matter to me if I go down? If I can't have Ulaala, I would be better off dead.'

He began to walk towards them, his ears forward, his tail erect, his hackles raised. When he got a little closer he curled his lips back to reveal his teeth.

A surprising thing happened. The two *undermegas* stepped aside, leaving only the *mega*, whom Ulaala called Agraaga, standing in Athaba's way. Something had been prearranged, even before the two groups had met. This was not a chance meeting on the trail. This had been planned.

When two wolves fight to the death, it is a silent, eerie battle, watched in silence by the spectators. It became obvious to Athaba as he approached Agraaga, that the wolf was going to stand its ground. The two *undermegas*, one male, one female, moved even further away. Ulaala said, 'Let me . . .' but Athaba was already confronting Agraaga, who had also taken up a dominant posture. A body-slam, even a decisive one, was not going to end *this* conflict.

That fact almost took Athaba by surprise. There was a last pricking in his brain, a thought that even now he could turn and run, but it only lasted for a tiny moment. He knew he was going to do battle, whatever the outcome.

There was, after all, *nothing to lose.*

No sound could be heard except the wind soughing between the rocks. The two wolves, coats the colour of granite against the snow, stood on the landscape and stared into each other's eyes. They had decided, without a word being spoken. It would be to

118

the death. The spectators knew it too, even though the silence had not been broken. Since the first family of wolves had split into the first two packs, wolves had settled insoluble differences by single combat.

Athaba prepared himself mentally. He stood still, letting the wind riffle his guard hairs, gathering inner strength. He knew why this had to be – *now* he knew. His opponent was blocking their path to the south. If he walked away, all three would fall on him and tear him to pieces. Even if they didn't, he would lose Ulaala.

Agraaga, his opponent, wanted Ulaala for his mate. He had decided she was worth killing for and now the scavenger had challenged his authority over one of his own pack he had no choice but to do battle. Athaba attempted to circle his opponent, but the other wolf kept his posterior up against a large protective rock. The two of the made darts towards each other, testing reactions, then falling back quickly. Their eyes were locked. Athaba knew it was most important to concentrate on the eyes, in which movements could be seen and anticipated a split second before they were carried out.

One or two rushes were made by both wolves, this time a little more seriously. Athaba caught a nip on his lower lip, but the grip was not strong enough to hold. He in turn took away a tiny piece of furred ear from his second rush.

Athaba could not afford to be caught and held. His adversary was bigger, had more weight, and would use it to pin him down. Athaba himself had a wiry frame. He realised, not long after the fight had begun, that he was just a fraction quicker than his foe and he intended to keep his distance until he was sure of a throat hold.

After a few minutes of this, his big opponent seemed to run out of patience. He was on show, before his two *undermegas* and he had wanted to be seen to be in command of the fight. He made a decisive run at Athaba, his jaws clashing, attempting to get a hold.

Athaba skipped backwards, hit a rock, rolled. Agraaga leapt, but Athaba was on his feet in an instant. Athaba's teeth snapped together, into the flap of skin beneath the throat of his combatant. The weight of the other wolf drove his body into the ground but he knew he had to hold on, or he would be lost. For a moment he despaired, because he knew he had not got enough flesh in

119

his teeth to finish Agraaga. He twisted and thrashed, turning several times until finally he had flipped from under Agraaga's heavy body. Athaba lay at full stretch. Agraaga seemed to want time to recover.

No sound had been made throughout the combat. There was no growling, no snarling, not so much as a whimper. Threats remained unspoken. No quarter would be given, none expected. The time for mercy was past. They had both had the opportunity to turn dominant postures into submissive ones. The chance to surrender had gone.

Athaba knew his opponent was surprised to find himself in a desperate position. Now that Athaba had the advantage he intended to keep it.

Agraaga suddenly swung round and began raking Athaba's body with his hind legs. Athaba hung on grimly, even managing at one point to gain a better grip, though still not a decisive one. Agraaga rolled and Athaba went with him. Agraaga was obviously in great pain, but that alone would not end the fight. Pain would impair the wounded wolf's concentration.

There came a point when Athaba knew he would have to let his opponent go. He was the smaller of the two wolves and Agraaga could kick and roll all day, gradually wearing him down. He must not wait until he was too weak to keep his grip. Better to go for one killing blow while he still had much of his strength.

Athaba waited until he sensed Agraaga's concentration was not at its fullest, and then he went for the jugular. This was no fight for supremacy: this was survival. His jaws clamped on Agraaga's throat. He twisted, savagely. The warm blood spilled. Athaba held on to the northern wolf until the struggling ceased. Then Athaba let him go. Agraaga fell sideways as if struck by a blow and flopped on to the snow.

Athaba stepped back, knowing it was over. The body of Agraaga lay where it had fallen and before long it was as still as stone. Athaba was glad he could not see his opponent's eyes. He had killed one of his own kind and it felt bad. He knew he had been given little choice in the matter: even had he tried to walk away they would have fallen on him. But another wolf was dead and some of the responsibility was Athaba's. He was glad that it was over. Athaba turned to face the two *undermega's*. The battle was not yet over. This time Ulaala moved to his side, her hackles raised. She was ready to fight alongside her new mate.

And still, not a sound had been made.

The watching *undermegas* fled, disappearing over the ridge. Ulaala said, 'Quickly, we must leave,' and led the way to the trail ahead. Athaba took one last look at the body on the ground. A big wolf, to be sure. Yet he felt no elation in victory. Only a sense of shock and relief. This had not been of his making. If only Agraaga had stepped aside, allowed them to walk through! Such a decision, to fight or step aside, was so finely tuned that in the end it was almost a subconscious one.

In Agraaga's case, fatal.

Athaba joined his mate and together they hurried across the white landscape, through gulleys, around crags, over streams, putting distance between themselves and any retribution. There would be a meeting before a pursuit, and possibly the chase would never take place at all, if the big wolf had not been popular.

'Will they follow?' asked Athaba. 'You know your own pack better than I do.'

'Doubtful. As I said, there's not a strong wolf amongst them.'

'*He* was pretty strong, that one!' grumbled Athaba.

'Not strong in character. I was really quite surprised when he took you on. I didn't think he had it in him.'

Athaba felt a bad taste of pique in his mouth.

'Perhaps his late show of courage has changed your mind,' he said. 'Are you disappointed he lost?'

She glanced at him swiftly as they trotted along, side by side.

'That's a silly remark to make. I would not have mated with Agraaga if he were the last wolf in the high country. He was dull and stupid – and so are you, if you think I was impressed by him.'

Athaba stopped and now voiced the thing that was between them.

'You don't *have* to come with me you know. I've done the job you wanted done. Agraaga is dead. That *is* why you told me you wanted me in the first place, isn't it?'

The truth came to her eyes before it did to her throat. She stared at him for a long time, before she replied. 'I admit I wanted to be rid of Agraaga. I thought up this scheme, whereby I would find the outcast wolf, the one that had freed me from the fishing twine,

121

and use him to get rid of Agraaga. It . . . was not a seriously considered plan. I went looking for this outcast, and found him. As soon as I saw him again the idea of using him suddenly became what it really was, a monstrous idea, unworthy of anyone, even a female wolf who had been tormented and bullied from birth by an aggressive male.

'The male, Agraaga, made this she-wolf's life a miserable existence. To make matters ludicrously worse, he suddenly decided he wanted to mate with the one he had been bullying for so long.

'Still, his brutality could not be put aside. He *would* mate with the female – Agraaga would have Ulaala – but on his terms. There would be no courting approach. He would tell her that she was his and he would kill any other wolf that got in his way. And she would still suffer his bites, his body-slams, his vicious unreasoned attacks.

'Then she found a wolf who was gentle and kind. A male wolf who did not seem to need to impress with his physical strength. She ignored her feelings at first, thinking them base. To mate with an outcast! Her pride stepped in the way and blocked her path. Finally, she tossed her pride aside, treated it for what it is, a shabby no-account thing. She knew she wanted *him.*'

Ulaala looked Athaba in the eyes and he saw the honesty was still there, in hers.

'I do want you, Athaba. I have behaved very badly, very foolishly. I'll understand if you want to walk away from me.'

He was silent for a while, then he spoke.

'Whether I want to or not, I can't. You're the only she-wolf that has ever paid any attention to me.'

'I don't know that I like the sound of that. You mean, you can't get anyone else, so I'll have to do?'

There was amusement in her tone.

'No, not at all. Look, I'm not good as this sort of thing, talking about it all. Let's just start from here. We're off to begin a new life. The old one is behind us. Agraaga is gone, and there's nothing more to worry about.'

He set off at a brisk pace, she beside him.

'The only thing that worries me,' she said, after a while, 'is that he *was* headwolf at the time. They may come on account of that.'

Athaba stopped and regarded this she-wolf with some irritation. It appeared she was going to be exasperating company.

122

'Wonderful! *Headwolf*. And you didn't think to warn me?'

She halted and shrugged. 'Would it have made any difference?'

'That's not the point.'

'Yes it is. You were going to fight him anyway, whatever happened.'

Athaba did not deny this because he had the awful feeling that it was true. Had he been spoiling for a fight? Certainly the anger that had been building up inside him over the last few seasons was now gone. Well, he had had a right to be angry, hadn't he? Rejected, exiled, treated like a parasite?

But to have killed one of his own kind!

Yet he could see no way he could have avoided it. He wanted Ulaala and she wanted him. That wolf, the headwolf Agraaga, had been determined to stop them. There was no way around that. Except . . . perhaps if Athaba had volunteered to join their pack, in order to be with Ulaala? No, impossible. They would *never* have accepted him. The fight just had to be, and to the death. If Agraaga were not lying on the snows at that moment, Athaba certainly would be. There *was* only one way it could have ended.

The travelled during the sunless hours, which were still long, using scent and sound when the light was poor. If the northern wolf pack followed them, they failed to catch them. Athaba felt close to the earth now that he was travelling again. While he was scavenging with the ravens and amongst the waste bins of the humans, he lost his connection with the landscape. Now he was back in tune with the vibrations of the natural world. He was familiar with the plants under the snow, and could smell the rocks. He listened to the fast-flowing streams that cut their own paths through his world. They told him many things, from the kind of weather that was behind them, perhaps following them, to the contours of the land ahead. A flow that increased in volume and speed meant melting snows at the source, perhaps a warmer wind on its way. The sound of the flow ahead could indicate a rise, a fall, a curve. There were nuances of these, and other aspects, which would be lost even on the indigenous humans that hunted and fished the same world as the wolf. Neither Athaba nor Ulaala could have explained the process by which they gathered knowledge, and kept themselves informed on what was happening around them. Their sources were so many and varied – the wind direction, its strength, scent, sounds, the stirring of a leaf beneath the snow, the flight of a bird, the movement of the earth, the feel, the weight, the taste of the air – a thousand seemingly unrelated occurrences were imbibed and assessed subconsciously by the wolves and connected their nerve ends to the environment.

The pair travelled swiftly, but without overstraining their physical capabilities. They rested when they felt ready, hunted on the run, and kept away from the scent of man. Athaba had not felt so fulfilled since the hunts of his youth.

On their travels they came across a large hunt and had to deviate from the planned route. They went up into the mountains and found a cave in which to hide. The place was long and dark and smelled vaguely of human markings, but it seemed safe enough, especially at that time of year. The summer months would be different, because it would be more accessible to both humans and other creatures.

Outside the cave, the wind played savage games amongst the rocks, but inside it was still. Athaba could sense the timeless movements of the stone around him, could hear the water creeping through the caverns, falling to unfathomable depths, rushing through narrow passageways. There were echoes trapped down there, bouncing from rock to rock, trying to find an exit to the outside world.

The two wolves caught small rodents in the crevices, and even ate beetles and other crawling things. It was not wholesome fare, but it fended off starvation. While they rested they told each other their life stories, finding them fascinating even though there was nothing terribly extraordinary in them. The cave listened and added its own sounds, told its own story, though neither of the wolves could understand. All they could divine was a sense of history that made their minds turn in on themselves. A history of boiling rock, steam, mould and form, strange creatures that no longer existed, bears, men and dogs. One of the world's natural shelters, the cave had been used for seasons out of time, by all manner of beasts. There were ghosts in there that resembled no living creature on the face of the earth. There were shapes and shadows that would turn the bravest heart to snow. There were secrets, blood secrets, that would turn the staunchest creature to ice.

Yet, there was also a sense of peace. It was not the cave itself that had created a dark past, but those that used its hollow confines. The cave was neutral: it took no sides and welcomed any wayfarer to its bosom. A traveller's rest that offered sanctuary from the storm. The cave made itself available to human hunter and quarry alike. Athaba allowed himself to be cosseted by this universal friend of those that journeyed through the long nights, the long winters of the high country.

When it was time to leave, he almost regretted having to go.

'We could make this our den,' he said.

Ulaala was not such a dreamer.

'The hunting is poor around here. We have to think about feeding our pups.'

Athaba felt a jolt of delight go through his body.

'What was that?'

'Our pups,' said Ulaala. 'Oh, you didn't know, did you? We've been travelling so hard and fast . . . I meant to tell you. Anyway, you should have noticed the difference in me. Don't I look like a mother to be?'

'What? Yes. No.' He could hardly think straight. Pups! His own pups. So all that earth and fire had not been simply for the pleasure of the moment. He was to be a father, the head of a pack. That was something to tell the sky about.

His head went back and he howled to the heavens.

'Quiet!' said Ulaala, looking round nervously. 'There are humans in the vicinity. Do you want to tell them too?'

He puffed out his chest.

'I don't see why not. I mean, I'm the wolf with fire in his loins. Hunters? I chew them and spit them out.'

'So you're the only he-wolf that ever gave his she-wolf pups?'

'No,' he said, earnestly, 'but these pups will be the greatest little wolves that ever stood upon the tundra. You wait and see. They'll change the world.'

'Well, I'm glad you're so pleased. I thought you might be a little jealous. You know I'm going to have to give them a lot of attention, and you won't be the only wolf in my life after they are born.'

He thought about that.

'I can see I shall have to be more unselfish in the future. I think I can manage that. Just think of it though! Our own pack. I can't wait.'

'So,' said Ulaala, 'the den . . .'

'Well, we can't make it around here,' he said briskly. 'The hunting's much too poor in this district. I'm surprised you even let me consider it. No, no, we'll move on . . . are you all right? I mean, can you travel in your condition?'

She snorted through her nostrils.

'I've travelled this far, haven't I? Of course I'm all right. On you go.'

So he led the way from the cave, euphoric in the thought that he was going to have pups, be a father, have a pack. Just a few short months ago he had been a raven-wolf, his own pack all dead and gone, his life over. Now here he was, his life beginning again, and the promise of pups in the air. He did indeed feel fortunate.

Chapter Eleven

Once they were in a suitable area, finding a place to den became a matter of urgency. It had taken them some time to travel south and Ulaala was heavy with her unborn litter. She began to get testy and irritable with Athaba, as she worried about a warm dry place in which to give birth. A place where she could feel her pups were relatively safe from harm. There were strange things happening inside her which were affecting her personality. She regarded the whole world as a potential menace and yet had no real quarrel with anyone, least of all Athaba, whom she frequently snapped at. During the rest hours she became miserable, certain that he would leave her because she had become a mean-tempered female. She needed him desperately. That was what was so strange about her feelings: she wished Athaba would go away, yet she wanted him by her side. How could you have both? How could you even contemplate both? Athaba gave her the choice pieces of meat after a hunt: she guzzled them down without a word of gratitude. The soft meats were necessary for her young to be born strong, full of iron. She saw him watching her with anxious eyes, knowing he cared for her and her condition, yet she was unable to respond with anything but words like, 'When are you going to find us a place to den . . .?' And when he did discover reasonably suitable areas, she rejected them, angrily. They were not quite right. There was always something, some little thing which bothered her. It might be that the entrance was too exposed, or the den just a fraction too far from water, or the ground a little too damp. She knew she was being fussy, but it had to be the perfect place. She wanted full confidence in it, so that she could forget about the world and have her pups without worry.

While Athaba did not fully understand what Ulaala's problems involved, he realised that everything was a crisis to her at this point in time and put it down to the fact that she was feeling insecure outside her pack. She told him once or twice that she was not herself, that having pups inside her did unusual things to her nature, but his comprehension on such matters was limited and he preferred to find more practical reasons for her attitude towards him. Once he had found the right denning area, he told himself, she would settle down and become a little happier. Then there was the litter. It must, he acknowledged, be uncomfortable having to carry so much weight around in one's belly. Certainly, he could not imagine what it would be like. Ulaala sometimes tried to explain to him that far from being uncomfortable, this was a pleasant way to be. Athaba decided she was just being noble, that such a bloated state just had to make one feel awkward and cumbersome. He put his faith in the den and just hoped the pair of them hadn't made a mistake in running away together. He could not imagine they could go on like this for the rest of their lives.

Finally, he found it, the place for which they had been searching. When he led her to the small clearing, with the stream running at the base of the nest of rocks, and asked her if she could see the opening to the den, he knew by her whole demeanour that it was the *right* place, and heaved a sigh of relief. Now he hoped she would relax a bit and start to put the world into proper perspective.

There was an improvement in both of them, once the den had been built. Athaba recognised a change in himself as well as Ulaala and realised that he too must have been tense, strung up, for once they were safely established in their new home something flowed from him into the sandy earth and left him feeling so much better. His frame of mind altered considerably. He felt ready to tackle anything.

Ulaala was still anxious a lot of the time, but it was a more gentle expression of worry. A sort of preoccupiedness which bothered Athaba much less than the taut moods to which she had been subject during their trek.

'It'll be all right,' she said to him tenderly, one night after they had eaten and were preparing for rest. 'Once the pups have been born, it'll be all right. Mothers get fretful, especially before the event . . .'

He accepted her word for that.

Even as the pair had been building their den in the nest of rocks, they were aware that there was a hunter further to the south. They were attentive to this danger, but knew it was pointless to move on. They would not find a better, more secure place to den. When they had left the north, it had been barely the end of winter with a hint of spring in the air. It was now the beginning of summer and the pups were almost ready to be born. In the summer, the hunters were active everywhere, so it was a case of find, settle and hope.

Luckily, they did not have to do a great deal to the natural cavity in the rocks in order to make it comfortable. Normally, they would have dug a hole in well-drained soil with a small entrance, a short dog-leg tunnel, and a dry chamber at the end. There would be no bedding. As it was, there was a cave in the cluster of rocks, the entrance of which was overlapped by the mottled, pitted monoliths, forming a natural camouflage. The outcrop was on a sandy hill, easy to dig. Athaba and Ulaala had widened the tiny entrance, which must have been formed in the *Firstdark* by a fountainhead, and scoured out the chamber within.

There were in the area, moose, beaver, marten, muskrat, caribou and bison, and, of course, all the smaller game. It was rich country during the season. There were also bears, which brought back some nasty memories for Athaba, but he intended to steer clear of the devils. A red fox came nosing around the rocks shortly after they arrived but Athaba soon put the creature on its toes and running. It kept stopping and looking back as if to say, 'You don't own the landscape!' The trouble was, he felt as if he did.

Contrary to normal procedures, normal behaviour, Ulaala and Athaba devised new howls to use alongside the traditional ones. In any other pack, the composing of new howls would be regarded as profane, since the songs of the ancestors were supposed to be complete in themselves. There was a whole set of howl cycles which were sacred and needed, it was said, no improvement.

But Ulaala and Athaba were not 'normal' wolves and had their own very radical ideas about life. Athaba said that for too long wolves had been automatically accepting what was passed on to them by their foreparents, without question, and had lost the initiative and inventiveness of those early wolves. They had become set in their ways, soulless, unthinking, blinkered, stolid. It was time to reassert the values of original conceptions.

The pair of them had made a start on this extremist programme, by inventing new howls. These were secret-pack-howls, the meaning of which was only known to the two of them. There were love howls, and warning howls, and howls just to clear the heart of exuberance. There were mournful howls for depressing times and racing, clipped howls for exciting moments. There were dream howls, to clear the head of fantasies, and dark-and-light howls for clarifying the soul. There were *hot* howls and *cold* howls. This tonal language of the wolves had been developed over many eons and though some of the other canids shared the ability to indulge in this complex and harmonious skill, none could match the wolves for depth and range.

It was not just the formation of each note that required talent, but the interpretation of each nuance of sound. It was as important to develop the *ear*, as it was the throat. Some wolves set out from birth to become *listeners* and were highly respected for their ability to interpret sound. A human, caribou or bear might think they have heard the same note nine times in succession, but a wolf with a reasonable *ear* would be able to distinguish subtleties between each note and form a mental picture of the Howler's message.

Ulaala and Athaba practised their skills on cold clear nights when their cries rang out amongst the rocks and echoed along gulleys. They found a Howling Rock near to the den which was perfect for Swallowing-the-moon. (This was a traditional howl whereby the Howler tried to entice the moon down to the Howling Rock using songs of promise; beautiful songs that had been composed especially to attract the soul of the sun. The idea was that if the moon ever came close enough, the Howler could suddenly break off in mid-note and swallow *Groff's* work for good and all, thus robbing men of their night light. Although there were witnesses to testify that some wolves had been *very* close to achieving this goal, no wolf had yet succeeded in swallowing the moon. It had become, like most traditional activities, more of a hypnotic game than a serious attempt at revolution. Wolves who played it became intoxicated, drunk on their musical attempts to draw the sun's soul from the heavens, and the mesmeric effect of watching the moon moving closer to their open mouths made them giddy with excitement. In fact, Athaba wondered if he would have the courage to actually do it, should the moon ever get within snapping distance. After all, the wolf that swallowed the moon would have a full stomach indeed and the dull light from its belly, shining out on the snows, would lead man to wolf.

What would they do with such a wolf? Cut it open, perhaps, to release *Groff's* lantern?)

It was better to treat it as a game.

These were also anxious days, wondering if the birth would be good and without complications. Athaba fussed around Ulaala so much so that she took to finding a place to sleep on her own. They slept for long hours, sometimes in the den, sometimes out in the sunshine. Athaba hunted and cached many of his kills.

One evening he went hunting. When he returned, the pups had been born. There were two males and four females. Six beautiful deaf and blind wolf pups. He had a pack at last, his own pack, *their* own pack. Life was complete.

Ulaala, though she was very protective towards the pups, became more like her old self. She was a mother first, but the pressure had an outlet and the relationship between her and Athaba improved, became even better than it had been when they first met. Athaba felt fulfilled too. Not so long ago he had nothing, and now he had a whole family. It was a miracle. It was difficult not to feel intense pride in Ulaala and the pups. He wanted to shout about them to the forests and mountains.

Eight weeks after the birth, when the pups had been weaned, Athaba's life fell apart again.

He was out hunting, and had crossed a muskeg – a basin of rock in which a bog has formed – rich in plant life. There was bog rosemary, skunk cabbage, marsh marigold and the carnivorous insect-eating sundew, all of which he had sniffed, searching for the scent of some recent prey. His tread across the sphagnum moss, with its cushioning layers of wood peat, was naturally springy and light. On the far side of the muskeg was a grove of lodgepole pine mixed with mountain hemlock. He paused to study this with suspicion. The breezes played around the tops of the trees, but there was no other movement so far as he could see. He went back to sniffing the small trails across the moss, through the highbush cranberry plants. Suddenly, his head came back as a strong scent offended his nostrils.

There, beside some sedge, were the footprints of a man.

After the initial shock to his olfactory organ this did not bother him unduly, since not all men were dangerous, of course. It was probably best to *treat* them as if they were, but there were those who ventured out gunless and harmless, to do whatever humans did with themselves in that part of the world. He remained

131

cautious but continued his hunt. He found several pools around the muskeg with some shrikes and yellowlegs moving amongst the rushes, but he wanted something bigger than birds.

At noon he came to a stream from which he drank. There were fish in the water, but after a few desultory attempts Athaba gave up trying to mouth-spear them. They were too quick for him. It was not a hot day, there being a lot of cloud cover, and consequently the fish were lively.

He left the stream and continued down a dry gulley, overgrown with dusty weeds. It was at the end of this gulley that he caught a very powerful whiff of native hunter. This was no southerner, white and pallid-skinned, clumping over the landscape in coloured shirt. This was a local hunter, who knew the earth as well as any human could. He was giving off that odour which told Athaba that the man was out to trap or kill wild animals. It was sweat-smell of a particular kind. Yet, there was another odour, another hunter's smell, but this one was not native. Athaba had no doubt this was a *tandem* hunt. A southern hunter being helped by a native tracker. The situation was as bad as it could be. Powerful weapons *and* good tracking skills.

Athaba came out of the gulley and began trotting towards some rocks. A breeze brought another wave of odours. The hunters were very close. He had to find some cover. He could not smell the scent of a machine, so that much was in his favour. Obviously they could follow, but only on foot.

At first he began heading back to the den, but then he veered off sharply, thinking that if they managed to keep up with him, he would be putting his mate and pups in great danger. It was better to circle the den, to try to find some area where the landscape was full of hiding places.

Suddenly, he hesitated. Something was very wrong. The strong scent of native hunter was carried to him on the wind, almost like a gift. Why would a skilled local be upwind of him? That didn't make sense. And there was no southern hunter smell of smoke and flowers. Where had *he* gone to? If Athaba turned around, avoiding the native, then he might find himself in an ambush.

For a moment, he did not know what to do. Finally, he veered off again, to the west, keeping under cover of a ridge. When he broke out the other side, he found the southerner waiting for him. The gun was already levelled.

132

Athaba began running, at the same time waiting for the sound of the gun. His heart was pounding, but he did not panic.

There was no loud report. All he heard was a 'plopping' sound, and then he felt a sharp sting in his rump. Instinctively, he nipped at the pain, thinking to find a hornet. Instead, it was some man thing that was stuck in his muscle.

He went on for six more paces with the object dangling from his rump, then a dizziness overcame him. He staggered. The world swam around his head. He fell forward, his legs suddenly becoming boneless. The skies folded over his eyes.

It was believed amongst Athaba's kind that at one time the native hunters were once wolves themselves. It was their eyes that gave them away: they still had the eyes of a wolf. Possibly some *utlah*, tired of being a raven-wolf, consulted the fox mystics on the dark arts of shape-changing. After sneaking into a cave and selling something, perhaps the meaning of a sacred howl, the raven-wolf had been given the secret. It had crept out on to a moonlit landscape that sparkled with ice and snow; where shadows were thick and black; where streams either raced in torrents or froze solid. This was a landscape that was hostile to man and therefore safe from invasion. It had crept into the land of the midnight sun, transformed itself into a human. Other *utlahs* had followed suit. This new kind of man, this exiled wolf in disguise, could live on the tundra or in the country of ice to the north, as well as any indigenous creature. This kind of man could track and hunt almost as well as a wolf, though during the act of transformation, some of the skills had been lost. *Almost* as well as a wolf. This new kind of man – a human as close to the earth as any wild thing – lived alone on the tundra, in the snows, for a very long time. So long was it, that wolves began calling them the Only People, since it seemed that the march from the sea of chaos had been halted somewhere a long way south of the tundra. These were the 'only people' who could live in the high country. Of course, they were cold in their new naked form. They began to hunt their former kin, to get back the skins they had lost.

The southern hunters, being devious creatures however, were not to be stopped by a few degrees below zero, permafrost, or raging blizzards. Eventually they found methods of fighting the cold, the loneliness, the barrenness of the northern landscape. They even reached the glacial country where the ice rumbled across the land and broke its snout in sections that floated away over the cold oceans. They came with their dogs and devices and began to establish supremacy in the land that had resisted them for so long. Even the Only People were unhappy at the inevitable invasion, but like their former kin, could do little about it.

Athaba's mind swam with the image of a wolf changing into a man, and a man changing into a wolf. The two images blended. Gradually light seeped into the corners of his eyes. He felt sick and groggy. His throat was dry and his nose was warm. He would have slept only there was a feeling of alienness about him which he wanted to dispel. Slowly, he opened his eyes.

Looking down on him was one of the Only People, the native hunter that had been with the southerner. The eyes were sympathetic: a wolf's eyes. Athaba could see brittle winters in those eyes, the deep frosts, the swirling ice, the white winds. They were narrow, crinkled at the corners, and set in weathered skin. A lock of black hair had escaped the hunter's furry wolfskin hood and was like a dark smudge on his brow. The hunter showed his many teeth. Athaba could smell his breath, smell a thousand foreign scents. He backed away, snarling. He needed to get back to Ulaala and the pups. His mate would be concerned by his absence. If these hunters had no wish to kill him, then it was necessary he leave at once, and return to his pack.

His posterior came up against a barrier and he turned and snapped at it in his weak state. He went forwards, then sideways, flinging himself in all directions for a moment, and being blocked each time. He lay down again, panting, dizzy. When his strength returned he tried again, and the hunter's barking infuriated him as he struck barriers each time. The hunter stood up, tall as a giant, over him. Athaba wanted to leap up high and rip open that barking throat, get at those curled lips, those teeth.

It took some while to realise he was entirely surrounded, enclosed by a thing made of thick metal wire. Never having seen one before, he had no name for it, but he had seen and heard of fishermen's nets – had found them and worried them on the ice – and this thing appeared to be a metal net. They had him trapped. Outside the wire net was the open landscape. They had not yet taken him anywhere.

He lay on the floor of the trap and looked up at his captors, the one with the eyes of a wolf and the pallid-skinned southerner with

134

a fire-stick in his mouth. The southerner's scents were atrocious and made Athaba want to retch. There was a gun at the man's side which smelled sickly as well as metallic. A shot from that weapon had robbed Athaba of his senses. The southerner's teeth were showing too now and he barked rapidly at the native hunter, while still looking down at Athaba. Then Athaba started as the face came down to peer more closely at him. He waited for a second, then leapt and snapped at the wire just below the face.

The white hunter jumped back, his teeth had disappeared behind his lips and his complexion grew paler than before. Athaba saw the quick flush of fear on his enemy, smelled it on his body, and was triumphant. Not so powerful, these southerners, when you took them on face to face. They were jerky creatures, no fluidity about them. Then, annoyingly, the white hunter showed more teeth, pointed and barked in a high rapid tone, and the signs of fear were gone from him again. Athaba's triumph had been a short-lived thing. Never mind, he could watch and wait, and repeat the performance. He had the feeling that these southern humans did not like sudden movements or surprises. What Athaba had to do was remain immobile, seemingly docile, then go for the face that came down to meet his own.

He was not going to give in without a fight.

When his strength returned he attacked the thick wire that surrounded him with renewed vigour. He wanted to get out, get back to his Ulaala, the she-wolf he had only just found! It was a cruel fate that had kept him bereft of company for so many seasons, given him Ulaala, a perfect mate, and then snatched it all away again.

All he succeeded in doing was breaking a tooth.

The native hunter came over to him once and kicked the metal net with his soft boot.

Eventually, Athaba heard that appalling noise and his heart raced as a bird machine dropped, thundering from the heavens. He was going to die after all! They were going to rain metal on him, *dak-dak-dak-dak-dak*, from the sky, and there was no way he could escape. The noise was appalling and nearly drove him out of his mind. And there were ragged winds tearing at the snow, pulling at his fur. Unnatural winds, that knew no real direction, crazed winds that had been driven insane by the noise of the machine and twisted in on themselves as they tried to escape its terrible whirling wings. It was all clatter and panic and rushing

135

blood and mind-screaming and confusion and ugly smells and noise and noise and noise . . .

Once again he flung himself this way and that, bruising his body in the futile attempt to breach his prison. *Ulaala*, his mind screamed, *what are they doing to me*? He *had* to get out, get back to his family. The pups . . . his mate . . . they were waiting.

They put wooden staves through his net and lifted him up under the swirling wings of the giant metal bird. So big! He had not realised how big these flying machines were. The native hunter put some slivers of meat through the wire but Athaba ignored them. He was too terrified to eat. What were they going to do to him? Was he to be swallowed by this metal monster? The noise. The noise. The noise.

Once he was inside the flying machine, the din increased, and all he could do was lie flat and wish to die. He was miserable, terror-stricken and defeated. The vibrations of the machine made his head spin. He vomited on the floor, not caring about the stench. Then his stomach fell rapidly away from him, dropping downwards. There was a feeling of instability, as if he were dangling from a string of meat by his teeth. If he let go, he would fall a long way, down to the middle of the earth. Cold air rushed around him. He closed his eyes and his head spun. If he could have torn out his own throat, a quick death, he would have done so at that moment.

The racket seemed to go on forever and Athaba despaired of ever being free from it. Then there came a heavy jolt and eventually the clatter became a clangour and then, a miracle, it ceased altogether.

Again Athaba's prison was lifted on poles and he was carried to a ground machine and then taken on a short journey to a building. Inside the building were bright lights and warmth. Food was given him, and water taken from a small metal fountainhead that worked to the command of the southern hunter's hand. Athaba still refused to eat or drink. He was too unhappy and confused. Unfamiliar odours assailed him, some of them causing flutterings of panic, but things were too bad to follow one individual line of terror through to its natural conclusion. There were also many strange sounds around him. In the wild, any one of these scents or sounds might have him bolting, but since there was no where he could run and a multitude of fears hissed and bubbled inside him, he did nothing but turn his face to the wall and wish to die.

Eventually, thirst forced him to lap some of the water from the metal dish. Not rainwater, meltwater, bogwater, nor even streamwater that had gathered some salts on its journey through the rocks and earth. This liquid had a strange taste, as if it had been poisoned with *bad* salts. Water seasoned in a hollow stump did not taste that bad. Water from the sac of a freshly killed caribou tasted sweeter. It smelled too, of one of those odours only found in the vicinity of men. Athaba waited for the poison to have an effect on his body. He was glad they were killing him this way. He could just let his chest weaken and his head fill with mist.

Nothing happened. He was disappointed. Water that smelled like that, with such a slippery softness to it, surely had to be bad? But it seemed it was just water, after all.

He began to miss so much that he had taken for granted when he was in the wild, never having been deprived of them before. Simple things that he had thought part of the natural order of all lands, all places. The air for instance. Why was the air so still? Where was the wind with its freshness and its tingling scents? Even in the back of the deepest den, there was a stirring, a draught of outside air. What about the sounds of the earth? The ticking of insects, the cry of the birds, the sound of snow and ice? What had happened to all those noises that came from the sky: the eerie whistles and the sound of the stars calling to one another in high-pitched voices? In here the atmosphere was like dull metal, dense ice. He might as well be buried in rock. Where were the sweet smells of his lost landscape? Where was the sun, the moon, the darkness? What were these strange hot lights buried in the metal sky above his head? None of it made any sense to him.

Most of all he missed Ulaala and the pups and spent much of his time fretting about whether they were coping without him. He had let his mate down. She needed him to hunt or watch the pups while she did so. The young ones would be in danger every time she had to go out to find food. These thoughts were so distressing he often howled, but though a human looked in on him occasionally they took very little heed of his mournful cries.

At other times he became angry and furiously attacked his prison. The meat they had left him was caribou. He disdained it. His carrion days were over. He was a headwolf with his own pack. How dare they give him meat fit for only ravens? Was he to go back to being a scavenger again? Let them throw it to the weasels and the ermines.

The native hunter came back and kneeled down, looking in. Athaba tried to frighten him with snarls and snaps, but the hunter merely narrowed his eyes. *You don't scare me*, said those grey eyes. *I know you, wolf. I know your ways. I have been you.* Then the hunter reached in for a sliver of meat and retrieved it quickly. He put it into his mouth and chewed on it slowly.

Athaba watched the jaws working.

I won't eat, he promised himself. He might have drunk the water, but he certainly wasn't going to touch their foul meat. He would leave it there until it stank and the flies were feasting on it.

Why didn't they kill him now?

What were they waiting for?

Nothing made sense to Athaba, who had never heard of a human hunter capturing a wolf alive. Perhaps they were going to use him for some ceremony: kill him slowly? Roast him alive over one of their fires. Watch his eyes sizzle and his tongue burst into flames? His imagination could work overtime in such a place.

Chapter Twelve

For a long while Athaba could think of nothing but Ulaala and the pups. How were they faring without him? Were they getting enough food? Was Ulaala managing to protect the den from intruders? These thoughts went round and round inside his head, driving him crazy. He knew he had to escape somehow, but it seemed impossible. For days he gnawed at his prison, trying to bite his way through the metal. It was the only thing he could do, but it was a useless exercise. All that happened was his gums bled and later his jaws ached. The frustration he felt was intolerable. Never before had he been so restricted in his movements and there were moments when he thought he would choke on indignation and rage. In his head were snow-peaked mountains, wide tundras, valleys, hills, open forests. In his eyes were walls within walls. The scents that attacked him were of steel and concrete: dull, cold odours with an offensive metallic sharpness to the former and a heavy dustiness to the latter. There were noises, too, which made him start every so often: clangings and bangings, roarings and rattlings, snaps and cracks. None of these was in any way familiar and consequently he was always tense, always on the edge of anxiousness.

In certain drugged states, however, he momentarily forgot he was confined and got up from a deep sleep to dash himself against the wires, not remembering they were there. At those times he went berserk. He had never been entirely enclosed before in his whole life. Suddenly his world had shrunk to a tiny place which stank of Athaba. Some of his faeces did not drop through the holes in the floor and his urine smell clung to the thick wire. While these odours would not have bothered him ordinarily, when they were fresh, they made him anxious when they went stale. He wanted to get away from them, hide them under the dust, but there was no dust to dig inside his prison.

When he was having one of his bad days, flinging himself around, crazed with frustration, the southern hunter would come

139

and try to calm him. This man did not seem to like him being distraught and seemed worried that he would injure himself. Since the man had been responsible for putting Athaba in this position, the wolf was at a loss to understand the reason for concern. Still, the man came, and tried to soothe him with quiet barking and growling. He willed the human to put a hand inside the prison so he could bite it off at the wrist. Athaba promised himself that if ever he and the southern hunter ever confronted each other in normal circumstances, Athaba would not hesitate to tear some holes in his flesh.

Eventually, to his own distress, Athaba began eating. It was the beginning of the end for him. It meant that he had accepted his fate, that he knew he was never going home again. Hope died. He even gave up his tantrums. There was nothing to do but lie on the grid and become nothing. He was not a wolf any longer. He was not even a raven-wolf. He was nothing.

The time passed in greyness. He was transferred to a stronger prison with bars. A dirt-tray floor helped to improve the atmosphere. He had a fit shortly after this move which appeared to cause great consternation amongst the humans. This left him with a wish that the fits were voluntary and that he could control their comings and goings. It would be satisfying to throw a fit when there were people crowded around his prison, waiting for him to do something spectacular. It would give them something to ogle at. He might even be able to arrange a little foaming around the mouth, pretend he had some deadly disease, like rabies. Now *that* would send them scuttling for the exits. It would probably also ensure his quick execution. Not a bad thing.

They put him to sleep shortly after his fit and he was vaguely aware of a man in a white coat taking things like spittle and blood from his body. For a while the southern hunter underwwent great anxiety, pacing backwards and forwards alongside the prison, and stopping to stare in through the bars. This activity ceased abruptly after a day or so. The hunter appeared to have shed his worries.

From time to time, people came to look at him, other humans from outside the large place in which they kept him imprisoned. Sometimes the southern hunter would accompany them – the native hunter seemed to have disappeared, for Athaba had not seen him in days – and point to Athaba. The humans would bark and show their teeth, some of them shaking in that peculiar

140

way. Athaba felt humiliated by these visits. He was sure they were mocking him for being trapped, and that the hunter was bragging because he had captured a mature wolf.

There was one visit that Athaba did not mind. A child would come to see him, with dark hair and bright wondering eyes. Athaba had seen native hunter children from a distance, playing near their homes, practising for when they became adult hunters. This child was the southern hunter's child. He could see the similarity in the bone structure and smell it in their scents. The hunter was always fussing with the child, touching its hair, and whenever Athaba made a noise in the back of this throat, the child would reach for the adult's hand.

But the eyes were full of curiosity and wonder as the child watched the wolf pacing his prison or lying on the floor with his head on his paws. He made Athaba think of his own pups.

One morning there was a stirring of excitement in the air and Athaba knew that something momentous was happening. He paced and spun in his small prison, stopping occasionally to look to where the southern hunter was standing, other men around him. Clearly the hunter was organising something.

A man in a white coat came and shot one of those sharp devices into Athaba's rump. It made him drowsy but did not rob him of his faculties completely.

At mid-morning a ground machine rolled through the great doors pulling a platform on wheels. Carrying poles were slipped through slots in the side of Athaba's prison and he was lifted up and placed on the platform. Then a short journey began to where a flying machine stood.

It was not one of those that dropped out of the sky, but one that had to run along the ground before taking to the air. Certain types of bird had to do that, could not take off vertically.

To Athaba's consternation he was transferred into the belly of this great machine. It was huge! In the sky they looked only as large as a hawk, though they got a lot bigger when they landed on their skids on the ice. Man's machines seemed to have the facility of expanding or shrinking, depending upon the way in which they were being used. Athaba was not surprised that they got smaller once they were in the air because birds did the same. It was probably something to do with flying itself:

a need to be as light as a seed in order to remain floating on the wind.

However, though these winged machines were bigger on the ground than in the air, close to this one was absolutely enormous. It was like a great cave inside: a cave smelling of metal and other materials used exclusively by men. Athaba's prison was strapped down to the floor of this cave, along with wooden cases and boxes and metal objects of strange shape and design. The wolf could not even guess what some of these things were and was too sleepy to pay them much attention anyway.

Along both walls of the cave were little round holes through which Athaba could see the blue and white sky.

After a very long time, the small child came and looked in through the entrance. It waved its hand at the wolf, its eyes wide and round. Then two humans climbed on inside: the hunter and another man. (A cloud-dweller?) They disappeared into one end of the machine.

Noise and motion. Noise and motion.

Athaba began to feel as sick as he had done on the other flying machine as his stomach plummeted and his ears began to hurt. He howled – a long tremolo – and swallowed, which seemed to relieve the pain in his ears. The noise did not cease for an instant and Athaba flattened himself on the floor of the prison, certain that he was going to slide over the edge of somewhere and fall a long distance.

After a while the noise had a mesmeric effect and Athaba was able to sleep fitfully.

The noise stopped abruptly! A terrible sensation entered Athaba's head. He began sliding down to the front of his prison, until he was bundled up against the bars. Then the floor seemed to go almost level again. There was a kind of whistling silence, a feeling of floating for a moment, and finally the world burst open, spilling noise, light and air. Athaba blacked out as his body slammed hard against the end bars.

He awoke feeling cold. There was the sound of the wind. The affects of whatever had been pumped into his bloodstream were now gone. His barred prison lay half on the jagged edge of the flying machine and half on the snows. It had broken loose from its restraining straps. Looking around him, Athaba wonder whether

142

another giant flying machine, perhaps a raptor, a predator of the species, had torn this one to pieces with its claws. It had been decapitated. Broken crates and boxes were everywhere, out on the snow.

The hunter came to look at him. Athaba could see the man was in a state of shock. His eyes had a dark spiral look to them. The hunter ran fingers through his hair, rubbed his face, and then began gathering up bits of clothing and putting them over those he already wore. He moved amongst the debris gathering items and stuffing them into a bag. There was no sign of the other man.

Athaba tried to stand and found one of his legs hurt. It would not support his weight without an excruciating pain shot through his whole body. He lay down again.

Darkness came. The hunter made a fire a short way off. Athaba did not like being so close to burning wood (and whatever else gave off that awful stink) but there was little he could do about it. He was able to lick through the bars at the snow, to get some snow to quench his thirst. The hunter seemed to have forgotten about him and no longer provided water, let alone food. Athaba was not at that time too hungry, but he was quite thirsty. A bird came close to being dragged through the bars in the middle of the night.

The following day the light came over an escarpment like something brittle and sharp. The snow was patchy and beginning to melt. Athaba was able to get a few more laps.

The hunter was busying himself, making a kind of sledge with shoulder straps, but Athaba had never seen these used by the natives where there was little or no snow, and he could see hard work ahead of the man. He could also see the second human now. He was lying still on the ground. One of his legs was missing and his head stuck out to the side.

When the sledge was halfway through, the hunter tried pulling it over the rocky ground. It stuck, several times, and the man got angry and kicked it to pieces, before sitting down with his head in his hands.

A while later he was busy again, piling rocks on the body of the dead human. He heaved and grunted during this activity, having to take off some of his clothing while he worked. When it was completed he tied two pieces of metal together in the middle and stuck them like a small tree into the mound of stones.

They stayed there again the next night and Athaba began to get desperately thirsty. He howled and whimpered, pleading with the man to get him some water. The hunter simply raved at him at first, and threw stones at the side of the dead flying machine when he got too noisy.

The man had a light and came to him in the middle of the night. After staring at him for a long time, the hunter went away and returned with a dish of water. He pushed it gingerly through the bars. Athaba lapped at it greedily and not at all grateful.

Athaba was now a little incensed that could not get free. It had been different while the prison was inside one of the men's buildings, but now they were back in the wild. Heeee could smell the scents of the land, feel its spirit. Naturallly, he wanted to be out there, running with the wind. He sensed he was a long way from home – a *very* long way – and he wanted to begin the walk. If he died getting there, so be it, but he was eager to be on the trail, despite his painful leg.

Two more days passed, during which a flying machine was heard, but at a great distance. The man danced like he had an insect in his ear, waving his arms and barking hoarsely at thhe sky. He had a fat-barrelled gun which he tried to shoot into the air, but it did not seem to work and he screamed and threw it into the flames of the fire, whereupon it exploded with a bright red flash. The hunter was showered with bits of flaming twig and Athaba could smell his singed hair. Again he danced, but this was a different dance.

The buzz of the distant flying machine died.

The hunter stood looking forlornly up into the clouds where his brothers lived, probably wondering why they did not come down and help him. He was clearly needing some sort of help.

No more machines appeared.

Finally, the hunter began to walk down the gentle slope, heading westwards. He stopped several times, looked this way and that, shook his head and seemed to make a decision before continuing. On his back he carried an overfilled pack.

Athaba howled his anger after the man.

When he was at the bottom of the slope, and small, the hunter turned and looked around. He stood still for a very long time before taking off the backpack and starting the long climb up the slope again. When he reached the flying machine, he stood by Athaba's prison. He smelled of sweat and the flies were bothering him. Finally, he reached down and did something to the end of the prison, and stepped back several paces quickly. Then he went off at a jogging run, occasionally looking over his shoulder.

When he was halfway back to his pack, he stopped and turned and stared.

Athaba, lethargic through lack of food, staggered to the end of the prison and nosed the bars. They moved. There was a space for him to leave the prison. He limped through the gap and out onto the ridge.

The hunter turned and began walking away again.

Athaba watched him for some time, then went over to the mound of stones and nosed around. A smell of rotting meat had been coming from the place for a while now.

Then the wolf left the heap of rocks, to follow the hunter down into the shallow basin where he could smell water. He walked three-legged mostly, only putting down his paw when he forgot there was something wrong with it. On the way he scented lemming. Immediately, he lay down and patiently waited for the creature to come within striking distance. It ran under a rock. The boulder was not very heavy and he nosed it over, snatched up the lemming, and fed for the first time in days. Near where he caught the lemming he smelled the metal, wood and other scents of a man's gun. The object had obviously been flung from the site of the crash, out onto the slope, along with many other things. The hunter had been unable to find it, though Athaba had seen him searching the whole landscape while the wolf had been starving to death in his prison.

Athaba left the spot without any regrets. He didn't like the odour of firearms. It was best to put distance between himself and any weapons of man.

In front of him there was the hunter, now going north. The man seemed to have no idea of where he was heading, no sense of direction whatsoever. Athaba was aware by his demeanour, his scents, his movements, that the man was full of indecision.

Now that he was free, all thoughts of revenge had fled from Athaba's mind. The wolf was no longer interested in the southern hunter. They could go their separate ways and never see each other again. All thoughts were for home which lay beyond

145

horizons and horizons. Athaba did not know whether he was a month or a season or a year away from his den, but he did know that the country around him was so unfamiliar that he had never heard tell of it shape. The whole geography was new to him. No itinerant creatures had ever described this area.

Yet the actual composition of the landscape – the rocks, soil, the general appearance – told him he was in a world similar to the one he had left behind. He knew from the ravens, who spoke to migrating birds, that there were lands with far different faces. Lands that were hot and green, with waxy plants that sweated under a fierce sun. Lands that were covered in grasses, green or gold, that swayed under shallow breezes. Lands of nothing but sand, where not a thing grew. He had heard about these places from the ravens, had at first dismissed them as lies, but the black birds were so insistent that he realised there was more to the world than the timber country and the tundra and the permafrost.

The temperature told him he was further north than where he began, but not out of touch with his old world. They were moving into the season for the long day. At the present time the light was hazy on the horizon, with slanting silver-grey streaks forming a kind of wall from the clouds to the earth. Somewhere beyond that wall was a familiar landscape, familiar scents.

The hunter picked up a rock, threateningly as Athaba passed within a short distance from him, but the wolf disdained even to glance in the man's direction. If the man thought Athaba was going to honour him with an attack, he had rocks in his head as well as in his hands. Such thoughts were for captured creatures who needed thoughts of revenge to stay alive, not for free beasts, who could outrun any two-legged fiend without a gun. The man was a miserable specimen of animal life and not worth a short pause.

Athaba limped down to the stream, nosed through some tall reeds, and drank the first sweet water he had had since his capture. It went down coolly, filling his belly. He wanted to hear it slosh around as he walked, and lapped until he was thoroughly satisfied. Then he stared along the braided water, watching it tumble through stones, sweep around a curve. Colourful insects danced over the spray and birds came in to feed. Athaba snatched at a small fish, missing the first time, then

146

catching it. A morsel only, it slipped down in a single gulp. The place was humming with life. This was not a landscape on which he would starve. A flock of ducks came arrowing over his head, to land with trailing legs on a stretch of shining water ahead.

No, he would not go hungry.

PART FOUR

The Long Walk

Chapter Thirteen

In the early summer the tundra is a waterland. The permafrost is like a layer of bedrock not far below the topsoil and surface meltwater has no drainage. It remains where the ice has thawed, open to the heavens, forming lakes and pools, streams and flows. Flatlands are covered in hammered silver sheets, or veins of shining mercury, looking as if they have been wrung from the clouds by some artistic sky-creature, concerned about the brown stains that are left behind when the snow departs.

On these decorative stretches are waterfowl, millions of them, covering the shallow lakes, wading in the streams and rivers, splashing through the pools. The waters are thick with fish and insects, especially mosquito larvae. This is low, windswept country. The tallest shrubs are the dwarf trees, not much bigger than a hare on its hindlegs. Here and there a swath of short willows or stunted birch breaks the monotony of the landscape.

The terrain makes for difficult travelling on foot. The ground is boggy marshland and sucks at the walker. At best the wanderer finds spongy moss to form a springy path under his feet. Those who do not know the firmer tracks flounder in the sticky marsh. Where the granite or gneiss pushes a rounded shoulder through the sediment, it is easier going, but still normal distances can take up to ten times longer on the tundra than on more solid landscapes. Here, there are big skies, mostly clear, in which a mind can lose itself. Here the midnight sun rests like a giant molten ball on the edge of the earth, as red as iron straight out of the forge on the first day of creation.

Athaba's injured hindleg slowed him down. The damage felt muscular, rather than to do with a fracture or dislocation of the bone, which gave him some hope that if he showed consideration towards the limb it would mend.

Since the daylight hours were long, there was little problem with maintaining visual contact with the landscape. The wolf picked his way over the mosses and lichen, trying to keep to firmish going where possible.

In the early morning of the second day he stalked a small rodent for a serious length of time, only to have it snatched from in front of his nose by one of those pirates of the sky, a jaeger. As the buccaneer of the air swooped on his quarry, Athaba leapt, thinking to have both bird and mammal for breakfast. The jaeger was too quick for him and he merely received a shooting pain up his damaged limb for his trouble.

'One of these days,' he growled, as the robber flew off. 'I swear I'll eat feathers and all!'

Hunger gnawed at this belly. In his present condition Athaba was ill-suited for hunting, but if he did not hunt the situation would worsen. He came to a small desert of gravel and spent some time nosing under stones and finding beetles. This was not ideal wolf fare but it was better than nothing. Beyond the gravel was one of the thousands of lakes. On the edge of the lake were some red-throated loons, the dark chestnut band under their necks appearing black from a distance. Athaba immediately went down on his underhairs and began belly-crawling towards these unwary creatures, inching himself painstakingly along through white-tufted flowers and alpine plants.

By noon he was within striking distance of the birds. Out on the lake the geese and ducks cruised, and if they knew of the danger they failed to warn the loons. Perhaps it was none of their business? They, after all, were safe enough in deeper waters.

Sunlight angled from the surface of the lake turning half to blinding metal. Athaba's inching had been reduced to fractions now. All he had to do was wait for the right moment to spring.

The warm sun on the patterned plumage of their backs and flanks lulled the birds into a dreamy state. At the appropriate moment, Athaba leapt and went berserk for a few seconds amongst the panicking fowl. When it was all over, three birds lay dead around him. He began eating one of them straight away. Having finished one, he started on another. Once the second one was under his waistline, he was too bloated to eat the last of them.

He took the third loon and tried to cache it in a safe place. The ground was unsuitable for digging, though, and all he could do in the end was cover it with ferns. It was not a very satisfactory piece of work.

152

He continued on his journey, around the lake, a little more glow about him. The scents of wild flowers and ferns, of waterbirds and rodents filled his nostrils. He almost felt like his old self again.

After traversing the shore for some way, he scented the hunter, and turned to witness his cache being uncovered. The man stood, looking guilty, holding the bird by the neck and staring at Athaba. The wolf wondered what to do about it. Should he attack the hunter for stealing his cached meat? In their present state, Athaba was probably the stronger, but his instinctive fear of man was hard to overcome. There were also practical reasons why he should not attack. Although the man was in a weak state he would undoubtedly fight for his life, perhaps injuring Athaba in the process. Athaba had to be fit for a long journey: he could not afford to carry more injuries than he already had. Also, what was to be gained by such a move? He had eaten two birds. It would be a while before he could manage the third. Athaba wondered why he had bothered to hide it in the first place, since it was doubtful he would return this way ever again? Habit, probably.

It would be foolish to attack the human.

Athaba decided to rest for a while, since his injured leg was giving him trouble. He lay down in the sedge at the edge of the lake and watched the man tear feathers from the bird with frantic hands. Then the human tried to bite at the raw flesh.

He wants to be a wolf, thought Athaba.

This was clearly an unsuccessful attempt at feeding himself, for the man made various sounds of disgust and then began looking about him. He gathered some dried vegetation, of which there was little, for some time until he had a pile. Then taking something out of his pockets, he put a flame to his little pyre. There was a swift *whumph* and the grasses burned away before the hunter was able to do more than singe the bird's feathers. A look of consternation appeared on the man's face.

Athaba rose quickly and trotted away from the place. The smell of fire awakened a feeling of panic in his breast which made his limbs tingle with nervousness. Athaba walked into the shallows of the lake, glancing behind until he was sure that the fire was not heading in his direction, before stopping again.

He turned to stare at the man.

Next, Athaba saw a flash of silver, like a fish breaking water. The man had taken out a blade and was cutting the underside of the bird. He extracted the liver and some other pieces of offal

153

and stuffed them into his mouth, chewing on them quickly. The next moment the wolf witnessed the man being violently sick. Evidently, his hunger was not sufficiently advanced for him to overcome his revulsion of raw still-warm liver. Not for the first time Athaba wondered at the weak stomachs of southern men. Why was it that they had to burn their meat before they could keep it down? The local people, who had once been wolves, could still eat raw flesh, especially fish, but the southern hunters always made a fire and roasted their meat. They were such delicate creatures, and without their weapons, so puny. Really,, they were to be despised rather than feared. Why, if wolves had weapons that could kill at a distance, then men would be the prey!

After a further time, the hunter succeeded in making a small fire out of rags from his clothing, and some other pieces of material from his backpack. He managed to burn the outside of the bird enough to be able to take some bites out of it and hold the meat down. Athaba saw him tear up some of the lakeside plants and gnaw at the roots.

The wolf now realised why he had not been fed over the last few days. Although the man had had food, at least up until two days ago, the amount was not adequate for both creatures to survive on. Supposing the hunter had expected rescue within a short time? One of those flying machines? Then he had to eke out his supplies and cache food for a period of time.

A wolf will feast and then go days without eating. Evidently men were not able to do that. This man was as starving as Athaba had been before the divers were caught.

Next, he watched as the hunter found two large stones and began crushing what was left of the bird between them. He smashed and pummelled at the meat until it was in thin splattered slivers, which he was able to feed to himself a tiny piece at a time. There was no more vomiting. The hunter seemed to have solved his own problem for the time being.

The man now stared back at the wolf. He seemed to have regained some of his former arrogance or, at least, confidence. With his hands he threw a shower of feathers into the air, letting them fall on his head and shoulders. He barked at Athaba: a triumphant sound. It was as if he had done something remarkable, like catch the birds himself, instead of just taking carrion from another hunter.

'A raven-man,' sighed Athaba. 'And a happy one.'

Then it was up on his feet again, a test of the injured limb, and the long walk continued. Behind him, the human hunter packed hastily and followed in the footsteps of the wolf. From time to time Athaba sniffed the air and smelled the closeness of the man. What was going on here? Why didn't the man go in a different direction, one more to his advantage? If he, Athaba, had been the human, he would have headed south. Athaba was going west because he believed that his pack was somewhere in that direction.

There were two possible answers. Either the man did not know in which direction south lay, which was unlikely, or he knew he could not survive alone. Perhaps he needed Athaba to show him the way across safe ground? Perhaps he believed he could not survive except on the wolf's leavings? Whichever it was, the man had obviously decided that his best chance lay in following the wolf, at least until some better plan turned up.

They circumnavigated the lake together. By the evening Athaba was exhausted. Yet he had travelled only a short distance that day. It was going to take forever to reach his home country. Surely death would overtake him first?

He knew he was going to have to harden his spirit to stone if he was going to complete this journey. He sensed his pack was a long way off – just how far was beyond any reasoning – and he was going to have to take each day one at a time. There was no use in dreaming of reunions, or wishing for an end to his walking. If he let his spirit go soft on him, his stamina would fail and he would fall into despair. The thing to do was set himself targets – a far hill, a distant lake – and tell himself that once he reached each particular point he would reassess his position, set a new goal. That way the journeys were finite. There was a clearly defined purpose: to reach a target within his capabilities.

He found a small plateau on which to rest.

Along the horizon, the red mane of the sun brushed the dark landscape. Northern lights flickered in the sky like wayward fantastical fireflies. Athaba heard the clatter of rocks as the hunter finally caught up with him.

The man knew his place, however. He stayed just beyond the plateau edge. His scent was slightly offensive to the wolf but it was getting more acceptable as time passed. The southern hunter had made a good start at growing back into nature,

155

becoming more a part of the tundra and less a human carrier of the stink of civilisation. Tundra soil smeared the man's clothing, his boots, his leggings. The scent of the moss was on him where he had lain in it. Clean wholesome tundra air was scouring his skin, filling his pores with its moisture. There were seeds in his hair and there was dirt between his toes and fingers. He was growing into nature, and nature was growing into him. Nature had a lot of work to do, to get this human fit for wolf nostrils. After all, the last ten thousand years had been spent softening this two-legged beast, removing all traces of the good earth from his person. There were millions of scrubbings, teeth-brushings, nail-filings, haircuttings, bearrd-clippings, shavings, tweezerings and orifice cleansings to correct. All this unhappy work had to be reversed. The man had to be blasted with grime so that his skin was clogged with dirt which was not so easily removed. He had to be toughened under the sun, in the wind and rain, to get rid of his tenderness. His hair had to grow, to collect dust on its follicles. His nails had to lengthen, gather soil beneath them. His lungs had to expel the smoke and fumes of the cities.

Nature had made a start on this necessary process but still had a long way to go.

In the late evening there were bothersome insects. Athaba could hear the hunter slapping at them and grunting. Then there was silence. Sometime after that, Athaba rose and padded over the distance between them. When he reached the hunter the man was lying on his back, his throat exposed, one arm draped over his eyes. He was fast asleep.

Athaba nosed into the backpack and retrieved the remaining bits of his bird. He took them back to his own place on the plateau and crunched the bones to get the last of the meat. A splinter went up into the roof of his mouth. This made him panic at first, wolves had bled to death on bone cuts in and around the mouth, but after a long time of working at it with his tongue, he loosened it sufficiently to enable him to spit it out. He should have remembered about the danger of bird-bones. He knew it all along, but it is difficult to obey old rules under new circumstances.

When he woke, Athaba limped across the top of the plateau. The sky was as clear and deep as an upturned lake above his head. A falcon circled above and then wheeled away to the south. Down on the shining tundra ahead and below was a crazed pattern of brooks and becks, cutting the land up into patches. Dwarf alder

156

swept downwards in a rush of light green to the tangled masses of grey fern below, as if it were trying to drive a wedge into the lowland plants.

The man must have been watching and waiting for the wolf to stir because he followed in its tracks immediately. When Athaba descended from the high ground to the marshes again, the man was not more than ten lengths behind him. The hunter's breath was laboured and his civilised feet slipped on rocks smoothed by glaciers during a time far off, during the new red dawns following *Firstdark*. Engines of ice had cut grooves over this remote world before men had even begun to hunt wolves with spears, let alone drop on them from the sky in machines. Man and wolf were travelling a landscape cracked by the frosts of a million long dark winters, incised by the reaches of northern ice that had since retreated, worn smooth by rumbling giants and imbedded with massive rocks that were now left stranded.

When they reached one of the streams, the man stood and stared down into the water. Athaba knew he could see fish: greybacked shapes that moved amongst the stones. The backpack was taken off and placed on the ground and the hunter entered the cold waters. He stood, poised for a few moments, before snatching at the fish. After several attempts, he was still empty-handed. Athaba watched him, wonderingly.

Then the wolf went to the water's edge and mouth-speared a grayling within a short time. He ate the fish slowly, his eyes on the man downstream. A second fish followed the first. By now the hunter, was standing with his hands on his hips. His expression was a cross between admiration and fury. Athaba speared a third fish and let it flop around on the bank. He kept his eyes half on the man and half on the gasping fish. Gradually, the hunter moved towards him. When the man was three lengths from him, Athaba swallowed the fish, almost choking in his efforts to get it down quickly.

There was a cry from his raven-man, as if to say, 'Will you leave me no carrion? Will you eat every morsel before my very nose?'

Athaba entered the stream for the fourth time, stabbed, stabbed again, stabbed yet again, and came out with a fish. He held it in his mouth until the man had backed away, hope shining in his eyes. Athaba left the water and dropped the fish on the bank. Then he deliberately lay down beside it.

The hunter began creeping forward again until Athaba lifted his head and stared hard.

Finally, the human could take no more and began shouting and throwing rocks. Athaba picked up the fish and splashed into the stream as the hunter came running forward, all fear of the wolf swallowed by his hunger. When the man got close, Athaba accidentally dropped the fish into the water where it shimmered back to life. The hunter threw himself on top of it, struggling to get his hands on the wriggling piece of silver. Once, he almost had it, but it slipped out of his fingers and flashed away on the current, leaving him on his knees.

Athaba shrugged at this peculiar behaviour, and continued his journey, well fed.

The temperature dropped during that day and the wind rose. When they came to a gravel plain, the man fell to his knees. Athaba thought he was finished, had walked himself to a state of exhaustion, but he was suddenly aware that the man had found something. A howl of triumph came out of the human mouth. The hunter began popping things into his mouth and then searching around amongst the scree on his hands and knees.

Athaba knew then what his raven-man had discovered.

Birds' eggs.

He began limping forward, anxious to be on his way. The hunter looked up and there was consternation in his eyes. Athaba knew he had given the human a dilemma. The man could either stay and search amongst the stones for more eggs or follow the wolf. Athaba knew that the southern hunter had no real sense of place or direction. He was relying on the wolf to lead him. The man finally seemed to compromise.

A hobbling chase began, with the human trotting after the limping wolf, at the same time pausing occasionally to snatch an egg from the ground. The birds began to mob both creatures but that was the least of their worries. One was anxious to cover ground and the other to fill his belly. Occasionally, the human swung his pack at the carking birds but it was a half-hearted gesture, like swatting at clouds of gnats.

While Athaba rested, lying on his side on a warm rock, the man was having trouble with his bowels. There was no mistaking sound or smell. The hunter's diver bird meat had turned to water in his guts and he was groaning amongst the rocks.

A blood-red sun stayed with them, black clouds like dust storms over its face. The world smelled musty like a creature after a long sleep. At the end of the day man and wolf were nowhere on a vast landscape. They had covered but a fraction of the distance between them and their two respective goals.

During the night the wind rose in fury and came screaming over the flatlands with grit in her teeth. Man and beast sought refuge amongst the scant cover, in a small copse of stunted birch that had withstood many such hurricanes. The sapling-sized trees that had stood for twice a hundred seasons bent under the onslaught of the wind and broke it where they could.

There was not much sleep to be had with the rocks and stones rattling over the world.

In the night, there were dreams. Pups ran amongst his legs, jabbed at Athaba's mouth to make him disgorge their next meal. He was a father, doing fatherly things. There were howlings, pups learning the complex songs of their ancestors. The scene then switched to Athaba as a pup, composing his own original howl, taking this howl to his mother. His mother, wrathful, unforgiving, for wolves do not presume to *invent* new howls, new songs. It was against the laws of the pack to offer new compositions. The ancient songs were there for a purpose and all things new were regarded with suspicion. Did he think he was above his ancestors?

Athaba dreamed of his brush with mysticism: the burial of his father and other events. His problem had always been that he had been born with more spirit than other wolves. Not the spirit of courage, though he had some of that, but the spirit of the infinite. He had always been ready to acknowledge that not all things could be explained in practical terms, that there *were* aspects to life and death that could only be *felt*, experienced by the spirit or the soul, and could not be subjected to reason and logic. There were things to be either accepted or rejected that could not be accessed through the intellect.

It was this acceptance of a mystical side to nature that had kept Athaba going thus far, when many wolves would have turned their faces to the prison wall and slipped into death.

When he awoke, the wind was raging through the copse, almost flattening the dwarf trees with trunks no thicker than a man's thumb. Nearby sat the hunter, curled like a fossil left lying on the wastelands. He was whimpering in his sleep.

159

Did humans dream? It was something Athaba had not considered before. It was possible, he supposed. They were animals after all, in body if not in spirit. There, another whine. He was surely dreaming – just like a wolf.

Athaba had thoughts about moving on, but a fit overtook him and he was left so weak after it he decided to remain where he was for the time being.

Chapter Fourteen

Wolf began the next day's journey in the terrible wind, shouldering his way forward, anxious to make some headway despite his sore feet and aching hindleg. Man followed him, seemingly reluctant, for his complaining could be heard even above the noise of the wind. They struggled (not *together* for Athaba could not conceive of them as being anything but independent beings) over the landscape like two insects, making slow progress. Once, when the wolf looked back, the man seemed on his last legs, hollow-eyed and pale. There was little possibility of finding food that day and the human was obviously growing weaker. The wolf expected that the man would die soon.

The wind seemed to rob Athaba of all his energy. It forced air up his nostrils so that he kept catching his breath. It blew grit and sand into his eyes so that he had to walk with his head down, in a submissive posture. Despair gnawed at his determination like a carnivore. He found difficulty in ignoring it. The wind was a mother to wolves who relied on it for survival, but like most mothers she chastised her young on occasion.

Then something happened which could be called a miracle, except that unusual circumstances make possible that which might not take place under normal conditions.

Athaba, his scent and sound hidden by the high wind, stumbled upon a herd of caribou sheltering in a hollow. His immediate, instinctive reaction was to bring the nearest one down, before it could bolt. Running alongside his prey, he leapt up at its throat as the caribou herd tried to scatter, his teeth sank in and he gripped the flesh firmly. He hung on grimly until the unlucky beast's struggles ceased. The rest of the herd had stampeded, but he had acted instantly and his reward was a feast of meat. He could hardly believe it himself. His fangs were soon at work on the underside of the creature. When the man came, the innards of the caribou were exposed.

The hunter saw the caribou and made a loud sound, lunging in shoulder to shoulder with the wolf. Athaba's reaction to this was to snap at the intruder viciously but the man defended himself, holding his backpack in front of him like a shield. In the other hand was his hunting knife. There was a brief struggle, with the hunter holding out the pack and using it to push Athaba away from the soft meat. Athaba's impulse was to attack the nearest object to him connected with the man, whether it was a vital organ or not. That object was, of course, the backpack which he ripped and tore with his teeth. With wild eyes the man fended off Athaba's irritable lunges but seemed equally resolved that his own hunger should be satisfied, whether it cost him an arm or even his life. Athaba yelled. The man barked back. The smell of the meat was overpowering and driving both of them to a frenzy. Then the shouting and barking stopped. Both man and wolf were determined to get their share of the prey. With the wind still screaming around them they gave up their quarrel and fell to the meat again. Athaba grumbled and ate, aware of the proximity of the man, but was now more interested in filling his belly.

The human went to work, hacking at the stomach of the beast until he had freed it. He retreated with the sac of the quarry in his left hand. The backpack was ignored and now lay by the caribou. Athaba worried it just once more, then concentrated on feeding himself.

When Athaba glanced over his shoulder he saw that the hunter had slit open the stomach of the caribou and was feeding himself hand to mouth with the contents. The wolf knew that the recently grazing caribou's belly would be full of partly digested lichen. The human seemed to like this warm sludge and gobbled it down as if it were the best food he would get out on the wastes. Athaba had heard of local hunters doing this very thing when they had been short of food for a few days.

It was a passing consideration. Athaba fell to again, gnawing at the entrails and satisfying his own needs. Once he had finished the soft meats, Athaba stripped the skin from the thighs and began chewing on the more solid meat. At last he had a feast at his disposal and could gorge himself to contentment. This was the way things should be, with meat to spare. When this meal had digested, he planned to cache some of his kill, despite the fact that he might never pass that way again.

When his hunger had been dealt with, Athaba rested beside the carcass, using it as a break against the wind. The man cautiously retrieved his backpack and, when he thought Athaba was not looking, cut some meat from the shoulder of the caribou, lay down some distance away from Athaba. The wolf recalled their little struggle over the meat and how angry he had been at the intrusion. His feelings had not been aroused because another creature was taking from his kill. It was a matter of precedence. It was *his* kill and therefore the human should have waited until Athaba had eaten, had taken the choice pieces. In any case, the man was a 'pack inferior' and therefore had to be kept in his place. Athaba's strong sense of rank told him that subordinates who took liberties should be disciplined on the spot. No hierarchy had been discussed between the two creatures, obviously, but Athaba knew he was the superior beast at this point in time. All the strength was coming from him. All the decisions were coming from him. He was the hunter, the pathfinder, the leader. The man should have known that and kept his place, which was to eat *after* Athaba and when the wolf had eaten himself into a near stupor. Instead, the man had barged in with his offensive body odours and frantic clawing for the best bits of meat. It was no wonder that Athaba had been incensed. Such behaviour was unacceptable. If the man wanted to be headwolf, he would have to assert himself in ways other than fighting for the choice pieces of the kill. He would have to show that he had skills useful to the pack.

The gale showed no signs of dying: in fact it increased in strength. There would be no more walking until it had spent itself. They settled in, the man building a wall of stones to keep out the wind: a kind of half circle about shoulder-height to a wolf. Athaba watched this activity with mild concern. Was the human bringing his civilised ways to Athaba's world? If protection was necessary, it was usually obtained from some natural object, like a hollow in the ground or a boulder, or in Athaba's case, the caribou carcass. It was not usual to fashion artificial defences against the elements, even though the materials came from the natural landscape. Athaba wondered whether he ought to reprimand the man, but then decided that the stupid creature would not understand why he was being punished, so it was all a waste of time.

Sometime that night the wind began to abate. Athaba, curious, arose and went round the wall to look at the man. His fellow creature was fast asleep and warm in the circle of stones. Athaba was a little indignant at this since the caribou was obviously not as efficient a windbreak as the stones.

He padded back to his own place, however, thinking primly that unnatural objects were best left alone, despite the fact that they were better suited to the job.

'No wonder men are soft creatures,' he grumbled sanctimoniously, 'if they pamper their bodies like that.' He was glad, he told himself, that wolves had no hands, nor brains to invent such artificial devices. 'Why, we would soon deteriorate into dogs. No, no, I'm only too glad we can't build things like that monstrosity.'

He fell asleep again.

Athaba rose to the *rhonking* of geese, newly arrived on the tundra after flying vast distances. The geese wintered in southern climes, mostly islands. With them, out on the boglands, were golden plovers, stints, godwits, wheatears, grey plovers and turnstones. The waders, like the plovers and turnstones, stints and sanderlings, search like the wolf for meat. Savagery is not confined to mammal predators out on the tundra, nor to the hooked beaks and talons of the harriers. Wader birds are without exception all carnivores. They are the wolves, foxes, weasels and stoats of the waterlands.

Athaba was uneasy. He could smell his own kind in the air. There were wolves hereby. The last thing he wanted to do was antagonise some local pack and have to fight and run, perhaps being pursued from horizon to horizon. If at all possible, he wanted to evade confrontation and the best way to do that was to avoid contact altogether.

However, just as the man was climbing to his feet, a stranger appeared from behind a piece of medial moraine, followed by four others. The creature that was obviously the headwolf stopped some distance away and regarded Athaba. Then it came forward again, the others at its heels. As it came a little closer, Athaba's nose told him the leader was a she-wolf. Of the other four, only one, a yearling, was a male.

The headwolf halted, a little unsure of the situation.

'You have one of our caribou there,' she said.

A year ago Athaba would have already taken to his heels and left his kill to the pack. Since then a hardness had set in. Despite the good sense of his earlier promise to himself, he now decided he was not going to be bullied. Shunning a fight was one thing: running away from a direct challenge was quite another. There were advantages on his side. He knew how he looked: rangy and mean. He was an itinerant wolf and knew how to take care of himself. At the same time, he was not stupid. He knew that if all five wolves attacked him, he would not stand a chance. It depended upon how organised the pack was and whether they were prepared to suffer casualties. If they had not eaten for some days, he was in big trouble.

'The caribou are yours? I was under the impression that prey was there for the taking. Since when did wolves *own* caribou? One might own a carcass – for example, *this* carcass is mine because I brought down the beast – but I'm sure you wouldn't claim something which is obviously not yours?'

The she-wolf took a couple more steps, still not as confident as she should be in the circumstances.

'*You* brought this one down, *alone*?'

Athaba was torn between pride and common sense. He wanted the wolves to acknowledge his hunting skills, but at the same time it would be better to present a stronger front if he could. In the end he chose strategy over vanity.

'Not alone. I had the human hunter with me.'

The man was by this time hiding behind his pack. He was pointing a stick which he had cut from the dwarf willows, as if it were a gun. Both Athaba and the she-wolf stared at the southerner in amazement. What on earth did he think he was doing? He surely did not believe that wolves could be fooled into thinking a stick was a gun? Sticks and guns have quite different smells for a start . . .

'*That* helped you catch a caribou?'

'When I say *helped*, I mean the human acted as a beater, sending the quarry towards me, while I waited in ambush.'

Now the man had risen to his feet and was backing away from the group. Athaba decided to ignore him. The other four wolves were closing in on him slowly forming a hollow ring. He knew now that they were preparing to attack him so he turned lazily and trotted in the direction of the man, as if he did not care whether he was followed or not. He hated having to leave his kill to this pack but they would soon discover his injured limb, if they had not already, and this extra weakness would not do much to keep them at bay.

165

When he was some distance from the carcass, he discovered that one of the she-wolves was not far behind him. The approach was aggressive and he turned and faced her.

'Don't be foolish,' he called. 'Just because I retreated before a pack, doesn't mean I couldn't take on at least two of you and win. A single wolf? I would chew you up and spit you out. Go back to your own.'

'You're wounded. I saw the limp. *I* think that hunter shot you . . .'

'And then threw away his gun?'

'I don't know, but my standing in the pack would improve if I were seen to take you on and beat you.'

She advanced a few more paces. Then she yelped and jumped as a rock struck her on the flank. She ran back, then turned again. Another rock whizzed under her nose. Athaba could see the human hunter now, a pile of stones at his feet. In any other circumstances it might be a stupid thing to do, to throw stones at a fully grown she-wolf, but the creature was unsettled. To take on Athaba might have increased her chances of pack promotion but to attack a human required more than a whim. When a wolf and a man seemed to be acting in concert, that situation needed thoughtful consideration. It was better to walk away than get into something which might damage an individual's standing in the pack.

She called back, 'What are you, a *dog*?'

Athaba was more amused than angry by this question.

'Who me? Or him?'

The she-wolf disdained to continue the conversation and loped back to the carcass where the others were feasting.

Athaba felt it wise to put some countryside between himself and this pack and he continued on his journey across the desolate landscape. His leg felt a little stronger but he still had to favour it. The human followed on behind, stopping to drink at streams when Athaba did and moving on when Athaba moved.

For three more days they walked, resting only when they were exhausted. The sun hardly rested itself now, merely dipping below the horizon for a short time before reappearing. The whole world seemed an unsettled place. The tundra chittered with bird life. Lake surfaces rippled with fish. The air was full of insects. There were mists and fogs, and rain, when visibility fell sharply.

166

There were warm days when the blue sky seemed to be lower, closer to the ground.

The wolf caught small mammals for his food but the man fed mainly on fish. He had learned to dam a stream with rocks at two points, to isolate a stretch of water. Then he would divert the flow upstream of his trap, digging out a channel in the soft earth with his fingers. Once the watercourse had been altered, his trap would drain leaving any fish caught between the two dams, flopping in the shallows. The first time he did this, the man did an extraordinary thing. He threw one of the fish to Athaba, keeping two for himself.

Athaba let the gift lie where it was, not far from his nose, while the man gathered brushwood from a forest of dwarf birch and made himself a fire. He watched the human wash himself in the stream, the water droplets clinging to his face fur. The smell of the cooking fish made Athaba's saliva glands active. It had been spitted on a stripped dwarf tree and suspended over the fire. The southern hunter turned it lovingly, roasting all sides of his meal. When it was sufficiently cooked for his taste, the human lifted it off its rockstand and held it up – a gesture to Athaba – before sinking his teeth into the flesh. Scales decorated his face fur now and warm juices ran down to drip on to his clothes. He was showing his teeth in that way peculiar to humans.

Athaba wondered what to do about his gift. If he took it, would he lose some of his independence? What would be the position between him and the man? How would it change their relationship?

As it was, Athaba preferred to think of himself as travelling alone. If another creature wanted to trail along behind him, that was nothing to do with him. However, the man had helped drive off the she-wolf a few days previously and was now throwing tidbits to him. The only time Athaba had accepted something from a human was when he had no choice: when he was captive. Would this give the man the idea that Athaba was *his* creature? No, there was one other time Athaba had taken from humans: when he was a raven-wolf. He had scavenged from the waste bins outside the huts in the ice country. Surely this was the same thing? The man did not want the fish. He had too many to eat at once, and this one would go rotten on him and he would be unable to devour it later. Wolves could eat rotten meat, but not men. Humans had delicate constitutions, as easily disturbed as the stomachs of pups.

This was waste food. Why leave it to the birds?

In truth, the smell of the cooked food had been driving Athaba crazy, and once he had swallowed the fish he felt guilty. The she-wolf had been right. He *was* a dog. He had become one of man's creatures. Never again would be feed from the hand of a human.

Yet this man was different, wasn't he? The tundra had grown into his skin. His smell was no longer as bad as it had been when they were first thrown out of the sky together. He had the mosses and lichens in his fur, the dirt between his fingers and toes. He washed his body in surface meltwater. His mind had changed too. He had grown more contemplative. At least that was Athaba's observation. The wolf had watched the man watching the midnight sun watching the world. Tranquil skies put the human into deep reflection, had him staring into their mottled redness of an evening with his chin cupped in his hands. The southern hunter was more like a native now, alert to scents and sounds which would have previously escaped his attention.

The man's shoes were now so worn and rotted they had fallen away from his raw and bloody feet. He had tried wrapping rags around these soft appendages at first, but this invention only worked for a short period of time and he was running out of material. For a whole day now he had been completely barefoot. He hobbled a little and spent time washing his abrasions and blisters, but he did not whine now as he had in the beginning of the march. Before the walk was finished, if he did not die, the man might become a wolf.

Athaba's own injury wavered from improvement to worsening, depending on how hard he drove himself during the day's walk. He longed for familiar scents to come over the horizon which would tell him he was nearing his journey's end, but these never came. In his heart he knew he was still many days, perhaps months, from his old stamping grounds. It would not do to give way to despair, however, for that would surely finish him.

While he was thus engaged in thought, the pack they had encountered a few days previously caught up with them and began to ring them. The man caught sight of them almost at the same time as Athaba himself was aware of their presence. Neither of them panicked. Instead, the man gathered more brushwood and built up the fire until its blaze was flicking upwards with long tongues. Athaba saw his companion place some smooth river stones right in the middle of the flames. He then settled at a distance from his work. It seemed to Athaba he was waiting for something.

Athaba gathered together vestiges of strength that he knew he would need in the coming fight. He was going to die, just like the man was going to die, but *he* wasn't going to sit down on his bottom playing with rocks and just waiting for his throat to be opened.

Just as the pack was closing in, there was tremendous CRACK from the area of the fire. It sounded like a rifle shot. Athaba leapt in the air and ran twenty paces himself. The wolf pack just scattered over the countryside, splashing through pools and across bog. There were two more 'gunshots' from the direction of the fire which had Athaba running circles, wondering whether to join the pack in their flight or stay and find out where the man had found a gun from.

When he was brave enough, he went back to where the hunter stood, stirring at the flames and barking in triumph. The man shook his fist at the retreating wolves. Athaba was still bemused. He had no doubt that a trick had been performed: there was none of the odours normally associated with firearms, in or around the fire. Something had been done but what it was remained a secret between the man and his work. Something to do with stones and fire.

Fire was not a thing wolves were fond of anyway since it was almost always associated with men. Brush fires could be started in the forest by lightning but mostly fire was the work of man's magic, one of his evil tools. Man and fire had almost always gone together. No other creature possessed the sorcery which would enable them to conjure heat and flames from wood and dried plants. Sometimes, even men lost control of their devilish art and forest fires raged killing both human and beast. Wolf lore said that man had not brought the secret of fire with him out of the sea-of-chaos but had acquired or stolen it since. There was one idea that said that the southern men had found a way to trap fork lightning during thunderstorms, and were able to break each jagged spear into tiny pieces, which they kept in small shiny containers like the one this southerner had with him.

However, the natives had been making fire from two pieces of wood for many hundreds of seasons before the southerners ever arrived with their metal containers: this was in the songs going back through a thousand great ancestors. There were those, too, who had witnessed both natives and southerners rubbing tiny splinters of wood against a hollow block of wood resulting in a flame. These hollow blocks, made of thin bark, had been found and nosed by brave canids, but the mystery of their ability to create fire remained unsolved.

So far as Athaba was concerned, it was best to treat it as sorcery and forget reasonable, logical explanations.

The next day, he and the magician left the scene of their triumph over the wolves of the tundra to continue their quest for the home of their kin and kind.

From that point on, the man's physical state underwent a gradual deterioration. He was attacked by mosquitoes, ravaged by them, until his skin was raw. The female insects fell upon him in their thousands and feasted on his blood, gathering their protein. Athaba knew from wolf lore that on the tundra there is not just one but some forty different species of mosquito. All of them were out for blood. Athaba suffered as well as the man, but the effects were not so terrible. The man was driven nearly insane, scratching and making himself bleed. The cuts festered.

Athaba liked his man better when he was crazy. It made him more acceptable somehow, less of a threat.

When the mosquitoes were at their worst, the midges came, so thick that neither man or wolf could draw a breath without filling their nostrils with little black bodies. They were like dust in the air, like powered stone. Their bites were not so dramatic as those of the mosquitoes, but they were an irritant just the same and there were more of them.

Along with the midges came the black flies: small dark insects with short legs, broad wings and humped backs. Like little demons they came straight from hell, their savage bite almost as toxic as that of a wasp. Indignity piled upon indignity. Man and wolf were drawn closer together in their fight against the common enemy, though they were able to do little in retaliation. They offered one another sympathy in looks and gestures. The swarms were unrelenting and there was now no darkness in which to hide and lick one's wounds.

170

Chapter Fifteen

The wolf finally gave the man a name.

There had once been an ancestor of Athaba's who was accused of having human characteristics because he preferred cooked meat to raw, was obsessed with roast beef and boiled bacon. This forefather had been killed while attempting to steal a ham from a human encampment. His name was Koonama.

So the man became Koonama.

Of course, Athaba did not even try to communicate this to the man. It was merely his way of accepting that the human was now part of his pack, his responsibility as headwolf.

Chapter Sixteen

And they came to a river, swollen with recent meltwater and rushing in torrents. It looked impassable. Since the beginning of their journey they had skirted lakes, waded through streams and braided rivers, splashed across wide shallow pools and slept on wet moss. Athaba was beginning to hate water. Normally, water did not intrude upon his life. Water was an essential commodity in frequent, small amounts, but beyond that it was barely considered.

Out here, in the wetlands, it became first a nuisance, then an annoyance and finally unbearable. It was omnipresent and formed barriers across the country which the two travellers could well do without. Athaba would have liked some fox-god, such as A-O, to reform itself out of the water, and thus rid the land of the stuff. He felt it a shame that wolves did not have a god of their own, otherwise he could have asked such a god to speak to his fox colleague and get something done.

Koonama looked at his headwolf as if it were the canid's fault that a river blocked their path, as if Athaba should feel personally responsible for this latest outrage of nature.

'No one asked you to follow me,' said Athaba to the dumb creature at his side. 'I didn't promise you smooth passage across the wilderness. All I'm trying to do is get myself home. I'm not responsible for you.'

This was no longer true, and Athaba knew it. Koonama was part of his pack now, and as headwolf he was responsible for all that occurred on the trail. He was the pathfinder and it was up to him to find ways and means of surmounting any barriers they came across, or avoiding them altogether, if that were possible.

However, Koonama looked down into his eyes, as if he understood. Athaba was convinced that at times the human *did* comprehend what he was saying. At least, he often reacted in the way Athaba wanted him to. Perhaps such a reaction was just automatic, not denoting any real understanding on the part of the human? It didn't really matter. Koonama was a kind of company for him, not *exactly* a companion, but he was there.

With a loud unexpected bark, the wolfman threw his pack on the ground, stared at the white foaming water with his hands on his hips, and then kicked a stone petulantly out into its currents. Then he dropped to the ground. A cloud of midges and mosquitoes followed him down, biting him in every conceivable place on his body.

Koonama looked as exhausted as Athaba felt.

Athaba found there was a kind of rhythmic pain, a repetitive pattern of agony, which set in with walking. When he stopped for the day, in the evening, his body was numb. During the light-darktime, when a sort of peace settled over everything, his body began to thaw, so by the time morning came everything from paw to nose to tip of tail ached. He would drag himself to his feet, stumble to the nearest watering point, and drink. If he had anything to eat, he ate. Then he would begin to walk again. Gradually the aches disappeared, to be replaced by actual pain which started on the pads and in the joints, and juddered through the body. Since walking has a rhythm, pain too has a motif. It almost became addictive. Athaba knew that if something went seriously wrong, a thorn in one of the pads, or a torn ligament – something that had to be rested for more than a day – he might never be able to walk again. It was not the actual walking that was agony, but the stopping. Once he had halted he would notice how light his head felt, how dry the joints of his legs were, how sore his pads. Should he have to stop for a whole day, a stiffness would set in which might be impossible to overcome when the time came to walk again. The longer the rest, the heavier and more difficult to overthrow becomes the lethargy. It became a permanent tenant of the body and mind. Before long, life itself seemed a weary burden, and he felt that it would be a better thing just to stay on the same spot, to die there, and enter a world where there was no need for walking. That state of mind, when death becomes more attractive than life, is more dangerous than the bullet.

It is only rhythms that keep us going.

Koonama tried entering the water, but soon sank up to his thighs as the river took the silt from under his feet. He turned and reached for a rock on the back, using it frantically as an anchor to pull first one leg from the sucking mire, then the other. His

173

sweat-smell told Athaba how relieved the human was to get out of the swirling waters.

Athaba studied the thick eddies himself. They looked solid things, like twisted white wood. There was no way he could see himself swimming through them. If he stopped, and waited until the flood subsided, he might not get back on his feet. *He* was going to walk, south along the bank of the flow, to find a crossing point upriver nearer the source.

Turning, he began the detour. Koonama groaned and followed, no doubt realising that there was no alternative.

They plodded on, staying on relatively dry ground, for two days. Food was not a problem: there were other creatures for whom the river formed an impassable barrier and some of them had halted, bemused or irritated by this wall of water, at the bank. They were easily caught. Even Koonama managed to chase a hare into the water, then grab it. The wolfman was becoming quicker, despite his tiredness. He looked leaner and meaner than ever, his eyes brighter, and set in a face that had once been pudgy and flaccid, but was now narrow and angular. The arms were muscled and stringy, the legs wiry.

He was a little mad, of course.

He tried to talk wolf talk sometimes, and when he received no answer growled away to himself in his own rambling way. He threw stones at things he disliked, like the river, or objects that annoyed him, like the stars. The wolf, used to loneliness, having experienced a great deal of that terrible inner emptiness during his seasons as an *utlah*, did not succumb to the attractions of losing his reason. He envied the man in a way. Madness was a wonderful escape from the ravages of loneliness: it provided imaginary companions with whom one could argue and converse. Lack of food only left the stomach empty but lack of company hollowed the body, the head and the heart, leaving a void that was startling in its size. The wildernesses of the spirit were vast places, more desolate and bleak than any external land. They were charred areas where forests of feelings have been burned to black ash and there was nothing left to explore. They were infinite vacuums of darkness where not even a star shone to break the monotony. That was why the man threw stones at the stars, because he envied the night sky. He wanted one within him.

It seemed to Athaba that Koonama was becoming more animal than man. When they stopped to eat, Koonama would tear at his

174

food like a wild beast, and bend down to drink at the water's edge like a real wolf. When the march had first begun, the man had been fussy about where he took his water and used cupped hands to drink from. None of that now. His hands were as black as his face and not to be trusted as a utensil since the bony fingers would not hold water.

He made beds from sedge and moss, but some animals and birds did that so this did not lower him in Athaba's eyes. He still walked on two legs, but Athaba did not expect the impossible. He still used his eyes more than his nose or ears, but was *becoming* more in tune with these latter senses.

There was indeed hope that the wolfman might save himself, if they spent a season or so in getting where they were going. Once, they had been hungry for several days when they came across the carcass of a caribou. Other predators had been there before them, and the parasites too. All the meat had gone and just the bones and horns remained. However, the beast had been in velvet when it was killed, so Athaba began stripping this covering off the antlers with his teeth. Koonama, possibly near to starving, copied the wolf. Between them they chewed and swallowed every last shred of the membrane, and afterwards Athaba felt proud of the way his pupil was coming along. He ate like a wolf, slept with the alertness of a wolf, was almost as hairy as a wolf, drank like a wolf on all fours. If Koonama would just throw away those silly coverings and could learn to walk on his knuckles, there was no saying what he could accomplish in the way of wolfery.

Eventually they came to some high ground where the river narrowed and the ground was solid. Koonama crossed first, his pack above his head, and was washed away. He went tumbling downstream, losing his backpack, and had to fight his way to the far bank. He made it, collecting by the look of it, some cuts and abrasions. Then the wolf went.

Athaba did not try to cross between two points. He allowed the torrent to take him downstream, much further than Koonama had gone, gaining a length across for every six sideways. Eventually his paws touched firm ground and he struggled from the water. The wolfman joined him later.

They spent the night sheltering behind a ridge, during which the man grumbled and raved in his sleep. There was some

175

darkness, after which the wolf climbed the ridge to get the lie of the land beyond. When he reached the top he could scent humans. In the far distance, lights were embedded in the ground. There was a settlement not half a day's walk from the ridge. Even closer, a road wound its way across the flatlands below, to the south-west.

Athaba lay on the smooth crest of the ridge and studied the landscape for a long time, before trotting down to where the man was muttering and thrashing. He found himself a crevice in the rocks and went to sleep.

When they awoke sometime later, almost together, Koonama went back to the river to bathe his feet. He seemed obsessive about his feet. Athaba went to drink. Then the wolfman fed on water plants. He was good at holding things down these days. Not much came up any more, though the other end of him was not always so lucky. He tended to suffer from recurring diarrhoea.

The day's walk started shortly afterwards.

Athaba struck out north-west, to avoid running into humans from the settlement. He kept the pair of them below the hill, out of sight of the road and the houses beyond. It was his duty as headwolf to protect himself and Koonama from human hunters. Koonama followed closely behind him, keeping pace with him. Athaba's hindleg still gave him trouble, but was not nearly so bad as it had been in the early days. The fits were still with him, but infrequently.

This was not the first time Athaba had been aware of the proximity of humans since the walk began. Previously he had smelled parties of hunters, closer to them than the settlement had been. However, he and Koonama had been lucky. The hunters had not so far caught the scent of the travellers. The pair of them passed within a few yards of one abandoned encampment but the hunters had been good at hiding traces of their journey. The ashes from their fire had been buried and all other signs wiped from the landscape. Athaba saw Koonama's nose twitch on this occasion as they passed by the spot. No doubt the wolfman could still smell the traces of charcoal in the earth. Koonama's expression at the time was one of puzzlement but the area was soon behind them, and thus forgotten. They lived almost moment to moment, and the last river, the last batch of dwarf trees, the last scent of sage, was history as soon as it was out of sight, smell and hearing.

176

Athaba was good at *his* job, which was to weave a silent path between human settlements so that the pack remained undetected. This job he performed with unswerving diligence and the pair of them managed to avoid all contact with humans. This he did for the good of the pack.

It did cross his mind once or twice that Koonama might possibly wish to catch a nostalgic glimpse of his old-world fellow creatures, but really that was not Athaba's concern. Survival was the overriding all-important rule, and wolves did not survive by inviting contact with men. His man had become more wolf than human and therefore had to sacrifice any sentimental desires for social contact with his former life. This was necessary both for the good of Koonama as well as for the good of the pack.

Two days later Koonama had a fever. He fell during the afternoon walk and lay with his face in the moss. Flies gathered around the sores on his cheeks and feasted in the cracks of his lips. The wolf walked on, leaving the wolfman behind.

Athaba splashed through pools and across country until the man was out of sight and scent. His olfactory sense was full of the odours of moss and lichen. His eyes were fixed on the distant horizon and his neck muscles remained rigid. He heard only the call of his pups, the howl of his mate. There was a lot of country between him and his home and he had only half a lifetime to cover it in.

The sky above him was striated, like ice scored by rocks. A dirty-ice sky, solid in appearance but with a depth to it: ocean ice, almost unfathomable. Across such a sky migratory birds travelled twice a year. Why did they bother? Why risk death time and time again to travel thousands of miles from one place to another? Why not find some place that suited them all the year around? But, in the early spring and late autumn, something shifted in the heads of the geese, the stints: a tilting of the brain's axis, an equinox of the mind. Shortly afterwards the air became full of beating wings. Birds swarmed liked bees and went south or north, depending on the season.

When he reached a cairn that had been built some time ago by humans, traces of man-scent on the stones, weak as they were, jerked some subliminal trigger in the wolf-brain. The light twisted behind his eyes and the subsequent action was involuntary but undeniable. He retraced his spoor across the bogs. He did not himself understand why he was returning to the sickbed of the wolfman: something had clicked in his brain, like the seasonal signal to a migratory bird, and he had obeyed it without resistance. There *was* no denying it. A bird flew south, Athaba retraced his tracks across the tundra.

Athaba went back to where Koonama lay on the soft wet bed of the tundra and waited, he knew not why, for either death or recovery.

That night Athaba lay near his charge, wanting to be on his feet and travelling, yet somehow held to this place. Wolves have never been very good with the sickness of others. They prefer to turn their backs on it. A sick pup will often be killed. At best they did what Athaba was doing: they stayed around the ill creature, studying the sky, the plants, the water, as if wholly unconcerned by the suffering close by. *This is nothing to do with me*, was the impression they gave. Athaba, despite his own experiences of being ostracised from the pack because of his fits, was at heart no different from other wolves. Like the rest of his kind he had an unreasonable dread of illness, of any creature that was not functioning normally. Abnormal behaviour worried him and presented him with fears he did not know what to do with. *If I ignore this*, he told himself, *it won't visit me too*.

Koonama shivered or sweated alternately, sometimes snatching at the air as if he were catching mosquitoes. Delirium caused him to thrash and moan as if he were grappling with strange invisible monsters. Perhaps he was? If so, he won, for the next morning the fever appeared to have subsided. The wolfman looked thinner than ever, but his eyes were clear.

There was a weakness about him which told Athaba that they would not be going very far that day. Athaba went off and ran down a hare, bringing it back. He ate his share, leaving the rest for the pack. The wolfman stirred himself long enough to make a fire. Then he partially cooked the tough meat, before devouring it.

Koonama seemed concerned about his little container of flames. He kept holding it up and peering at it, then nodding his head mournfully. Athaba was at a loss to know what was worrying his pack. After all, the container still produced fire. So long as it did that, where was the problem?

The days were beginning to get darker and colder. Koonama's old clothes were in tatters, but he kept some of the pelts of

178

the kills and wrapped them around himself. Even to Athaba's nostrils, used to rotting meat, he began to develop an odour fit only for a six-month-old carcass. What worried the wolf was the fact that other predators – perhaps bears? – would be able to scent Koonama from a long way off. There was nothing to be done about it though. The wolfman had to keep himself warm or he would die. To Athaba's eyes he certainly *looked* better. The skins acted as a camouflage and when the pair of them were hunting together, Koonama was able to move upwind of the prey, while Athaba waited downwind, ready to ambush. It was not the way wolves normally hunted, but it was developed between them because the wolfman was useless at stalking and running down prey. A wolf might follow prey for days, stopping when the quarry stopped, patiently awaiting the right time to attack. Koonama would run at the prey and give up the moment it took to its heels.

So, some time after Athaba had run down a young musk-ox and the man had skinned it and made himself a cloak from the pelt that hung with shaggy matted knotted hair, they began their teamwork. Even to the wolf the wolfman was a ghastly sight. Athaba could imagine what went through the mind of any prey that was ambushed by the pair of them. First of all it would be aware of an awful stench riding on the back of the wind. This would have the creature up on its toes, alert and ready to bolt. Then there would be a rustle, a movement amongst the distant dwarf willows. The small trees would tremble and shimmer in the eerie light of the northern day. One or two birds would bullet from hiding places. By this time, the quarry would be an instant away from flight, nerves tingling like electric insects, tendons so taut they hummed in the breeze. Then this *thing* would suddenly leap up on its hindlegs – this ghastly *thing* which had no real shape and from which bits of flesh and skin dangled horrifyingly – this *thing* which would let out a warbling shriek loud enough to frighten a bear – this stinking creature from some other world, with bright eyes, even white teeth, and waving limbs.

If the prey did not have a heart attack or freeze on the spot, it would fly across the soggy turf, uncaring of anything but getting away from the monster that had sprung from the earth before its very nose and eyes. Athaba would be waiting, crouched behind one of the *roches moutonnées* that littered the landscape and spring on the unfortunate beast, thus realising its worst nightmares.

179

When the wolfman was ready, they continued with their long walk across the tundra. Athaba wanted to make good headway before the autumn, which was not far off, began to shake itself loose of sleep and walk across the landscape.

Koonama too must have been aware of the coming cooler weather, perhaps glad of it since wherever he went a cloud of flies and other insects followed. No doubt the cloak was partly responsible for the gathering of these pests around his head. He must have wished for the yellow dryas to wither and decay, so that the flies would leave him alone and disappear back into their hidy holes.

Mists began to roll across the landscape with hearts of soft light. These fallen clouds would leave Athaba and Koonama dripping with moisture and would cause the creases in their joints to become sore with rubbing. So many discomforts, yet they went on, deeper into the western sky. It had become a way of life, to move in the same direction, day after day.

Chapter Seventeen

First there was Cle-am, the Long Hot Wind, followed by the fox A-O and the wolf Sen Sen. These three were responsible for shaping the earth, giving form to a nebulous mass. When the word reached the sea-of-chaos, where humans were moving through an inner darkness, a jealousy was given birth. Humans were not world shapers and were able to do little with the murky sludge at the bottom of the waters in turmoil. They coveted the earth and were prepared to kill any bird or beast that stood in their way.

At the height of the wars following *Firstdark*, in which wolves were being slaughtered by the ten thousand, there was one called Ranagana who felt there must be another way to make peace with the humans. He was aware of the failures of others, to negotiate with *Groff*. Ranagana had heard of those who had spoken with dogs and cats and had tried to find a way they could meet humans halfway. No political change had come from any of these attempts and Ranagana lay down in a cave on the hillside and being a wiser wolf than most, indulged in original thought.

At the end of many nights of turning the problem over in his mind and discarding that which had been attempted and that which would not work, he decided to go out into the world and seek advice from other creatures.

Ranagana had come to this conclusion: that not all men wanted to kill wolves for the same reasons. That various groups of humans each had different reasons for wanting wolves dead.

There were those who hunted wolves for their pelts. These were a deadly breed of man but were not mass murderers. In the normal course of events, wolves would not be too concerned at having such an enemy. Trappers were not intent on genocide, for that would rob them of future livelihood. If there were only trappers in the world of humans, the wolf would be in no worse a position than any ordinary prey.

There were those humans who were not concerned about wolves who lived out in the wild and killed them only when they encroached on human settlements. These, too, were not intent on massacre, only on protecting themselves and their property.

Finally, there were those who wanted to exterminate the whole wolf race because they feared and hated the wolf.

This last group were the most dangerous and responsible for the terrible slaughter that swept like a swath over the landscape. Dogs had told Ranagana that certain humans wanted to annihilate wolves because of the way wolves hunted and killed.

'They're horrified at the way you tear out the throat of your quarry. They're appalled at the savagery they witness when you hunt.'

The wolves were at a loss to understand this.

'It's the way we were made,' they replied. 'Other creatures do the same and they're not persecuted the way we are. Look at the big cats! What do they do that's so different from us? What about humans themselves? They even *skin* their kills.'

'Well,' said the dogs, 'unfortunately you're not as endearing as a leopard, nor as majestic as a panther. You look savage *all* the time, whereas a big cat can hide its claws in velvet and purr and look as though it wouldn't harm a butterfly. Humans will excuse their own actions – they don't even consider them because they're for the good of the human race which they believe is god-like and does not have to account for its actions. So, you won't get anywhere by comparing your own actions with theirs. Even the fox can get away with more than you because it does it out of sight of the humans. If foxes could *just* leave livestock alone, they might not be bothered at all. No, I'm afraid there's no real logic behind human hate of wolves, any more than there is behind their fear of spiders. A tiny little creature which a human could squash between finger and thumb, yet they go in terror of it. Fear of the spider, hate for the wolf. These are inexplicable prejudices which will never be conquered.'

Ranagana did not believe this. He felt if wolves could manage to become remorseful about their way of hunting, they might become more acceptable to humans. It was certain they could not change their *ways*, for they had to eat or die, but they could change their *attitudes* and show the humans that they, too, like men themselves, thought hunting and killing an

182

unfortunate necessity, a disgusting business to be done behind closed doors.

Ranagana had heard of a weasel, another creature despised by men, who had come to the same conclusion and had undergone a change in attitude towards hunting and killing its prey. He went to see this weasel, to discover whether wolves could undergo the same change, the same process. This is what he heard.

'Most humans think I'm bigger than I am, but I'm not. I'm little, slim and swift. There is much blood in my history: we are, after all, the children of Mogascunga, the forest god. He picked me as the king of the weasels and gave me the task of saving us from the dark two-legged menace that is now abroad in our world.

'So I began to meditate on all those activities which disgust our enemy so much. I began telling myself that it was wrong to like the taste of blood – weasels have this thing about blood – even though blood must be shed to get meat. I began to convince myself that I needed to atone in some way, for my behaviour, though it is natural enough for a weasel to love the taste of blood. I began to tell myself that it was an *un*natural desire, that I was in some way a freak of nature with inherent evil characteristics which had to be scourged.

'I used to lie awake in the grass, under the moon, defying the owl. Around me the night was a turmoil of fear and dread, whispers and secrets and hidden tremblings. There were hard, sharp eyes out there. Claws and teeth, fangs and talons. A swirling blackness, a storm of dark red passion. There were snouts out there, catching the scent of prey. There were ears out there, listening for the rustling of quarry. Smells came to my nostrils, of leaf and bark, of sap and still water, blade, stone, clay, fur, feather and flesh, of bracken and gorse and fungi, of warm warm blood.

'As I lay there, my mind was in the same tumult as the night around me. I smelt the blood and my senses screamed with delight. I needed it. I needed it. Yet, I had developed this sense of guilt, I had to suffer this terrible remorse. "Those poor creatures." I would think to myself, "I drink them dry and leave them like husks to shrink, wither, and blow away. I am a demon, but a demon with a conscience." Can you imagine such a mind, that craves the red viscous river flowing through tthe veins of his victims, yet once the deed has been done, the craving satisfied, the guilt flooding in? Sometimes I think I shall go insane. There is a worm that burrows through a weasel's ear and into his brain. Creatures who suffer from this worm go blind and mad. I have the same madness, and my lunacy comes not from a real parasite, but from that worm called *conscience*. Some god somewhere has cursed me with this unreasonable imagination. Since I have indoctrinated myself with man's feelings on the subject of blood, I am able to change places with my victims and experience their feelings on being confronted by a creature like myself.

'Yet, the next time the bloodlust is high again, I fail to heed the voices. I push my conscience to the pit of my brain and go forth with needle-sharp fangs, to prick their pulsing arteries.

'Humans do not like me. I sense their revulsion very strongly. Most of them have never seen a weasel, but still they have this deep-seated loathing for me and my kind. They find me exotic but I am something to be disdained. Humans do not like creatures with sharp teeth and a heady desire for blood. They believe me to be a mammal almost the size of a stoat, but I am quite small and neat. A stoat is huge in comparison. I have tiny bright eyes. I have tiny white teeth. I can stand on my hindlegs and my willowy dancing has mesmerised a thousand rabbits. I have heard their screams close to my ears. I have pierced their jugulars. My soul is stained with dark patches. My soul is a leaf with cankerous blotches.

'There is much blood in my history, which was why I was chosen by Mogascunga.

'Mogascunga is a weasel-god. He is the rot that creeps over the forest floor, a dark presence in places of shadow, a stagnant pool. You can touch and see Mogascunga, and you can hear him, but most of all, you can *smell* him. Have you seen a tree fungus grow black and rotten on the bark? *That* is Mogascunga. Have you felt the slime that grows at the edge of still dull water? Have you heard a scraping or slithering near your hidy hole on moonless nights. *These* are Mogascunga. Have you run from a place where alders have locked into each other and odours of death hang from their crippled branches, choking the glade? This, too, is Mogascunga. Not a pleasant god to have, but one does not choose one's gods.

'So, I am a weasel with a conscience and a revolting god.'

Ranagana, on hearing this story, went sadly back to his cave. It seemed it was possible to develop a conscience regarding natural ways, but in order to do so you had to go mad, lose all reason. And in the end, would men respect you for it? No. They still despised the weasel, even though he had given away his mind in order to reach a compromise. They still despised the weasel, though they knew nothing about him, not even his size.

There was no answer to man's hatred.

Chapter Eighteen

Autumn on the tundra is a sight which burns itself into the brain: the hot reds of the fireweed blaze across flatlands that seem only a salmon's leap from infinite. The scene has a calming effect and has the power to promote patience. Apart from the migrating birds, it is a time of stillness and tranquillity. It is a short season that, contrarily, appears to be eternal: as if it is and always has been forever autumn.

The wolfman had had a recurrence of his fever and once again the wolf had stayed by him. It was true that while the human thrashed and moaned, Athaba kept his distance. This kind of behaviour was both distressing and worrying. Once a silence had descended upon the sick wolfman, then Athaba crept back to his side and licked his brow. Koonama was hot and dry. Athaba realised it was necessary that the sick creature be given water if he was ever going to recover.

A braided river cut through the ground not far from where Koonama lay. There was no way the wolf could get the water to the wolfman, so he dragged the wolfman to the water. When Koonama's head was close to the rushing torrent, he must have picked up the sound of the flow, or the smell of the water, for he stirred himself long enough to drink. Athaba began a vigil by his resting place. There was the thought that the human might starve to death, so Athaba regurgitated food for Koonama, the way he used to do for the pups of the pack.

Such ministration did not go unrewarded. On an evening when pastel colours covered the sky, and northern lights fell like curtains, forming a backdrop, the wolfman rose to his feet. He had been getting steadily better, steadily stronger, and was now ready to walk again. Athaba had decided that if Koonama was to survive the coming winter, they had to get down to the tree line, where the game was more plentiful. There were wild sheep to the south, and goats. There were also plenty of bears and humans.

Splashing over a shallow lake one day they came across another wolf. By the look of him, he was an *utlah* with no pack behind him. He stopped some distance away from the two and when he began to walk again, he veered from his original path, as if to avoid them. Athaba went out to intercept him, wanting some information on the path ahead. The other wolf seemed uncertain but as Athaba got closer it slowed its pace. They stopped some ten lengths from each other.

'Where are you going?' asked Athaba.

The grey wolf rumbled in the back of this throat, then said, 'Never mind where I'm going. What are you doing with a human?'

Athaba glanced over his shoulder to where his pack was waiting patiently, standing in the shining waters, looking lean and lost.

'Human? Oh, him? I'd forgotten . . . he's part of my pack. I'm travelling across country looking for the other part. I'm headwolf of . . . well, never mind.'

'But a *human*. Say, he's not one of those creatures raised by us, is he? You hear about these things – a she-wolf finding a human child and rearing it with her pups.' The stranger shook his head gravely.'It never works, you know. They always revert.'

'No,' replied Athaba, 'you've got it all wrong. You see, he originally captured me, put me in this prison-cage, but the vehicle he was carrying me in went wrong. I don't know what happened, but we found ourselves stranded on the tundra. Now I'm trying to get home.'

The other wolf came closer now. His fears of the human seemed to have been stifled by Athaba's explanation, or perhaps it was just a case of curiosity? He told Athaba that his name was Moolah.

'I thought you were a dog at first – a man and his dog. That's what worried me. You don't often see a man and his wolf, if you see what I mean. No, no, don't get me wrong, I *know* you're not his wolf. From the sound of it, he's *your* man. What I don't understand is, why you're travelling with him? I mean, you say he's part of your pack, so you've taken responsibility for him, but does he pull his weight in the hunt? Where do you put him? Shoulder? Flank? Tailwolf, perhaps? I'm not trying to be sarcastic, you understand, I'm just curious. I mean, if a wolf doesn't come up to scratch, he's out, or she's out, depending on the gender, right? Out. Full stop.'

Moolah paused to scratch himself behind the ear.

Athaba said, 'So you've been banished from your pack?'

Moolah's head came up quickly.

'What? What's that? Why do you say that? Who told you lies like that? What did I say? What? Don't look at me like that. I don't need your pity. I never wanted to be in the pack in the first place. I was always different from the others. They were jealous of me, that was clear enough. When you have talents out of the ordinary, you're bound to make enemies. So I was a little vague about hunting! Hunting's not the be all and end all of everything, is it? Some of us can hunt, some of us are better at other things, like story-telling. That was my job, only – only – '

'Only what?' encouraged Athaba, gently.

The other wolf looked thoroughly miserable.

'Only I was *too* good at it, see? I told all the old tales, all the traditional stories, but I have this imagination see. I – I embellish a little, pepper the story with my own little additions, make it more exciting, more colourful . . .' He stopped and blinked, and looked away to where Koonama was still waiting.

'And in the end,' said Athaba, 'you made up *new* stories.'

Again, the head jerked up and round.

'Eh? What are you, some kind of sorcerer? How do you know all this? You've met my pack, haven't you? You've been talking to owls and weasels. Who's been spreading lies about me?'

'I understand,' said Athaba. 'I really do understand. I was an outcast too, an *utlah*. They used to call me the raven-wolf, because I ate with the feathered parasites that followed behind the pack. But I came out of it. I have my own pack now.'

'What, *that*?' said Moolah, nodding contemptuously towards Koonama, who was now stamping his feet. He looked a strange sight, with his musk-ox cloak hanging from his skinny shoulders; his pale face and dark-ringed eyes; his legs bare from knees, covered in red swollen bites.

'Koonama is a good hunter, in his own way, which you are not,' said Athaba, 'by your own admission. So don't go spitting on something you don't know anything about. Besides, he's not the whole of my pack. I have a mate and six pups, too, when I can find them.'

188

'Name? The human has a name? Isn't that overdoing it a little? Humans don't have names. That's *silly*. You'll be talking to him next.'

Something, a hunger for social contact, stirred within Athaba. He had not realised how much he missed discussion, how much he yearned for a conversation.

'Listen, evening's coming on,' he said. 'Why don't you spend the night with us? Talk a little. I haven't talked to anyone in such a long time. Yes, I *speak* to Koonama, but of course I don't get any sense out of him. He understands one or two commands, but it's just the tone of the word he knows. What do you say?'

Moolah looked at Koonama dubiously.

'I don't know – I mean, he's *still* a human, no matter how much you trot around that fact. I'm a firm believer in the saying "you can tame a volcano more easily than a human". Even dogs tell you, you can't trust humans in general. Oh, they all say they know and admire individuals amongst them, but,' he nodded in a sage manner, 'in general they're a bunch of crazy killers. They'll kill anything, whether they're hungry or not, whether they can even eat the prey, or not. It doesn't seem to matter to them. Something on four legs? BANG. Kill it. Then decide what to do with it afterwards. I mean, they can always throw it to the ravens and the coyotes, if they find it isn't of any use to them, can't they?' Athaba found his sarcasm entertaining and again he pressed the other wolf to keep them company for the night.

Moolah studied Koonama. 'Are you sure he won't go for me? Has he got a gun under that ox-skin?'

'Can you *smell* a gun?'

Moolah shook his head.

'Well, I was never very good at that sort of thing. It's why I'm not good at hunting, you see. I don't know what people mean by *smell*. I know what it's supposed to mean, I think, but . . .' he shrugged.

Athaba was suddenly consumed with pity for the other wolf. For Moolah to have survived to adulthood must have taken enormous reserves of mental strength and initiative. Athaba could not imagine how one *could* manage without the most important of the senses. To be blind, yes, or even deaf – but not to scent the world? Why, it was impossible to form a picture of the landscape without using one's nose. Athaba would not know which way to turn without his ability to gather information

189

about the landscape and its creatures through his sense of smell. On those days in his life when he had been ill and his nose had been dry or blocked, he had been so miserable and helpless he had been close to despair.

'Come on. You must need a good talk, too,' he urged.

Moolah shrugged.

'Oh, all right, if you insist. Have you got any food?'

'My wolfman's carrying two hares.'

'Wolfman, eh? Koonama, the wolfman? Bizarre, very bizarre. Can you get him to bark for me?' Moolah, fell in beside Athaba, and they trotted to where Koonama was standing. 'Will he yap if I ask him to?'

'No, but his howls are coming along. I'll show you later. In the meantime, let's find somewhere to stay for the night. Where's your pack, by the way?'

'Lost,' said Moolah, miserably. 'I lost the spoor one day when they were crossing an ice field. Never picked it up again, even though I circled and circled.'

'Of course,' said Athaba, remembering that this wolf did not follow by scent. 'Well, I found I was better off without my lot, even though it was a wrench at first. Bit like being born again, isn't it, except that there's no pack around to help you grow up?'

'You're *so* right,' replied Moolah, excitedly.

Koonama fell in beside the wolves and began trotting with them.

Athaba continued, 'Oh, yes, I remember that day. My whole pack was slaughtered by a sky human – came down in a machine and *dak-dak-dak-dak-dak*, there they were, all lying bleeding in the snow. Not one of them alive. I didn't know what to do. I mean, I had been outside the pack for several seasons, but you know how it is, you tag along – you're still *part* of it, even though it's a detached part. Once they had gone, I felt as if I'd been cast adrift on broken pack ice. Floating over the ocean, not knowing where I was going. Just spinning gently on a platform of ice, subject to the wind and current.'

'Exactly!' cried Moolah.

They came to a nest of rocks and settled down, the wolfman leaving one of the hares and taking himself off somewhere alone. He came back a little later and curled up on the ground close the Athaba. Athaba knew this surprised Moolah, though the other wolf said nothing. The sky was scored with lights as they began their discussion.

'What lies ahead of us?' asked Athaba.

'Timber country, mountains, if you keep going south that is.'

'And the game?'

'Moose, sheep, the usual. Some good waterfalls where you can wash the dust off your coat. Pike in the streams, and pickerel and grayling. Geese and ducks on top.'

'Bear?'

'Grizzly and black bears. Don't mess with them, if you can help it.'

Athaba nodded. 'I don't intend to. I think we'll strike west again now that we're almost at the tree line.'

'Where are you trying to get to?'

Athaba described the landscape which had been his stamping grounds since a pup. Moolah was a well-travelled wolf, having been itinerant for several seasons. He knew his own country well and had talked to other travellers. When Athaba spoke of the Howling Rock of his homeland, Moolah said he had heard of it.

'That's just somewhere north-east of volcano country. I've never been there, but I've heard tell of it. I've always been fascinated by volcanoes. There was a bald eagle once, he spoke a little *Canidae*, and he told me about these hills that spit fire. Always intrigued me.'

'You mentioned volcanoes before, when you were talking about men being untamable. What exactly are they?'

'Well, they're places where the rock has turned to liquid and pours from the ground. The eagle called the rock *lava*. When it cools, it turns into all sorts of things, like pumice stone. Pumice is so light, it floats on the water . . .'

Athaba's head came up.

'Pumice? It floats?'

'That's right.'

Aksishem: 'the stone that floats'.

Athaba said, 'And this *lava* – it can be said to "run" because it's liquid, right?'

'True.'

'What happens to trees that get caught in the flow of this lava?'

'Well, they burn I suppose. Lava is very hot – fiery rock.'

191

'But if they got pressed down, underneath all that rock, became like rock . . .'

Moolah looked puzzled.

'Then they would be – *rock.*'

'And would sink in water!' cried Athaba.

Startled by this outburst, Moolah moved away.

Athaba said, 'Don't be alarmed. I've just learned the answer to a riddle given to me by my father. All these years. Listen:

> I am –
>
> the stone that floats,
> the wood that sinks,
> the rock that runs,
> the air that stinks
>
> – what am I?'

'A volcano of course,' cried Moolah. 'That's pretty clever. Yes, "the air that stinks" – it does too. The eagle said it makes your eyes water, the smell is so pungent.'

'That's it then,' said Athaba, and fell silent.

After a while Moolah said, 'So, what does that tell you? The riddle I mean?'

Athaba thought for a moment.

'Nothing. Nothing at all – except that my father made that up I think, which puts him in your category. I wonder if he kept his talent for doing such things a secret from the pack? I expect he did, otherwise they would have banished him, like they banished you, for inventing new stories.'

'Lies, they would have called them.' nodded Moolah.

'And my father told me that rhyme. He must have known I was a little like him – inclined towards a mystical nature. When you get these stories of yours, I suppose it's difficult to keep them to yourself?'

Moolah snorted.

'Almost impossible. They have to be told, you see. They trip out of the brain, on to the tongue, and there you are. It's like there's another creature inside me. I get so excited when I make one up. I want to tell the whole world. I suppose some of it's because I think I'm such a clever devil and want everyone else to know what I can do.'

192

'So my father had to tell someone, and he chose me. Mother knew about it, of course, this secret side to him, but she obviously managed to keep it from the rest of the pack.'

Moolah agreed.

'If your pack was anything like mine, you only had to twitch without there being an established ritual, and they came down on you. I think I'm well rid of them – and you of yours too. I quite like the itinerant life. I think I'm a rover by nature. Yes, it's dangerous, moving around without the protection of the pack, but where isn't there danger in this life? Sometimes a pack will draw attention to itself simply because of its numbers, whereas a lone wolf will escape.

'Anyway,' Moolah sighed, 'I have to tell you that from all I've heard, – well, you're a *long* way from home. You certainly won't make it before winter sets in. Maybe not even before next spring, depending on the hardness of the weather.'

Athaba was dismayed. He felt as if a tree had fallen across his heart.

'But we've come so far!'

'You've come so far, but the edge of the world is further, my friend. This great land of ours is vast – vaster than vast – and from one ocean to the other . . .' he shrugged. 'I'm sorry, but I thought you ought to know.'

'Koonama will never make it.'

'Best to abandon him. He's only a human after all. And you. He imprisoned you. Why should you feel any responsibility for him? Better to leave him.'

Athaba thought about this. Since it was true that the wolfman would not survive the whole journey, it seemed kinder to abandon him now than drag him on until he dropped. It required a decision which Athaba did not want to make. There was no doubt about it: the human would not last very long if Athaba were not there to help with the hunt. Without their guns or fishing rods these humans were hopeless hunters. He *might* manage to survive the autumn. But the winter? Never. His belly would turn to ice within a few days.

'I don't know,' he said, wearily. 'This is such depressing news. I kept thinking we would hit something recognisable soon, that home was just over the next lake or river. So far our travels have been mostly through the season of full light, but we're moving towards the season of all darkness. What *am* I going to do with him?'

'I wish I could help. Anyway, if you take him to your home, he won't last a minute. If my memory serves me well, that's the area patrolled by Skassi's pack.'

Athaba was jolted by the sound of the name.

'Skassi? I knew a wolf by that name once. He was killed in the high ice country.'

'Well, from what I hear, this Skassi is the most savage wolf to come amongst us for a long time. He's dedicated to the destruction of mankind. His pack numbers between thirty and forty wolves – one of the largest packs ever – and they roam the countryside looking for humans to attack and kill.'

Athaba said, 'Why? I mean, we have always been enemies, humans and wolves, but such action will only lead to more hostility. There are humans out there who are not concerned by us and leave us alone. Does this pack attack them too?'

'*Any* human. Children, whatever. They say Skassi has a hatred for men that goes beyond all considerations. He collects renegades and coerces other wolves to join his group. Once they've killed, the lust of human blood sticks. The whole country is in a turmoil. No wolf, whether part of his pack or not, is safe. The humans are striking back, of course, but they're hitting the wrong wolves. Innocents on both sides are dying.'

This information further served to dampen Athaba's spirits and raise his anxiety level. His family, his pack were up there, where this Skassi was creating mayhem and havoc.

'Does anyone know why Skassi hates men so much? I mean, none of us has any love for them, but we all have to live in the same world.'

Moolah stared hard at Athaba.

'It's said that he was out hunting alone one day, up in the northlands, when his whole pack – his family pack – was slaughtered to a wolf. A massacre. Not one of them remained alive. From that moment on he vowed to kill ten humans for every dead wolf in his old pack. When I last heard, Skassi had attacked a group of southern humans – the type that only visit the north and jabber a lot – harmless creatures that don't even carry guns. They use those small black boxes instead, which just click instead of firing bullets. Two of these people were torn to pieces by Skassi's pack. . . there was a lot of human blood let that day . . .'

'Skassi,' said Athaba to himself. 'Is it possible?' To take on the human race was sheer madness, whatever the injury to the nation of wolves. Men had proved, time and time again, that when their kind was threatened they became completely ruthless. They would move with cold efficiency towards eliminating the wolf and removing any threat for good. Those who tolerated wolves, even those who *liked* wolves, would not deter those who had called for their extermination since the first battle after the *Firstdark*. When they were ready, men would move across the land in a swath, cutting down all before them. Was this indeed his old arch enemy, the Skassi he once knew?

The news was extremely grave. It meant that Ulaala and his pups might be in danger from huntsmen looking for Skassi. All the more reason he had to get home quickly.

'Thanks for the information,' he said to Moolah.

The other wolf remained silent. No doubt he was thinking that he had given his advice and it could be either accepted or rejected. They fell into silence for a while, both unused to talking at length and finding company awkward to deal with. Then the itinerant opened the way again.

'You mentioned a Howling,' said Moolah. 'I haven't had one of those in ages. How about it?'

Athaba agreed, but his mood was such that he wanted to begin with a mournful howl, a dirge of sorts, and positioning himself firmly in a sitting position, his head thrown back, he began:

'OOOOOOooooowwwwwooooOOOOwwwwwwwWWW . . .'

Moolah joined in. The wolfman, Koonama, woke, and on hearing his companions howling, waited for the chorus and came in with his own slightly inferior howls. He sat in his haunches, like the wolves, with his arms like forelegs straight down in front of him, knuckles touching the moss. He threw back his head, and:

'HHHHoooowwwww-howwww-howwww-oooo uuu uuu uuu oooOOO . . .'

Soon Athaba's despair had been washed away temporarily by the joy of howling, and he chose a howl which was full of rapture, a howl to the beauty of autumn. Koonama's face was ecstatic: he was obviously completely entranced by his own role in this joint activity. He listened, he copied, he followed the others. There was happiness on his face. Once, he burst out into one of his songs, barking away to a *kind* of tune. Athaba had heard humans doing this and making shrill music with their lips. However, he and Moolah showed their disapproval at this unethical departure from the Howling, and reprimanded Koonama with a short display of aggressive postures and one or two nips. The wolfman soon learned to remain with howls, rather than depart into fiendish human barking, eerie enough to disturb any ancestors of ancestors. Athaba was very pleased with Koonama. He seemed to have a natural feel for the rhythms and nuances of tone necessary to impart the full feeling of any howl. Of course, there was a roughness to it and Koonama would not have gained any status in a pack with his renditions so far, but he showed pup-like promise, considering he was, after all, a human. There was potential there. He was certainly as good as many domestic dogs Athaba had heard.

'UUUooooOOOOllllloooOOO owwwwwwwwwwwwwwwwwww . . .' howled Koonama.

'That's it, that's it, swallow the moon!' cried Athaba, and Moolah shook his head as if his ears were full of tics, looking first at Koonama and then at Athaba, as if he were not quite sure how he had landed himself with these two creatures: whether this was indeed real, or whether he was dreaming.

When the Howling was over, Moolah told a story, delighted to have an audience, especially one appreciative of a newly fashioned tale. It was a story of wolf as the hero, the vanquisher of great evil. Koonama sat and listened as if he were hanging on every word, though when Athaba cared to look deeper there was a complete lack of understanding in the wolfman's vacant eyes, which was a shame because it was a good tale.

'The world was in its infancy at the time,' began Moolah, 'a pup that had yet to grow to wolfhood. At that point in its history only tiny creatures like krill and plankton lived in the sea and the land was crowded not only with the creatures we see on its hills and in its valleys today, but with walking fish. There were herring and salmon, running around on legs, and squid and octopuses (who never lost theirs) roaming the pastures, grazing on grass. They didn't look a lot like fish as we know them. Certainly they were as separate from other life forms as birds are from beasts, in that they had scales and preferred rainy days to sunshine. They seemed to bathe a lot too, in the streams and lakes, so were halfway to becoming watergoing creatures. Their legs, too, were of all different sizes. Some had long spindly legs and moved about, their bodies just above the tall grasses, as if they were floating. They ate the windblown seeds of dandelions. Others were closer to the ground, the bottom feeders on short rounded legs, and sucked on rotten windfalls.

'On the whole, the fish communities were a peaceful lot, not bothering other creatures too much. Except for the sharks, that is, who lived in caves and preyed on travellers. They would attack anything and everything, sometimes simply for the sake of bloodlust. They fell on birds and beasts in great numbers, dropping from the ledges of mountains and tearing their victims apart with unspeakable savagery. Then they would trot back up to their high caves on short stumpy legs, their crescent mouths gleaming and their triangular teeth dripping gore. In those far off seasons, they had short blunt tails which leaked a yellowish acid, and this viscous fluid killed any plant on which is dripped.

'Everyone went in fear of these landsharks, and because the creatures were so successful at killing, they multiplied very rapidly. Finally, there was a truce and a conference arranged between all the other carnivores, who were close to starving because the sharks were killing off every living thing. Bears and wolves and big cats were among the most bitter in their condemnations of the dreadful killer fish. Finally, one of them, a she-wolf named Grensa, was elected to issue a challenge. To do this she had to travel across many lands, to reach the Great White Shark who was the acknowledged leader for all his kind.

'On her journey, Grensa had to deal with many shark foes, not the least of which were hammerheads, tiger sharks, grey sharks and whale sharks. When she arrived at her destination, bleeding from the feet and scarred from her battles, the Great White himself was there to meet her. She told him this:

'"I have come to challenge you to single combat. If you win and I lose, all the other carnivores of the earth have agreed to begin eating grass and to chew the cud. This will leave more meat for the sharks. If you lose, however, you must agree to eat only plankton and krill from that moment forth."

'The sharks were ignorant of many things, for as you know one only increases one's knowledge about the world by talking to itinerant creatures such as birds, and sharks ate things on sight before a word could be uttered either way. Consequently, the Great White had never heard of *plankton* or *krill* and asked what they were.

197

'"Why, they're animals," said the wolf, appearing surprised at the question. "I'm sure you must have eaten them at some time. There are millions and millions of them. In fact, they're probably the most numerous of all the world's creatures."

'That didn't sound too bad to the shark, though of course the wolf had omitted to add that plankton and krill are minute lifeforms that live in the ocean.

'So the challenge was gleefully accepted, and the wolf Grensa fought with such courage and ferocity that she defeated the Great White Shark and won the world for the mammals and birds. When the sharks were told what plankton and krill were, they screamed that they had been tricked and refused to keep the promise of their dead leader. However, there is a Final Judge who steps in at certain times: someone greater than men, greater even than the giant *Groff*. No one has ever seen this mighty being, who always causes an eclipse of the sun before doing some work in the world, and indeed whether male or female is a question that has never been answered.

'There was an eclipse, during which all the sharks were cast into the sea by their tails. They knew then that they could not escape their fate, but came up on land one last time, to drive all the fish-creatures into the waters with them, so that they would have meat to hunt in their new home. In the general stampede, certain mammals, like the porpoise, the dolphin and the whale, got caught up with the fish and ended up in the ocean with them. None of these mammals was frightened of the sharks, once the habitat of the killers had changed from mountain caves to watery grottoes. So the whale, porpoise and dolphin remained in the oceans and still live there today. On the other hand, seals, sea lions and walruses could never make up their minds entirely, and still spend half the time in, and half out, of salty waters.

'Thus Grensa is one of the great wolf heroes and her spirit roams the Far Forests at the right shoulder of Shesta, the mighty warrior-priestess who defeated the dog-king Skellion Broadjaw after the battle of Steep Slope, in the canine wars following *Firstdark*.'

Chapter Nineteen

In this land the light falls in soft slanting columns. It reveals the colours of the tundra, the burnt sienna reds, the saffron yellows, as if through a mist. The same hues in southern climes would be harsh on the eyes, but here on the tundra they are gentle and soothing. It is a light which softens rugged peaks like the first snows of winter, rounding edges and blunting points. Here, where cold, dense air produces the looming effect of bending rays, images of distant mountains are pulled above the horizon and hang, clear and still, against the sky. Here, the waters are so glassy that sunlight is able to bring flowers on the beds of streams into bloom.

In this wide open land, the distances are vast beyond parallel. Even when you reach a place you want to be, you may not yet be there. It is a land where the imagination is the best guide to distances and where horizons always seem the same.

Athaba was extremely distressed by Moolah's information that he and Koonama were a long way from home. Each day, after rest, they had risen and begun their long walk home. In Athaba's mind's eye was a vision of home not far beyond the next clump of dwarf alders, or rise, or river. There was never any real disappointment, because there was always the 'next' field of cotton grass, or swath of dryas, or glacial waterway.

Now he knew. He was still a long long way from home, even though he seemed to have been walking forever. He went down to a pool to drink, before despondently rousing Koonama. The wolfman was slowing him down, too. Without Koonama he could make twice the distance each day. He had to decide very soon whether or not to put the wolfman out of his misery. It would, of course, be kinder to kill him quickly than to leave him to die of illness or starvation.

Athaba said his farewells to Moolah.

'You won't travel with us?' he asked. 'I don't understand how you manage to hunt at all with no sense of smell. We could help you find game . . .'

Moolah said no.

'I've been on my own so long now, I wouldn't know how to live with other wolves. As for feeding myself, well I suppose a pack would not praise my kills, but I manage to survive. You have to rely on sound, even sight, to indicate where prey might lie. When it's a matter of survival, you soon learn to compensate for losses.'

'Well, it's your choice. Don't be put off by Koonama – he's really quite harmless. He's been with me so long now, I swear he thinks he's a wolf.'

'No, it's not him, though I do find his presence a little disconcerting. It's me really. I like to live alone. I don't have any responsibilities towards anyone. I can do as I please without so much as a word. It's a solitary life – no, that's not quite true – it's a *lonely* life, but it's one I've become used to. Good hunting, anyway, and I hope you find your home.'

With that, they parted, Moolah setting off north and Koonama and Athaba going east.

The way was ridged and rough, with mountains to the south. There were bound to be more humans in this area and Athaba decided to rest early and start early, using the dark hours (short as they were) in which to travel. Early on in their trek, an owl flew overhead and from its flight pattern, and the time of day it was airborne, Athaba deduced it had been disturbed by something. That something would no doubt turn out to be a humans: possibly a hunting party.

Mid-morning became dark and gloomy, as if the winter season were already upon them. The reason for this loss of light was that black clouds had begun to gather in menacing groups above them, threatening rain. A storm was pulling its pack together, in order to attack the land below. The pair found shelter just as the dark wolves of the sky began snarling and rumbling in the backs of their throats.

The rain did indeed come down: a cold, merciless rain that drove itself into the ground. Athaba and Koonama had found a cave in the side of a hill and they rested in the entrance, staring out at swirling wetness; at the lightning flashes that briefly lit the purple landscape. The inside of the cave smelled of bear, but Athaba was not too concerned by this as it was a very stale smell. Possibly the cave had once been used as a hibernation place by some bear which was now far away.

200

At one point in the morning, Koonama obviously became bored with sitting watching the storm and went further into the interior. There was quite a network of tunnels within the system and for a while Athaba could hear his subordinate scrambling about, occasionally barking, to which Athaba would give some comforting reply like, 'Don't worry. I'm still here.'

When the storm had cleared, Athaba called for Koonama.

He received no reply. He was suddenly aware that there had been silence back in the caves for some time. After waiting for a few more moments, hoping to hear some faint cry from the depths of the earth, Athaba went into the interior himself, anxious that they should be on their way now that the storm had passed over. It was pitch dark in the caves, but a wolf needs no light. It is almost impossible for a wolf to lose itself in such a place, even though it might be a maze, for he sniffs his way in and out. If he gets 'lost' he has only to follow his own scent trail back to the surface again, like a line of string.

Athaba followed Koonama's scent down through the networks of narrow tunnels. His subordinate seemed to have been trying to explore the whole wormery of the earth: his trail took Athaba into thin passageways, chambers, boxed corners, blind windows, chimneys. Finally, Athaba found him asleep in the dust of a small ledged chamber. Koonama'a breathing was raising the cave-dust in small clouds. Athaba went to him and said, 'Time to get up! We have to move.' When this failed, he did something he normally avoided. He touched the wolfman, rousing him with his nose.

On waking, the wolfman seemed to go berserk. He began screaming, the sound echoing through the caverns. Athaba backed away from this madness. Koonama had lost his reason in this closed area and was extremely dangerous in such a state.

'Calm down,' yelled Athaba, hoping the human would understand the tone, if not the words.

Koonama jumped up at this point and ran smack into a wall of rock. Athaba could smell the sweet scent of blood, which judging from the snuffling sound, was now pouring from Koonama's nose. This behaviour was making Athaba himself very agitated. The wolf had no idea how to handle this situation. There was no way he could communicate to Koonama that he should stifle his panic, follow, and the entrance would be found for him. All he could do was wait until the violent mental attack had worn down his subordinate and hope that he became passive.

Koonama thrashed around in the dust on the floor on the cave for some time. His wailing was pitiful to hear and Athaba was more than once a split second away from attacking the creature that was causing him so many problems. Then, to Athaba's relief, the wolfman began to crawl around, touching things. He found the exit to the chamber and followed Athaba's growling. Every time he stopped, Athaba would encourage him with more sounds. In this way he kept the wolfman moving all the time, towards the entrance to the caves.

It took an age to get the wolfman just a few lengths and through the right exits, since some of them forked into blind passageways. Once, a fit of trembling came over Koonama, and Athaba thought his subordinate was going crazy again but the nervous bout ceased and they were able to continue.

When they finally reached fresh air, Koonama gave out a sobbing sound and ran into the daylight, falling on his face in the rain-sprinkled moss. That was when Athaba blacked out and presumably had a fit, because when he came to (that sweet time of funny faraway dreams) the wolfman was standing some way off, looking very concerned. Athaba could see the caked blood on Koonama's upper lip, and the bruises on his face.

This incident added to Athaba's doubts about Koonama. They had been together for so long that Athaba had begun to think he could turn the human into a wolf, but underneath that superficial wolfish look, Koonama was still very human. No wolf would have panicked like that simply because he was in a confined place, in darkness. He would have sniffed, got a mental picture of his surroundings, and made his way to the surface. Such behaviour, the way Koonama had acted, was dangerous for the pack and could not be tolerated.

When he went over to where Koonama was standing, the wolfman immediately displayed submissive postures, because he knew he deserved to be punished. Athaba, however, did not chastise his subordinate. He had decided it was time that they parted company. In one, maybe two days, he was going to have to kill Koonama. The wolfman would not be able to keep up with his fast pace and would drop behind. There would be plaintive callings (it had happened in the past) but this time Athaba was determined.

As if he had realised his headwolf's intention, Koonama put in an extra effort to stay with the moderate pace that day. He trotted when necessary, never letting Athaba get more that ten lengths ahead of him. When they rested, Koonama always got up first and began the journey, so that Athaba would have to overtake him to get back in front. When they came to the long resting place at the end of the day, Koonama rolled on his back and let his hands flop like wilted flowers, the way Athaba did sometimes when he was scent-rolling on the ground. The wolfman was trying to make himself endearing to the wolf, trying to say he was sorry for being such a problem.

Athaba ignored him. After the next long rest he was going to do what was necessary. It was something he thought he would never do to a pack member of his, but after all, Koonama was *human*. It was not as if he were a real wolf. To abandon Koonama was, of course, cruel and unthinkable. The pity of it all was that the wolfman had done so well, come so far, but now he was at the end of his energy. There was nothing else Athaba could do except to perform the final kindness.

That night he slept well apart from Koonama.

When he awoke, there were two fish by him for his breakfast. Koonama had been up to his old trick of damming a stream and snatching fish from the shallow waters. Koonama ate his fish raw now and was already halfway through a grayling. He showed his teeth to Athaba.

Athaba ate the fish then went down to drink. He took in the scents of the land as he refreshed himself, smelling the cold coming through the rocks and up from the permafrost beneath. Not far below the ground the thick frozen layer was beginning to join forces with the surface cold in preparation for the winter. Soon the whole landscape would be solid ice, the braided rivers would grow sluggish and then gradually come to a standstill, the lakes would turn to plate and then disappear, becoming part of the whole mass. Ice droplets would hang from air flaked with light snow. Hard times were coming, and creatures would die.

A man with only a musk-ox cloak would certainly freeze to death very quickly.

At the end of that day, Athaba had almost changed his mind again. The wolfman was obviously trying to make amends and was doing his best to keep up with his headwolf. It was as if he knew that Athaba had plans for him and was doing his best to frustrate that decision. Athaba was mystified as to how Koonama could know. Perhaps the wolfman smelled death in the air and was determined to cling on to life until the very last moment? He stared at Athaba with sorrowful, almost accusing, eyes. But what if it were left? The wolfman could drag the pace down to a stop. He looked as if he were on his last legs even now, with his swollen ankles, his puffy knees. The lids of his eyes were like hoods and were bitten raw by insects. If he did not fall down, he would probably go blind. Yet, it *was* difficult to kill him.

However, Athaba finally decided it was necessary. He postponed it until Koonama was asleep. The wolfman always slept on his back, with his throat exposed. Athaba did not want a struggle, for the sake of his companion. The deed had to be done swiftly. If Koonama resisted then Athaba might have to tear at a protective limb and cause more pain than was needed.

However, before this could come to pass, something happened, something put itself in their path, which Athaba regarded as a sign.

They came across a road.

As soon as he saw it, the man fell on his knees and began sobbing. He rolled in the gravel, as if it were mud, and cast it into the air so that it fell like hail around him. Athaba was mystified by this behaviour. What good was a roadway to them? Yes, it was easier going than the tundra, but you could not follow such communications because men used them all the time, for their vehicles, their machines.

Nevertheless, Koonama began walking along it and kept turning and gesturing for Athaba to follow.

The wolf decided to stay with the wolfman for a while, but as soon as something came along that road he knew he would be off across country.

Nothing did come that evening. They walked well into the lateness, until after darkness fell, and the road stayed long and empty, shooting away into the distance. They made good time though. When Koonama eventually decided he would obey Athaba's instructions to stop, they settled down by the side of this flat strip of man's work. They had reached a junction now, where the gravel road met an asphalt surface that crossed it.

Athaba lay awake, under the stars, waiting for the sound of the change in Koonama's breathing which would tell him his subordinate was fast asleep. Out in the night, there were whisperings, as creatures crossed the man-made barrier on their way from one landscape to the next. There were the swishings of wings

204

as nightbirds flew overhead. When the time came, Athaba rose and padded softly to Koonama's side. Sure enough the wolfman was on his back, his thin throat exposed to the elements, as if offering it to carnivores in a gesture of trust.

Athaba studied the white flesh under the starlight. One swift movement and the jugular could be torn open. Koonama would bleed to death in a very short time. It would be a kindness. It would be a merciful death . . .

Yet he could not bring himself to do it. Something, some weakness held him back. He stood there, over his charge, ashamed of himself. Had Koonama been one of his pups, he would have *had* to do it or suffer terrible remorse. Yet he was prepared to abandon this creature who had been with him longer than his pups. He owed Koonama a swift death, but something stronger than this debt was keeping him from fulfilling his duty.

The failure heavy on his mind, he padded back to his resting place, to stare at the sleeping form of the wolfman.

Just before dawn there were lights in the distance.

Athaba heard the sound of the engine before his subordinate and tried to force Koonama into shelter of some rocks. The disobedient wolfman refused to acknowledge the order. Instead, he stood in the middle of the road, a strange expression on his features as the vehicle got closer.

Athaba turned and began trotting back out on to the tundra. Koonama called to him, but there was no way he was going to stay and fight with Koonama against hunters. When man came, the best thing to do was run.

He was aware of the truck slowing down at first, as it approached the ragged wolfman. Then the wolf heard the engine race again. There was a clanking and grunting from the beast-machine as it speeded up, and Athaba turned to see Koonama leap out of its way in order to save his own life. The humans wanted nothing to do with this strange thing that had crawled out of the swamps of the tundra.

There were obviously second thoughts. It slowed to a stop, some twenty lengths beyond the wolfman. Koonama ran towards it. Someone leaned out of the vehicle, then finally jumped down.

Koonama pointed towards Athaba.

The man who had caught him followed the finger and shook his head, urging his captive wolfman into the vehicle. Koonama was going to be taken away and put in a prison-cage, probably

205

like the one he had kept Athaba in. Athaba was certain that the humans would not take back into their fold a man who had become wild, who had forsaken them for the wolves, who was a traitor to his kin and kind. If ever a wolf turned domestic dog, other wolves would kill it as soon as it tried to return to the wild again. Surely the human race had no use for a creature that was neither human nor wolf, but part of both? Surely it could never again trust a man with a wolf's name, whose loyalties were towards its headwolf and its pack? Koonama, in order to survive, had sold his soul to the wilderness. Athaba was convinced that the wolfman could never rest again, but he would hear the call of the wind over the tundra, the soughing of the breezes through dwarf willows. He would wake in the middle of night, hearing the fish breaking the surface of the water and the myriad bird life out on the lakes, in the reeds along the shores. His lips would crave the meltwater from glacial streams, his tongue the taste of freshly caught hare. His human spirit had been eroded by the landscape and replaced with something else, something not human.

Athaba left that place, heading away from the road and out into the wilderness again. He wanted to be far away when his wolfman was thrust into a prison. Koonama, he knew, was terrified of confined spaces and would go completely mad. And it was Athaba's fault he was there. It he had done his duty, Koonama would never have had to suffer such indignities. Athaba was mortified at his own lack of resolve. Such lack of moral fibre was more fit for a dog than a wolf.

Athaba now travelled alone and his thoughts were ever for Ulaala and their pups. While he had responsibility for Koonama, he had something else to think about, something to occupy his mind as the long walk dragged on and on. Now he had nothing to distract him, the frustration of time and distance ate away at his spirit. He had to acknowledge to himself that Koonama had helped him, simply by being there.

A day after he had left his subordinate to a terrible fate, Athaba found himself facing a distant range of mountains. These had to be crossed and since he had no knowledge of where the passes lay, he knew that more time would have to be expended in seeking a path through these rock giants.

At noon the sky turned, first purple, then black, and it was obvious a storm was coming. The sky began to fracture with fork lightning and thunder opened holes overhead. Athaba sought shelter just as the first large drops began splattering the ground around him. Another delay. It seemed that apart from men, nature and the weather were also against him, determined to keep him from his pack.

He sat under a rock hang, the dreary landscape before him. The mountains were hidden in the rainstorm now which lashed the countryside with its wet flails.

The lightning continued to flash and crackle across the heavens as he waited impatiently for the storm to cease. Sometimes it hit the earth and snaked along the ground as if seeking entrance to a lower world. He did not fear the lightning. It meant little to him except that it hurt his eyes occasionally, if he was staring right at a spot as it leapt to light. The thunder was disconcerting, but unless it was directly overhead, nothing more. He had known wolves who would shiver and shake in hidy holes while a storm was in progress, but he was not one of those.

Towards evening, the sky began to clear, and a red soreness took the place of the bruises left by the thunder. The world smelled musty and earthy, the rain having brought certain vapours to the surface. Generally, it was a pleasant odour, as if the world had been dipped in a herbal lake and had emerged, not cleansed, but soaked in aromatic juices. Athaba began walking again, sniffing the air as he went, delighting a little in the change that had taken place. It was almost as if *hope* had been added to the atmosphere along with the new musky scents. He went up on his toes, deer-trotted for a while, his spirits replenished.

That night he did not pause for rest, having considered his time spent under the rock hang as much the same thing, though of course he had not been able to sleep through the violence of the storm. He took time out only to hunt. There was a new urgency to his travels. He began to worry, not about what was in front of him, but what was behind him. He had been seen by men and they would blame him for converting Koonama from a human into a wolf. They would surely be out for revenge?

Athaba knew that some men did not need very much of an excuse to begin a hunt. It all depended upon what type of community the human settlement was, that the man had been heading for. If they had time on their hands, there would be time to hunt. Athaba needed to put plenty of space between him and that possibility.

207

When darkness came he followed a stream which he knew must have come from higher ground. Once he reached the mountains he would be safe from men.

The waters gurgled and clattered beside him, possibly trying to tell him something, but no one knows the language of the landscape and Athaba simply used the sound as a guide. He tried not to dream of his journey's end, but sometimes it was impossible to keep the pictures out of his head.

PART FIVE

The Feral System

Chapter Twenty

In the distance were the mountains, muffled by snow that had turned purple in the last of the day's sun. They rose out of the tundra as if they had been pushed up overnight, their shoulders crackling as they hit the high frosty regions. Athaba headed towards these, his paws springing on the reindeer moss. He knew he was being chased, he had smelled them as he crossed that trough. There were men with guns and dogs behind him: they had been following him for some time.

His heart was pounding a little in his chest, but he was strangely calm considering that this was the first time he had ever been tracked down by dogs. Previously, hunters like Koonama had just come across him by accident, and (in that instance) had captured him before a long chase had time to take place. No, he was not panicking. His adrenalin was high, naturally, but he wasn't overwrought or even too excited. He knew he had a job to do if he was to keep ahead of his pursuers, and it would not help him to get too feverish.

Soon the grasses and mosses gave way to lichen, then ahumic soils, and finally he was running across the stony area which served as an apron to the mountains. The larger pebbles, forced to the surface by the constant movement of the soil, slowed him down a little. They were painful on his pads and slipped from under his paws, so that he jarred his legs.

He stopped and turned, looking back over the glacial valley, exposed without its ice sheet. The wind was crossways to the run of the valley and he only got whiffs of scent. They were definitely heading in his direction though.

He found a shallow gulley which rose gradually at first, then more steeply towards the corrie that had been the birthplace of the glacier. This would provide cover as he climbed the ridge. It was cold in the gulley, which still retained snow. Without any further hesitation, he plunged on to this hardened snow and began travelling up the gulley. If they were tracking him with malemute dogs, the icy regions of the trench would not hold his scent for very long, and the malemutes were not really trackers. They could pull a sledge until eternity came and went, but their noses were not up to wolf standards. Nevertheless, he had a lot of respect for malemutes: they were not pampered house dogs. They worked, ate and slept out in the same conditions as the wolf, curling up in the open snow at night and dragging sledges by day, often through blizzards. Their strength was mostly in their legs and shoulders, rather than their jaws, but they were still a force to be reckoned with, especially in numbers. Athaba had no desire to test the courage of these creatures.

Athaba wondered vaguely if the hunters had any kind of mechanical back-up. A vehicle would not be able to follow him up the mountain, but they might have thought he was running the length of the plain below. He hoped they *had* thought that. A frustrated hunter whose quarry keeps doing the unpredictable will often give up before time.

He continued climbing. Below him the mat vegetation spread over the valley. A month ago it had been covered in clouds of black fly, so thick they were like dark smoke; and before them the even denser and larger cumulus-like towers of mosquitoes. Both these insect swarms had driven Koonama crazy. They had not bothered Athaba as much as the wolfman, except in his ears and around his mouth. Now these two pests were gone and the air over the distant tundra was clear and sweet and cold. When he looked back, the figures were moving swiftly across the brown flatlands, rich with the colours of berries. There were about five of them. One of them had two dogs on leads.

Only two? Well, that was something in his favour. They wouldn't risk letting just two dogs go after him on their own. Obviously they were just using them to follow his spoor. Wait until they hit the cold rocks and snow where any scent was faint and transient.

When they reached the bottom of the mountain, he was up on a ridge and travelling quickly. A chip of rock zinged away just to his front and then he heard the sound of the shot echoing around the spurs and gulleys. One of them at least had a high-powered gun. When he kept on running in the same direction, another shot shattered a stone in his path. He swerved and took a line down by a rockfall. A ptarmigan ran out from behind a boulder, but this was no time to think about food. If he was not swift and single-minded he was going to die.

At the next mass of detritus he lost his footing and skidded down the scree, hurting his old hindleg injury. The men were behind the ridge now, and unable to get a sighting, but he had no doubt they were following very quickly. It might have been an idea to double back, except there were enough of them to leave one behind as a rear guard, so Athaba abandoned that idea. It was not worth the high risk. What he had to do was get them stumbling about amongst the foothills while he was back down on the flat and running. In that way he could put considerable distance between them. What he wanted was to cross over to some point away from the direction they had come, in case there were more back there, possibly with a vehicle.

His head was clear and he knew what he was doing. There was still no panic, despite the guns. His life depended upon remaining cool and thinking his way carefully through the problem. Ragisthor would have approved of that. Funny, he had not thought of his old mentor for such a long time. It was the chase that had brought him back into Athaba's head. The memory of that time when he and Ragisthor had encountered hunters together.

At the bottom of the other side of the ridge, he limped out on to an autumn snowfield where a huge herd of some half-a-thousand or so caribou were keeping cool. They saw that he was preoccupied and not interested in them, so there was no stampede at that point. The wolf crossed behind the herd, aware that he was a dark target against the snow, but hoping to get on the other side of the caribou. One or two nervous ones skittered around a little as they caught his scent, but there was no panic. They would be aware of him and ready to take flight, should he change his course.

The herd would shield Athaba against a sighting by the hunters and though the caribou would no doubt bolt when the men came blundering down the ridge, the subsequent confusion could only work in his favour. The dogs would certainly become uncontrollable for a short time as they smelt the fear of the caribou and heard the drumming of the hoofs, the cries of terror.

The grassy slopes formed a wedge that drove a green point into the grey ridges. Athaba wanted to be back amongst the rocks where his colour would help hide him and there was cover to use. Out on the snowfield he was an easy target.

As was expected, when the men appeared on the far side and began descending, the caribou took off, first scattering, then pulling together and thundering the length of the dip in the wedge. There were barks from the men and Athaba hoped they might be more attracted to the idea of shooting caribou than a lone wolf, but he heard no shots. The hunters were determined, it was obvious, to get *him*. He was their goal and they were going to let nothing stop them. Men were not persistent without a reason. They would kill at a whim, but they would not follow a single creature over tough terrain, ignoring other more attractive kills, unless there was something very strong giving them a purpose. He wondered if his guess had been right, that they were angry because he had turned one of their kind into a wolfman. It was possible. Anything of that nature was possible. He had not heard of it happening before. There were those stories of human babies reared by wolves, but in those cases the wolves had helped an infant to survive. *He* had changed an adult from a hunter into a subordinate pack member: a hunter who looked unhuman in his musk-ox cloak and skin covered in sores and wild matted hair.

Athaba's leg was jarring on the stony ground now and becoming more painful by the minute. Had he been on the flat and his leg uninjured, he might have made a speed which would leave the humans standing – providing there was no vehicle – but in the mountains the going was rough and sometimes slippery. He could still keep well ahead of the hunters, but they were persistent creatures. They would keep coming and keep coming until he was boxed in, in some canyon, or out on a plateau with a sheer drop at the end.

He passed an area where there were recesses in the rocks, not quite caves. There was a thought that he might hide in these until the hunting party had gone home, but then if they were really that determined they might bring dogs up here and sniff him out.

Athaba decided against the caves and went for another ridge which had possibilities on the other side. If he could just find a narrow crevice in the rocks, which would allow a wolf to squeeze through, but not a man, then he stood a chance.

He scrambled up to the saddle, only to find that the ridge dropped away on the other side in a sweeping slope, with no cover whatsoever. Not even a tor or piece of moraine was available to hide behind and get some sort of a breather to enable him to reassess his position.

The ridge fell away to a spur to his left and he decided to follow this down. It was no use climbing higher, up into the snows and the steep-sided walls of the mountain. He had to keep going over the ridges, looking for some situation that might save him. When he was halfway down, he scented one of the hunters. Probably the one they had left to prevent any doubling back. After waiting there for a while and realising that Athaba was not going to be fooled, he had come round the bottom of the two spurs and was waiting for the wolf to descend.

The party was behind him and the back-up man in front.

There was only one thing for it, and that was to throw himself down the talus and hope he did not injure himself.

He went down on his bottom and began the slide in a dignified manner, but soon lost his grip and tumbled head over heels until he landed in the shale at the bottom.

The hunting party had just made the top of the ridge, further up, and they saw him and began barking to their back-up man, no doubt trying to convey the information that if he ran around the bottom of the spur he would trap the wolf between them.

Athaba shook himself and began sprinting for an outcrop. All of a sudden he felt a rush of exhilaration. The adrenalin began flooding through his system. He was going to make it! On the far side of that outcrop he could see that the foothills fell gently away again into another valley. Wide tundra stretched out before him. If he could make that and not worry too much about his hindleg, he could certainly outrun the men's guns. They would be exhausted by now anyway, and there could not possibly be any vehicle in that direction when they had come from the opposite side of the hill. He was going to make it.

He passed the outcrop going at speed and was soon out on the mosses of the tundra, feeling the grasses whipping at his legs. Men were such oafs when it came to hunting. Without their machines . . .

At that moment, at that precise moment, he heard it. The terrible swishing clacking sound from the sky. A man was coming down from the clouds. The air machine swept down like a monstrous hawk, ready to stoop on the running wolf. Athaba felt the cold black shadow move back and forth over his body, as if this bird of prey were toying with its quarry.

215

Athaba was determined to keep on moving. He would die in mid-stride. They would not find him waiting for the bullet.

The machine passed overhead for the last time with a roar and a clatter, turned, and hovered alongside him as he ran. The grasses flattened submissively around him. Athaba glanced up and saw the rifle being aimed. Behind the man with the gun was a familiar figure, watching for the moment of the kill.

Koonama!

The wild face with its wild eyes stared down on him, long unkempt hair flailing in the wind created by the machine. Bony fingers, white at the knuckles, gripped a rail. The mouth was open, a red gash in the grey and ginger hair.

What was this? Retribution? Revenge? For what? Without Athaba the wolfman would have been captured by humans long before now. For leaving him, possibly, to the fury of his kind? That was it. Koonama was trying to get back into the good graces of his human pack. He had gone back to his *megas* and offered them a sacrifice, to show he wanted to make amends for his treachery. He must have told them he would deliver the wolf that was responsible into their hands.

Their eyes locked and Koonama barred his teeth in triumph, the way humans did on such occasions.

What have I done to you that deserves this? thought Athaba.

Now the wolfman watched as the gun was pointed, the trigger squeezed, and the . . . the *dart* struck his headwolf's flank. It dangled from Athaba's side like a dead hornet.

A now familiar dizziness overtook Athaba.

Not again, he thought, as he staggered the last two or three paces, the sound of the machine drowning out his howl. *Not again!*

He fell on his side, panting, as the machine began descending just a few lengths away. Athaba tried to retain some strength in his body. He wanted to be conscious when Koonama leaned over him, so that he could rip the throat out of his erstwhile companion. He wanted it to be the last thing he ever did. After which, they could shoot him. Better to die than be imprisoned again. Better . . .

Chapter Twenty One

Athaba awoke to find himself once more in the prison-cage that he vowed he would never see again. Perhaps not the *same* prison, but one very similar. Once more he was fed and watered through the bars and once more he fell into a pit of despair from which he believed he would never emerge. The days slipped by, each much the same as the last, until almost a month had passed. Then, one day, he had a visitor.

It was Koonama.

The wolfman's appearance had changed so much that Athaba hardly recognised him. All the hair had gone from his face and he was fatter and looking much healthier. The sores had all but disappeared, but where they remained there was some sweet-smelling mud covering them. His skin glowed, his eyes were clear and bright, and for some reason he kept crinkling the skin around their corners, and around his mouth. He stood by Athaba's cage and growled and barked at him in a soft tone, for all the world as if he were trying to talk to him.

Athaba wanted to kill his erstwhile companion.

Koonama was in fact no longer a wolfman, but a human complete. The wolf did not understand these men creatures at all. If a wolf had become half-man, other wolves would *never* accept it back into the pack, no matter what it promised or produced in order to make amends. There were no half-measures amongst wolves. Once your loyalty had been diluted even just a little – a raindrop in a pond – you were finished. But here were the humans, taking one of their traitors back, just as if he had remained faithful to the species every moment of his life.

In fact it was obvious that he was welcome! There were many gestures displayed which Athaba had observed during his last period of captivity: such things as backslapping, teeth-showing, loud repetitive barking, hand touching shoulder, hand lightly striking shoulder, hugging. Koonama had a female with him who constantly did the hugging thing and kept touching his head-hair. She also made clucking noises at Athaba but the wolf ignored this mockery.

Again, Koonama supervised the carrying of his prison-cage out to an air machine, and accompanied Athaba into the sky. Athaba idly wondered whether they were going through the whole thing again, but this time he was not drugged and would try to watch what happened when they dropped out of the clouds and hit the earth. Perhaps he was caught in a cycle of events from which he could never escape? Perhaps he was really dead? Maybe that first time he had been shot and killed and this was the world that you went to afterwards? There were no Far Forests, only a kind of locked circular movement which took you across the tundra up into the air and across the tundra again, for all eternity. That was surely it.

He was wrong.

The machine touched down lightly this time. The prison-cage was lifted out and Koonama stayed by it until the sky man was back inside his machine. Then Koonama opened the door and gestured for Athaba to come out. Athaba was very suspicious. Was he being set up like a target for guns of other huntsmen? He bristled and moved to the back of the cage. Again, Koonama made a gesture which Athaba interpreted as 'come outside'. Then he thought, what choice do I have? I can either rot in this cage or go out and face whatever is there.

So he went forward and out into the open. The air was sweet and fresh. No guns blasted holes in his pelt. Slowly he walked away from the cage, towards the trees, trees that were somehow *familiar* to him. He sniffed and below the fumes of the aircraft and the men he found smells he recognised. There was a rock he knew, not three lengths away. Ground shapes, undulations, flats he had traversed before.

He saw now what was happening. Around him were the sitka spruces of his old home. It *was* his old home. Koonama had brought him back to the place where he had been captured by the southern hunter and his native guide. This was where the dart had struck him in the rump and he had staggered and fallen into the deep black pit of unconsciousness. Not too far distant was the den where his mate and pups were waiting for his return. His heart flooded with anticipation.

Koonama showed his teeth and waved him northwards to where his den lay.

218

Athaba regarded his old pack member for a few moments, then turned and walked away with dignity, neither running nor strolling. A kind of high-stepping deerwalk, springy but not jaunty, firm but not rigid. When he reached an outcrop of rocks he looked back to where Koonama was standing. His ex-captor was very still at first and then, as if on an impulse, the man raised his head and let out the howl that they had used when Moolah had parted with the pair of them on the edge of the tundra: it was the *farewell to the brother wolf* call which ended in a triple tremolo. Athaba could see that the human's eyes were shining and thought he was showing his teeth, the creases were only around his mouth.

Athaba returned the howl and then slipped between the rocks. Shortly afterwards he heard the sky machine leave, heard its wind amongst the treetops. Finally, there were only the sounds, smells and sights of the wilderness.

Soon he was on his way northwards, to his mate and his pups. The anticipation in his breast was tremendous. *Now* he could allow himself the luxury of dreams, to picture the faces of Ulaala and the pups, when he strolled up to the den. Should he howl first, to warn them of his coming? One of their secret howls, perhaps, so that she would not think it was another wolf usurping his position as her mate? Or perhaps not. Perhaps surprise might be the best tactic?

What joy there would be that night, though, when he was back by her side. And the pups would have forgotten his scent, and be puzzled by his presence. They would come into the den, one by one, and look at him, sniff him, and wonder what induced their mother to let this raggedy stranger share her bed. And when they found out who he was, their father, they would tumble over him, licking his jaws, nipping at his mouth.

He couldn't wait. The long walk, the reversals, the pain and suffering, the disappointments, they had all been worth this moment. The excitement in his breast was overwhelming, so that his breath came out in short sharp pants. His expectations were as brilliant and wonderful as the northern lights.

Suddenly he was in the clearing and at last the crop of rocks was in view. His nostrils filled, searching for the scent of his loved ones. He was home. He was in the place he never thought to see again and a miracle had come true. There had been mountains, lakes, rivers and wide wide flatlands between him and his mate, and he had crossed them, put them behind him. The improbable had been overcome, conquered.

He took up a high-standing stance on a rock, again filling his nostrils with the smells of his den. Then again, and yet again. Anticipation began to melt away, to be replaced by hope, and finally by dread. Nothing. The ground was blank before him, around him. Once more he sniffed, hoping for the scent he wanted, no matter how faint. Once more the hope drained and was replaced by a feeling of gloom.

Something was badly wrong – there were no wolf odours!

Athaba ran forward, entered the den.

It was empty and cold.

Athaba still tried to fool himself with hope at first, thinking that Ulaala had gone hunting or perhaps taken the pups for a drink at the stream. Going down to the brook and he lapped some water himself, but there was no she-wolf there to welcome him. No sign of the pups either. (They would be over five months old: hardly pups any longer!) The tree-covered slopes to the south were beginning to sing in the wind. A norther was coming in with snow in its teeth. Athaba stared at the tumbling waters of the beck as it danced over his paws. Around him the rocks had a few secrets but they never gave anything away. It was all very bemusing. What to do? He had become, in these last few seasons, a wolf who lost himself in action, a doer that hated to remain too long in thought. But his situation required a *lot* of thought. He couldn't just go rushing around in circles, hoping that serendipity would lead him to his family. A plan was required.

Back at the den again he sniffed around, inside and out, for a long time. The marks were old, the scents stale. His mate and pups had left a long time ago. It was pointless searching the ground around the den for a trail. Any spoor would be cold, impossible to follow. The temptation was to rush blindly into the trees and keep running. He wished he were an eagle or some kind of bird. Surely they *never* lost their kin. They could float on the wind, looking down, and see the whole world spread out beneath them, like a wolf from a high mountain peak. Rivers, forests, tundra, lakes, these would have shape and form up there, would present no barriers. If only he were an eagle!

A blizzard was building up: the first of the winter. He went inside the cold empty den and lay in the chamber, wondering what to do. For too long now he had been thinking of his home-coming and in all those thoughts not once had he considered the fact that the den might be empty. In his mind it was as if time had stopped for Ulaala and the pups, and no changes had taken place while he was absent. In fact the size of the pups would have surprised him since he still pictured them the way he had left them.

Of course, when he *really* gave it sensible consideration he realised there was no reason why his pack should still be in the den. They obviously thought he was dead. Given that this was the case, it seemed reasonable that Ulaala should leave an area with which she was unfamiliar to travel north, where her old pack were. With her mate dead she would want some help with protecting her pups.

Her old pack?

But she had aided in the killing of one of the males and run away with the perpetrator. Would they accept her back into the pack after such a deed had been committed? More likely they would fall upon her and punish her for desertion and other crimes. What about the pups though? They would be an asset to any pack: six healthy pups. (Providing, of course, that they were all still alive. He hadn't thought of that before.) Maybe they would take her back on sufferance if she took the pups with her?

Where else might she go?

It was possible that she had gone south, looking for him perhaps, or to find a home in the forests. This was something to keep in mind, although she would need a very secure hiding place to keep herself and her pups safe from humans. Usually, there were not many hunters around during the winter: a few, but the woods were not crawling with them once the snow came. Now that Skassi had turned man-killer, the world was not a predictable place.

He felt daunted all of a sudden. Having been on his long journey with Koonama, he knew how vast was the landscape around him. To the east, from which he had come, was almost infinite tundra. There was no reason not to suppose that the same unlimited lands lay also to the west. Here and there were ranges of mountains forming impassable barriers. Also rivers, but these would happily be frozen during the winter and presented no real problem.

221

Still, if he let his mind range over the size of the area of search, his head began to spin. It was possible that fifty lifetimes would not give him enough time to carry out such a search.

What choice did he have?

None.

He needed his mate, his family. Somewhere Ulaala was struggling to feed his pups and he should be with her, at her side, providing. They needed *him*. If he knew he had to spend the rest of his existence this side of death simply in looking for Ulaala, that task would still have to be carried out. Could he just shrug his shoulders and make his home here? Or do a cursory search of the surrounding woodlands and hills? Or even search for a season, then give the thing up as hopeless?

None of these.

He had to search until he found her, nothing less.

He decided to confine himself initially to a spiral search from the den outwards, hoping to come across some signs of Ulaala that were not cold. The more he thought about it, the more he convinced himself that she would not have gone without leaving something to tell him where. What he had to do was go out and search the area minutely for any marks.

He was not a wolf to sit around and pine. He needed to be working at something, even if that something seemed hopeless. He could talk to other animals, find out if anyone knew where she had gone. She could not have travelled a long distance without *someone* being aware of it. And if the distance was short, so much the better, he would find her all the sooner. Optimism suited his personality much better than confusion or despair. If he had to tear the stars down from the night sky, or swallow the sun to get them back, he would do it.

Awaking in the den the next day, he was aware that there had been a heavy fall of snow outside. That deadened snow silence was all around him: the world had been muffled. At the entrance the cold white crystals had pushed themselves inside and formed a plug, which Athaba dug out fairly easily since the snow was still loose and light.

Once out on the landscape again, everything seemed to have taken new positions overnight. The earth had a new language. All previously visible landmarks had been erased or altered. Yesterday's pattern of smells, which is a wolf's map of the immediate world, had changed. It had been simplified. There was no complex interwoven mat of scents: just fine fresh threads running to and from definite directions. Normally the smell-pattern took time to analyse, but after such a heavy snow fall only the newly laid odours were available, along with visible spoor.

There was a clarity to the air, the dust of dry days and the mists of damp nights having been borne to the ground by the heavier snow. The light, such as it was, was soft and rounded, producing hazy shadows on the surface.

Athaba was again a little despondent as he made his way through the white blanket, sometimes disappearing into a drift, at others ploughing his own path between rocks and trees. Any signs Ulaala had left him were now buried deep beneath the surface. All summer Ulaala's movements had been lying on the ground, waiting for him to find them, and after just one night they had been obliterated. Her spoor, her scent, any deliberate marks on tree or rock. He found a weasel shinning up a rock.

'Do you know of any wolves in the area?' he asked the weasel in its own language.

The weasel nodded.

'To the north,' it said, its eye wide.

He asked the same question of a wolverine and got the same answer.

Hunger forced him to hunt for some of the time, but he tried to combine this with his search of the landscape.

When he found nothing of value to him in the immediate area, he decided to start to make his way northwards, beyond the areas of white and black spruce, and even the cottonwoods, and into the bare rock ranges. The world froze before him as he walked. Ice floes came together to form sheets and fields of frostfire. There were fewer creatures abroad, some having gone underground. Foxes passed him in the night, their lean shapes almost part of the darkness. He envied the fox and its ability to be satisfied with its solitude, wondering why wolves were cursed with the need for company. On his journey into the dark regions of the north, he trapped a raven in a hollow between two rocks.

'What do you know of wolves in the area?' he demanded of the raven in its own tongue.

'Meee? Arrrk. North, try north.'

'Which pack? Is it the wolf Skassi's pack?'

The ravens being followers were familiar with the different groups of wolves, knew the location of several packs within flying distance, and often changed from one camp to another as the hunting fared better or worse. This one knew of Skassi's man-killers and told Athaba they were now in the mountains to the north-west, having to winter in the less accessible areas of the country. Fierce winds, as well as glaciated heights, gave any human hunting parties great difficulties in tracking the pack. Skassi's wolves reputedly used the high windy ridges and rugged canyons normally only favoured by wild sheep, in order to stay out of reach.

Athaba's former rival had made the landscape ten times as dangerous for any four-footed traveller than had previously been the case. Normally, there were patchworks of men out hunting for various reasons, some of them poachers, some of them hunting with authority. Never before, however, in wolf memory, had the human communities risen in such numbers and with such single-mindedness. It seemed that every two-footed mammal with a gun was out searching. And the creature they were looking for? The wolf.

Of course, they were killing other creatures as well, such as moose and caribou, with more abandon than usual. But in their eyes was the image of the wolf. They wanted the skins of those who had turned (unthinkable!) to killing men. Despite the fact that humans had left a trail of murder since their emergence from the sea-of-chaos, they were almost insanely self-righteous about their own prerogatives to life. The death of a bear, seal, wolf, or other creature was often necessary, occasionally perhaps regrettable. The life of a human? Why, that was a-b-s-o-l-u-t-e-l-y sacred! A human life was the most precious thing amongst all the billions of lives on the planet. A million whales, ten million seals, innumerable wolves, did not make up a single human life. Those who took a human life were hunted down with a ferocity and determination unmatched by any other situation. Men protected their species with a fanaticism not found in any other animal.

Only men were allowed to kill men, and then only in great numbers. When one man killed another man, he was hunted down like any animal, but when hordes of men killed multitudes of their own kind, that was acceptable.

This attitude might have bemused the beasts of the field and the birds of the air who could have felt indignation, except that they had long since ceased to wonder at the vagaries of man.

Now and again they accepted that men went crazy with fury when the blood of their own kind was spilled.

Athaba travelled with great caution, using secret ways and hidden paths, to reach his destination in the north. Like the others, he accepted that the situation was an unusual one, and that when Skassi had been caught, and a period of adjustment had followed, things would settle down to normal once again.

And they *would* catch the killer pack, eventually. They always did. There would be no rest for man nor beast until Skassi's skin had been stretched between a set of poles and left to dry.

Athaba battled through the snows, over ice fields blasted by screaming winds, through gales scouring out valleys and blizzards raking the mountains with their savage claws, to the gates of the high north. There he set about systematically trying to find Ulaala's old pack.

They had not, of course, remained in the same spot where he had left them, but he knew they would be somewhere in the region. He had to travel almost to the shores of the iced-over ocean, before he found traces of their whereabouts. He had no real plan in mind, except to find one of their number – a flankwolf perhaps – who would tell him whether Ulaala was back with her pack once again.

Athaba was aware that his own life was in danger from the pack he sought, remembering he had killed one of them. There were at least two other members of that pack who would recognise his scent: probably more since he had criss-crossed their territory with his trails in the times when he was a raven-wolf. So he had to move with extra caution and attempt to cut a single wolf out of the pack. A youngster if possible. Athaba wanted no fights. He needed to keep his strength for travelling and physical injuries were the last thing he needed at that time.

He kept an attentive eye on the ridges, especially, looking for a silhouette. Occasionally, he heard a solitary howl and moved in its direction, only to find his target had disappeared. It was almost as if they had known he was coming and were playing a game with him, tormenting him.

Chapter Twenty Two

It took a whole month for Athaba to locate the pack. One of the problems of finding Ulaala's old pack was that Athaba might have difficulty in confirming their identity. He had to rely on his memory of their marks, their scents, from the previous winter. There were one or two other packs in the region which confused such identification. However, he finally found what he believed to be the right group and did one or two surveys of their den from a distance.

The pack had found a cave a long way to the east of their previous den. The cave was in a valley, so Athaba was able to get up to a ridge and observe them without being too obvious. They would, of course, eventually pick up his scent. Their reactions to this he could only guess at. They might be wary, even afraid of him, since he had killed one of their skilled warriors, but then again they might still be harbouring cold anger towards him and might hunt him down in numbers to exact revenge. It was impossible to decide what they would do, really, since the dynamics of packs alter drastically with changes in leadership. Athaba seemed to recall that Ulaala considered her pack leadership to be weak: that power swayed back and forth between uninspired headwolves that lacked the kind of personality to form a strong cohesive group with firm policies. It was a strange world which produced, in some packs, three or four charismatic potential leaders, any one of which was strong, capable and inspired. In such a pack, the struggle for power was occasionally bloody and savage, depending on how close in years the contenders were. Other packs might go for many seasons under indifferent leadership: wolves who dropped in and out of the headwolf position, having no forceful intentions and no positive interest. Such packs displayed a distinct lack of innovative methods in both hunting and surviving. Instead of 'I will brook no opposition in my desire to be headwolf!' it was 'Not me again? I did it last season'.

Athaba's observations under the cold light of an ice moon, under the single-eye stare of the dog star, led him to believe that Ulaala was not with the pack. He caught no scent of her (a scent he would know instantly), no sound or sight. All he saw were pack wolves moving in and out of the cave, going to or returning from, the hunt.

But he had to be sure. He could not leave the place without first being absolutely certain that she was not of their number. It was possible, of course, that she was sick and remained in the cave. He tried to decide whether any of the pups might be his, but he had been away so long, his offspring would have grown considerably, developed different scents.

He lay for days without food, watching the cave, using the wind to lift the pack scents to his nostrils, and finally deciding which of the wolves below he was going to follow and confront. This was his plan, to choose a victim, track it and then corner it in order to obtain some information.

One wolf in particular looked something of an outsider. She was scruffy and had one ear bitten in half. Her dealings with her contemporaries almost always led to a quick snapping and snarling contest, before one of them went away submissively. The grey she-wolf had a dark streak above her right eye that was probably a birthmark. The guard hairs beneath her body almost dragged on the ground. Athaba could not decide whether she was submissive or vicious, or both, but once he had decided on her, there was no going back.

He studied her movements, noting when she left the cave for water, or for hunting, and whether anyone went with her. This was the main reason for choosing Birthmark. She was hardly ever accompanied. For some reason none of the other wolves liked going on hunts with her. When he was satisfied that he had all the necessary information on her movements, Athaba took to the snows and found himself food, digging up lemmings and voles.

Once he had fed and watered himself sufficiently, he went back to the ridge and watched for Birthmark to leave the cave. She did so that night, under a moon the colour of coagulated blood, crossing the rugged white landscape going east.

Athaba followed her.

Birthmark's spoor in the day's fresh snow led between two rock overhangs well out of sight, smell and sound of the den. Beyond this gateway was a canyon, walled on three sides. Athaba entered cautiously, thinking that this was an excellent place to trap his victim and force her to tell him all she knew about Ulaala. When he slipped through the gap, he found to his astonishment that Birthmark's tracks ceased just inside the canyon. But her odour was there. He looked up into the darkness. He couldn't think where she had gone, unless she had sprouted wings and flown to the moon. Athaba stood there, perplexed for a moment, his eyes scanning the canyon, her scent filling his nostrils. Where was she? Was she invisible? Was she hanging from the nose of the night by a hair-thread? The whole situation was so uncanny it made the hairs on his ruff stand out. What should he do? Call her? Where would she answer from?

'Why are you following me, rot your nostrils?'

The voice made him start. It came from somewhere behind and above him. He whirled, to find her on a ledge just inside the gap, where she had obviously leaped on entering. She looked down on him with contempt.

'I asked you a question, why are you following me? You've been watching our pack. The others couldn't understand where the whiffs of wolf-stink were coming from, but I marked you soon enough, up on that ridge.'

Who was following whom?

'Why didn't you give my position away?'

Again that look of contempt.

'Tell them anything? I'd rather puke on their pups. I'd rather pee in the drinking water. Why should I tell that bunch of wormbrains anything? What would *they* do with it? I'll tell you. They'd run around in circles sniffing their droppings and wailing, "What shall we do? Oh, what shall we doooooo?" From my days as a pup, I've heard the same song whenever a decision had to be made. They make me vomit, those sanctimonious turds. "For the good of the pack," they whinge.' She snorted. 'For the good of the pack, my rear end. Since I was a yearling I decided to have nothing more to do with them. I hunt when I feel like it, for myself and nobody else, and if they get stuck with a rogue moose, they get no help from me. I wouldn't give them the tics out of my left ear. And as for mating,' she shuddered, ' I wouldn't touch one of them with *your* scraggy haunches, let alone mine.'

Whereupon, she dropped off the ledge and gave him a heavy body-slam, sending him skidding across the snow.

'Come on, why the tracking? I could bleed to death from a cut on the tongue waiting for you to answer. Swallowed it? Cough it up with your liver, quick, or I'll tear your snout off.'

Athaba stared at this fascinating creature with her half-an-ear and black birthmark on her scruffy brow. Why did he have to pick one like this? She was clearly a little crazy, but they obviously hadn't got the courage, or perhaps the ounce, to order her from the pack. To say she was a non-conformist would be to understate the case. She was clearly so much an individualist she put all other rebels, including Athaba, in the shade. In his own pack she would have been torn to pieces before she was six weeks old and the bits scattered over the widest stretch of tundra the pack could find.

'Listen,' he said, squaring his shoulders and gathering as much dominance as he could muster, 'you'd better be careful. I've killed one of your pack already. I want some information . . .'

'Killed?' she sneered.

'At the end of last winter.' It wasn't an act he was particularly proud of, but he needed to get the upper hand in this confrontation, without too much fuss. 'Ulaala . . .'

'Oh, that was you, was it? Ran away with bitch-pretty, eh? Listen, puppy-fat,' she gave him another body-slam which almost bowled him over, despite her skinny torso, her lack of weight. 'I could have killed that cottonball by *blowing* on him. He was about as tough as a sandpiper's egg. Understand me? You're not talking to some rat-killer now, rangy, you're talking to me, Tolga, and this bitch-nasty will tear your eyes out and spit them down your throat. Got it?'

Suddenly, he had had enough. He ran at her and body-slammed her until she spun off her feet. Then he grabbed her by the throat-ruff and dragged her in a circle around the canyon, finally hurling her bodily along a slide of ice, so that she turned circles three times before coming to rest.

She climbed groggily to her feet.

'So you want to fight?' she slurred.

He charged her again, body-slamming her on to her back, and then stood four-square over her, barring his teeth just above her throat.

'Just let me . . .' she panted, struggling to get to her feet. He kept her there with his weight on her. Non-conformist? She disobeyed all the rules of wolf-fighting. Once an opponent had you on the ground with his teeth at your throat, you were supposed to submit – or die. He didn't want to kill her. That wasn't at all necessary. All he wanted was for her to agree that he was the dominant animal.

'If I could just . . .' she wriggled and wormed, trying to get into a position to bite him.

'LOOK!' he roared. 'KEEP STILL. What do you think you're playing at? I could have killed you half a dozen times. You've *lost* – don't you understand? There's no way you can win now. Just accept that fact, like any wolf would.'

'Never,' she panted. 'I'm not *any* wolf. I'm Tolga, I'd rather *die* than submit.'

One of those, he thought wearily. One of those creatures that actually meant what they said. She *would* die, rather than submit. What was he going to do?

In the end, he stepped away from her, letting her up.

She climbed to her feet, obviously still a little winded.

'Why did you do that?'

'What?' he thought she meant why had he attacked her.

'Let me up? Why didn't you rip my heart out. I would've done if it was you on the ground.'

'I don't want to kill anyone. I just need some information. All I want to know is if Ulaala has been back here.'

Tolga sneered again.

'Run away, has she? Couldn't hold her, eh? What's the matter with you? Not passionate enough for her?'

Athaba kept his patience with difficulty.

'Nothing like that. I was captured just after . . . just after last spring. By humans. I escaped but had a long walk back to my home country. When I arrived she was gone. She probably thinks I'm dead. Now I'm trying to find her.'

'Why bother? Plenty more insipid females in our pack. Kill another *mega* male and take his mate. You could make a hobby of it, attacking and killing males and running off with their mates. Sounds like fun. I might even give you some help. I could spy for you. Find out which females are most attached to their males, and you could go for them. No point in inflicting pain unless you do it properly, is there? Why, I could . . .'

'I just want to know if you've seen Ulaala.'

'Haven't seen, smelled or licked her rea. . .'

'That's all I wanted to know.'

He turned to leave, but she called him back.

'Look, I like you. You've got the makings of a good outcast.'

'I *was* an outcast, still am. I ate with the ravens and ran with the coyotes.'

'So. Just as I thought. A wolf of character. I *knew* there was something about you. A mange on strong dependable wolves who follow the rules, give me a ruffian like you any time. Listen, a raven told me a story, that some of the *utlahs* are running with the hybrid swarms in the south. Maybe the insipid little bitch-pretty has gone down there?'

Athaba was despondent at this news. He seemed to have been walking forever. Perhaps his whole life was going to be one long walk, from day to day, from month to month, from season to season? It was a daunting prospect. Nevertheless, he rallied enough to complain.

'Why do you *keep* calling Ulaala "insipid"? She has plenty of fire – more than most wolves. She's certainly not insipid.'

Tolga said, 'Next to me, she is.'

'A fully grown rabid black bear would be insipid next to you.'

This remark was taken as a compliment, for Tolga gave him a nudge with her shoulder.

'Don't flirt with me, you *fellow*,' she murmured.

'I – I won't. Listen, something has been intriguing me about you since I first saw you. That mark above your eye – were you born with it? Or is it a scar of some kind?'

'Are you trying to mock me?' she said, her tone suddenly very savage again.

'No. Not at all. I was just interested.'

She stared at him for some time, then grunted.

'To tell you the truth, I'm a little sensitive about it. It ruins my good looks. I'm inclined to bite the ears off any scabby creature that mentions it. I got it when I was a pup. Some puffy-faced hunter found the den – not really hunters, they just had guns – they stank of fermented berries and couldn't walk straight – the pack was loose – it was summer – we were alone with my mother. They shot her as she tried to protect us, then they began digging us out. They took my brothers and used them as target practice, pushing them on to sharp stakes in the ground and then shooting them to pieces. When they picked me up, I bit off the end of a scurvy finger and there was a lot of screaming and shouting and blood dripping on my coat. Finally – may their

231

kidneys dry up like old nuts – they took me to their fire. Just as they were about to push the end of a red-hot spike into my eye, my father came out of the darkness and savaged the arm of the man that held me.

'So, he missed with his brand, but caught me above the eye, burning a wound there, may his bladder swell and burst in his gut. As you can see, it's never gone away and I have to put up with a lot of mockery.'

'You escaped! That's incredible. And your father too?'

'Yes, he got away that time. But they came back in their dozens and hunted us down relentlessly. They got my father in the end. You can't wound a human and get away with it. The only wolf who can do that is Skassi. Have you heard of him?' Her eyes shone. 'You must have heard of him. Skassi and his pack of renegades? Now there's a wolf I admire – for leading our kind against the men. They've looked under every stone in the land and *still* they haven't caught him. They come in their hundreds, on foot, in vehicles, in sky machines. You must have heard – seen? When you go south, you'd better steer clear of the eastern range. That's where Skassi is, I believe, up in the mountains. Every day new wolves join them. Probably go myself soon . . .'

'Thanks for the warning, but I already know about Skassi. In fact, I think he's an old rival of mine, from my former pack. We fought once.'

'And that's when you were cast out?'

'Yes, but not because of the fight. There were other reasons.'

'And Skassi let you go, without killing you?'

Athaba saw that a misunderstanding had crept into their conversation, and though he was a modest wolf, he felt he ought to put it right.

'Just a moment, Skassi didn't beat me – I thrashed him. It was me that walked away. I wasn't chased, not by him. It took the other members of his group to do that.'

Tolga looked at him askance.

'*You*, beat *Skassi*?'

'I said so.'

She yawned in his face.

'Well, I'm afraid, my prince of story-tellers, that's a bit too looooooong to accept, that one. Let me tell you, I have *seen* Skassi, which I'm sure you will too, one day. Skassi is the most magnificent wolf that walked the earth. He's a fighter beyond comparison, without parallel. No one has *ever* beaten Skassi. Do you think he's the leader of fifty hard, mean renegades for nothing? You ball of cottongrass fluff, Skassi's body is marble and his soul granite. He's been hit by bullets on three separate occasions, and he just ignores the wounds. They heal over. He's invincible.'

'He's certainly very lucky. He and I are the only survivors from our old pack.'

She yawned again.

'Was that before, or after you, what was it? "thrashed" him?'

'After.'

'Sure,' she sneered. 'The day it rained death from the sky machine, you . . .'

'I was the raven-wolf, following a long way behind the pack.'

Her jaw suddenly dropped open. When she finally did speak, it was in a tone of awe mixed with uncertainty, as if she couldn't be quite sure whether to throw herself at his feet and praise his name, or dismiss him as a liar.

'You – are - *Athaba*?'

This took him aback a little. She knew his *name*. When he had been in this area before, he had had no name. He had been the Outcast. Only his scent was known to Ulaala's pack.

Tolga continued, still in the same cautious tone.

'Skassi tells – tells that you went over the edge of a cliff. That you could not have survived such a fall.'

'Here I am, with the luck of dogs. I have been as fortunate as he, surviving as many encounters with men as he has. I've never been shot, and I don't wish to be, but I've been in their hands and had a human shoulderwolf for a time . . .' he stopped as he realised he was bragging now.

Tolga's mouth hung open again, but after a few moments she closed it with a snap, as if trapping a lone mosquito.

'Now I *do* know you're lying. A human wolf? Listen, I don't know what your name is, herring-head, but it isn't Athaba. Skassi speaks of this Athaba with great respect. They once ran together until circumstances drove them apart. He often calls for the spirit of this Athaba, to assist him in the fight against men. "Athaba," he says, "had the heart of a bear." You? *You* look as though you've got the heart of a cabbage. Athaba wouldn't go chasing over the countryside looking for a female, for a start. Not the Athaba Skassi speaks of. You demean him with your

233

silly lies. You demean my hero Skassi. We have a great leader at last – not since Shesta, the warrior-priestess who killed Skellion Broadjaw, has there been such a hero amongst us. Not since the *Firstdark* battles on the southern plains has there been a creature with Skassi's strength, his fortitude, his courage.'

'Let me tell you something, Tolga, before we part for good. There is more to fortitude than fighting, there is more to courage than killing. Skassi has courage and fortitude, and strength too, but they're misdirected and certainly, from the way you're talking, overrated. There's nothing supernatural about Skassi. In fact he's more down to earth than I am. You talk as if he's on some holy mission from . . . from some god of the mountains, some fox-deity that has finally turned to unbelieving wolves to carry out his bidding. Skassi will get a lot of canids slaughtered for nothing: for a revenge that will neither satisfy nor heal. I hate the men who slaughtered our pack, too. They're a poison in my blood. But they are gone, we'll never find them. They are scentless. They are lost to us. All Skassi will succeed in doing is stirring up fury amongst the hunters, and they won't be satisfied until every wolf is an empty pelt stretched between drying poles.'

'You *still* say you are Athaba?'

'I don't have to prove that to anyone,' said Athaba, and he rose and walked from the ridge, down through the snows, heading south. On either side of him the white walls of the hills protected him from the wind. When he was quite a way from Tolga's den, he heard a howl.

He turned. She was standing on a tall rock.

'Skassi *needs* you, Athaba,' she called. 'He needs you!'

Athaba turned and continued walking. That night a blizzard came in obscuring all his senses, but despite the danger he kept on walking. He wanted to reach the south before midwinter. The further he went, the warmer it would get, of course, but not *that* warm. The danger would increase, too. In the south were men beyond number. Skassi. His former rival was making a hard life that much more difficult, *rot his soul*, Athaba thought, catching a little of the flavour of Tolga's character for a moment.

Chapter Twenty Three

In the far off times just after the *Firstdark*, when wolves were making songs of all the geography of the earth, songs that were maps of the world which would show future generations where to find waterholes and soaks, and at what time of year; songs that told descendants which plants and fungi could be eaten and which could not; in those far off times, there were still primal forces loose in the world. Some of these forces were great evils who followed the humans out of the sea-of-chaos and into the world of the wolves. Even the men themselves were not able to deal with the terrible powers alone. They had, of course, brought with them their shamans and wizards, their witches and warlocks, their magic men, their sorcerers, but many of these were untrustworthy and some sided with a great evil dedicated to the destruction of both ordinary man and beast.

These nebulous entities who occupied the nightmares of all living creatures, had once lived in the dark sludge at the bottom of the sea-of-chaos, and should never have found their way to a world of light and air. Left in their own environment, they were harmless beings, unable to evolve into anything more than a huge bubble of foul, heavy gas. Let loose in the atmospheres of the earth, they moved sluggishly over the surface of the globe, until they came to a place where there was goodness and joy. In such a place they settled, bringing corruption, disease and decay. In such a place birds and beasts began to experience unrecognisable fears, and wake from terrible dreams. In such places, the rot began which would eventually destroy all living creatures and turn green fertile land into a bog where only mists could stay.

One of these places was Hidey Wood, a region much further south than where the wolves are today, where deciduous trees mixed with conifers in a temperate climate that grew a multitude of fungi and flowers amongst the grasses between root and leaf. Where toothwort grew and titmice lived.

All manner of different creatures lived in Hidey Wood which

235

was one of those last retreats from the onslaught of men. It was a place rich in vegetation where oaks broadened their shoulders and hornbeams filled the spaces between.

At this time, most of the men lived on the plains where they were busy erecting huge stones, both hewn and rough, in circles of all sizes, which would help to drive out the primal forces of evil that had escaped the sea-of-chaos. One or two, however, were impatient to begin living in the woodlands. So it was that a man came to Hidey Wood, and though he settled down peacefully enough and took just sufficient from the wood for his own needs, a Great Evil had followed him from the central plains, chased there by the magic rings of wood and stone.

This Evil settled in amongst the rotting humus of the woodland floor, in the dark shadows thrown by tree and fern, beneath the stagnant pools of water poisoned by dead leaves, under ancient roots, in abandoned holes, behind the webs of spiders. There, in the heart of the wood, in its disparate parts, the Evil festered and began sucking the life from the lush greenery around it, draining it of all vitality. The man saw this and called on the woodland creatures to do something about it, otherwise he would have to burn Hidey Wood to the ground and set up a stone ring on its charred remains.

It fell upon two creatures, normally enemies, to find a way to defeat the Great Evil. One of these was Issa, a weasel, a creature with a facility for languages. The other was Katanama, a red kite. Elected by the other creatures of their home, these two were instructed to put aside their differences and find a way to rid the land of the Great Evil.

Issa was a slender, rusty-coloured female, forever busy searching the holes and hollows of Hidey Wood for prey. One of her favourite foods was snails which she found among the coltsfoot and catkins on wet mornings. Her lithe body was often seen snaking swiftly over the forest floor, looking for mice and voles, ready to go for anything smaller than a badger or bigger than a beetle.

Katanama was a kite who soared above the woods, hanging on the wind, sometimes so still up there that others often thought him lifeless, his wings too rigid to let him fall. Katanama preferred dead things to live, and in his lazy way he was glad of the man that had come to the wood for men are wasteful creatures and keep scavengers like kites in their daily meals.

236

These two, left together, consulted a mystical fox named O-sansan, on the way to rid the woods of the Great Evil which loured over and lurked in their forest home.

O-sansan consulted the green slime on the bark of the alders and investigated the possibilities of the creeping fungus in the cracks of the blackthorns. Finally, she spoke:

'We need a wolf,' she said, 'to do battle with this entity. Only the wolf, of all the fighting creatures of our north-western lands, has remained pure of heart. The wolf seeks no alliance with men, asks for no favours, concedes no territory willingly. The wolf has remained uncorrupted, its spirit strong, its soul unblemished. This evil thing that has come to Hidey Wood can only be defeated in mortal combat by a wolf with an unimpeachable spirit. Even so, that wolf is not guaranteed success, and will need to have great courage and fortitude. A spiritual warrior. You must find such a creature and persuade him to journey to Hidey Wood, to do single battle with this Evil.'

This seemed clear and simple enough and the two creatures began a search of the nearby countryside. The weasel went in all the holes, dens, earths, dreys and other places of darkness she could find, and the kite took to the airways and searched the open plains for sight of a wolf.

After many days it seemed clear that though there were wolves in the area, they had been driven into hiding by the presence of man, and indeed were rapidly being exterminated. These wolves dared not leave their pack and spent all their hunted days avoiding huntsmen. They were poor creatures, with damaged spirits, and not of any use to the Hidey Wooders. The pair went back to O-sansan.

'Ah,' said the wise old vixen, 'this is man's doing. He has driven the bravest wolves far north, to the distant mountains, and left this land bare of their presence. You must travel many days and nights to find the creature we need.'

When the kite and the weasel had left the fox, they began their journey north. However, the kite was obviously much faster than the weasel who made very slow progress over the terrain. Finally, the kite landed by the weasel called Issa and said that they must think of another way.

'You're much too slow,' said Katanama. 'At this rate we shall both be dead of old age before we rid the wood of its evil.'

'What do you suggest?' asked Issa.

237

Katanama rustled his squared buzzard wings, clicked his hooked beak and shifted his weight from one claw to the other: a beak made for tearing pieces of meat from a carcass, claws made for vice-like gripping, each with a set of sharp talons.

'I suggest,' said Katanama, 'that I carry you the way I carry my food. I can grip you in the middle with my claws and we can fly to the north country together.'

Issa was not sure about this. Although Katanama ate mostly carrion, he was not above hunting small creatures which were still full of life. He was a scavenger, but a predator too. Once he had her in his talons, he might forget himself for a moment. It would only take one jab of that vicious curved beak and Issa would be kite meat.

She voiced her fears.

Katanama conceded the possibility.

'However,' he said, 'I cannot fly to the north alone because even if I find the wolf, I shan't be able to speak to him. You have a gift for languages. You speak my tongue and you know *Canidae*. It is essential you travel with me. I have given my oath not to harm you and I shall not break my word deliberately. In order to make sure I never forget myself, you must constantly remind me of our mission. Just keep saying to me, "Remember the wolf!" as we fly along and you shan't come to any harm.

So Issa was gripped gently in those strong talons and lifted from the ground she had never before left in her life. As she rushed skywards, the land flattened below her and spread itself rapidly in all directions. The trees became dots, the hills bumps made by moles, the rivers silver slow worms. The suddenness of the lift took her breath away and for a while she was so frightened, so awed and overcome by the experience, she could not speak. Fields were like fallen leaves below her and the whole scene was one of terrible beauty. Finally, she fought against the wind that rushed up her nostrils, down her throat, and was able to squeak out, 'Katanama, remember the wolf!' whenever the claws began tightening around her slim, lithe waist.

The world rushed under them. They flew through rainstorm and windstorm, through cloud and mist, through clear skies and dark, over seas and strange lands, until they came eventually to the land of the wolf.

Here, the country was mountainous, and there were eagles and falcons, the wildcat and the lynx, wolverines and martens, all manner of predator that hunted and killed like the weasel, but were not averse to a little weasel meat now and again. Issa told Katanama that she trusted his claws more than the landscape below, full of its bands of predators, so they searched the snows, the caves, the timberland, in the same way that they had reached the high country, with Issa in Katanama's talons.

Here and there among the passes, in the valleys, on the hillsides, amongst the snows, were packs of wolves. Each time the pair came across a pack they would descend and call for a wolf to rid them of the Great Evil that had come to Hidey Wood. Wolves would stand and listen, and then either order the pair away or ignore their pleas. It seemed that nowhere in the land of the midnight sun was there a wolf prepared to do battle with an unknown entity from the sludge in the sea-of-chaos. Certainly not for a tatty old kite; certainly not for a bloodweasel whose appetite for red meat surpassed their own; certainly not for a MAN.

So the pair went from pack to pack, Issa reminding Katanama of their mission from time to time.

One day, when they had despaired of finding the wolf they needed to rid them of the presence in Hidey Wood, Katanama saw a carcass that had been abandoned by a pack. The rotten meat was being picked over by ravens and kites, coyotes, and one lone wolf. Katanama was hungry and suggested they descend to eat. Issa agreed, always anxious to keep her transport well fed.

They dropped beside the carrion and Katanama began tearing at the meat with his beak, while Issa waited at a safe distance. While she was sitting there, preening herself, the lone wolf came to her. He was a sorry-looking creature, with a moth-eaten coat and tics. Flies bothered his head in clouds. His eyes were weak and watery and he constantly flicked at the air with his stringy tail.

'I have heard,' he said to Issa, 'that you and the kite are seeking a champion, to drive out some kind of evil from your homeland.'

'That's true,' replied Issa, eyeing this raggedy creature without interest. 'We need a wolf, a spiritual warrior capable of meeting with this entity in mortal combat. Do you know of such a wolf?'

'Let me first explain who I am,' said the wolf, settling on his haunches. 'I am the raven-wolf, the *utlah*. I have no name because I am no longer of the pack. I call myself "the Outcast" and am all the *utlahs* that ever were or ever will be. We are one creature because we have been reduced to our basic selves and at this level there is no difference between us. There are many outcasts but only one outcast. Do you follow?'

'I think so,' said Issa.

'Now let me put this proposal to you,' said the Outcast. 'I have nothing left for me in this world. I have undergone the worst possible punishment, including death, that a wolf fears. I have been cast out, banished, from my pack. I may smell, hear, see my old life ahead of me, moving through the mists, but I may never enter it again. I am alone. Not solitary, like the fox, but *alone*. You, who are not a pack animal, cannot imagine how that feels. It is the end of all things. Blackness, misery, utter hopelessness.

'Then I heard of your mission. Hope sprang into my breast. I am the Outcast, I am a thousand wolves who wish to redeem themselves. Trust me with this quest and you have not one, but great numbers all under a single skin. I wish to travel to this far country of yours, to do mortal combat, and even die in the attempt at ridding your land of this foul presence.'

Issa was a little taken aback by this speech and while her common sense told her that this poor scruffy creature could not possibly be a match for the Great Evil of Hidey Wood, she began to see that she might not have a choice. It was actually the Outcast or nothing. So she told the wolf, yes, he was the chosen one, and a small flame came into the wolf's eyes. He straightened his legs, firmed his shoulders, lifted his tail, and set off towards the south.

On this journey the Outcast met many outcasts, and since they were one, he told them of his mission, and they too left the ravens to walk the long walk to a place they had never seen, to help creatures they did not know.

The journey from the land of the midnight sun is so long and hazardous that only one in a thousand might complete the task. It takes a four-footed creature over mountains so high that to pause would be to freeze in one's tracks. There are rivers between that are as wide as seas and seas so vast they seem to have no shores. There are torrents and forests thick with hunters, and great divides that fall to the centre of the earth. There are places where the rock is molten and the earth too hot to tread without burning one's paws. There are deserts of sand and deserts of ice. There

240

are places where a wolf must cross deadly waters on ice floes and places where there is no food nor shelter from a blinding sun.

On the journey the Outcast died many times, but since he was of great number he lived to walk on. His dry bones decorated the wide deserts of dust, his frozen form became blocked in ice, his drowned corpse was washed on to bleached sands far from his homeland in the high north. He died, and lived, and each time he left this world he became spiritually stronger because while his number reduced his soul remained whole.

And the journey itself built and strengthened his spirit within him. The nature of his quest, his mission, purified his soul. So by the time he came to the edge of Hidey Wood, many months later, he was indeed a single wolf. A single wolf with a spirit so vast that it preceded his tangled form, and though, when the weasel saw him moving across the ridge of her landscape, she was both amazed and impressed, his ragged mangy body gave her no hope in the coming battle. She did not know that a thousand wolves were in that ravaged pelt: a thousand wolves of great courage, fortitude and endurance. For they had set out on a hopeless journey with a torn spirit and in poor physical condition to carry out an impossible mission, and though they had fallen in great numbers, they had reached their journey's end with the last body that remained to them.

And the Great Evil felt the wolf coming, and IT knew of the Outcast's worth, and was afraid.

It went out to meet the valiant wolf and on a scruffy patch of turf one of the most horrendous battles of all time took place. There were attacks and retreats, victories and defeats, and neither the terrible entity from the sludge at the bottom of the sea-of-chaos nor the outcast wolf would give an inch of ground. Darkness swirled over the land, great storms came and went, ferocious winds tore at the landscape, pits yawned and the earth trembled as the two fought on.

Finally, utterly exhausted but still struggling, the wolf triumphed over the dark presence and chased it deep into the depths of the earth. The raven-wolf then lay on the battleground, to gather his strength, while the creatures of Hidey Wood called out their praises. Issa and Katanama and the vixen O-sansan were given due deference for their part in ridding the forest of the otherworld creature, but the wolf was lifted above all as the great champion of the land.

241

And the man heard the singing and the chanting, listened with envy to the praises heaped upon the wolf, and he took his weapons in a jealous rage and killed the wolf, thus performing one of the most treacherous deeds of the time just following the *Firstdark*.

Such a dastardly act did not go unpunished, for the Great Evil that had been defeated by the wolf, because of the nature of the man's deed, was able to enter the murderer's head and remained there until he died – raving mad, dissolute and worthless – with not a single creature to mourn him over the whole globe.

Chapter Twenty Four

Athaba turned south once again, unfamiliar paths of the wilderness becoming familiar to him. He began to recognise rocky outcrops that he had passed before on his way north or returning south. He saw a bear cave on the trail and the day after had one of his fits. He wondered about that: why just the thought of a bear should send him into a blackout.

At one point he saw five wolves kill a bull moose, bringing the bellowing giant crashing down in a tangle of broad antlers, flying hoofs and clashing teeth. The wolves were too preoccupied with their task, and later their meal, to concern themselves with Athaba. The smell of blood was in their nostrils. He watched them eat, then take chunks away with them, back to wherever they had their den. When they had gone, the scavengers appeared out of the windblown topsnow and moved in, but Athaba was now a little too proud to join the beggars at their feast of scraps. He waited until the carcass had been left alone, before descending from his rocky outcrop and stripping the last fibres of meat from the bones. He saw that one of the great horns had snapped under the weight of the falling body. The broken piece was as large as his own flank. Such a mighty beast, the bull moose. He decided it must have been sick to have been overcome by the wolves. Even then it had gone down fighting, trumpeting through those cavernous nostrils, a thrashing storm of dark hide and slate-grey pelts. Athaba had known wolves killed by moose. Once he had found a rival pack member with broken ribs and legs, lying under a tree. Round about the dying creature were blood patches and moose hair. The wolf expired just as Athaba arrived but it was obvious that a battle had taken place, and at least one wolf had come off badly. There was no sign of a carcass at the scene.

A raven came while he ate but he prevented it from crying out and attracting any of the nearby pack by asking if it knew so-and-so, or such-a-one, names of ravens from his days as an outcast. The bird was intrigued by this wolf who was into the culture of the scavenger and knew all these ravens, and kept shaking its head saying, 'Nein, nein. Ich weiss nicht, aber Retteltelt? Weissen sie er? He vos vun sonnoffabisch, ja?' The moose tasted good and Athaba rather enjoyed his chat with the raven. It reminded him of the old days which had now gone into some misty region of his brain. When he thought about it, the old days had been pretty bad, but he had lived through them, survived, and now that they were past they took on a different quality.

The winter settled like iron on the land and he fought his way through windstorm and blizzard, down through the tree line and over the mountains. Where the hill were too high to cross, he sought a way around them. He passed small human settlements, both temporary and permanent, and kept clear of the inhabitants and their dogs.

In the late afternoons, which were just as dark as the nights, he stopped to rest beneath rock outcroppings and in ice hollows. When he had rested for long enough, he continued, using the darkness as a screen to hide him from any hunters who might be foolish enough to brave the cold.

Each time he met a canid, Athaba asked for news of his mate, and each time the answer was the same. No one knew of Ulaala nor any female wolf with six pups.

Finally, he reached the wide belt of land between the wilderness and the city where he believed the hybrid swarms were roaming: those huge packs of mongrel coyote-wolves and dog-coyotes, with a sprinkling of dog-wolves. He had been told that the size of the packs sometimes reached up to sixty or so in number. They lived, and died, raiding the human settlements, scavenging and killing rats and other game. These packs of mottled hue, made up of members whose size and shape varied as much as their colouring, swept through the countryside in hordes, the raggedy bandits of the canid world. They were the swashbucklers of the suburbs, full of bravado and completely lacking in any kind of discipline. Every so often the human population would become annoyed with them and a 'dog shoot' would cull their numbers. But they were irrepressible and rose again in just as great a number until the cycle closed once more. They lived the kind of life many domestic dogs and responsible pack wolves envied but were too conventional to follow. Any wolf story-teller worth his or her salt would always have a new tale to tell about the hybrid swarms of the south. Any wolf *undermega*

244

still young enough to find the idea of a cult group exciting, would entertain the thought that 'if the worst came to the worst' there was always the prospect of joining the hybrid swarms.

One of the greatest swarm leaders of all time, who even featured in the songs and chants of conventional pack howls, was Rory Hightail. This magnificent cross between a red setter and a wolf once led his swarm over high mountains and across a sandy desert, losing only seven out of sixty-three of his band. The hunters that had been after them, among them Rory's mother's master, turned back after three of their number perished of thirst in a dust bowl. Rory Hightail's swarm roamed the woods of the north-west for a time, before moving to the outskirts of another city to renew their raiding tactics again. Once more the citizens rose against them and this time Rory's band forded a river in flood, throwing off their pursuers. For much of his life Rory Hightail was a true swarm leader: bold, audacious, intelligent and full of good humour. He had been known to rescue pups from certain death, snatching them up by their scruffs on the run. His mates (of whom it must be said there were many) would hear no word against him, which said much for his private life. His lieutenants would have flung themselves from high places had he considered such an action necessary.

Rory Hightail, spawned somewhere amongst the trash cans of the suburbs, became a canid legend in his own lifetime. He thwarted humans time and time again, leaving them either frustrated and angry or perplexed, always in some place he was not. He swept across the countryside avoiding the guns with dogside cunning and wolfhalf stealth.

Rory Hightail died of natural causes at the age of sixty seasons and his bones lay somewhere on a platform of rock from which the lights of a city could be seen twinkling in the distance on clear nights. Some said the wind blew round them, not through them, in deference to his respected remains. His memory was held as hallowed by both dog and wolf, one of those rare hybrids who bridged differences between the two, rather than widened them.

Athaba was crossing a stretch of waste ground uneasily, swimming in a river of unfamiliar scents, when he saw a group of canids clustered on and around some rusting vehicles. They were all kinds of breeds, some of them unrecognisable, hidden beneath pointed noses, blunt snouts, motley colourings, ragged coats, sharp eyes, stubby legs. Athaba doubted whether there was anything even approaching a thoroughbred amongst them. They were draped, rather than lying, on their metal beds. They looked like beggars, thieves, ripthroats and ragrunners, but there was a decadence about them, in their indolent poses, which reminded Athaba of his old mentor, Ragisthor. They had the same cynical expressions, the half-amused, almost contemptuous twist to their mouths. Athaba felt that if he were to ask a question of them, they would all yawn, simultaneously, into his face. Surely these were trash-can pirates; buccaneers of the scrapyards; privateers of the waste lots? Was this indeed a hybrid swarm?

He approached them slowly, anxious not to drive them off, nor to invite attack. In any case, the car hulks worried him. He was extremely distrustful of anything that smelled of human, even if it appeared to have been thrown away.

About twenty lengths from them he stopped. There were about forty or fifty of them. They suddenly lost their idle stances and he saw sinews tighten, muscles appear. Without actually moving from their places, or even changing their positions, they looked alert and ready either for fight or flight.

After regarding Athaba for a long time, one of the creatures climbed to his feet and trotted forward. He stayed at a safe distance but near enough to talk.

'You a wolf?' said the speaker, who looked like a squared-off woolly hound of some kind.

'Something wrong with that?' asked Athaba.

The dog sat on its haunches and scratched behind its ear with its hind leg.

'Nothing *wrong* with it. Just, we don't see many wolves around here. This is not exactly wolf country. I thought you types needed the forests and the tundra? You won't find many moose around here – only mouse.'

'I'm looking for the hybrid swarms. Are you – those over there – are they a hybrid swarm?'

'Hybrid swarm?' again a vigorous scratching. 'You're a little out there, wolf. So far as I know, the hybrid swarms are way way down south.'

Athaba's heart sank. 'Could I walk there?'

'You'd die trying. I'm talking distance here. How far have you come?'

'From the northern coast.'

The dog made an appreciative noise and scratched his wire-curly, squared-off jaw.

'That's quite a distance, but if I'm not mistaken you need to go ten times that to reach the hybrids, maybe even twenty. I know of a dog who comes from down there – hopped a train – have you ever seen how fast a train moves? Faster than a truck, anyway. You've seen a truck?'

'Yes, I think so. I've seen land vehicles.'

'Well, a truck's a land vehicle all right, and it can show anything on four legs its rear end in seconds. A train's faster and my friend was on that train for days. You understand? There's no way you can walk it, wolf. Say, you got a name?'

Athaba was aware that the rest of the swarm had crept forward a little and their ears were pricked. They did not look particularly dangerous as individuals, but their numbers were worrying. There was one sharp-nosed sleek hound who eyed him with what appeared to be strong hostility. Athaba already felt extremely uncomfortable this close to a human town and these dogs still carried the faint whiff of domesticity about them.

'Athaba. I'm called Athaba.'

'My name's Lucky,' said the dog, renewing his scratching. 'I'm mostly-airedale.'

'You aren't hybrids?'

Lucky looked round at the others then back again.

'Us? Naw. We're feral dogs, is what we are. Ferals are domestics gone wild. We didn't like the cosy life, or got kicked out for one reason or another, so we *act* like those hybrids – or maybe they act like us? Anyway, we're just ferals. Why do you want hybrids especially. You got a grudge? You going to kill someone?'

Athaba sighed.

'No. I'm looking for my mate and our pups. She was supposed to have come south, to join the hybrid swarms. Now I don't know what to do. Who's the dog looking at me as if he wants a fight?'

Lucky turned and stared, then turned again to face Athaba. He spoke almost in a whisper and it was obvious he did not want to be overheard.

'The one with the pointy face? That's Rip. He's the closest thing we've got to a leader around here. He's mostly-borzoi. They used to hunt wolves you know.'

Athaba kept his eye on the mostly-borzoi.

'What's all this *mostly* stuff?'

Lucky looked at him with a surprised expression and then nodded.

'Oh, I see what you mean. Mostly-terrier, mostly-poodle, mostly-alsatian? – well, you see, we're not pedigrees, nowhere near. We're mongrels, a mixture of every dog under the stars. We're downtown trash, conceived, if the truth must out, in some dirty alley or backstreet by two passing strangers, one of which just happens to be on heat at the time. A quick no-introductions mating, probably between two mongrels who couldn't trace their ancestory back past their parents, if that far. Only, you got to have a few illusions, see, so we look at each other and say, "You got a lot of borzoi in you, right?" and the dog in question usually answers, "Oh, that? Yeah. My grandfather was a pure bred," or some such lie. Makes us feel like aristocracy, see? Everyone needs posh ancestors. No one likes to think he comes from the trash cans.'

Lucky's voice suddenly increased in volume, probably for the benefit of the other dogs.

'There ain't no such thing as a mongrel round here. Every-body's got a history in them. Mine's terrier history and I'll fight anyone who says different.'

The rest of the ferals crept forward then, all except Rip, and began nervously sniffing around Athaba, who remained rigid and uncomfortable. He was not used to a bunch of scruffs going over him like he was one of their own. Somehow, however, he knew that he had to endure this treatment by these suburban hounds if he was going to get anywhere with them.

One of the females said her name was Pippa.

'Why don't you stick with us for a while?' she said, 'and we'll help you look for your family.'

Lucky said, 'Yeah, join up with us for a while. We'll put the word out around the streets, see if we can come up with anything. In the meantime, a few names – this here's Daniel, he's a cross between a retriever and a spaniel, which must have been *some* mating, but we don't mention it because he gets huffy. This here's . . .' and so the names came at him, but Athaba knew he would never remember them all. His head was in a whirl over the certainty that he had made a mistake in coming south. It was impossible that Tolga had confused hybrids with ferals, and that Ulaala was running with one of these dog packs. There were some big dogs but a wolf could not get lost amongst them, or even mistaken for a husky or alsatian. Humans in these parts would know a wolf when they saw it. Such a discovery would raise a hue and cry amongst the men and hunting parties would be all over the area.

The mostly-borzoi spoke.

'Maybe you've forgotten, Lucky, but there's a shoot due about now. You want to drag this wolf into a shoot? We know how things go, but he would be dead within minutes.'

What was this, thought Athaba, the dog Rip worrying about his position as leader? Perhaps he was worried that Athaba would take over his exalted status? The narrow bloodshot eyes of the mostly-borzoi regarded Athaba from a distance and it was difficult to read the intention behind them.

'He's right,' said Athaba. 'I don't like towns. I don't know anything about them. Even just standing here makes me nervous. I'll get back to the wilderness, where I belong.'

The mostly-airedale looked disappointed. It seemed he had taken to Athaba. Lucky seemed to accept him without bothering about the differences between them. He was one of those rare creatures who made friends within seconds of a meeting.

'Run with us just *once* then, wolf. You'll never get another chance to run with a swarm. Come on, what do you say? Never mind old Rip over there. The shoot's not due for a few days yet.'

'What is this *shoot*?'

'When the townspeople get together and come out here with guns to cull the swarm. They never get many of us. Some poor loafers, often travellers just passing through.'

'*Me* if I'm not careful,' said Athaba.

The mostly-borzoi nodded slowly.

Lucky pleaded.

'Just one run?'

Athaba gave way to foolishness.

'Let's go then,' he said, realising he was being very stupid, but wanting to get something out of his system. He had been on the trail for so long it was good to agree to something which was both irresponsible and exciting.

The pack gathered at a corner and when all the dogs were out of the yard, Rip yelled, 'Let's go,' and the swarm of ferals swept along the empty road, swirling with small whirlwind snows.

There were few buildings this far out of town and these were mostly shut tight. They were not human habitations but places where goods and machinery were stored.

The dogs swerved round a garage and Athaba saw a creased human face at a window, but they were soon past and the gas station fell away into the hazy windswept snowscape. He admitted to himself he liked the excitement of the run. It was not like hunting with the wolves. That was an orderly affair, well organised. On a caribou or musk-ox hunt he knew exactly what his role was at any given time. They might follow a herd or single for three or four days, stopping when the quarry stopped, but always remaining within reach of the prey. These were wearing-down tactics. Or they might attack at once, if they caught the herd by surprise. Or the move would be a pincer attack, or flushing strategy, or any number of well-tried ways of ensuring a kill. In every wolf's head was a series of field moves which had been drummed into him or her from birth. The possibility for error was minimal, the danger almost non-existent. Hunting was about survival, not about bravado. Each wolf, from his given position, knew exactly what was expected of him. Only unforeseen circumstances, like the time they met the bear, provided any deviation from the norm. The only real excitement came from being switched from, say, flankwolf to shoulderwolf when another member of the hunting party was injured. Or when one plan was obviously failing and a back-up was suddenly brought into play.

Running with the dogs was completely different. For a start, a wolf hunting party usually consisted of about five or six. The feral dogs numbered something like fifty. It was a heady experience, sweeping through the outskirts of a town amongst a swarm of excited ferals. It was as if they were an irresistible force, looking for an immovable object to smash aside. The windswept snow whistled past his ears, the ground whisked by under his paws, and he knew that any human seeing them would be frightened out of its wits. There was a feeling of power, of getting his own back on the humans. These dogs were taking the fight into human territory, not waiting for men to come out looking for them. They were rash, brash robber-dogs. They were the marauders of the streets. Admittedly, they were only knocking over trash cans, but it was the *style* in which they did it which was exciting. They ran devil-may-care on the edge of the wind, bowling over any

250

loose upright object that got in their way. Cats went into their high-leg-stance-fur-on-end-spitting pose, hissing, '*Le guet-aspens!*' as they were surprised by this motley band of reckless tearaways. Athaba loved it when he saw a feline preening itself on a gatepost, only to transform itself suddenly from a soft furry bundle into a stark-furred thorny demon. Domestic dogs froze in their tracks or ran for cover, yelling, 'Clear the streets, clear the streets, the wild ones are coming!' Town birds took their wings, squawking, '*Die hunden hunderterlei kommen* . . .' A tame rabbit in a hutch drummed the plywood wall with his hind legs, screaming, '*Papao! Papao!*' It was a truly exhilarating experience.

Rip, the leader, then led them through the courtyard of a roadside restaurant, and as if it had been planned, swept around the back to get to the trash cans. Metal bins went flying across the yard, spilling their contents on to the frozen ground. Dogs grabbed what they could, mostly beef bones and chicken carcasses. Some of the smaller dogs, like Pippa, paused long enough to lap up sloppy waste. There was a yelping from the humans inside the building as the dogs busied themselves amongst the garbage, running off in all directions once they had something in their mouths. Athaba was petrified by the noise and commotion, wondering which way to dash, regretting his rash decision to join these mad creatures on their run.

Suddenly a screen door went crashing back on its hinges and a man appeared in the doorway.

He had a shotgun in his hands.

There was a double explosion, twin flames leapt from the barrels of the gun.

A dog went somersaulting through the air, torn almost in half by the heavy-gauge shot. It hit the snow in a mess of broken bones and bloody flesh. The back legs twitched.

The rest of the dogs began leaving the scene immediately. Athaba was caught at the rear of the swarm and had the mass before him, blocking his exit. The man was staring at him now with round eyes, and Athaba knew that the human could see a wolf amongst the ferals. He started his run, but had to pass the man who was now fumbling with his weapon. The shotgun was raised, the barrels pointing at Athaba. The wolf heard the clicking sound as the man pulled the triggers, over and over again, following his flight with the muzzles. The weapon was unloaded,

251

but the man was so obviously electrified by the presence of a wolf he was reacting without thinking.

The swarm made the edge of the wilderness without further incident and Athaba was ready to keep on running. He paused only to catch his wind.

'Where's Pippa?' said Lucky, panting.

The dogs all lay panting between the piles of planks and bricks of the yard. They looked around.

'Pippa!' dogs began calling, until Rip told them to shut up.

'You want to bring the whole human population out here?'

No answer from Pippa.

After that, those dogs who had bones began eating, as if everything was back to normal. Athaba was stunned, shocked by the suddenness of the loss.

Athaba went over to Lucky.

'Was it Pippa who was shot?' he asked.

Lucky looked up for a moment and his eyes said yes.

'Why doesn't someone say something?' said Athaba.

'We – we don't mention those who leave us,' said Lucky, his eyes not meeting Athaba's. 'It's not done.'

'She didn't *leave*. She was blown to bits.'

'All the same, it's not good for morale to talk about it. She's gone, and that's that. Talking about her won't bring her back. We'll only start getting morose and scared and the next time we go out we'll fall down on the job.'

'Fall down on the job? You sound as if it was a well-planned raid or something. Lucky, all we did was run out there and rush in. What could go wrong with that? Or rather, what could go *right* with it? The only thing it's got in its favour, is surprise.'

Lucky didn't look up.

Athaba next went over to Rip.

'That was your fault,' he said. 'You led the swarm into the yard.'

Rip looked up from gnawing on his bone. He was clearly embarrassed because he only met Athaba's gaze for a second before turning away.

'Hey. No one's responsible for anyone else, okay? The bitch didn't have to go. She had a choice. Get off my ground, wolf. Find someone else to blame.'

252

'You knew you held sway, Rip. You knew the others would follow you.'

Lucky was beside him now. His voice was quiet.

'Look, Athaba, leave Rip alone. He feels bad, can't you see that? Listen, we're *not* wolves. We're not even thoroughbreds. We're a motley bunch of scavengers doing the best we can to live in the only way we know how. If we could, we would go out there and bring down caribou, but we can't. We know what we are. Scruffy strays is what we are. It's all very fine for you to come in here with your "noble canids" image, but most of these dogs have been whipped or beaten until half out of their heads. You think they would be here if they could live in a comfortable home? Sure, one or two of us are freedom freaks, but the majority are simply ill-treated house dogs, either tossed out or forced out.'

Athaba looked around at the sorry crew of dogs, as they stared at this minor confrontation. His heart felt heavy.

'I'm sorry,' he said, moving back to his place. 'It's nothing to do with me. I'm an outsider.'

The darkness became thicker as clouds moved over the area. There was a sleet coming down which froze on contact with the ground. Everyone lay around as close as possible to keep warm. Athaba wanted to get back out in the wild country again before they came for him with more guns.

Poor little Pippa. Her hair had been matted. Her ears had been full of tics. Now she was dead, cut in half by buckshot.

When the feast was over, the dogs left the yard one by one, intending to take up residence for a while in some other part of town. They had no doubt the man with the gun would be out with his cronies, armed to the teeth and looking for revenge.

Rip bid a gruff goodbye to Athaba and told Lucky he would see him again soon. The mostly-borzoi then left the yard. Only Lucky and Athaba were left.

'Where will you go?' asked Lucky.

'Up into the hills beyond the town for a while. Want to come with me?'

Lucky shook his head. His eyes were wide. Athaba knew the dog would refuse the offer to join him. It was an impossible arrangement, a dog and wolf travelling together. Or was it? A wolf and a man had done as much, though by accident rather than design. Still, he could see by Lucky's eyes that the thought of leaving the swarm and going alone with a wolf was a terrifying one. Exciting, but terrifying. Athaba was sure that it was not the danger which would deter the feral but moving out of his environment into an unknown land. An animal might face an army on his own stamping grounds but quake before an inferior opponent elsewhere.

Lucky said, 'What will the other wolves think? You bringing a dog along with you? Even if I am a mostly-airedale – a superior breed.'

'What other wolves. I haven't got a pack. I can't just join up with any old bunch of wolves, you know. We're not all great friends and allies. We respect each other's territory – mostly – but keep to our own packs. If I tried to force my way into another pack, or maybe even just approached them on a friendly basis, I might be killed. I would certainly be driven away, unless they were desperate to recruit new blood, which doesn't often happen. An old wolf like me? They'd laugh me out of the den.'

'I see,' said Lucky. 'Anyway, no thanks, just the same. I'm a mongrel. I belong in the suburbs. I wouldn't know what to do with myself out in the wilderness. Just the thought of it fills me with apprehension. Thanks, but no thanks. I'll stay here and work something out. I need a bit of order around me, the smell of humans and things human, like houses and cars and streets. This is my world. I guess once a townie, always a townie.'

'As you wish. Goodbye, dog.'

Lucky's square jaw dropped open. The wiry hair on his head was catching the drifting snowflakes: white amongst the grey curls. His eyes were bright and he lifted his head.

'Goodbye, wolf.'

They parted and went their separate ways, one going south, the other, north.

As Athaba travelled over the snowpacked foothills which led to the mountains, he thought how fortunate he had been during his life. Yes, there had been a great deal of distress, tragedy even, but for a wolf he had known much. From amongst his two main enemies, men and dogs, had come two friends. From amongst his friends and relations had come several enemies. The world was obviously not just *this* and *this* – sometimes it turned upside down, to become *that*. It was a strange thing, this memory-scent of things past. He had forgotten some of the names and smells of those close to him in his family pack in the early years: wolves he should have remembered. Yet he knew he would never forget

Koonama, or Lucky, both of whom would remain part of his olfactory recall for the rest of his life.

The light snow became heavy and the wind increased in strength until a blizzard was in progress. Athaba dug himself a hole in a drift and curled inside where he was soon warm. One thing was certain, the man with the gun would not follow him in such weather. He hoped it was the same back down on the outskirts of the town whose lights he could still see. That way the dogs would be safe, too.

What an adventure that had been. It was one he could never tell to another wolf without either being derided as story-teller or losing their interest because there would be no comprehension of what had actually happened. He could imagine such a conversation.

'So, you entered this human place?'

'Yes.'

'By force, of course. You were caged, or netted?'

'No, I went in – to steal scraps.'

(A funny look enters the other wolf's eyes.)

'You went in? How? Don't they have wooden barricades at the entrances to their dens?'

'We didn't go right inside, only round the back of the dwelling.'

'We?' (Narrowed, suspicious eyes.)

'Me and the dogs – feral dogs – that's domestics gone wild again. There were fifty of us.'

'Dogs.'

'Yes, ferals.'

'You like dogs?'

'Yes, no, not necessarily. It was an act of defiance, don't you understand? We were trying to take the fight to man himself. It was a great victory, a canid victory, fought by dogs and a wolf, against men. They should sing about it in songs. There should be a howl, a fox chant, telling future generations that not all the fights were back in the era of the *Firstdark*.'

(A knowing nudge.)

'You see yourself as a hero then, leading this group of mongrels against the guns.'

'There *was* a gun there. It was aimed at me, the trigger pulled, but it failed to fire. And anyway I wasn't the leader. That was a mostly-borzoi named Rip. An irresponsible hound.'

'You braved men's weapons to get, what is it, scraps?'

'Yes, I suppose so.'

(A shake of the head.)

'You must really like burned meat.'

'And *you* have the brains of a marsh toad.'

(A stiffening.)

'Is that necessary? To insult me simply because I refuse to take your wild imaginings seriously?'

'Yes, absolutely. The most necessary thing in the world.'

'Well, I . . .'

Oh, yes, he could see it all. This was something he was going to have to keep to himself for the rest of his life. He wondered if he would even tell Ulaala and his cubs – if he ever found them again.

Outside his hole the wind cried, mourning the deaths of a thousand thousand wolves with a loud white voice.

PART SIX

The Manhunter

Chapter Twenty Five

Once more Athaba travelled into territories unknown, this time moving sharply westwards in the hope of picking up some information on the whereabouts of his pack. A small trickle of doubt was running through his mind at this time, as to whether the object of his mission was still in existence. There was, of course, the strong possibility that Ulaala and the pups were dead: killed by hunters, or by other wolves. As he crossed glaciers that rumbled down self-made chutes in the mountainside, travelled soft snowy wastes, walked through magnificent ice-walled canyons fashioned by nature into temples, he considered this possibility. Did it make any difference to his search? Not unless there was proof of such a tragedy. If someone he knew and trusted told him that they had witnessed the death of his mate and pups, well then, it might make a difference to the way he spent his time. It might have, but since there was no such information available he didn't actually know whether such news would stop his feet from moving. He thought it *might*, but he wasn't absolutely certain. Perhaps he would carry on wandering in the hope that the informant was mistaken? It could be that the dedication to travel was now so deeply ingrained that it was impossible for him to stop without there being a good reason. His body was now tuned to the rhythms of the walk, the trot, the run. Remaining still had his legs twitching.

The land groaned under the press of ice. In the winter all is hard and brittle, slabbed, sheeted, layered. Even the wind seems to come in blocks to body-slam any creature that is foolish enough to stand in its path. The foxes have names for all the winds, even the small swirling gusts and the high whistling airstreams, but wolves have no time for such niceties as names. They, too, rely on the winds for information, but they know the wind can be a savage, destructive thing and their relationship with it is ambivalent.

In the winter the land claims everything for itself, even lakes and rivers turn into part of the solid earthscape. They crystalise, stretch their shoulders, and form themselves into icy lengths or wide plains, their summer fish trapped deep below somewhere in the coldest regions of the underworld. They live a season of safety below the reach of wolf mouth-spearing, or bear paw-spearing. Athaba often wondered why wolves did not copy the bears and find some cave or earth-hollow in which to wait out the winter until the game was plentiful again and the fish were not icelocked beyond reach. Such a sensible way to treat that white season with its fangs of ice and talons of wind.

One dark day, when he was travelling through a canyon being raked by the claws of a norther, he heard a howling.

This was not an unusual occurrence. He often passed through territories of his brother and sister wolves, but this song stopped him dead in his tracks. He recognised it even though it was not a traditional howl. He recognised it as one of the songs he and Ulaala had composed together, that season long ago when the pair of them had set up the den.

Athaba veered from his path to search the hills for the owner of that voice. There was only one: it had not been a chorus. He eventually found a small cave in the side of a mountain, large enough for a wolf. Standing outside this tunnel, he let out the same howl he had heard just a while earlier. For a long while nothing happened, then he heard the click of a stone being dislodged. He waited patiently.

Finally, a face appeared, framed by the rock.

'Who are you?'

The speaker appeared to be a yearling or thereabouts and Athaba had no time for pleasantries.

'Never mind who I am. Where did you learn that howl? Answer me quickly or I'll rip you from tail to throat!'

'What's it to you?' the speaker said boldly, but at the same time his face retreated into the darkness.

Athaba was convinced he had found the member of a pack that had come into contact with Ulaala. If they had harmed her, this yearling was going to pay the price. He was in no mood for socialising. He wanted information. He was in urgent need of the truth.

'I'm coming in there, wolf, so if you have something to say, say it now, before we fight. Do you hear me? Only one of us will leave this place . . .'

260

A nose appeared and the voice said in an aggrieved tone, 'Why do you have to be so hostile? I'm not harming anyone.'

'Are you alone?'

'I might be.'

The yearling was obviously alone and afraid and trying to be brave about it.

'Come out, NOW,' commanded Athaba.

The young wolf crept from the hole, shivering a little.

'I'm not afraid of you,' it said. 'My father taught me to fight and if I have to I'll fight *you*.'

'Your father?'

The yearling drew himself up.

'My father was a *headwolf*. I'm going to be a headwolf one of these days. He was a great fighter. He even fought Skassi once, and *beat* him. Skassi told me so himself. Skassi's not ashamed of being beaten by my father. He says my father was one of the meanest *utlahs* that ever roamed the icefields of the east.'

Athaba had begun to realise who this terrible father was.

'Well, I'm a little sick of hearing about this father of yours. What about your mother. Is she still alive?'

'My mother is the mate of Skassi and she's a mean wolf too,' said the youngster proudly.

Cold jaws closed around Athaba's heart.

'Your – your mother is Skassi's mate?'

'When my father was killed by hunters, she had to find another mate . . .'

'What's your name, youngster?'

Again the yearling drew himself up.

'Yanthra, son of Athaba and Ulaala!'

The jaws came together, crushing the organ in his chest. His Ulaala was now the mate of his old enemy. This was the cruellest bite from the teeth of fate he had ever received. Before him sat the fluffy creature he had left two seasons ago, no longer fluffy, but now a grown yearling. Yanthra.

'What about your brothers and sisters?'

'They're part of the pack.'

'Pack? You mean Skassi's rogues? The mankillers?'

'Freedom fighters, not rogues. Skassi doesn't like them to be called that. Skassi says they're going to wipe the existence of men from the face of the earth, so the wolf packs can live and roam in peace once again. He says that things are going to return to the way it was in the *Firstdark*, before men came out of the sea-of-chaos, before *Groff* stamped his foot on the land. Skassi says he's been chosen as the wolf to herald in the *Lastlight*. Skassi says . . .'

Athaba growled.

'Damn Skassi! I'll have his liver. Recruit *my* pups would he? On a suicide mission? Damn him, I'll tear him open and spread his lights over the snow.'

'Ha, you couldn't . . .' then the yearling stopped. 'What do you mean, *your* pups?'

Athaba muzzled the yearling under the chin.

'Youngster, I'm your father. It may take a bit of believing, but I am Athaba, the meanest *utlah* of the eastern icefields.'

The yearling regarded him for a few moments, then scratched behind his ear. He did not seem to know what to do. Then he asked, 'How did you meet my mother?'

'I was an outcast when I met Ulaala and she was from another pack. She was caught in the fishing line of a native hunter and I helped her to get free. I fought one of her pack, a wolf named Agraaga, and killed him, in order that I could take your mother with me to the south.'

Yanthra's jaw fell open, then suddenly pounced on Athaba and gripped him by the jowl, rocking his head to and fro for a moment. When he let it go, he cried, 'You *are* my father! You're alive. No wonder you knew the secret howl. Only mother and my brothers and sisters know the howl. She said you two made it up together and no other wolf would know how to do it.'

'Calm down, youngster. Let's go inside your little cave and you can tell me all about everything.'

Yanthra nipped him again and again.

'My *father*,' he howled, the sound echoing along the canyons. 'My father's back . . .!'

'Mother never really believed you were dead,' said Yanthra, once they were inside the small but relatively warm den. 'I could tell. She only said that to us because we kept asking where you'd gone. Even now one of us catches her looking out from the highlands, over the valleys, watching for you coming home.'

Athaba said, 'Well, I've had a long and weary search for both your mother and yourselves.'

With that he proceeded to tell his son all that had befallen him since leaving the den that day long ago. The youngster listened, wide-eyed, to the stories of his father's travels, occasionally asking a question or two, but in the main just listening.

When Athaba had finished, he saw that Yanthra was drooping and could hardly keep awake. The excitement of finding each other had taken its toll of both of them. He was disappointed because he wanted to hear the tale of what had happened to his mate and her pups after he was captured. However, he knew that Yanthra could not give a coherent account in the state he was in, so he decided to let the yearling rest first.

'Sleep now,' said Athaba, 'and then you can tell me what happened to all of you after I was taken by the hunters.'

Even before the words were out, Yanthra's eyes had closed.

While the yearling was asleep Athaba left the den and went out into the night. He slipped down into the valley and hunted under the moon, refreshing his worn body. His chest felt heavy and his head light, but he had at last found a positive trail to his mate Ulaala and his pups. That was *something*.

But Yanthra said she was the mate of Skassi now. Did that mean she would not want him, Athaba, if he walked out of the snows and into her life again? He could hardly blame her. Any other female wolf would have marked him down for dead long ago. Perhaps she had? Maybe his son was reading too much into a mother's unspoken words? Perhaps she looked down on the valleys for another reason, nostalgic for a life that was past, but knowing that it was *past*? Once a wolf had mated with another wolf, then feelings might be transferred? Was he too late even for that? It was the season *now*. Not that it mattered to him, except that Skassi would have a stronger claim on her and she might feel bound to honour that claim. There were no strong feelings of jealousy in his breast, only a yearning for his mate that he wanted desperately to be fulfilled. He *deserved* it! After all he had been through, he deserved some peace and happiness, surely? But things don't work out that way, he knew. Deserving something did not necessarily make it happen, especially when *two* creatures were involved. If you wanted something badly enough, you could go out and work for it, get it, or die trying. So long as it was just you and no one else. But you couldn't make up someone else's mind for them. No matter how much you might want a she-wolf, if the female didn't want you then you could turn yourself inside out trying to attain the unattainable, it would make no difference.

Out on the snows of the valley the wind was chill, but his coat was thick and he remained warm now that he had some food inside him. He wandered around amongst the white forms, trying to decide what to do. Should he wait and hear his yearling's story before he made up his mind? Or should he leave now, head west again, and not bother her any more? His turning up at this time might cause her more agony and perhaps she was tired of making decisions.

Athaba might have done this, had she been with any wolf pack but Skassi's. As it was, he saw her as doomed anyway. Of course, men were hated creatures and revenge was the one thing all wolves dreamed of. But, no matter how hard you tried, you couldn't win. They would get you in the end. Skassi knew that. He was an ageing wolf determined to go down with the blood of men on his teeth. Rid the world of humans? Skassi was telling youngsters stories in order to get them to follow his suicidal schemes. Wolves had wanted a leader for centuries: a headwolf unafraid of the hunters' guns who would take them into battle and halt the advance of the bipeds. It was a forest dream, a flimsy wisp of flame from the midnight sun, insubstantial. Wolves had lost the fight many centuries ago, in seasons out of time. They had fought and died and eventually settled for perpetual retreat, moving ever backwards as humans needed more room for their brood. The most they could hope for was to find a region so inhospitable that men would not want to live there, under any circumstances. The northern icefields were like that and had stopped the advance for many seasons now. Of course, it was not greatly desirable country for wolves either, but losers could not be choosers.

So, he did not feel he could leave his Ulaala (*his*? Ulaala) with Skassi without first giving her the choice between them. He did not feel he was doing her a disservice, since if she stayed with Skassi she was doomed in any case. He might even stay with her, near her, so that they might die together.

One thing was certain, he promised himself, his pups would not stay. He had to meet Skassi if only to wrest his now yearlings from the mad wolf who wanted to take all others down with him along the road to destruction. That much was sure. Next season, the offspring of Athaba and Ulaala would be running for game in the east, whatever Skassi had to say about it.

Having made his decision, Athaba began walking back to the den, to be met by an anxious yearling.

Yanthra said, 'I thought I had just been dreaming – that you hadn't come back after all. Then I saw your tracks in the snow and smelled your scent, and thought you'd gone away again because you didn't like me . . .'

Athaba nipped his erstwhile pup.

'Silly creature. I had to hunt and have some time to think. Have you eaten yourself?'

'I had a cache, up in the rocks.'

'Good. Now, you haven't told me what you're doing out here? Why aren't you with your mother and siblings? Did you get lost?'

Yanthra hung his head.

'Well?' said Athaba.

A low dejected voice said, 'I ran away.'

'Why?'

'There were wolves there that didn't like us. They only let us into the pack because Skassi said to, but whenever his back was turned they bullied us. We're not cowards,' the head came up, '*I'm* not a coward. We fought back. But they were bigger and stronger – tough old . . . well, wolves like you, Athaba, but not so . . . understanding.'

A wave of tenderness towards this youngster went through Athaba and for a moment he promised himself he would fight any *mega* that had made Yanthra's life the misery it obviously had been. Then he realised that would be a foolish thing to do. He would not allow himself to be diverted from the task he had set himself. The important thing was to get the yearlings away from the pack.

'Some of the she-wolves were the worst,' said Yanthra with feeling. 'Mother made them go submissive when she was around, but you know, there's hunting to be done and raids to make.'

Athaba went cold inside.

'Your mother has been on raids? Against humans?'

'No, raids against other packs. We haven't been with them long enough yet. Skassi was going to start attacking human settlements again in the spring, once the weather had turned.'

Relief flooded through the older wolf.

265

'Well, we'll see about that. In the meantime, let's get back to the den and you can tell me the whole story, of how you left the timberlands and what happened once I had gone.'

'I will,' said Yanthra, heading back for his cave.

Athaba followed behind the eager yearling.

Chapter Twenty Six

Yanthra could see that his mother was very anxious when his father Athaba did not return that night. Although still a pup, Yanthra was aware that warrior-hunters like his father often stayed away from the den for days at a time, so he wondered why Ulaala was so worried. It was possible that she had smelled something on the wind, something too subtle for the youngsters to catch. He mentioned it to his favourite sibling, Riffel, and she said seriously, 'I'm sure I caught a strange scent today. You don't think father has attacked some humans, do you?'

Riffel was still of an age when she thought her father was invincible and the only thing that stopped him killing bears and humans was a generosity of spirit.

There were two more female pups in the den, Torka and Grisenska, and the male pups Mook and Wassal. They were all healthy, strong wolves, who would live to adulthood providing they did not meet with an accident or get taken by an eagle or a lynx, and though the situation appeared normal to the pups they knew their mother and father considered the litter to be a lucky one.

Grisenska was the largest and strongest of the six pups and it was to her that Ulaala entrusted the den that night.

'Lie by the entrance,' she told the frightened Grisenska, 'and attack anything that tries to come in. Don't let any of the other pups go out. You understand me?'

Grisenska nodded her head and Yanthra could see his sister was desperately unhappy. They had never been left completely alone before and the fact their mother was prepared to risk leaving them unprotected for a while was an indication that Ulaala was extremely concerned for her mate.

Their mother left a short while later.

They all lay around the dog-leg tunnel, not even whispering, but completely wide awake. Grisenska carried out her duties, guarding the entrance, despite her nervousness. Every sound beyond the den had her pricking up her ears. Something snuffled around the hole outside for a while, in the middle watch, but whatever it was the creature did not attempt to enter the den. There was still a strong scent of mother wolf in the air and no animal in its right mind would risk entering a dark place where a mother wolf was guarding her brood.

Yanthra knew that his sister would die protecting them and thought how unfair it was that she had been born just a little bit bigger and stronger than the rest of them. Due to that small accident of birth, she took on responsibilities at a very early age, for the whole of the sibling group.

Apart from the unknown snuffler, the night passed uneventfully. Ulaala returned before noon. She brought food with her, regurgitated it for the pups. She seemed calmer than before but strangely distant.

Grisenska asked, 'Did you find father?'

'I found no signs of him,' replied Ulaala, bluntly and truthfully.

Over the next few weeks Ulaala became extremely thin. Having to feed the pups by herself was an enormous task and Yanthra often felt guilty because he was always hungry and for ever at her muzzle. It was essential that the cubs began solid food as soon as possible, and Ulaala did everything to encourage this, pushing soft meats before them.

Not only was their mother losing weight, but as the pups grew larger they needed more to sustain them and so had to hunt for themselves. The problem was, of course, they were not very good at it. They needed a great deal of practice.

Finally, Ulaala ceased sitting outside the den, watching the horizon during the little rest time she was able to make for herself, and stated that the family must move.

'We have to find another pack,' she said. 'I can't feed you all, you can't feed yourselves yet, not properly. I want you strong and fit. We need others to help you hunt. You need adults to go out with and learn from. I can't do it completely by myself.'

So they set off in a north-easterly direction where another pack was known to be denning. The journey was hazardous and on the way they lost Torka who was carried off by a fast current in a river. There was no knowing whether she lived or not, but Ulaala was stricken with guilt for a couple of days and neglected Yanthra and the others in her grief.

They found the pack up on a rise amongst some rocks. There were seven of them, all adults. Their breeding den had been discovered by hunters last spring and thought the pups had not been killed on the spot, they had been stolen. Two wolves had died during the pillage, trying to defend the little ones. The rest of them had been out on a hunt and came back to find the mother of the pups had been slaughtered and the clown of the pack, a wolf known as Giggagim, bleeding to death. Giggagim told them what had happened before he collapsed and drifted away to the Far Forests.

'They caught us unawares – came in on a machine – shot Filfa straightaway. I tried – went for them – shot me too. Took the pups in sacks. They – they were just about to – to skin Filfa when the rest of you returned. Left us. May be back, soon . . .'

The pack left the area immediately and never returned. They had lost a whole generation and were very bitter about it. Ulaala went to negotiate with them and found the three males and four females very willing to take the family in. She knew they were not so much concerned about her, and had she been alone would have thought twice about letting her stay. The pups, however, were a different matter. Five strong new wolves, soon to be *undermegas* were what the pack had been missing. The oldest wolf was twenty-eight seasons and the youngest, before the pups arrived, twelve seasons. The fresh blood was expected to revive the pack and set it back on course again.

The pack headwolf was a female called Sirenka, a relatively sharp creature who liked everything in its place, especially pups. She was firm, fair and ruthless with those who stepped out of line. As headwolves went, she was not unusual. In fact the male who sometimes took over from her, when there was need for a different set of skills, was immediately transformed from a gentle, dozy creature who played with the pups and taught them silly games to a stern autocrat who frightened the life out of them. There was something about leadership which left Yanthra thinking it was not the best of ambitions for a carefree wolf like himself.

He told Mook, 'Who wants to become a crusty old wolfer like Sirenka or Miggamak? Soon as they're in charge, they turn into bad-tempered monsters, body-slamming wolves out of the way and glaring at us if we so much as dribble in front of them.'

Mook, who was Sirenka's favourite, did not agree with him.

269

'I *want* to be a headwolf. You get all the best bits of meat and you can tell others what to do.'

Riffel said, 'Yes, you'd like that, wouldn't you? Well don't think you can boss me about.'

'I will, if I'm headwolf,' cried Mook.

Wassal put an end to the argument by stating something quite obvious that had been missed by Mook.

'You're not *likely* to achieve such an ambition, brother, sad as it may be to you. After all, whoever heard of a headwolf called *Mook*. It's not a name that inspires a pack. The only one of us who's likely to make such an exalted position, let's face it, is Grisenska. She's serious, she's got the right attitude, and she's a BIG pup. Put all thoughts of leading out of your head, Mook, and settle for top shoulderwolf.'

'Maybe you're right,' muttered Mook, whose stomach governed his existence. 'Maybe a shoulderwolf doesn't work so hard and gets the next best choice of meats. Grisenska doesn't care what she eats, anyway, she's interested in quantity not quality. If I'm her top shoulderwolf, then maybe I'll get the best anyway.'

'IF, you're top,' said Yanthra. 'But to do that you've got to beat Wassal, Riffel and me. Think you're up to it?'

'Try me!' cried the pup, and another of the interminable wrestling matches began in the dirt beside the den.

So it was that Ulaala and her pups became part of another pack and though their mother fitted uneasily into the hierarchy of the group, the pups (being pups) soon adapted and became favourites of one or another adult.

One night Yanthra was lying beside his sister Riffel when their mother returned and went to join a Howling Chorus on the high rocks. Yanthra listened to the songs for some time and then said to Riffel, 'I'm going to ask them to do that one mother taught us, you know, with the high pitch that drops suddenly at the end of the howl?'

'No,' said Riffel, sharply. 'You know mother said that's a secret between *us* only. It's our father's special howl.'

'Our father's dead,' said Yantha.

'Even if he is, which isn't certain, it's still to be kept a secret. Those other wolves wouldn't understand. You're not really supposed to invent new songs, only sing the old ones. Listen,' she added, 'how *sad* mother sounds . . .'

Yanthra listened to the howls of Ulaala, and even though he was only a pup, he could recognise the melancholy behind those notes.

'Yes,' he said, 'she's missing father, isn't she? Do you think she'll ever stop? Missing him I mean?'

Riffel said with some authority, 'If you find a true mate, a *really* true mate, you never want anyone else. Mother and father are special, I think. Ulaala will die watching the hills for signs of Athaba returning.'

'I think that's a bit much,' said Yanthra. 'I mean, I know she's missing him now, but she'll get over it. She'll find another he-wolf.'

'*Never!*' said Riffel with some feeling. 'She'll never forget father. You he-pups have no souls.'

'Well, we *have*,' said Wassal who had been eavesdropping, 'but some of us have more soul than others.'

'Are you meaning me?' cried Yanthra. 'I've got as much soul as anyone else.'

'Prove it!' said Wassal, and the inevitable tumble ensued.

After that conversation Yanthra watched his mother and saw how deeply she was feeling the loss of his father. He wanted to do something to comfort her, but he didn't know how. Once, he nuzzled under her chin and said innocently, 'I can do it the way father used to,' and saw such pain spring to her eyes that he never did anything like it again.

Ulaala was barely tolerated by the adult wolves of the pack she had joined. Yanthra saw her being blocked from drinking water, shouldered aside at the kill, moved from sleeping-place to sleeping-place as the other wolves changed their minds about the most comfortable spot on which to rest. She never complained, probably because she was fearful of her pups being turned out of the pack, even though she was bigger and stronger than most of them. Being a northerner, she had developed broad shoulders and strong leg muscles. She could have taken most of these timber wolves apart, but suffered the indignities they bestowed upon her for the sake of her pups. Yanthra knew it irked her though, that she had to take these insults. She was a proud wolf, of good antecedents, and a rugged upbringing had given her a physique which any headwolf might have envied.

She told the youngsters a story of her youth, when she was an *undermega* and had been trapped on an ice floe, moving

271

out to sea on the currents. Eventually, she knew she would have to swim for it and plunged into below-zero waters, to leg-paddle to the land. Halfway back she thought her muscles would seize up on her and she would have cramp and drown, but she kept her eye on the bank and willed her legs to keep moving.

When she hauled herself out on the snow, she was elated in a strange way, as if she had passed some kind of test.

'I felt I could have taken on *Groff* at that moment, and punished him for being the instrument of men.'

Mook looked around him nervously.

'Doesn't *Groff* live near us? I've heard the adults say he was given a palace of ice in the snow country. This is the snow country, isn't it, mother?'

His mother said, '*Groff* was betrayed by those who gave him life. The humans stopped believing in him and he turned to mist then blew away on the four winds.'

'Can humans bring him back again?' asked Riffel.

'I think they've forgotten how. All this was long ago, seasons out of time, just after the *Firstdark*. Things have changed since then. Things have changed quite dramatically. Humans were almost animals then, and only had one or two weapons, like stone axes and wooden spears. Their heads were full of magic and they used the magic to hunt us down. They used to draw pictures on the walls of their caves, of men killing deer and wolves and bears, and the next day these pictures would come true. Things they believed in then, like *Groff*, did come true *because* they believed. Humans had no doubt in their magic in those days. If you believe strongly enough in something, it is said to always come true because that's how things happen. Someone once believed in the world, and there it was. It's a good job for us that humans now have doubts. When you want to create something you can't afford to have the *tiniest* little doubt that it's going to happen, or it won't happen.'

Yanthra said, 'Well, I know father is still alive. I *believe* it. Athaba will come back to us.'

Ulaala hung her head a little.

Wassal said, 'Can't you see you're upsetting mother?'

'I can't help that,' Yanthra replied. 'I can't help what I believe, can I mother? If I could, then I wouldn't believe in the first place. Isn't that right?'

272

'That's true,' Ulaala said, licking his face fondly. 'You mustn't mind me – I don't have the faith of the young.'

['And I was right, wasn't I?' Yanthra said to Athaba. 'I was right all along. Wait until we see that Wassal. I'll make him swallow his tongue all right. I *knew* you would come back. I saw it in my dreams. And it's *true*.']

Ulaala and her pups had been part of the new pack for two months when an event occurred which caused them to change direction yet again. First, two of the wolves were shot by hunters, and the pack moved eastwards, towards the mountains. When they reached a low valley, they rested for a few days, to hunt. One evening, when the stars were clear as points of ice, a strange headwolf walked right into the midst of them, flanked by two shoulderwolves. A wolf with a cinnamon-coloured coat.

The moment Yanthra smelled and saw this wolf, he knew he was witnessing an extraordinary creature. The headwolf was not as big and strong as Sirenka – in fact he was quite lean with a faintly insouciant look about him – but his manner was striking. It was full of confidence. His tread was firm and even. He held up his head and stared into the eyes of any wolf that had the audacity to study his form. There was no suggestion of faltering, or excusing himself for entering the temporary den of another pack. His demeanour dared anyone to challenge him.

Yanthra knew, within those few brief moments, that there was not a wolf among them that night who would survive combat with such a creature. This was a wolf that had killed a man. This was Skassi, the leader of the manhunters, the rogue wolf of the east.

Not a member of Sirenka's pack said a word. They waited for the rogue to speak. They all knew who he was and most of them were overawed. The legends that had sprung up around this wolf in just a few seasons were passed from pack to pack, from forest to tundra, from the icefields to the mountains, and all who heard were impressed. For the first time in a century of seasons, ten centuries of seasons, a wolf had arisen who promised to lead his kind out of persecution. It was an incredible covenant, taken seriously by almost every wolf in the land. There was a buzz in the air, of zeal, enthusiasm, fanaticism. Wolves were talking of driving mankind into the sea, beyond the snow line, down to the depths of the south where they belonged.

Skassi stopped opposite the pups and stared hard.

Yanthra quaked under those cold, hard grey eyes. They seemed to find some fault with him and he fully expected the rogue wolf to order one of his shoulderwolves to 'rip out the throat of the audacious one' but still the pup could not take his eyes from the headwolf's face.

'You,' said the great Skassi, seemingly with a throat full of gravel. 'Your name?'

'Yanthra.' 'Riffel.'

They had both spoken together, thinking that each was the one to whom Skassi was speaking.

'Be quiet,' said the soft voice of their mother, from behind them. Ulaala had come up silently and was in a protective position, guarding her pups.

'My name is Ulaala,' she said.

'These are your pups?'

'Yes.'

Still the rogue wolf stared with narrow eyes at Yanthra.

'One or two of them have familiar markings. Someone in my old pack had a slate-blue colouring such as that little one . . . you, your name?'

This time Yanthra knew it was he who was being addressed.

He did not know why he answered so formally, as if it were some occasion such as an initiation or a ceremony. Perhaps it was an occasion of a kind, if not a ritual? It certainly felt like one.

'Yanthra, son of Ulaala, son of Athaba,' he said, proudly.

Skassi turned and stared even harder. After a long while he spoke again.

'Ah, yes. Athaba. I see him now. I see him in your mane and tail, and in your jaw.'

The rest of the pups were looking at the rogue wolf with round eyes, wondering what was going to happen next. Was this famous rebel going to kill them all, for being sons and daughters of Ulaala and Athaba? It certainly seemed like it. They stared into the ferocious eyes, at the savage fangs, of this terrible wolf of wolves, and waited for his condemnation.

'I knew your father,' he said at last. 'We were raised together, we fought together. We even fought each other. We have been enemies all our lives.'

The pups waited, as still as stones, while Ulaala moved closer to them, stood amongst them.

Skassi then said, 'I distrusted your father. I thought he stank of mysticism and magic . . .' he paused, and looked away, to the north-west for a moment, before continuing with, '. . . but he had aspects of character I've never seen in another wolf,' the voice was almost wistful, ' – tenacity, fortitude, endurance. He was a wolf who refused to lie down and die where any other would have given up hope long before . . .'

'That was my Athaba,' said Ulaala, with fierce pride in her voice.

Skassi's head came up.

'Was?'

'He's dead.'

'Have you seen his carcass? Were you there?'

Ulaala looked taken aback.

'No?'

'Then don't be so certain, she-wolf. That outcast has a dozen lives, and all of them disreputable. I wouldn't be surprised to see him walk across those hills one day. I know, you see – we're from the same pack – we're of the same blood. Only the guns can kill us, only the guns *will*.'

'He was shot by a hunter,' said Ulaala.

The narrow eyes closed and opened, slowly. Skassi looked as though he were thinking, deeply, of some subject beyond the ken of other wolves. His eyes had distances in them, greater than the leap from star to star. There was frostfire there, too, burning coldly from within.

'Shot?' said Skassi. 'Show me the pelt, show me the holes. I see him coming, out of the blue mists, one day. Did you hear that I am able to see into the future? The forests talk to me . . .'

This all sounded a bit strange, to Yanthra, after his father had been accused of the sickness of mysticism and magic. It sounded very much like Skassi had the same complaint.

275

Chapter Twenty Seven

Skassi went to Ulaala and sniffed her as one might sniff a mate. There was silence amongst the wolves that watched in anxious anticipation. No one quite knew what Skassi wanted: why he was visiting at all. Certainly this act of nosing around a female of another pack, without even having had an invitation to the den, was a breach of protocol at the very least.

No one moved or made any objection to this blatant display of bad manners. There was not one amongst the pack who dared show any hostility towards Skassi and his two shoulderwolves. Ulaala herself must have felt the humiliation strongly, because she alone spoke.

'Don't do that!' she said.

Skassi ignored the remark and then motioned to his two pack members that they were leaving the area. As he walked out, through a gap which led to a mountain path, he said to his shoulderwolves:

'Bring the pups.'

The two wolves, a male and a female, whirled and began rounding up the pups like a dog with sheep. Confused, the pups gathered into a group. Ulaala shouted: 'No!'

Skassi turned and said, 'They either come with me, or they die. Which is it to be?'

'I'll kill the wolf that touches them,' she warned.

Yanthra's heart was beating hard at this point. He wondered if there was going to be a battle between his mother and these three strangers, because it was fairly certain that the rest of the pack would not help them. Then he heard his sister speak.

Grisenska said, 'Don't mother. It won't do us any good if you are killed. Let's go with them?'

Skassi said, 'You may come with them, if you wish.'

Ulaala was crouched, ready to launch herself at the shoulder-wolves. Yanthra could see the torment in her eyes. His mother had to make a decision between attacking those who would take her pups from her, or allowing them to be taken and to go along with them. It was a choice between almost certain death and permitting Skassi to turn her young ones into renegades. Skassi had killed humans. There would be no rest for him or those that followed him. Humans would turn the world inside out rather than let a mankiller get away. They would shoot down every wolf on the tundra, in the forests, in the mountains, if that was the only way to ensure that the culprit was punished.

To Yanthra's surprise, his mother's taut coiled form slowly relaxed.

She said, 'I'll come too'.

Out on the trail the pups stumbled along through the darkness with the shoulderwolves nipping their flanks to keep them moving. Although they were used to being without daylight at this time in the seasons, the path through the mountains was unfamiliar to them. Even Ulaala slipped occasionally, on patches of ice she could not see in the dark.

They travelled a long way, through passes and over glaciers, until they came to a place where the trail dropped away, downwards into a hidden valley. As they descended Yanthra looked up the sheer face of the mountain. He could not see the top which disappeared into the blackness above. All around him the iron rock rushed silently downwards like black waterfalls. Surely this was a place where rivers of stone fell to earth from some lake above the clouds? Perhaps somewhere above their heads was the palace which had once been given to *Groff*, carved from ice and snow, and perched on a plateau of frozen cloud? Cottonwood trees of white mist grew from fissures and crevices as he watched. These expanded slowly: ghostly dim shapes that eventually became part of the night. This was an eerie land of shadows within shadows, where moulted darkness clung to the rocks and the ground dropped away to places that saw no sun.

In the gravel beds they passed were buffaloberry and crowberry shrubs which hid scuttling shapes. When the light of warmer seasons came there would be poppies and fireweed and coltsfoot scattered over the passes, but now there were no flowers to scent the air or colours to pattern the hillsides. It was a dreary journey which filled the hearts of the pups with heavy sand.

Skassi led the group, occasionally pausing to howl, the sound echoing round the white natural walls of the canyons. From the

277

distance came the faint sounds of answering howls, informing them that there was no danger.

Yanthra felt afraid as he and his brothers and sisters entered the area of the den. Dark silent forms of strange wolves could be seen in hollows and dips. Although there was menace there, the overall feeling was one of deadly resignation. These were wolves who had renounced worldly wants and had prepared themselves for an early death. There was no fear in them. Such feeling had been replaced by a philosophical acceptance of martyrdom. The oath that was only whispered out of curiosity amongst wolves in the forests and on the tundra was buried in their hearts. It had changed them from beasts that run from men to beasts that pursue men. The hunted in them had become the hunter. Yanthra regarded these wolves with great awe, wondering how they could reach the state of mind that was evident in their posture, their eyes.

Skassi called the whole pack together. His control over them seemed absolute. They obeyed him as if they were entranced. His hold over his pack appeared to have its sources in mysticism rather than physical discipline. The sheer power of his personality seemed to draw the wolves from their rest and place them in set positions around himself. For a wolf that seemed so fiercely opposed to anything which smacked of cabbalism, Skassi was strangely reliant on some invisible method of persuasion which even Yanthra found irresistible. Even when not staring into those terrible eyes, the pup could feel the presence of this wolf leader, like a stale hot wind that will not be denied existence. In the end, the pup had to look up again, to find those eyes and wonder about the compelling influence behind them.

'I have brought these pups here,' said Skassi, 'to give us a second generation of mankillers. Before the spring, I want each of them to be aware of their role in life. One pup will be allocated to a *mega* whose job it will be to educate that pup.

'There is also a new she-wolf amongst us. Her name is Ulaala. She is to be my new mate.'

Yanthra saw his mother start at these words, and he guessed she was about to voice a protest when another female suddenly let out a loud shrill sound, followed with the words: 'I am Skassi's mate!'

There was a short answer from Skassi.

'No.'

From that moment on Yanthra witnessed a silent vicious war between his mother and this female who had once been the mate of the headwolf. It was pointless for Ulaala to say that she had no desire to be Skassi's mate. The lord of the wolves had spoken and his word was law. The she-wolf, Nidra, spent her whole time trying to bait Ulaala into a fight, taking savage bites at her when Skassi was not around. After a time Ulaala began to retaliate and it seemed that neither she nor her antagonist was going to back down before one lay dead at the other's feet.

Yanthra himself was at first allocated to a stern but clearly disinterested wolf by the name of Ginnant, who taught him the rudiments of fighting men.

'When you attack from the front, be sure to zig-zag. Go *under* the weapon – go for the stomach or lower – rather than leaping for the throat. While you're in the air you have to pass the muzzle of the gun and the hunter would be a fool not to blow you apart at that moment. If you go close to the ground, weaving, and up from below, you will destroy his sense of security. If he misses you with his first one or two shots he'll start to panic and his instinct will be to back off or turn and run, and then you've got him for sure.

'However, it's best not to attack from the front if at all possible. Attack from the rear or the flank. Go in fast and silently – only fools bother with battle cries. Avoid the limbs, even if they thrust a boot at you, or raise an arm to protect themselves. Our instinct is to go for the nearest part of the body, but you have to overrule such reactions. Again, try to get between the leg and arm, in the side, and tear out his kidneys. Once you sink your teeth into his flesh, *don't* let go. Twist and turn, spin, but don't let go until the meat comes away in your mouth . . .'

'Have you ever killed a man, Ginnant?' asked Yanthra.

The wolf looked at him with weary eyes.

'That's not the kind of question you ask of a *mega*. Now, repeat to me what I've just told you, then go off and practise. I'm a little tired today . . .'

Yanthra did as he was told.

The den of the renegades was neither a place of despair nor a camp full of bravado and swaggering wolves. It was a grim place, where the business of killing for the sake of revenge was taken seriously. Sometimes, Yanthra felt he was in some dark

279

dreamworld. His mother (and father when he had been around) had taught him that wolves did not waste their time on useless hunts which were not likely to result in food. Wolves, he had been told, should be opposed to anything which was not for the good of the pack. Hunting men was definitely not good for the pack. It was an extremely dangerous, possibly even suicidal, method of obtaining meat. Whatever else men were, there was no denying their intelligence. They had ways within ways that left the brightest wolf on earth blinking with astonishment.

This pack was not even concerned with eating men, once they had been killed. In fact the instructions were to leave the area as soon as possible before human hunters arrived with more of their deadly weapons. The whole idea of waging war against humans was insane. It was a war that could not be won.

However, this pack consisted of wolves who were dedicated to the destruction of men. Yanthra was not about to go up to Skassi and say, 'I think you're quite wrong, because . . .' The headwolf would burn him where he stood with those fiery eyes.

So, Yanthra did as he was told, but at the same time felt as if he were acting out a role in someone else's nightmare. He was afraid much of the time and woke from rest with a leaden feeling of doom in his breast. There was a greyness to life that would never again see colour. A kind of suppressed panic existed in Yanthra's breast, and he knew it was in his brothers and sisters, too. They took the lessons that were forced upon them, but with reluctance, looking for their mother the whole time.

Ulaala came to Yanthra during rest time one day.

She whispered in his ear.

'I've spoken to your brothers and sisters, now I'll tell you. We have to get away from this place, but we can't do it just yet. When the spring comes, you must be ready and watch for my signal. You'll all be stronger then and the weather will be better for travelling. Don't give up now.'

Hope entered the pup's heart again and from then on he went about his duties with a little more enthusiasm. Ulaala had promised them they would escape and his mother always kept her word.

Before that could happen, however, Yanthra found he had to make his own plans for escape.

The pack woke after a general sleep to find Ginnant's body stiff and lifeless. He had died, soundlessly, during rest. There

280

were a few flecks of blood on his lips to suggest that his lungs had not been in the best of condition. His death left Yanthra without a tutor and to his (and Ulaala's) horror, Skassi insisted that Ginnant's replacement should be Nidra.

The she-wolf who had been displaced by Ulaala from Skassi's 'side' could not wait to get hold of one of her rival's pups.

'I'm going to make that little devil sorry you're his mother,' whispered Nidra to Ulaala. 'He'll wish he died at birth. I'll teach him, all right. I'll teach him the meaning of suffering . . .'

A fight followed this remark, and the two she-wolves had to be forcibly parted by shoulderwolves. Skassi was very angry and would not listen to Ulaala's pleas. He insisted that Nidra would not dare to harm the pup when she knew the youngster was under Skassi's protection. But the wolf leader's mind was somewhere else most of the time. He was becoming increasingly difficult to reach, both in a mental and physical sense. There was a high rock on which he lay and always this was guarded by two of his shoulderwolves. Approaches from other pack members were discouraged. Skassi divorced himself from the petty squabbles of the pack and when Yanthra looked up at the rogue headwolf, almost always occupying his lofty position above the den, it was obvious that the *mega*'s thoughts were on some distant place beyond the ken of mere pups. The eyes belonged to some time in the past: there was no future in them.

Skassi's indifference to all pack politics which did not directly concern himself left the field open to the sneak bullies and life became uncomfortable for most of the pups and especially for Yanthra. In fact he was tormented so much by Nidra that he made his own plans for escape. Almost a yearling now, the pup grew stronger by the day and one rest time, without saying anything to his mother, he slipped out of the den area and made his way back through the mountain passes to where the old pack were still wintering.

When he arrived with his alarming tale, however, they turned him away. They were afraid that Skassi and his renegades would follow the pup and retribution would fall on any who gave Yanthra shelter. They gave him food and returned him to the trail.

The youngster made his way back into the mountains, to a place where food was to be had, albeit in small quantities. He survived from day to day, all the time expecting to be followed and forcibly

281

dragged back to Skassi's hideout. However, dark days passed and no wolf came up the trail, until his father arrived.

'And that's the whole story,' said Yanthra to Athaba. 'Of course, it's not really the *whole* story, but all the important bits are there. What shall we do now?'

Athaba mulled over what his son had told him. The situation was certainly very grave. If he did not get to Ulaala and the rest of his pups before spring, the hunters might very well get there first and kill the whole pack. Then again, Skassi would probably move on once the weather improved, and it was difficult to say which way he would go. Spring was not now far off. Cracks of light were appearing in the long night.

'I don't know,' he said, truthfully. 'It'll require a lot of thought. We'll talk about it when you've rested.'

There was another problem which had to be considered. Although Yanthra had indicated that his mother was not happy at being told she was Skassi's mate, she and Athaba had been apart for a long time. Too long. They hardly knew each other, if the truth were to be faced, even though they had had pups. How long had they *actually* spent in one another's company? A season only. There was no reason why Ulaala should retain any feelings of loyalty towards Athaba. She might even have forgotten him. He was dead to her mind. A pup's eyes are always clouded by the certainty that its mother and father are fond of one another and wish to be together. This might not necessarily be true. Ulaala may have formed an attachment for the rogue leader. After all, even a youngster like Yanthra had been able to recognise that Skassi had immense charisma. Such personalities, however misguided and dangerous, were often fatally alluring to normal wolves. How else had Skassi managed to mobilise a huge pack of mankillers?

For his part there would never be any other mate for Athaba but Ulaala. However, he could not reasonably expect Ulaala to feel the same way about him. After all, he had 'deserted' her when she needed him most, when the pups needed both parents. When she found out he was not dead, she might even be angry with him, for allowing himself to be captured at such a time.

All this was conceivable.

He had to prepare himself for such a disappointment, but one thing was certain, he could not leave his pups to be slaughtered and he knew Ulaala would agree with him on that issue. She had told Yanthra that she planned to take him and his siblings away when the spring came. If Athaba did that for her, she could then choose whether she wanted to stay with Skassi or join him and the pups. That seemed to him to be fair. He had to give her the choice and not use the pups, who would be yearlings by then anyway, to force her back to his side.

He thought about other matters.

He might have to fight Skassi. That did not bother him as much as it should, but there were wolves who would rush to the assistance of their great leader. Athaba might be confident about a victory over Skassi (and even that was not certain, since fanatics tend to have a suicidal strength to draw on), but he certainly could not fight a whole pack. This meant he had to choose his moments very carefully indeed. It would be no good marching in and demanding the return of his pups. If he was not leapt on and torn apart at the time, the pack would be warned and ready for him.

Skassi himself seemed now to be the wolf on the tower of rock who communes with his ancestors but not his fellows. He sounded – deranged. There had been others like him in wolf history. In the end they reached a stage where they believed themselves invincible, omnipotent, unbeatable. In the end they were destroyed by themselves as much as by any enemy. If Skassi had detacheed himself from his pack and was now spiritually isolated, there would be no reason in him. His compassion would have been burned out. His uunderstanding of his kind would lie buried under the great weight of his own self-importance, his sense of a sacred trust, a mission sanctified by the voices of his ancestors. Voices that now occupied his head and drowned the sound of pack.

How had Skassi reached such a state . . .?

Chapter Twenty Eight

Skassi heard the sound of the gunfire from the middle of the frozen lake. It did not go on for long, but he knew from its repetitiveness that it was devastating. He left his quarry and raced back to the snowbanks. It took him an age to reach the spot where he knew he would find the pack. By that time the sound of the air machine was circling in from the east, but he would not have cared greatly if it had been directly overheard. There was a terrible feeling in his chest. Instinctively, he knew that the world had changed within the last few moments.

On reaching the slope where the corpses lay, he stared about him in bewilderment for a while. Then he went up to the nearest dead wolf, a womb-brother. Megilla was on his underside, the right way up, his limbs splayed out from the four corners of his body. He looked like he was forming himself into a cross. His head was flat on the ground, mandible resting on the snow, with his nose pointed to the north. The eyes were open and staring. Along his back were four large ugly holes which had oozed thick blood. This had frozen on contact with the cold air.

'Megilla,', said Skassi, nosing him under the chin.

The head flopped to the side.

Skassi went rapidly from one to the other of the pack until he was sure that they were all dead. Then he ran away from them, still in a state of shock, and wandered around for a while without any set purpose. At one point he came across Athaba's tracks in the snow and with hope fluttering in his breast, followed them. But they ended at the edge of a cliff and when Skassi looked over he could see nothing but snow beneath. He sniffed Athaba's spoor, ascertained that it was indeed his old rival, then left the place sadly. He was now convinced that he was the only member of the pack left alive.

There was the sound of the flying machine returning. The wolf hid behind a rock overhang and watched as two men go out of the machine and then threw the bodies inside. When all the corpses were in the flying machine, it took off again, slipping up and sideways into the white sky until it was lost from view.

Skassi headed south and walked for two days without a break. Then, exhausted, he fell to the ground and slept where he lay. On waking, he found himself to be extremely hungry and went on a hunt, which kept him busy. Once he had fed, however, the full impact of the last few days hit him so hard he physically staggered.

He knew he was alone.

That thought – the idea that he was alone – was almost enough to drive him mad there and then. For the first time in his life he appreciated what he had done to Athaba, when he had caused him to be banished from the pack. Yet Athaba had still trailed after the pack: knew his kin were close by. It was *the* most terrible experience, to be alone, and if there had been a cliff nearby he would have dashed over it in that moment, simply to stop the hollow ache in his heart and head. He felt as if all the space, the emptiness of the tundra, were *within* him. Somehow, all those geographical wastelands had moved from outside to inside, and his heart lay on their bleak desolate flats and ranges, enclosed by nothing.

For a long while he just kept heading south, picking up food as he went. There seemed to be a sense of purpose in him but he had no idea where he was going or why. He simply travelled through the darkness as though it were a tunnel until he came to a human village. The night that he arrived at this place, which could have been any human habitation, he rested on a hill amongst some trees and waited until dawn.

Skassi had a wakeful dream that night, of the land that he loved. The land of the caribou, moose and snowshoe hare: creatures that ran through boreal forests of white and black spruce, larch, birch and aspen. The land of the red fox that hid itself amongst alder and willow, where the air was full of raptors who used the sky as a great swing, to stoop and rise, stoop and rise, in magnificent sweeping arcs. Born to the sound of giant slabs of ice crashing together, Skassi needed no gods to awe him, no supreme beings to amaze him. The natural forces around him, that filled the sky with white dust and thunder, that populated every plain and taiga, every field of cotton grass where seas of white stretched beyond even the imagination, were enough to humble him and give him a sense of his own insignificance in the world.

He had always distrusted mysticism because he felt it robbed the wolf of his appreciation of the real world, which had wonders enough for any creature.

What beast, listening to the song of the ice, that eerie creaking as temperatures changed, could doubt that the earth was the only god? It did not matter what the season, there was always wonder over the land. Sometimes there was golden moss in the muskegs and fireweed spreading like red hot lava around the throats of broad lakes and oxbows. Sometimes the ground was covered in multicoloured berries and purple spruce cones that had dropped from their needled mothers like pieces of midnight sun. Sometimes, on windy days, there were seedling threads, wispy-white, filling the air.

Then there were the mountains, that was the great god earth rolling his shoulders slowly over seasons out of time. On the lower hills, greenery, and moving skyward the huge grey slabs of rock that supported and maintained the glaciers, winter's children.

No mysticism could match such grandeur.

Skassi was dedicated to the land in which he lived and the one dark stain upon it, that spread wider each season, was man. He intended to do something about that blemish. It was time to begin eradicating it.

The sun came up, late in the day, and Skassi left his knoll to go down amongst the houses. He went down amongst the enemy with no thought in mind at that time but to see what kind of creatures they were in their own dens. What kind of beast it was that had wiped out his whole pack in the blink of an eagle's eye. He knew they hunted wildfowl on the tundra, where the lakes were covered in ducks and geese. They ate those. He knew they liked to shoot the hare for its meat and the caribou for its coat. In that they were no different from the wolf. Why, though, sweep through a whole herd, or flock, or pack, and cut down every living thing for no apparent reason? This was the great mystery of man which he wanted to uncover.

The people remained out of sight. Then as he was passing a house a human stepped out on to a porch and down the steps to the ground. The human was watching its feet, careful of the slippery stairs and afterwards the icy street. Finally, when it was about two lengths from the wolf it looked up from its boots and met Skassi's eyes. There were a few moments during which they simply stared at each other. Then the human face twisted and it began to scream in a shrill voice. The two-legged creature's eyes were now wide and wild, and its mouth open and red. Whether man, woman or child was not evident, not to Skassi whose whole attention was taken by the noise this human made, rather than noticing height or form.

The screaming penetrated deep into Skassi's head. Skassi's brain flattened in his skull, his eyes went dark. The shrieking terrified as well as incensed him. The sound was like thorns behind his brow. He acted instinctively. He fell upon the screaming creature, swiftly tearing its throat. The act was over in a second: one lunge and then away towards the foothills.

Before he was fully up the slope above the town, a hunt was in progress. His pursuers were many. They came out, some ill-equipped, to get him before he disappeared into the wilderness.

At least, he thought, licking the blood from the corner of his mouth, they now have a reason.

How easy it had been! Why, these creatures were no more invincible than lemmings. When you caught them by surprise, they were virtually defenceless. They didn't even have horns. The arms flailed uselessly and the legs were not made for swift movement. The caribou was quicker, more formidable. They had no teeth nor claws. The hawk and the lynx were better armed.

The guns and machines made men what they were, and if you caught them without metal in their hands, they were easy kills!

Skassi escaped because it was winter. Although his pursuers returneedd to their homes and prepared themselves for a long hunt, he was by that time out of their reach, well into the mountains. He found a cave in which to hide, knowing that the falling snow would soon cover any tracks. Still in a high state of excitement, with his heart racing, he lay in the darkness of the narrow tunnel and considered his act of rebellion.

Yes, it had been so easy! This was the thing that surprised him the most. Since he had been a pup he had been taught that humans were to be avoided because they were the most dangerous animals on the earth. Yet he had wounded, perhaps killed one of these creatures, with very little effort at all. And it was over and done with so quickly it was almost frustrating. He had wanted to savour the act.

Now that he had time, he went over the attack in his mind. The human had stepped out of the dwelling, dressed in furs. From behind it, from the open habitation, had wafted a mixed human stench: a disgusting compound of odours which included sleep, food, sweat, and many other stale smells. This was so strong and revolting that Skassi almost turned and ran from it.

Skassi had no idea what sex the creature had been, or whether it had been a mature human, or one not fully grown. He had seen the look in the eyes change from puzzlement to fear, once the creature had realised that he was not a dog but a wolf. He had *smelled* the fear. It had swamped his senses, making the adrenalin surge through his body. There followed the screaming sound. Then the creature had raised its arms in front of its face, as if it knew that Skassi was about to leap, to protect itself.

That movement had acted as a trigger on Skassi's reactions.

He had felt the power jolt through his body. He sprang and though his body weight was only three-quarters that of the human, bore the biped to ground. There was noise coming from the creature's throat, but Skassi soon stopped that. He would have liked to have dragged the human along the ground, gripping with his teeth and twisting and turning the meat with his jaws, shaking it. Of course, that would have meant his own death, because the human's pack came out shortly afterwards to find out what was troubling one of its own.

The proof was now there. Humans were far from formidable foes. They were in fact extremely easy to kill, once you got them without their weapons. Skassi felt he had exploded a myth that had protected these creatures for a long time now.

Of course, if they *did* have their machines and guns with them, then men were *very* dangerous. But the times one came across them when they were unarmed were not infrequent. Perhaps their resources were finite? Maybe they only had a limited number of these weapons and if you kept on the move you could avoid those with and kill those without? There was a thought! Organise the wolves into mankilling packs.

War! War against men.

His nostrils burned with excitement. His brain swirled with fantastic images. The audacity of the idea was heart-stopping. Skassi would not only have his revenge, he would find a place of fame amongst his more illustrious ancestors. He would be a legend amongst wolves, outshining even the great warrior-priestess

Shesta who had triumphed over the dog-king Skellion Broadjaw in the battles after the *Firstdark*. To be one of the immortals!

But, he quickly reminded himself as this shining image threatened to take him over completely, his main purpose would be to teach humans a lesson. To show them that they could not massacre the pack of Skassi without being punished.

In his hole in the rock, while the air machines were searching for him, and dozens of humans tracked him on foot, he made his plans. When he came out and began looking for recruits, he found his scheme to be self-generating. He had attacked and, most likely, killed a human. Those men who had come after him had shot and killed anything that even resembled a wolf. There were now wolves in the region who had lost their mates, or pups, or pack members. He found bitterness amongst his kind and used this to gather wolves to his cause. Of course, the grieving wolves had no idea the shootings had been the result of an attack by him on the human settlement. And left to themselves they would normally have licked their wounds and found a new hunting ground. But Skassi sought them out, fuelled any anger he found with strong rhetoric. He convinced them that the time had come for wolves to make a stand, that they should fight instead of run.

'We can't ignore our dead forever,' he blazed. 'We have to honour them with retaliation. Show them we care. Put your paws in my prints, follow me, and I will show you the blood of our enemies, staining the earth . . .'

When he had five good wolves he took them to a place where two men were testing rocks with strange devices. It was a remote area, without even a road, and the wolves waited until the men were busy hunched over their work, then attacked them from all sides. The humans had not been expecting such an ambush, and one of them went down under three wolves, in a flurry of arms and legs. The other managed to get hold of a digging implement and fought back bravely, until the wolves had to let him go. They had savaged his right leg and the man had to limp his way over the landscape. So far as they knew, he survived, because they themselves were directed north-west by Skassi, who saw the need to vacate the vicinity before the place was swarming with human hunters.

With his own sense of purpose came a fervour, an intenseness, that he found was persuasive. There were many who resisted his call to the fight, but those that did come were fanatically pro-Skassi. His word amongst them was absolute law. He chose the most dedicated amongst them to be his personal bodyguard, his ever-present shoulderwolves. Over the seasons he built his pack into a powerful fighting force, which somehow managed to stay one jump ahead of any pursuit. They went for soft targets: people out on the trail armed only with small black boxes; single dwellings far from settlements; sleeping campers protected only by canvas tents.

The more humans the pack ambushed, the more wolves were hunted and killed, sometimes members of his own gang of rogues. Relatives of the dead were easy to recruit in the wake of counterattacks by the humans. The pack grew to immense proportions at times – fifty, sixty – though there were desertions in the beginning. He stopped these by tracking down wolves who had had second thoughts, slaughtering them, and feeding them to the ravens.

As the pack grew, so Skassi withdrew from his creation more and more, until he would only venture down amongst them on such occasions as a long march or big battle. His bodyguards fiercely protected his isolation and became silent powerful figures themselves.

One of the reasons Skassi withdrew into himself was because when he was down among his wolves, he began to have doubts about whether he was doing the right thing. Not doubts about killing humans, but concerning whether he should have taken these hunters from their various homes and turned them into warriors. The term 'hunter-warrior' had always been used, but until Skassi had formed his pack it was more a reverent title than an accurate description. Now there were wolves who really were 'warriors' in the old sense of the word. Skassi was responsible for this and hated the immense guilt that went with the uniqueness of his creation. Had he still been a headwolf of a conventional pack, he would have had an accepted traditional framework of laws within which he could govern. As it was, he had to make his own rules, and he spent much of his time brooding over decisions – whether they were right or wrong – his thoughts evolving into circular obsessive arguments which never went outside his own head. He had no other wolf he trusted enough to discuss such issues with and scorned advice from those close to him. His shoulderwolves, the guardians, he regarded as loyal but lacking in the sort of higher consciousness that was necessary to consider such lofty matters. He knew that any attempt at discussing motives, and rights or wrongs, with other wolves would only put doubts into their minds about their leader's sacred mission. 'If Skassi isn't sure,' he could imagine them thinking, 'why are we doing this thing?'

No, it was essential that he gave an outward show of being utterly dedicated to the overthrow of man; absolutely convinced of the purity and rightness of their cause; completely self-assured and confident. To display less than these was dangerous to the whole enterprise. So the irresolution had to remain hidden. The brooding had to appear to be something else: the great leader considering weighty matters, affairs beyond the ken of normal wolves. He had to detach himself from them so that his uncertainties did not sow seeds of doubt amongst his warriors.

Unfortunately, his solitude fed those very things which had forced him apart from his pack and he knew that his reason would be eroded by them if he was not strong. So, he spent nights in vigil, convoking his self-esteem and instilling within himself a sense of his own importance, his own uniqueness. He often dreamed about his old pack. It was as if those wolves of his younger days were the last of a pure breed. Once they had left the world there remained behind only rogues and ruffians. He had a very strong feeling that Athaba was still alive. That his enemy of yesterseason was still roaming the land, scavenging, fighting, hunting, surviving in the way that Athaba knew best. When they had both been members of the same pack and Skassi had been respectable, he would have had as little as possible to do with the *utlah*, Athaba. Now he was a mankiller, however, the situation had changed. He needed terrible rogues like his old pack enemy. Give him a dozen Athabas and he would have no need for all these motley wolves that came to him these days. Athaba may have been a mystic and a deviant, but he was also a ferocious and fearless warrior. Such wolves were hard to find. Not only that, he was blood kin. Skassi missed his old pack so very much. To be able to talk to a blood cousin again, one who remembered the old names, why that would be worth the moon.

So Skassi dreamed, and grew more disdainful of his followers, grew more distant from them as the nights passed. By the time he had recruited Ulaala he was beyond the reach of any criticism or advice.

291

When spring was not far off, Skassi called his pack together and told them they were going south.

'The humans in this region will gather in strength and come looking for us once the passes are open to them. We have to keep on the move, stay ahead of them. They will expect us to go north, to use the protection of the weather, but we will go down amongst them and wreak havoc. Tomorrow we set forth across the raw country for the forests of black spruce where the beautiful saxifrage and lousewort grow, where the pine needles spike the soft light of morning. I shall lead you, my hunter-warriors, to great victories in the south and your names will be whispered amongst the living with awe and amongst the dead with reverence. You are the chosen ones who will liberate the world.'

A great howling of approval followed this announcement which, typical of Skassi's recent speeches, was delivered in a high lofty tone. Since the last summer such communications had become grand and eloquent, touched with sentiment and studded with colourful phrases.

Once the howling was over, Skassi returned to his resting place on the tower of rock to brood on his decision.

The next morning they set off through the mountains, heading south. The pups, almost yearlings, were encouraged to keep up with gentle nips. Swiftly and silently, they travelled across frozen landscape pausing only to form brief hunts and provide themselves with food.

Skassi travelled at the head of his numbers, his shoulderwolves around him like the four points of the compass, preventing any contact with the rest of the pack. Orders were sent back through them, since Skassi would not speak directly to ordinary wolves once they were on the trail.

Just before they left the mountains, while they were still in a deep pass, they had a Howling. Five wolves formed a chorus and there were to be solos by several others, including Skassi. Although the headwolf remained aloof from the pack the majority of the time, he still regarded his own voice as superior to most others, and like all artists wished to share his gift with the less fortunate. During a pause between songs, there was an ominous rumbling from above.

'What's that, thunder?' said one of the listeners.

'Quiet!' commanded a shoulderwolf. 'The chorus is about to begin the second howling.'

The ground began shaking at that point and the noise from above became louder. Small lumps of snow fell, exploding into powder on impact with the ground. Suddenly, the wolf that had been told to remain silent, shouted.

'AVALANCHE!'

The slopes above responded to his yell with a roar of their own and then wolves were running in all directions. Mostly, they headed for the exit to the valley, running at right angles to the descending tons of snow. Some, however, tried to outrun the flow. They ran further down the slopes in their panic and were engulfed in the monstrous flood of white. It took their racing feet from under them, flowed over them, buried them, and then proceeded to pile itself on top to a crushing thickness.

Those that ran counter to the avalanche managed to reach safety. Among these were Skassi, Ulaala and the pups. They turned, to see nothing behind them but a vast overspill of white snowpowder, which filled the air with sparkling clouds. Finally, when it had all settled, the face of the land had changed shape. It was smooth and flat and hid several more secrets beneath it.

'Shall we try digging them out?' cried Nidra.

Skassi asked, 'How many?'

A flankwolf did a count.

'Six of us missing,' he said.

Skassi said, 'They can't have survived such a fall. It might take us days to dig them out and they'll be dead by that time anyway. We have to leave them.'

'But,' cried Ulaala, 'what if one of them is near to the surface? Shouldn't we at least try?'

'A waste of time,' said Skassi.

Again, Ulaala tried to protest, but received a body-slam from one of the shoulderwolves. She was hustled into line, and the pups with her, and the march south continued. She heard Skassi remark to one of his guardians, 'Six is not too bad. We were lucky. Not a disaster, anyway.'

'Unless you happen to be one of them,' she called, unable to help herself, and received another slam. Skassi ignored her. She had noticed that he had the ability to pretend deafness when he did not wish to comment on something.

There were no more incidents until they reached the tree line.

293

Chapter Twenty Nine

Yanthra and Athaba set out on the trail towards Skassi's strong-hold just as the snow was beginning to slip from the slopes. The pair of them moved cautiously, careful not to go too close to the edge of the track in case a fall of snow took them by surprise and carried them into the drop. They travelled quickly, without pausing to hunt, having eaten a day previously.

When they reached the site of the den they found it had been vacated, probably a few days previously.

'We're too late,' said Yanthra in despair.

Athaba replied, 'Don't worry. We'll follow them wherever they've gone. The trail will still be fresh enough to leave a scent, especially by such a large pack of wolves.'

So, they sniffed out the direction and found it to be south. Then they set off in pursuit, hoping to catch the pack before it got too far. However, just when they were getting close Athaba had one of his fits. This was such a bad experience for Yanthra that the young wolf ran off and hid in the rocks. It took Athaba a day to find the pup.

Yanthra began trembling the moment Athaba discovered where he was crouched.

'Don't come near me,' he said.

Athaba was both upset and shaken. The fit had been a bad one and had left him weak. He knew he must have looked quite devilish, as he lay on the ground twitching and convulsing. It had obviously scared his son quite a lot. He himself could remember nothing, of course, except the dreams he always had during these bouts which were vivid and not always unpleasant. Ulaala had once described to him what he looked like when he went through a series of these paroxysms.

'You shouldn't be afraid of your own father,' said Athaba. 'I could never harm you.'

'Well, what is it then? What were you doing? I thought you'd been poisoned, or shot, or something. Your eyes went all white.

294

They rolled upwards. And you were shaking so bad your teeth rattled. What was it?'

'When I was not much older than you, Yanthra, I fought with a bear. Skassi was there too. He was the one that got us into trouble in the first place, just as he's getting a lot of wolves into deep problems now. We had to attack the bear to get him to let Skassi go, because he was being squeezed to death. Unfortunately, I got swiped. Have you ever seen a bear's paw, son? Not close up. Well, I can tell you it's as big as a wolf's head, and a lot harder. I felt as if I had been clouted with a tree trunk. My head buzzed. I lost track of time and what I thought had been a few days, turned out to be nearly a month.

'Anyway, as a result of that bear hitting me, I began to get fits. That's what you saw me having – a fit. It doesn't mean anything except that I lose control of my muscles for a while. That's all. Once it's over, everything's back to normal.'

'But your tongue was hanging out. It was horrible. All slavery.'

'Just as I said, I lose control of myself for a while. It doesn't hurt me, except that sometimes I bite my tongue. Luckily I haven't bitten it off yet, so I can still tell you about this . . .' The attempt at humour failed because Yanthra still crouched at the bottom of the hole in which he had hidden himself, and seemed determined to stay there.

'Are you coming out?' asked Athaba.

'I don't know. I'm still scared.'

'Well, that's honest enough. The wolves of my pack at the time it happened were *so* scared they banished me. We wolves don't like the unusual.'

Yanthra said, 'Will I catch what you've got?'

'Certainly not. It's not that kind of an illness. It's physical, like a broken leg. You think your mother would have stayed with me if she thought her pups would be exposed to a nasty condition like this?'

'Maybe she hasn't seen you do that?'

'I can assure you she has.'

After a long while the pup was persuaded to leave the hole and then the pair of them went back to the trail. Yanthra still kept glancing at his father from time to time, as if he expected Athaba to have another of his fits while they walked. Athaba noticed these sidelooks and guessed that his son was still wary,

295

so he chatted about trivial matters, trying to distract the yearling. He was not successful. In the end, he turned and said in exasperation, 'Look, I'm not going to perform for you again today. These little acts only come when they want to, and they're always months apart, so if you want further entertainment you'll have to wait a long while. Is that understood? I'll let you know when the clowning is about to start again, and you can prepare yourself in plenty of time. I promise you next time I'll put on a really good show, just for you, all right?'

Yanthra got the message and hung his head.

They were both extremely thirsty by this time and not a little hungry. They found a thin stream that dropped from a ledge like a twisted vine, and satisfied their thirst. Then they each went off in search of voles and lemmings, to put their hunger to rest. When they rejoined each other, the younger wolf seemed to have calmed down.

'I'm sorry, father,' he apologised.

'Not your fault. I should have told you. Your mother used to keep you away from me when I had a fit, so you had no reason to know.'

'Did Skassi *really* banish you.'

'He and the rest of the pack. I was terribly distressed and angry at the time, but now . . . well, it was a long time ago. I suppose you could say I'm still an *utlah*. Once an outcast, always an outcast. The ravens used to call me "Outcast" and it became my name for a while.'

'Ravens? You knew some of the ravens?'

'Knew them? Why, we ate regularly together. We discussed life and its ways over the carcass of a musk ox or caribou. We picked through the bones of moose and put the world to rights.'

'You ate *carrion* father?'

'Nothing wrong with that.'

'Oh. I thought there was.'

'You mean you had been *told* there was, which is quite a different thing from thinking it out yourself. Never take anything you're told as being fact, son, unless you've considered it carefully yourself and come to your own conclusions. It doesn't matter if you're eventually wrong, so long as *you* made the decision and didn't rely on received opinion. Take note of *advice*, but decide for yourself. Now, we have to get back on the trail. If we wait around here, midnight's sun will catch up with us.'

296

'Midnight's son? Is that Skassi?'

Athaba looked at his pup and saw the innocence in his eyes.

'No, but it could be,' he said.

They found the place where the avalanche had occurred and there was a wolf there which had dug herself out. She was staggering around, still in a daze, after having spent some time under a weight of snow. As they approached her, they could see her knocking into firs and dislodging the snow held by the branches. When this fell on her in great wads of white, she jumped in the air, probably under the impression that another avalanche was in progress. They managed to calm her down and she told them her story.

'I was bringing up the rear. The tailwolf – horrible position but I'm under punishment for stealing meat – and then I heard this thunder. I looked up and saw the whole mountain moving, down on us. I ran forward, then backwards, panicking a little. By that time the snow was rolling over me like water. I struggled, then it went black. I think I must have been right on the edge because there wasn't a lot of snow above me, I don't think. The only thing was, I couldn't breathe, and it seemed to take ages to dig out sideways.'

Her eyes were round with fear.

'I could have been digging the wrong way, couldn't I? I could have gone *into* the mountain, instead of away from it.'

'Always better to trust your instinct,' said Athaba. 'Anyway, you're all right now. Do you want to accompany us to Skassi? We're on our way to join the pack.'

She shook her head.

'No. No. I've had enough. My heart was never in it anyway. I'm going back to my old pack, what's left of it. Most of them are with Skassi, but some stayed behind. A few of the old ones. I'm going back . . . I don't care if he hunts me down,' she added fiercely. 'You can tell him that, if you wish. I've really had enough.'

'I shan't tell anything,' said Athaba. 'So far as Skassi knows, you're still under the snow.'

Her eyes lost a little of their wildness.

'Thank you,' she said.

She left them, staggering back along the trail whence they had come. Athaba wondered whether she was ever going to make it. Someone who had survived an avalanche, however, might not be in good physical shape, but their mental reserves would be high. There is a kind of elation that follows a trial, immediately afterwards, and this is a deep source of energy.

The two male wolves continued on, past the valley.

It seemed that Skassi was never going to stop. It was over a month before Yanthra and Athaba reached a heavily forested hill that stood above a wide plain. It was a solitary height, not quite of mountain status, but imposing just the same. There were rocky outcrops on its slopes and clearings where the granite was exposed above the topsoil. Most of it was tree covered, however, even on the crest. It was on this summit that the pack appeared to be resting.

Even as Athaba and Yanthra reached the lower slopes of this wooded hideout, they were aware of a flying machine that was buzzing back and forth above the landscape. Skassi seemed to have walked right into the heart of hunter country on purpose. It appeared he was no longer interested in soft targets, he wanted to meet the human hunters on their own ground. It was suicide.

Athaba and Yanthra tracked the pack to the top of the rounded hill, but did not at first venture into the denning area. Athaba wanted to scout the surrounds before they revealed their presence to the other wolves. He told Yanthra to stay clear of the summit and to familiarise himself with the hill and its secrets, especially around the midriff of the slope.

At noon on the second day after their arrival Yanthra came to his father. He looked concerned, though to his credit he was not panicking. His news was grave.

'We're surrounded, father,' he said. 'There are men coming from the plains. They're all around us I think. I was out hunting and I did a circuit. Their scent is everywhere. They must be coming to do battle with Skassi.'

'Not so much a battle as a slaughter,' said Athaba.

He went out and reconnoitred on his own, keeping to the base of the hill, but testing the wind with his nose. From a high vantage point, he saw them in the distance, a curve of hunters wearing camouflaged jackets and hats, surrounding the hill. They were closing slowly, making sure nothing slipped through their cordon.

Athaba returned to where his son was waiting.

'I think you're right,' he said. 'They're moving in. They won't be able to see, hear or smell them from on top of the hill, and it doesn't look as though Skassi has posted any sentries down here. I wonder if he wants it this way? Why go up amongst the pines, where you can't use your senses to the best advantage? The smell of the rising sap is overpowering at this time of year and the ground is soft with pine needles. The trees provide cover for the hunters. Either Skassi is useless at this kind of thing, which I know he's not, or this confrontation is part of his scheme.'

'What are we going to do?'

'Well, we can't save them all, Yanthra. We'll be lucky to get away ourselves. We have to think of your brothers and sisters – and you of course.

'While you were out hunting this morning I was searching some of the upper slopes for a hiding place. I've found this small cave – just a crack in the rock really – faced by a tall boulder and well hidden. It was my intention to get the pups – sorry, yearlings now eh? – to get you all into that cave and then destroy your scent trail with my own, so that Skassi couldn't find you.'

Yanthra looked at his father with an accusing eye.

'How were you and Ulaala going to get away?'

'Well, you must accept that your mother might not want to go with us. She may have decided to stay. I *hope* she comes with us, but I can't force her. She's a wolf with a will of her own. If she does come, she can go with you in the cave. One of us has to throw Skassi off the scent and that's got to be me. I was going to run, down the hill, and lead them a dance out on the plains.'

Yanthra said, 'But you can't do that now. The whole area is full of hunters. You'll be shot out in the open.'

'I'll think of something. Now, what you have to do, is this . . .' and he outlined his plan, making sure Yanthra knew the part he was to play. When they had talked it over and refined it, the pair of them set off towards the peak of the hill.

As they walked they chatted.

'If we don't meet up again, though I'm sure we will,' said Athaba, 'I want you get word to your mother. Tell her the story of my disappearance and say I would never have left her on purpose. I think she knows that, but I want you to tell her anyway. Also, I've got a riddle for you to solve. Listen,

299

I am:

The stone that floats,
the wood that sinks
the rock that runs
the air that stinks.

What am I?

Yanthra stared at his father with a worried expression.

'I don't know. Is this a test, Athaba? If I fail, what happens?'

'Nothing happens. No, it's not a test. It's just a bit of fun. My father told me that rhyme, not long before he died. I never did work it out, not for myself. I had to have help in the end. *Now* I know what it means, of course. In those days, a puzzle like that was dangerous, because the pack Skassi and I came from did not like anything that sounded mystical. My father took a chance in playing the game with me, because if someone had heard, or I had mentioned it, they would have . . . well, he would have been in for a bad time. They were an ignorant pack, you see, and afraid of anything new, anything which required an understanding which was not born of practical everyday things. Progress in that direction was frowned upon. You weren't expected to use your mind for such things as mystical riddles, only for improving your hunting skills. Things like that . . .'

'So you won't scold me if I get it wrong?' asked Yanthra.

'No, of course not. You take your time, son, think it over. In a few seasons from now, you might . . .'

'Is it a *volcano*?'

Athaba pulled himself up short.

'Who told you that? Who told you? Was it your mother?'

Yanthra looked at his father innocently.

'No. I never heard it before. I just guessed. When we were with Skassi's pack, the wolves came from all over the land. Some of them talked about pumice stone which floats like wood. And I was told that where the earth cracks open, on some islands in the south, there is a stuff called lava which is white hot rock that flows like water . . . I just guessed. You're not angry?'

Athaba was aware he seemed huffy.

'No, no, not *angry*. Just surprised. I thought . . . I thought it would take you longer, that's all.'

300

'Sorry, father. Tell me another one and I'll savour it for a while.'

'I don't know any more,' replied Athaba.

'What about if I give you one? Um, what is it that draws circles in the sky, but leaves no marks?'

'Look,' said Athaba, relieved. 'We're coming to the end of the trail. The den must be just ahead. Now remember what I've told you.'

'You don't know, do you?'

'Don't know what?'

'The answer to my riddle.'

'I've no time for games now, son. This is serious business.'

'Oh,' said Yanthra, and he sounded disappointed.

'All right,' sighed Athaba, 'what is it? I'll never guess in a million seasons.'

'An eagle! Mother told us that. Clever isn't it?'

'Very clever,' Athaba snorted. 'Now, pay attention to our plan. Remember what to do.'

'Yes father.'

Chapter Thirty

With Yanthra close behind him and wanting to create as much of a diversion as necessary, Athaba walked right into the centre of the wolves. They had known he was there, of course. They would have scented the presence of two strange wolves in the vicinity, but since there were only two, against forty-three, there was little reason for the pack to be alarmed. This was one pack that was always open to new members. In any case, one of the two was hardly a stranger. He was a yearling that had deserted them.

Athaba stopped and looked around him. Skassi had chosen a forested spot. Underfoot was a thick layer of dead pine needles, forming a soft brown cushion. That was bad. Hunters could approach without being heard. The aroma of sap and pine needles was in the air, almost overpowering. That was also not good. Any attacking huntsmen could come from downwind and would have to stink for their scent to penetrate the smell of the conifers.

The sun came through the canopy of needles and patterned the ground beneath with shadows. Amongst these dark and light patches, lay many wolves, and around these wolves were the bones of several kills. Athaba's first impression of them was that they had slipped into apathy, but he knew he must be mistaken. This pack had so far outwitted the armies of hunters that had now tracked them down and ringed the mountain. They were simply resting before the next battle. This was their way of recouping, re-energising. They were a wanted gang of ripthroats and mankillers whose deeds would be sung by descendants, but whose season on earth was coming to an end. The world of men had been mobilised against them. The slopes below were crawling with trigger-happy gunmen who would turn over every stone, push aside every stem of cotton grass, lift even the mosses, until this pack was slaughtered to a wolf.

Suddenly, Athaba caught a whiff of a scent he thought he had forgotten. Ulaala! The conscious mind may have lost the fragrance of that she-wolf, but not the subconscious. He realised then that

302

he had been desperately hoping for that aroma to find his nostrils. It seemed he had been searching for that scent for seasons out of time. Now he had it and his mind reeled for a moment. He had told Yanthra to give Ulaala the choice of whether or not to accompany Mook, Wassal, Riffel and Grisenska, but now he wished he had said, "Insist on her coming. Say I hold her to all her promises. Tell her I'm sorry I was taken from her. Tell her anything, son, so long as she comes with you." But it was too late to change his mind. Yanthra had his instructions: lead out his brothers and sisters when the chance came and take them to the cave, lower down the hillside. "If your mother wishes to accompany you, all well and good, but don't press her," he had said.

Then he saw her, standing just a few lengths away. Her grey eyes were on him. He almost ran to her, licked her muzzle, shouted his joy at seeing her again after all those seasons. Instead he stood there, believing that his feelings were foolishly exposed for all to see, in his wooden stance, his awkward pose. He could express nothing. The words rushed to his throat, but there were too many, they jammed there, locked solid. There was a wish that others would stop their staring, get on with whatever tasks they were doing. It would have been easier to show his anger towards them than open himself to her.

Finally, it was she who spoke first.

'It *is* you?'

Her expression changed from perplexity to something else, something he had been hoping to see. In her face was a kind of hurt delight, as if she wanted to scold him, but was too overcome with emotion to say very much at all. He remembered then that she thought him dead and realised how much more difficult this was for her than it was for him. Her mate had strolled into the pack as if he had just been out hunting, gone perhaps a day, instead of back from the dead after several seasons.

'Yes,' he replied, simply.

Seeing her now, the journeys came back to him: seemingly endless treks over tundra and mountain, through snow and ice, in wind and rain. He remembered his bleeding pads, when he had been footsore, his flesh weary, his bones feeling as if they had been rammed together by some uncaring creature who wanted him to suffer. He recalled the agonising loneliness of the trail, the long, long nights, the dull days. The sight of her brought

303

back the times he had gone hungry simply because he would rather be nearer to his goal than spend the time to hunt. There were those times when hope had flared like sun in his breast, only to be extinguished shortly afterwards. Times when his mental and spiritual reserves were all but exhausted, yet still he knew he had to force his body forwards.

Yet now, now he saw that they had all been worth it.

'I thought, you were dead,' she said in a accusing tone.

'So did I,' he remarked wryly. 'It's not something I can tell you in a few moments, but I was captured by a man that day I left the den, and have been searching for you ever since.'

'It's good to see you,' she said, and he knew she meant it and that it would be all right between them.

At that point a sturdy-looking wolf came up to Yanthra.

'The deserter has returned, has he? I suppose you think you can work your way back into the pack by bringing along this broken down old flea-carrier? There's punishment due, yearling.'

'Who's this overbearing she-wolf?' asked Athaba of his son.

Yanthra scratched himself nervously behind the ear.

'This is Nidra.'

Athaba stared the formidable she-wolf in the eyes. He would not like to have to fight such a strong *mega*. He was getting too old for fights and she looked vicious. Other wolves were gathering around them now, and a lean male, probably one of Skassi's shoulderwolves, had come down from the summit of the hill. There was a hostile atmosphere building up. Ulaala came to his side. So did a tough-looking yearling with more meat on her than Yanthra had on him. This had to be his pup, Grisenska, the largest of his brood. He nodded approvingly at her. Then he turned his attention back to Nidra.

'You really should find out who you're speaking to before you wade in,' he said to the female. 'There are some wolves on this earth who look ragged and beaten because they've recently conquered the world. Some wolves have no need to look fit and strong because there's nothing they haven't done, and couldn't do again, and nowhere they haven't been, and couldn't return to if they wished. You don't take on the world and chew it up, to come away looking like you look now. Once you've done that, you look like I do.'

'You've conquered the world?' she sneered, but with less confidence than she had shown before.

304

'In a manner of speaking. You force me to brag. I've fought with bears and walked away. I've killed wolves larger than you. I've humbled one you hold in great awe, though to tell you his name would be poor manners on my part. I've travelled to the edge of the earth and back. I've fought with men in their own dens, and snatched their food from under their noses . . .'

'Have you ever killed a man?' she cried.

'No, but I've tamed one. I've taken a man and turned him into a wolf, turned him into a useful member of my pack. It's easy to kill. Try capturing a man and making him your own.'

'I don't believe you,' she snarled.

'I would if I were you, Nidra,' said a voice from behind her.

She whirled and Athaba looked up, at the same time his olfactory memory gave him further recognition signals.

Standing on the edge of the clearing was Skassi. A leaner, more rugged wolf than Athaba had left behind so long ago, but Skassi just the same. His coat had lost the sheen of the early years and his eyes looked weary and worldworn. He was flanked by two wolves who looked even more formidable than Nidra. They had shoulders to put a musk ox to shame. They looked as if they could crack rocks with their jaws.

'Come up, brother. It's good to see you,' said Skassi.

Nidra was looking as if a boulder had struck her between the eyes and she repeated, '*Brother?*'

'The wolf he told you he had humbled, was me. This is one of the old breed of wolves, one of the great ones. He has done all he said, and more. Look at him. Look at me. Do you not think we resemble one another? We have the same blood. We have the same spirit. Once we were enemies, because we were both ambitious. We come from a lineage that gives not a mote to rival, not a speck of dust, if it means stepping down. We have ancestors that walk the Far Forests with fire in their eyes. This is my brother, Athaba.'

'Athaba!' said several of the surrounding wolves at once, and there was awe in their voices.

They stepped back, giving him space, opening a path through the pines, to where Skassi stood. Nidra continued to stare at him with narrowed eyes, but eventually stepped aside herself. Obviously Skassi had passed on stories about him, had turned him into something of a legend. There was a touch of irony in that, considering what they had been to each other in the past. Athaba realised that as the only other surviving member of Skassi's old pack, he had to be more than just a wolf. If he was Skassi's 'brother' he had to be almost a god. He was glad now that he had bragged to Nidra about his exploits. Skassi would approve of that.

He began to walk towards Skassi.

'Brother is it, you old rogue?' he called. 'You didn't call me brother when we fought in single combat, those times back in seasons lost. I seem to recall that I was also humbled by you. No one's mentioned *that* yet. So far it's a draw – one each. Maybe we'll get to fight again before we die and find out which of us is the real wolf, and which the fake.'

There was a murmur amongst the avenue of wolves at this speech. Athaba knew what they were thinking. *He had dared to call our leader 'an old rogue'. He has the audacity to suggest he might be 'a fake'. Surely Skassi will have him torn to pieces?*

'Ah, but in the first fight,' called Skassi, 'I had the weight advantage. You were only a yearling then.'

'And in the second, I had nothing to lose, and you had everything. Yet you walked away with your dignity.'

'We were always too dignified for our own good.'

'And look at us now. Two moth-eaten old pelts held together by nothing but deeds past.'

Skassi shook his head, sagely.

'There are glories yet to come, brother, of which you can be part if you so wish. I would like my kin by my side. Not of the same womb, but of the same muscle and sinew . . .'

They were now face to face.

'Come and talk,' said Skassi, after a moment.

'We haven't got much time,' said Athaba. 'The hunters are working their way up the mountain. There are too many of them this time. We'll be cut down.'

'Perhaps, but there's still time to talk. Come up to the summit. We can watch their progress from there, and talk at the same time. You're looking fit!.'

'I'm looking terrible,' remarked Athaba, 'and you know it. *You* look terrible too.'

'Then we'll terrorise them with our joint appearance,' said Skassi. 'Come. Tell me about your travels. Your mate thought you were dead, you know. I said you weren't. I told her, they have to be giants to kill wolves like Athaba, and there have been no giants on the earth since *Groff* turned to mist . . .'

The pair of them walked through the fragrant-smelling pines to the peak of the mountain, where the winds wheeled and the air was clear. They passed no sprinkling of alpine flowers or scattering of dead cones without a sniff or a glance, and were for all the world like two wolves out for a daily stroll, with nothing more serious on their minds than the brightness of the sun and the aroma of the morning.

Athaba recounted his adventures to his old enemy, watching Skassi's expression changing as each new event was unfolded. On the summit they lay and talked, about Skassi's trials, about Athaba's tribulations, and about old times with the pack when they were both still young and in tune with their bones, with their muscles.

Skassi said, 'But this Koonama? I find it difficult to believe that a wolf can tame a man.'

'Not so much a wolf taming a man, but the man having to adapt to brutal forces of nature. If he had not changed, he would have died, and I think he knew that. But you? You really are a killer of men? If wolves do not train men, they don't kill them either.'

'Plenty of wolves have killed men.'

'But not sought them out, hunted them down. This is a very unwolflike thing to do, Skassi. You should give it up. You're leading all these other wolves into forbidden areas, on foolishly dangerous enterprises. Don't you see that? Can't you see how wrong it is to condemn these creatures to death?'

'They know what they're doing.'

'Only partly,' said Athaba. 'It's *you* they're doing it for, not themselves. They're not dedicated to your cause – they're dedicated to *you*, Skassi. You've got them mesmerised.'

Skassi, who had been getting irritated by Athaba's questioning, seemed to be pleased by this remark.

'Yes, it's true that I have a certain persuasive power over them, but the cause is good and right. I don't feel guilty about using any power I have to further that cause. Have you forgotten what men did to our pack? Our brothers and sisters, our kin? You and I are cousins, Athaba. Surely the same fury runs through your veins as does mine? I was hoping you would join me. Share the responsibility for heading this pack.'

307

Athaba wondered whether his son had yet managed to lead Grisenska, Mook, Wassal and Riffel out of the camp. He hoped they were well on their way to the small camouflaged hole, halfway down the mountain. Perhaps Ulaala was with them?

'I'm very honoured, Skassi. I mean that. Under any other circumstances, finding you alive and wanting me to join you – why, I would have been ecstatic. But I find this situation, I don't know, *unnatural* I suppose. Yes I felt the same terrible fury. When I saw our pack slaughtered I was blind with hate and hopelessness, even though I had not been part of the group for many seasons. I can't even imagine how *you* felt. It must have knocked your world off kilter. But this is not the answer to such feelings. Wolves do not organise wolves to hunt down men. It's not in our nature.'

Skassi's eyes narrowed and flicked to his two shoulderwolves who lay not far off.

'If you think it's unnatural, you must believe me to be insane. I once accused you of mysticism. I wasn't wrong then, but you seem to have changed a lot – sloughed your aura of magic like a snakeskin – so much so that now you appear to be accusing me of a similar vice. A mad wolf is a mystical wolf. There's no getting round that fact. Are you accusing me of being mad?'

'*Accuse* is the wrong word . . .' as Athaba was speaking there was a commotion amongst the pack below the trees. He pretended he had not heard this, since Skassi seemed to be taking little notice of it either. One of the shoulderwolves got up and wandered a few paces down the track to the den, but stopped there and merely listened for a while. Athaba continued '. . . I believe you are mistaken in your actions, that's all. This is not for the good of the pack, Skassi, this is for your own vengeance. It will feed no wolves, nor will it keep the pack safe. Quite the opposite in fact.'

Skassi shook his big-boned head.

'You disappoint me, brother.'

'I'm sorry . . .'

At that moment a wolf came hurtling through the trees.

'Skassi! Skassi! Hunters, below.'

The creature came skidding to a halt in front of them. Skassi motioned to his shoulderwolves that it was all right, and then turned his attention on the agitated intruder.

'Slowly,' he said. 'Now, what's this? Hunters?'

'Humans – guns – dozens – coming up – the slopes.'

Skassi was on his feet now.

'Up the hill?' he turned his savage expression on Athaba.
'You? You led them here?'

Athaba said, 'No, of course not. Why should I do that, and trap myself as well?'

'But you must have known they were coming.'

'I knew they were there, that's all. Yanthra and I were caught inside the ring before we even began climbing up here. We were surrounded. There's nothing I could have done. They were all round the hill. There's no way through them.'

'You could have warned me.'

'I could have, but I didn't. Now you know, without having to rely on information from me.'

There was still menace in the expression.

'Then why are you here?'

Athaba remained silent, but the messenger from the pack answered for him. He seemed strangely reticent and shame-faced as he delivered the following statement.

'The she-wolf, Ulaala, and her pups. They've disappeared. Nidra went after them, but hasn't returned.'

'This too? Why wasn't I told?' growled Skassi. He shook his head violently, as if he had warble flies in his ears. 'What's happening here? Communication seems to have broken down.'

'We – we didn't want to disturb you,' said the wolf. 'We thought we could handle things without bothering you.'

Athaba said, 'You're paying the price of distancing yourself from your pack now, Skassi. They were frightened of disturbing you. They would rather face your wrath later than sooner. You can't sit up here in the clouds and still have the same sort of control as a headwolf who sleeps amongst the pack. You've let it slip away from you.'

'I don't need lessons from you,' said Skassi.

The messenger was looking from one to the other of them. There was the sound of a rifle crack from lower down the slopes. Probably a trigger-happy hunter shooting at a hare breaking. The messenger said to his leader.

'We have to do something – organise – quickly,' he said.

Skassi motioned at Athaba.

'Kill this one,' he said.

'What?' cried the younger wolf. He stared at his leader in disbelief. 'This is the legendary Athaba. There's no time . . .' he looked behind him. 'The hunters . . . we have to . . .'

At that moment one of the shoulderwolves started forward, towards Athaba, his guard hairs bristling. He ran in a straight line and Athaba crouched to receive this onslaught. None of the other wolves moved. The second shoulderwolf merely watched her mate, as if she felt he could deal with this affair without her help. Athaba stared intently as the big male came flying through the mottled shadows. The shoulderwolf's lips were curled back, revealing his teeth, and there was a redness in his eyes that spoke of a brain which breathed the mist of death. There was nothing that would stop him now, not even a command from his headwolf. His mind had locked into the action of attack and his movements were almost mechanical in nature, though fluid in motion.

When he was about three lengths from Athaba, he suddenly spun over sideways, several times. There followed the sound of a shot immediately afterwards. Surprise, shock and agony appeared on the victim's face and remained in his expression as he climbed slowly to his feet. He looked at Athaba, accusingly, as if Athaba had been responsible for inflicting the wound. Then a second shot took him in the shoulder and once more he twisted, sinking on to his belly where he stood.

'They're here . . .' cried the messenger, unnecessarily. Then he too kicked up his back legs as he received a blast from a shotgun. Athaba slipped into the trees with Skassi close behind him. The pair of them dropped down low, into some undergrowth, and waited. Athaba's heart was beating fast. Skassi growled in a low voice, 'This is your doing.'

'No, it was your presence that brought them here. Now be quiet. You're a fool, Skassi.'

'We'll settle this later.'

'Quiet . . .'

They could hear the sounds of shots all round them now, and men were barking at each other. A wolf ran crashing through the bracken, seemingly blind, and into a row of saplings. A withering fire snicked through the young trees, cutting many of them to stumps, sending chips of wood and stone zinging through the air. Several more barks followed and a man thumped by in big boots, his feet missing Athaba's nose by fractions.

When he had gone, Athaba began sneaking down the hillside, heading towards the small cave within which he hoped was his family. Skassi came after him, keeping close to the ground.

Obviously his old pack brother was not so mad he wished to be executed along with all the other rogues that were lying around the slopes, pumping out their wolfblood on the pine needles.

Several times the pair of them had to stop and hide in thick brambles and ground cover, using the shadows to keep them from the poor eyes and even poorer noses of the human hunters. Noise was their biggest problem, but they were wolves enough to be able to use the mosses as padding whenever they could, and to avoid any dead branches. They slipped between old logs and under the arches of fallen branches, using their noses to guide them through the hunters.

The men themselves seemed to have broken the ring they used to surround the hill and were now in groups, crunching through the forests, turning this way and that, and probably more cautious now since there was a chance of being shot in error by one of their own kind. They kept calling from group to group, no doubt to ensure this kind of mistake did not happen, at the same time watching the shadows carefully for movements.

From time to time, shots were heard, echoing through the spruces. Each time this happened Athaba's heart jumped, thinking, 'That might be my young ones!' but hoping that his pack had made it to the cave under the guidance of his mate Ulaala.

When the pair of them were over halfway to the hole, they came across the carcass of a wolf. It was Nidra. She had not been shot. Her throat was torn open.

'Ulaala!' said Athaba.

Skassi muttered, 'That's not Ulaala . . . oh, I see. You think she killed Nidra?'

'She may be hurt. *That's* what I'm thinking.'

'She's dead, for certain. The hunters will have got her. She can't have got through.'

Athaba said, 'She doesn't need to get through. There's a hidden cave halfway down the slope. My son Yanthra has led them to the entrance and with any luck they're holed up there now.'

'I see . . .' said Skassi.

They continued through the ferns and bracken, slipping quietly along, staying under the canopy of the lower greenery. Finally, there was just a sunlit glade in between them and the rock overhang which hid the cave. Athaba stopped on the edge of the clearing. Crossing it was clearly going to be the most dangerous part of the journey. There was absolutely no cover and the

311

sunbeams would pick out and spotlight any creature going from one side to the other. He collected his thoughts, wondering whether to make a dash for it, or go cautiously, stealthily.

It seemed like the whole journey, all the journeys of his life, had led him to this moment. There was something about the shadows on the far side of the glade that troubled him. Something about dark within dark. He could smell no human, but then there was no wind. All was still and not a leaf fluttered or blade quivered. Was there a hunter there? Like all wolves, his sight was not his best sense. He waited and watched, for a movement. Listened for a sound. The shapes of the shadows remained still as death, silent as death. Surely a human could not remain motionless for so long? They were restless creatures, that relied upon poor use of senses. He was aware of Skassi, just behind him, knowing that his old pack member was patiently waiting for his move, not urging him at all, but content to remain where he was for seasons out of time if necessary. This was the old way of the hunt, with the leader showing infinite care and patience, choosing the time to move, exactly, to the moment, the *right* moment, whether that pulse was the last beat in the history of time, or not.

With his nerves taut, Athaba slipped out of the undergrowth and into the arena of light. He stood there for a moment, and then began to cross the centre of the glade. Skassi was close behind him. When they were three-quarters of the way across, Athaba caught the movement in the corner of his eye.

Incredibly, a hunter stood on the verge of the clearing, looking down the sights of his gun. How could that be?

There was no way Athaba could avoid being shot. He could not cover the distance between the spot he was on and the safety of the trees without presenting his full profile silhouette to the hunter. The man would have to be blind to miss him. Already the trigger finger was squeezing. Athaba knew he was about to die.

He waited a long moment before he saw a slight movement in the otherwise rigid face of the hunter, a relaxation. The barrel of the gun seemed to lower slightly. The man's eyes opened wider.

A breeze sprang up and the scent of the hunter came to Athaba: a smell he recognised instantly.

The man had been silent as a wolf, as quick as a wolf.

The reason was that the hunter *was* a wolf.

Koonama!

In that moment Athaba saw that *he* had been recognized, too, for the gun barrel was lowered even more, and a face frowned at him. Then the stance relaxed, the muzzle dropped. They stood, staring into each other's eyes, knowing who they were, amazed to find each other in this place of death.

Suddenly, there was a blur alongside Athaba.

'Run, Athaba. I'll get him!'

Skassi, racing by him, on the attack. Skassi, never short on courage. Athaba knows the thoughts, the instincts. *My brother wolf has frozen. I must make the kill.* Personal enmity aside, two wolves against the common foe. 'Skassi . . .!' The warning stuck in the throat. He has no words to call a halt. What words? What words? Time is needed. Long explanations. He tries.

'NO!' he shouts. 'Stop!'

'Don't worry . . .'

Skassi, halfway to the hunter, the gun comes up again, quickly. The big wolf, his own advice ignored, flies at the human's throat. Lean, hard, wolf body. Tight, narrow. Sunlight ripples along muscled flanks. Fangs bared, gums retracted.

Koonama remained, steady and cool, unflinching.

The muzzle of the shotgun flashed thunder into the hollow glade.

Skassi twisted sideways.

The rogue wolf crashed to the ground, thrashed a while, then lay still. Koonama pumped another shell into to the breech, sweating and breathing heavily. He stared at Athaba with a different expression on his face now. Having just faced death, the strain showed in every tense movement. A few moments ago, he and Athaba had been old travelling companions, caught in a conflict not of their making. Now they were again just man and wolf. Skassi's attack had shattered any fragile relationship that protected them from each other. Trust had evaporated. Now there was only the gun and the jaws, lead shot and fangs.

Athaba streaked to the edge of the glade as the weapon came up again. The muzzle followed him until he hit the greenery, but the weapon either failed to fire or the man remained Koonama for just a short while longer.

Then the wolf was on his way down towards the hanging rock, not pausing for a moment longer. He wriggled through the undergrowth on the far side and wormed down through the cracks in the rocks, to the entrance of the cave: a narrow slit

313

facing another boulder. He squeezed into the slit, having to twist his body into much the same shape that Skassi's carcass was in at that moment. Once inside, in the darkness of the cavern, he called out softly.

'Ulaala? Yanthra? Are you here?'

His heart was beating so loudly he feared that the cave would act as a device to send its echo outside, to the hunters that still moved over the slopes. He could feel its pounding in his chest and the throb of blood in the pulses behind his ears.

'Ulaala . . .?'

Chapter Thirty One

In the coolness of the cave, far from the sounds of the guns and dying wolves, Athaba found his family. Ulaala was there with the five yearlings, all sitting quietly and waiting patiently for their father to join them. They remained in the cave for two days, until they were absolutely sure there were no hunters outside.

Athaba left the hole and scouted for a while.

It was a fresh summer morning. The light angled through the spiky pines and laced the ground with shadows. Birds peppered the bushes. Small mammals moved over the forest floor, some stealthily, some rapidly. Athaba searched the woodland and found no trace of wolf or man.

Skassi was dead now and had taken many with him. Athaba could not decide whether Skassi was a hero or a fool. His old pack rival had, it was true, struck back at man. That took courage and determination. It took a strong spirit to say, 'Enough!' and to make a stand against the deadliest creature on the earth.

Yet, there was no way a wolf, or any other animal, could ever win against man. A battle perhaps, but never the war. The war had been won by the humans a long time past, seasons upon seasons ago, after the *Firstdark*. They had beaten the wolves and all the other creatures so completely that there was no turning the victory around, no matter how brave and how brilliant the leader of the rebellion. If Skassi had not believed that, he was a fool. If he had, he was at best utterly irresponsible, for he had populated the Far Forests with more souls than that mythical country had ever expected in a single day. The son of midnight had gone out like a wolf and had taken his pack with him.

Athaba sighed, then called for his own pack to join him.

While they were in the cave Ulaala told him that she had heard of an area where human hunters were not permitted to go. No vehicles had ever been seen in this place, and the flying machines never landed there – so she had been told by one of the wolves in Skassi's pack.

315

'This wolf said that bears and eagles and all manner of creatures live in this area, just north-west of here.'

Athaba was a little sceptical.

'No humans go there?'

'Oh, yes, they go there, but not with guns. They use those little black boxes which you expect to shoot things, but only click and nothing else. There are quite a lot of them, so you have to get used to the smell of man without panicking, but the wolf assured me that no animals have ever been attacked in this place.'

Athaba could hardly believe it.

'Not wolves, though. They would kill wolves, wouldn't they? I mean, I can imagine them leaving the bears alone, and the eagles, but they hate wolves too much.'

'Well, he seemed to know what he was talking about,' said Ulaala. 'He spoke wistfully of it and said he wished he'd never left, but he heard the call of rogue wolf and had to follow it.'

'Would we be allowed to hunt there? I mean, we have to catch our meat or we'll starve. Are you sure this place has not been put aside to breed cattle or something? Men do that, you know, keep tame and domestic stock. They can get pretty savage if you kill one of their animals.'

'No, these are wild plains and mountain country. It seems to be a place where creatures like us are left alone.'

'Sounds too good to be true, but we'll go there anyway. What choice do we have?'

So, with their sons and daughters, now yearlings and good at hunting, the pair set out for the plains with the mountain range as their hinterland. When they reached there, they found the word of the wolf was true.

The yearlings developed into fine strong *undermegas* and recruited other wolves into the pack, until Ulaala and Athaba found themselves headwolves of a pack of seventeen. That was before the new pups were born. After Grisenska had been a *mega* for one year, she took over as headwolf from her father, choosing a sturdy mate to aid her in the task. Although Ulaala was younger than Athaba, she too stepped aside and relinquished responsibility for the pack.

The pair of them would lie around the den of a winter evening, boring the youngsters with tales of prowess and Athaba would sing songs of the old days in his gravelly voice, as if there had been no other time, no other set of seasons.

When he told the story of the man who was turned into a wolf, however, the youngsters used to look at each other as if to say, *who's our old grandfather trying to fool with such outlandish fabrications?*

'Koonama,' he would tell them, ignoring the obvious nudges, 'was both man and wolf, and I often wonder how he fares amongst his own kind. I think he tells them a tale, of how a wolf and a man survived a long journey across the tundra. How the wolf kept him alive and reached down inside him to find an earlier creature, an inner man that had been dormant for so many seasons the outer man had forgotten him.'

'Perhaps,' one of the youngsters might say, '*he* thinks he turned a wolf into a man and gets it the wrong way round?'

'No, he would not do that,' Athaba would answer, 'because the wolf did no manly things, while the man followed the wolf in all its ways. If he thought he had changed me, he would have kept me after capturing me again. He knew he had not tamed me: I had tamed him.'

And there would be a restlessness amongst the youngsters, as he spoke these words, but he knew them to be the truth so it did not matter who listened or who believed.

Koonama *knew*, that was the important thing.